HEALING STONES

BOOK 4

HEALING STONES
Book 4

DIANE McGYVER

Quarter Castle Publishing
where imagination is magic
New Scotland, Canada

Lady Diane McGyver fell in love with the fantasy genre when at the age of 13 an awesome Dungeon Master introduced her to Dungeons & Dragons. From there, she landed in the world created by Terry Brooks, then journeyed into the realms crafted by Mercedes Lackey. By the age of 16, she was truly lost to magical lands and dreamt of one day living in one or two.

Her future goal is to write fantasy stories until she's 100 years old. She's already made plans to retire–at an early age–to write by the sea where she spent her childhood. There, she will live in a peel tower or a stone cottage and raise chickens, commune with trees and find adventure.

To learn more about McGyver and her books, visit her website: dianelynnmcgyver.com or follow her on Twitter (@Dragons_Novel).

Text Copyright@2020 Quarter Castle Publishing

Paperback ISBN: 978-1-927625-41-5
eBook ISBN: 978-1-927625-42-2

Cover Design: Diana Tibert
Interior Design: Diana Tibert
Published May 2020

Quarter Castle Publishing
Nova Scotia B0N 1Y0 CANADA

0120QCP0026

Please Note

This book was written using Canadian spelling. Diane prefers the old English she was raised on. So you'll read amongst instead of among, sceptical instead of skeptical and smelt instead of smelled.

Healing Stones, Book 4 of The Castle Keepers series, is a work of fiction. Names, characters (regardless of race), horses, places, events and incidents are either the products of the author's vast and wild imagination or used in a fictitious manner. Any resemblance to actual persons and animals, living or dead, or actual events, past or future, is purely coincidental. Many locations believed to exist in Nova Scotia—Glen Tosh, Wyvern, Goshen, Shulie—truly exist in this novel.

If you share a name with one of these fictional characters, the author apologises; there are only so many unique names on the planet. If you like the character, then you're welcome.

Quarter Castle Publishing bore the complete cost of publishing this book and received no financial assistance from outside sources.

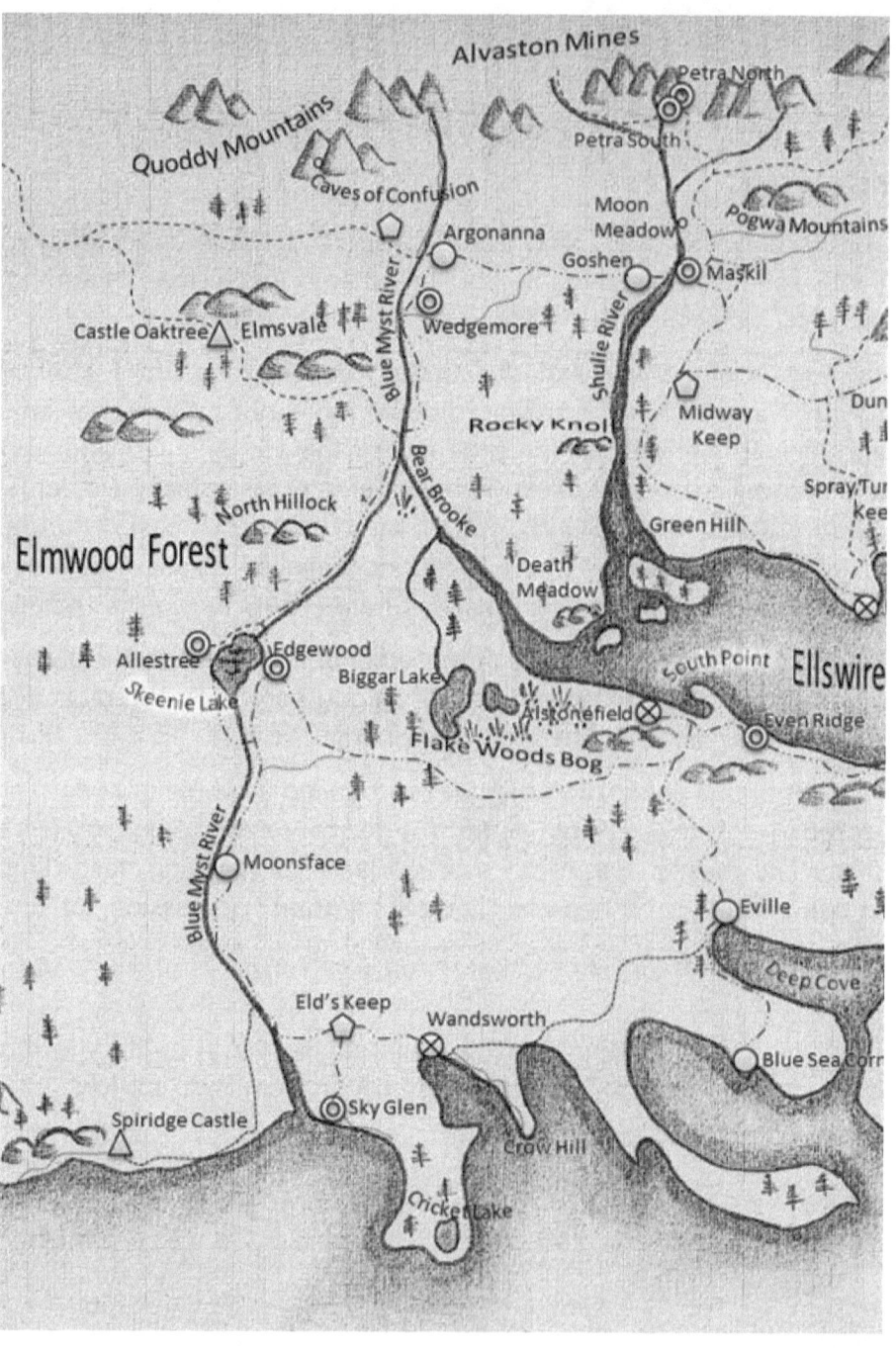

The moment you forget who you were,

the limitations and fears that held you back disappear,

and you are free to be whoever you want to be.

Dedication

To true love, wherever you roam.
Our time will come.

HEALING STONES

1

Moonsface Awaits

THE SUN HAD BEEN up for more than three hours, yet it had hidden behind billowy white clouds much of that time, stealing heat from the land and casting much of it in shadow. The cool temperature forced Isla of Maura to pull her jacket from her saddle bag. She didn't bother buttoning it; it was a warm day with a chill that would depart as soon as the sun peeked from behind the clouds. She'd be warmer if she did something other than stand next to the cold firepit and listen to McGuigan and Lyneth argue about the best route into Moonsface.

The obvious way, the one that took them directly into the large village on Blue Myst River, was the one McGuigan wanted to take, but Lyneth, who had been to Moonsface many times, insisted they take the narrow path around the collection of knolls. It'd add at least an hour to their travel time. Isla didn't care which course they took; she wanted to mount her two-bit horse she'd bought with money earned from tedious work and get moving. If they argued for another ten minutes, they'd have already travelled halfway through the long way.

"Everyone travels the main road." Lyneth, a woman of both human and elf blood, stood taller than McGuigan.

"You've said that." McGuigan Mulryan, who felt he should lead the party of three, stood on his toes to add height to his dwarf size. "It's a waste of time."

"I'll tell you what's a waste of time," said Isla, throwing her arms into the air. "Arguing." They glared at her, and she hung her head. She was youngest, least experienced, yet she had chosen their destination: Wandsworth. Lyneth was oldest, wiser about The Trail and had travelled this area of Ath-o'Lea before; she should lead the excursion. McGuigan's ego prevented him from accepting this fact.

After spending six weeks at Maskil recovering and reacquainting herself with home, they'd set out for the large city of Wandsworth with the hope of finding her long-lost friend, Liam Jenkins. He'd been sent there more than six years earlier after his das had been killed. His meeme had been murdered on the journey, leaving the boy, only thirteen years old, to live with his aunt and uncle, relatives he'd never met.

To finance their journey, they'd brought three packages, ones that needed to be delivered discreetly to shops in Moonsface. Lyneth, being the more experienced fighter, carried these packages in her rucksack.

The argument circled around to what had already been discussed, and Isla huffed and dropped to the large rock to sit and wait out the debate. Hearing a noise in the bushes, she looked to where the horses stood. She blinked, bringing the scene into focus. Someone mounted her horse, kicked it in the side and raced towards Wandsworth.

She leapt onto McGuigan's horse and sped after the cloaked figure. For five weeks, she'd tolerated her aunts' teasing and comments about her wardrobe to earn the money to get that horse; no one was going to steal it from her. She kicked McGuigan's horse, making it gallop, but her horse was faster and quickly out-paced her. They ran for a good five minutes, and she feared she'd lose the money she'd invested in the animal. She cursed under her breath, dreading the idea of having to work again to get another.

When she rounded a corner, she brought McGuigan's horse to a sudden halt, sliding and spraying dirt into the air before the gang that blocked the road. Her eyes grew wide as she realised she'd ridden into a trap. Ready to change direction and flee, she saw the man who'd taken her horse baulk and search frantically for an escape route. Feeling trapped, he stopped the horse and put his hands in the air.

"I mean no harm." The man's voice quivered, and he flung the cloak from his head, revealing long brown hair tinted with shimmering green. The young elf glanced nervously between Isla and the four heavily-armed men and their bulky horses that blocked his path.

"Except you stole my horse," yelled Isla, wary of the large humans leering at her. She prepared to bolt if the exchange went badly.

"A horse thief." The human with black hair, a healthy tan and a deep scar that ran from his left eyebrow to his cheek smirked. "Interesting. But not what we seek."

"It's what I seek." She put her foot on the young elf and gave him a shove, knocking him out of the saddle. He hit the ground hard and sent clouds of dust into the air. She grabbed the reins of her horse and turned. "Thanks for blocking his path." She started away, hoping they'd let her leave without dispute.

"A moment, please." The man with the scar spoke in a harsh tone. She half turned. "It's all I have."

"We seek someone. Perhaps you've seen him...being a hauflin yourself."

"Who do you seek?" She waited as he allowed the appropriate amount of time to pass to keep her in suspense.

"A man. Brown hair. Brown eyes. Young, like yourself. Maybe you passed him on your journey."

"The hauflin men I've met on The Trail were at least twice my age. Where's he from?"

"Wandsworth."

"I know no one from Wandsworth. This is the first time I've been to Moonsface, and I haven't gotten there yet." She frowned at the boy who dusted dirt from his trousers. "Thanks to this thief." She prepared to leave, not wanting to waste time with strangers who rose hairs on the back of her neck. His description of the male hauflin matched most she'd met, including Arthur. The ex-friend brushed her mind, and she forced him out. She searched for another who had strummed her heart strings long ago, and she'd not know who to sing for until she'd found Liam and listened to his song.

The man chuckled. "Moonsface awaits. Safe travels."

She nodded and rode towards McGuigan and Lyneth. Once out of sight of the men, she brought the horses to a lope. Although McGuigan might grumble, they were taking the long way to the village.

She saw her friends up ahead, McGuigan on the back of Lyneth's horse, and she ground to a stop. Leaping from the saddle, she shoved the reins into his hands, then jumped onto her horse.

"Lyneth, lead the way," she said. McGuigan opened his mouth to protest, but she hushed him. "Four mysterious men travel in our direction. Today, the long way is the better way."

Lyneth gave McGuigan a face and retraced their tracks. She travelled less than a mile, then entered a narrow trail that led away from the road.

Isla gave the road towards Moonsface one last scan to see if the four men were in sight. They weren't, and she guided her horse into the cover of thick trees and bushes. After a mile, Lyneth slowed, giving the horses a chance to rest as they meandered around boulders and large trees.

"You call this a trail?" asked McGuigan. "I call it a footpath at best." He glanced back at Isla. "Did those men appear threatening? Did they try to attack?"

"No, but they gave me a bad feeling."

He huffed. "We're travelling through the woods because of a bad feeling? It's going to take forever to get to Moonsface. It's more dangerous travelling like this than on the open road."

"Maybe, but I don't see four large humans with swords and scars marring their faces here."

"Humans?"

"Yeah. Not the friendly type."

He settled into the saddle, glancing back once before falling silent.

The coolness generated by deep shade forced Isla to button her jacket. She didn't care about the length of time it took to get to Moonsface; she was relieved they were moving. Although she was eager to reach Wandsworth to find Liam, she enjoyed The Trail, seeing new places and learning about the land they travelled. For five years, she'd been a prisoner of Blackvale Castle, and the monotony of that time made every trail, every person, every tree something different to see.

They travelled less than a mile and came upon a fork in the trail. Lyneth took the one on the left; the one that appeared less travelled.

"Where does that go?" asked McGuigan, pointing to the trail not taken.

"Moonsface." Lyneth didn't look back.

"Is it shorter?"

"In some ways."

"In length?"

"Exactly."

"What does that mean? Will it take us to Moonsface faster?"

"If we jog the horses."

McGuigan followed her, but he stared hard at the trail on the right. "Both trails are the same distance from the village?"

"You could say it that way."

"How would you say it?" Frustration laced his voice.

"The same way you would."

Isla hung her head. The constant bickering between them since leaving Maskil weeks ago made her think she'd be happier alone on The Trail. Her parents would disagree, but they didn't have to endure trail mates who persistently chose opposite opinions. These arguments never occurred when Elspeth led the group; no one questioned her authority and if they did, they had a darn good reason. Now, with no one to make the final decision, McGuigan and Lyneth wrestled for it like two mature female goats knocking heads to be the leader of the herd. She'd seen does fight until they drew blood, and they'd go at it again, before the wounds healed.

McGuigan fell silent after travelling a few minutes on the path, but when another fork appeared and Lyneth veered left, he stopped.

"Where does this trail go?"

"Moonsface." Lyneth slowed but didn't stop.

"Is it faster?"

"Not really."

Isla was forced to stop to avoid bumping into his horse.

"Not really?" McGuigan peered down the trail. "It looks for easier riding. Let's take it."

Lyneth stopped. "Do you not trust me to take the best trail into Moonsface?"

"I trust you will take the path that pleases you best, not what's best for us."

"I've been through here many times and—"

"You've said that," he snapped. "It doesn't make you an expert. It doesn't mean we have to listen to you." He pointed his horse to the right. "I say we go this way. It's easier."

Isla cursed under her breath. Kicking her two-bit horse in the side, she bumped her way past McGuigan and followed Lyneth. "Onward. Let's go."

"What?" His mouth hung open. "We're going this way."

"From here on, we vote. I'm with Lyneth. Two against one. Now follow or we'll meet you there." She ushered Lyneth forward. "We'd be there by now if not for the bickering."

A smile creased Lyneth's lips, and her horse walked forward.

McGuigan grumbled, turned his horse and followed. "I thought you were on my side."

"I'm on the side that gets us there safely *and* quickly." Isla glanced at him. "Pip-pip, young man." She grinned at the words Tam had used to hurry him up. Their time at Maskil had given McGuigan the opportunity to know his uncle, a man with dry humour, simple ways and a quiet manner. The relationship had instilled confidence and purpose in McGuigan. This made him more outspoken and in situations like this, more annoying.

"This is the less challenged path," said Lyneth over her shoulder. "Fewer travelers take this route. Trust me."

"I do," said Isla before McGuigan spoke. "We both do."

For the next thirty minutes, they rode in silence with no additional forks to cause problems. Isla relaxed and admired the landscape, the lush trees, tiny bunches of wildflowers and the birds singing sweet songs. A red squirrel ran in front of her horse and into a small bush. It emerged on the other side and raced towards an unusual tree. She stared at the mammoth growth; it was unlike anything she'd seen before. Relaxing her grip on the reins, she slowed the horse for a longer view.

The lower eight feet of the tree was all trunk, and broad, dark-green leaves concealed the top. Or was it a group of trees growing closely together? Countless trunks rose from the ground, both thick and thin. The maze they created provided protection from the elements and concealment from passersby. As she rode nearer, she marvelled at the roots squirming from the main trunks, gliding across the ground as if a nest of snakes of various sizes protruded from the wood.

She tilted her head, trying to make sense of the branches... No, roots growing from the outstretched branches. They grew at different stages, some a few inches long, others almost reaching the ground. Spell bound, she directed her horse off the trail and onto the forest bed covered in yellow needles.

"Why are you stopping?" growled McGuigan. "We don't have time for sightseeing."

"Why are you so eager to get to Moonsface?" asked Lyneth, who stopped to wait.

"No reason."

"With you, there's always a reason."

"It's nothing."

"Oh, it's something. Fess up, *young man.*"

Frustrated, he blurted, "I want to get rid of those packages."

"You're nervous." Lyneth shook her head. "Don't think of them."

"I can't help it. You heard the warning."

"The same I've been hearing for more than seven years."

He huffed. "Back when we had the strength to defend ourselves."

"You mean The Mercenaries." She cleared her throat, and her expression softened. "We're almost there. Stick to the plan, and we'll be fine."

"Shhh!" Isla dismounted and let her reins fall.

"What are you doing?" asked McGuigan. "It's a tree."

"You ever see a tree like this?" she asked over her shoulder. She stepped closer. A soft mumble or... What was that sound?

"It's the Nathair tree." Lyneth rested her arms across the horn of her saddle.

"Nat hair?" McGuigan grimaced. "Its branches look like dangling hair."

"Nath-air. And those aren't branches. They're roots. As it was explained to me, off shoots of the branches droop or grow downward and set new roots into the ground. This is a single tree and those trunks are roots grown from the branches."

"Strangest thing I've ever heard," said McGuigan.

"That's not the strangest," said Isla, walking closer. "It's humming or..." she glanced back, "groaning. It smells odd, and..." she peered closer, and a cold sensation raced up her arms, "it emits negative energy."

"It's a tree." McGuigan sat up and gathered his reins. "Let's go."

Her hand touched one of the branches, and her fingertips tingled. Stepping between the woven roots, she peeked into one of the cavities created by the clump of trunks. It was large enough for a medium size animal or a dwarf to lay down comfortably.

Her ears perked. What was that?

"Help."

She stood straight. "Hello?"

"Who you talking to?" McGuigan stretched his neck to see.

"I think there's someone inside."

"In the tree? Crazy."

She stared at him, her mind unfolding memories created long ago. "Your uncle Tam was imprisoned in a tree for years."

"That doesn't mean there's someone in every tree."

"Please, help me." Pain laced the barely audible voice.

Isla stepped closer, searching around the branches, roots and trunks. "Where are you?"

"Here."

She stood on a thick root and poked her head between the tangled branches. A dark set of eyes gaped at her from deep within. She tried to see more of the person, but only a narrow slit revealed the position. "Can you hear me?"

"I see you." It was a man's voice.

"How did you get in there?"

"Fell asleep."

Confused, she asked, "How long have you been there?"

"Three days."

She pulled back. He'd be dead in a few more.

"What is it?" asked McGuigan.

"A man. Lyneth, what do you know about this?"

Lyneth dismounted and came near. "He's trapped?"

"I think so." She scanned the area. "I can't see how he got in." She stepped off the root for a wider view, then grabbed a branch and yanked; it was solid. "I'll never break it." She kicked a branch, but it didn't budge. "What do you make of it?"

Lyneth scratched her head. "There's no entry. No opening to reach him. Did he say how he got in there?"

"He said he fell asleep. Doesn't make sense." She poked her face near the hole and gazed at the stranger. "Did you crawl in there?"

"No. The tree..." he gasped for breath, "grew around me."

"It grew around him?" She drew back. "Now *that's* crazy."

"Let's go," said McGuigan.

She stared at him. "What? We can't leave him."

"Not like we can help him." He leant forward and whispered, "He was probably put there for a reason."

"Possibly," said Lyneth. "We'll send someone for him."

"He might be dead by the time they arrive." Isla's mind raced. There had to be a way.

"We can't help everyone," said Lyneth.

She swung around and stared at the tree. If he was a bad man, the tree would claim him, but what if he wasn't? Her emotions fought against each other to decide the right thing to do. Walking away was easy, but...an uncertain sentiment rumbled within. Similar to how she felt when she'd discovered Willow in the dungeon at Vale of Avoca, she was unable to walk away. But how would she release him?

It was a tree, not a prison of stone. She withdrew her dagger and stood on the thick root. Her blade struck the branch near the opening, and the tree vibrated. She hit it again, and the tree shook.

Something wrapped around her ankle. It tightened its hold and curled around her calf. "Whoa!" She stabbed the thin root with her dagger. It flinched and uncurled. "What the..."

"Watch out!" McGuigan jumped off his horse and raced forward, his sword drawn. A dangling branch swooped towards her, and he cut it in half. "Get out of there!"

She jumped up, but another root grabbed her ankle and dragged her across the ground. Dirt and needles flew into her face, blinding her momentarily. Holding tight to the dagger, she stabbed the root repeatedly until it released her. She leapt to her feet and saw McGuigan and Lyneth battling roots that emerged from several branches. Roots as thick as rope seized her ankles and she slammed into the ground, losing the grip on the dagger. She scrambled to retrieve it, but her hand thumped against dirt as she was dragged away.

Screaming filled her ears, but in the rush to reach the dagger strapped to her thigh, she couldn't see what was happening. Roots threw her against a trunk and pinned her twenty feet in the air. Unable to reach her weapon, she pounded the tree with her fist, then kicked it.

Wiggling and pushing against the trunk, she found room to grasp the dagger.

The tree released more roots and branches, removing several of the bonds that held the man trapped within. Isla gazed down at him. His small size suggested he was either a boy of the dwarf race or a hauflin.

The tree shook violently, and branches flew rapidly about, trying to entrap those who attacked it. Leaves slapped against her as she leapt from one branch to the next. Roots that snagged her were quickly cut away. Branch by branch, she shortened the distance between her and the stranger. The tree exposed him further, and more branches lashed out. They knocked her off balance, and she fell until she latched onto a limb. Unable to secure her hands, she slipped farther, and landed on a branch beside the man's head. The top half of him had been exposed. He was hauflin.

A branch swept towards her, and she ducked in time to avoid it. "Your hands!" she yelled. "Are they free?"

McGuigan slammed into the roots in front of her. "Get away from here! Leave him!" He swung his sword and lopped off the end of a branch. "Its too much."

Isla shook the man's shoulder. "Can you reach up?"

Dry evergreen needles, dirt and bruises covered the man's gaunt face. His shaggy, dirty, damp hair stuck to his skin as if glued there. His torn shirt revealed scratches and minor cuts. Maybe McGuigan was right; this man was secured here for a reason, and those who had done so had put a beaten on him first.

Pain raced across his young face as he wiggled his arms free from his sides and lifted them into the air. "Help me."

"Leave him!" ordered McGuigan. "We can't save him. We'll be lucky..." a branch slapped him across the face, "to save ourselves." He ducked when the next branch flew towards him.

It struck Isla and flung her against a thick trunk. She hit with a solid thud, and it knocked the air from her lungs.

"Come on." McGuigan stretched for her. "Hold onto me."

The urge to heed his advice stalled her, yet abandoning the helpless stranger wrenched on her sympathies. She scrambled to her feet and leapt onto a branch near the captive.

"Grab my hand!" McGuigan cut down another branch. "Let's go!" He latched onto her and jerked her forward.

"Please, don't leave me... Isla!"

She froze and swung around, releasing McGuigan. How did he know her name?

"Please, I don't want to die." He reached for her with one hand and pushed against the tree with the other.

She grabbed the dirty hand and pulled. "Help me!"

McGuigan grasped the man's wrist and pulled him out of the tight hole he stood in. The quick discharge made him stumble forward and lose his balance. He fell hard against a series of roots and tore a hole in his trousers.

Isla tumbled backwards, dragging the man with her. His thin frame fell across her, and the strong smell of body odour swept through her air passages. In the dank aroma, she detected something familiar, but... She pushed him off and scrambled to her feet, dagger in hand. A branch struck her across the face, and she flew into the man, sending him flat on his back.

"This way." Lyneth stood before the tree, ducking the flying branches and cutting down those that came near.

"Come on." McGuigan grabbed Isla's jacket and pulled her to her feet. He turned and chopped off a branch as it swung near.

Isla drove her dagger into her sheath and reached for the stranger. He struggled to stand and appeared too weak to carry himself. She helped him up and draped his arm across her shoulder. They lurched forward with McGuigan following close behind, cutting the branches that flayed out.

Forty feet from the tree, they were out of range of the branches. Isla forced the man to travel farther down the trail until he collapsed on the moss. He lay on his stomach and coughed and sputtered, gasping for air and moaning in pain.

McGuigan led his and Isla's horses down the path and stopped near her feet. "We're not staying."

Lyneth followed close behind. "I agree," she said with ragged breath. "We need to get away from that beast."

"Finally, you agree on something." Isla rose. "Help me get him up."

"Up where?" McGuigan plugged his nose and eyed the filthy man that lay before him. "He stinks."

"You'd smell better after being trapped in a tree for three days?" She placed a hand on the man's shoulder. "Hey. You going to be okay?"

He slowly raised his head and propped himself up on his elbows. Through strands of thick brown hair, he stared at her. "That depends on you." He coughed and moved his mouth as if to gather spit.

"Water." She grabbed the flask from her saddle. "He's had nothing to drink for three days." She helped him sit up, then removed the cork. A familiar scent swirled in the air, and she leant closer as he lifted the flask to his mouth. "You..." Her gaze swept over his face, then stared into his deep brown eyes, eyes she'd seen before.

"Don't get too close," said McGuigan. "You might never get rid of that stench."

She brushed dirty strands of hair from his face, and her emotions ran wild. His hair was longer, his jaw more pronounced than in his youth and his thin facial hair concealed the wee scar on his chin, but his eyes were the same. "Liam?"

Uncertainty consumed him, and he gripped the flask tightly. His eyes grew glossy, and the little colour he had in his face drained. "I'm him." His voice shook as if he didn't want to admit it.

"Liam?" Lyneth leant close. "*The* Liam? The one we're going to Wandsworth to find?"

"The same." Isla scrutinised his body. His thin shirt and trousers were speckled with smears of blood, gashes and holes. The dirt and calluses on his feet indicated he hadn't worn footwear for weeks. A dark-blue stone shone above his button shirt, the same stone she'd fashioned into a necklace many years ago. There was no doubt this was the man she sought, but he appeared like he'd escaped from five years of prison at Blackvale Castle. He was nothing but bones. Three days trapped in a tree hadn't done this. "Are you ill? A disease?"

"I told you not to get too close," said McGuigan.

"No. I am well." He choked on the words, and it took a minute for him regain his composure.

She snatched a wad of cheese from her saddle bag and handed it to him. "Eat."

He hesitatingly accepted the food and watched her as he ate it slowly. Once the taste filled his mouth, he chewed quickly and took another bite.

"When did you eat last?"

He shrugged. "Four, five days."

"Where did you come from? Moonsface?"

"I passed through."

"Wandsworth?" He nodded, and she released a groan of disbelief. "You've walked from there? It'd have taken weeks. Why did you leave?"

"I set out to find you."

She studied his actions. He seemed to tell the truth, but there was hesitation. "Why now after all these years?"

"An odd feeling told me you were..." He thought before he spoke further. "The last I heard, you were taken from Maskil. I lost hope." He swallowed and absorbed the pain. "A dream or... I don't know. My hope returned."

"I spent five years in a prison." She jerked her thumb in McGuigan's direction. "He's the reason I escaped."

"You owe him?"

"That's been paid in full." She and McGuigan had come to terms with their relationship. They were friends, comfortable with each other to kiss if they wanted to, but... She reflected on her and Liam's past; they had not only kissed but pledged to unite.

"And now you are...?" he asked, his voice weak.

"Friends. Good friends. Maybe even best friends."

"Best friends." He let the words slip out as if remembering the time when she had called him her best friend. "I'm happy for you." He didn't appear happy; his appearance suggested anything but.

"Can we talk about this elsewhere?" asked Lyneth.

"He can eat on the way," said McGuigan.

"Are you strong enough to ride?" Isla offered him another drink, and he took it.

"I think so."

"He's not riding with me." McGuigan stepped back.

"He'll ride with me." Isla corked the flask and returned it to her saddle. "Help me get him up."

"I'm not touching him," said McGuigan.

"Your attitude is starting to grate my nerves." Isla gripped her fists. "Lose it."

"Or what?"

"Or else." She stared him down. "Help me get him up." She turned to Liam. "These are my friends. The mule-headed dwarf with the sass is McGuigan. This is Lyneth. She's leading this party."

"She is not." McGuigan stood tall.

She reached for Liam's arm. "Slowly. We'll get you to a place where you can rest."

He rose on shaky legs and rubbed his left thigh. "I lost feeling in them yesterday." He grasped her shoulder. "It'll take a day or so to get them back."

"We've got lots of time." She guided him to her horse. "I'll mount, and they'll help you up." After climbing into the saddle, she removed her foot from the stirrup and reached for him. "Easy. McGuigan, give him a hand."

He mumbled under his breath but helped hoist Liam into the saddle. "Phew." He stepped away quickly and waved his hand in front of his face. "You're riding last. I don't know how you stand it."

"Same as I did when you soiled your trousers when you tried the Light Spell."

His mouth clamped shut as the memory passed through his mind. "I'm still riding second." He jumped onto his horse and got behind Lyneth.

"When you're ready, we'll start." She glanced over her shoulder and when their eyes met, a familiar feeling resurfaced. Memories from long ago brushed her mind, igniting a smile. "I've thought of you often, wishing things I believed might never be." Her gaze fell upon his lips; they looked as sweet now as they had when he was thirteen. She sniffed the air. "You do smell awful. Before food, you will bathe."

A mischievous grin brightened his face. "I'm sorry. If I had known you were to find me today, I would have..." The ray of happiness that had lit up his haggard face evaporated, leaving him avoiding eye contact.

"It's okay. Soap is a marvellous product." She felt him slip in the saddle, and she brought her hand around to steady him. "Hold on. I don't want to lose you." He reached for the back of the saddle. "No, put your arms around my waist." She grasped his hand to move it forward and felt his thin wrist.

"I shouldn't." He held his hands to his chest.

"I'm giving you permission to do so. Please. Before you fall off."

Slowly he placed his hands on her hips and held them firmly. The horse stumbling made him slip again, and he wrapped his arms around her. He inched closer and pressed against her back, shivering as the heat from their bodies joined.

"Though time and distance separated us, I'm still your friend." She glanced over her shoulder and into his face. "It's why I came in search of you. Do you still consider me a friend?"

He pressed his lips together as his face twisted in anguish. "I've always considered you *more* than a friend, but I understand. We are only friends." He rested his cheek against her back and fell silent.

When she began her search for Liam, she had imagined several scenarios upon finding him. Her most popular was his smiling face, him sharing memories of their past years and him pulling her into his arms for a kiss that melted away the years and deeds, leaving them lovers and possibly mates. Rescuing him from a beast of a tree and finding him beaten, half starved and reluctant to share information was not one of the situations she had visualised.

"Take the less challenging path, she said." McGuigan grumbled and frowned at Isla. "It will get us there faster, she said." He pulled at the material around the hole in his pants. "You both owe me a pair of trousers."

2

The Village Pillory

LYNETH HALTED NEAR A babbling brook. She peered down stream and, in the distance, saw a small pool perfect for bathing. The first dwelling they'd meet on entering Moonsface was a quarter mile away. Their first delivery location was half a mile farther. They'd be there in less than an hour even if they stopped for the filthy hauflin Isla knew as Liam to cleanse himself of his horrible odour.

She'd smelt stench like that but not since leaving Blackvale Castle. There, it was sometimes impossible to bathe for seasons. She'd rarely seen soap, and the single outfit she'd owned was seldom washed.

"Why are we stopping?" McGuigan halted beside her.

She drew a calming breath to keep her patience with this boy who grew more irritating by the day. "To allow this man to regain his dignity."

His face twisted. "How's he going to do that here?"

She groaned. "Isla, take him down stream. There's a pool. Let him soak. You have thirty minutes." She dismounted and led her horse to the brook for a drink while Isla walked hers towards the pool.

McGuigan slipped out of the saddle and stood beside Lyneth to give his horse a drink. "I doubt he can wash the smell away." He glanced towards the hauflins, who went behind the bushes. "I've never smelt someone that bad that wasn't dead and rotting. How did he let himself get that awful?"

"Obviously, you've never been in despair."

He lowered his brow. "He could have washed in any stream or lake he passed."

"Easily said."

"Easily done."

"I smelt that bad or worse when I escaped Blackvale. Remember Isla's stink when you pulled her from that cell?"

He scratched his thin beard. "But...she had a good excuse."

"He does, too; you just don't know it. When you took Isla in your saddle that night, I questioned how you withstood the stink."

"I wasn't thinking of the stink."

"Neither is Isla now."

He cast his eyes down stream again. "Do you really think it's him? The Liam she's looking for?"

"She thinks it's him."

"He looks diseased, but..." he winced, "it feels more like he's running *from* something not *to* her like he claimed."

She gave him her full attention. "Very observant. You're growing wise, young man, or at least observant. I thought the same. Then I thought, maybe it's both."

"In his state, he's not a threat. If I slapped him, he'd tumble backwards."

"Physical strength is one possible threat." She leant closer and whispered, "Isla will be blinded by emotion, so it's up to you and me to listen and watch for the truth. Let's keep this to ourselves, okay?"

He stood straighter. "Understood."

"There is one advantage to finding this man here."

"What's that?"

"We don't have to go to Wandsworth." She grimaced. "I was there once, and I don't wish to go back. It's a dirty, rude city. Worse than Ellswire; it's bigger, more people. There are a few good neighbourhoods, but it's mostly too many people crammed into too little space with everyone pushing to get ahead. It makes for bad neighbours when you don't have space to relax without someone gawking at you."

"Maybe that's what he was escaping from."

"Possibly. I'm sure we'll learn in time." She saw Isla leading her horse along the brook. "Where's your friend?"

"Bathing. He wanted his privacy, so I gave it to him."

"You're certain it's him?"

"Yes. I recognise his scent."

"How can you identify it in his stench?" asked McGuigan.

"Somethings you know and remember."

"You're scent-bonded with him, aren't you?" Lyneth remembered the moment she bonded with Rod. She could find him if she was blind and lost in the stinkiest hole.

"What's that?" she asked.

"It's deliberately ingraining a person's scent within your senses. Sometimes it happens automatically. You've probably done that with McGuigan, your das...Kiefer. You know it's them by smell alone."

"In my life force? My nwyfre?"

"Yes, if you believe in such things."

"I do. And I did, a long time ago."

"You can find me without sight?" asked McGuigan.

"I can, especially when you haven't bathed for several days." She poked him in the ribs.

Lyneth chuckled. "He forgets that when we first found him, he was terrified to bathe because he didn't want to be alone on The Trail. Brac's tolerance wore thin, and he tossed him into a lake."

"That wasn't funny," he said. "That water was ice cold."

She shrugged. "We all laughed. Isn't that the definition of funny?" She remembered those days well. As a member of The Mercenaries, she'd felt safe on The Trail. She had made great friends and got to see more of Ath-o'Lea than she'd ever dreamt. Brac was grumpy at times, but he always lightened the mood with his unexpected actions and comments. She missed that. She missed Morwen, too. They'd become good friends during their time together. Rhys was the one who kept everyone serious, focussed, but he, too, had a playful side. Elspeth, well, she kept them safe, confident, and gave them purpose.

Again, she thought about going home to Inishmore and returning to her life and her family and avoid the dangers of The Trail. One thing kept her from doing so: Rod. He was still a prisoner of Blackvale Castle and although his sister Catriona, Isla and she had several plans in the works, it'd take time to see one through. Then she'd take him home, introduce him to her family and hopefully keep him there.

‰ ❖ ⍦

The horse and cart that travelled the narrow dirt lane that separated McGuigan from Ample Bothain stirred up dust, and the wind whirled it around and flung it in his direction. He sat on a wooden bench outside Eoghan Keep, waiting for Isla and Lyneth to deliver the last package. He didn't know what the leather pouch contained, and he wanted to keep it that way. It might be harmless, or it might have threatened his life. Once they were through, they'd get a room for the night and spend the day touring Moonsface.

He enjoyed the slow pace of the large village. Almost everyone he met was elf, so as a dwarf, he stood out and the occasional passerby stared at him. The citizens seemed content and the traffic, the little there was, moved in a civilized manner.

"Is this your usual method of surveillance?"

He gripped the edge of the bench and tried to ignore the man who sat on the other end wearing his clothes. When Isla had requested a shirt and pair of trousers, he refused, but her nagging finally forced him to surrender the items. He disliked Liam; the man gave off bad vibrations, or as Isla had said when she approached the tree, negative energy. He didn't know if the energy came from Liam or the tree.

"You don't have to like me."

"Good." McGuigan glanced at him sideways. "I don't trust you either. Just because you were Isla's friend when you were kids, doesn't mean you're the same person, someone she'd care about now."

"I'm not the same person." He released a heavy sigh. "I don't expect her to care. We're strangers."

"Then we understand each other." He kicked a pebble from the wooden sidewalk and sent it flying onto the dry, dirt lane. "She cares about me, and I'd do anything for her. That includes protecting her from people who she mistakenly thinks is her friend."

He nodded. "I'll hold you to that. Are you two..." he cleared his throat and gazed into the distance, "lovers?"

"We were. We're better friends. She's had another since, so don't believe she's waited for you. She's free to be with who she wants."

"I wouldn't think otherwise. She's better off." He fingered the stone hanging around his thin neck, and gloom darkened his gaunt face. His eyes grew glossy, and the muscles in his jaw twitched.

A twinge of regret pricked at McGuigan for speaking the truth and generating sad emotions. However, the man had to know Isla was free to love who she pleased. Time and prison had changed her. She'd fought horrible self-hatred for many moons before she came to grips with who she'd become. This man hadn't been there to help her through the terrible memories and haunting nightmares. He'd never know what she'd overcome to be the confident woman he saw battling the tree to free him.

"I could never hurt her." Liam gulped. "All I ask is a chance to give her the little I have to offer. My life is unimportant."

McGuigan swallowed hard. The man offered his life to a woman he hadn't seen for more than six years, one who may not care about him. Something stronger than love fuelled his motives, something more powerful than loyalty.

೫ ❖ ೮

Isla's mind drifted to the man sitting outside with McGuigan, and she jerked it back to focus on the two seasoned elves standing behind the counter in Ample Bothain. The little shop overflowed with a wide variety of food, and magnificent aromas filled her nostrils and made her think of the bakery in Maskil. When they were done, she planned to buy two of the fruit displayed on the counter. They were like nothing she'd seen before. They resembled an apple but were dark purple.

Lyneth had done the talking, gave the man the package in question and accepted payment. They were finishing up with a few niceties before the deal ended. The owners had flipped the sign in the window to CLOSED and had locked the door to complete the business transaction.

"We have a proposition for you." The man leant close. "If you can be discreet."

"We can." Lyneth glanced at Isla. "What does this involve?"

"We have a package we wish delivered."

"Where to?"

"A little valley on the south side of Knollton Mountain."

"Inglenook?"

"You've been there?"

"No, but I've heard of it. It's a trek. A good three weeks out of our way."

"It's a shorter travel than that from Maskil to here, yet I'll offer the same reward."

"But this is through mountains on rough trails with few places to resupply."

"We'll pay double," blurted the woman who tidied up the shelf behind the man. "It is worth it to us."

"Bess, hush." The man regained his composure. "We shall double it because we wish to see the *package* delivered quickly and safely."

"How big is the package? Will it fit inside a rucksack?"

The man glanced at the woman, who came to stand next to him. "It's... We assume discretion."

"Yes. We will tell no one, and we'll hide the package in a secure bag to ensure no one sees it."

He cleared his throat. "It won't be that easy."

"Goodness, Harry, tell her." She leant forward. "It's a boy; his grandnephew. We need him transported to his sister's home in Inglenook."

"A boy?" Lyneth hesitated. "That is another matter."

"But you can do it." Bess pursed her lips. "He brings us nothing but bother. Our children are grown; we've no inclination to raise another."

"Excuse my mate. Deaglan is active. He's been with us since his mom passed, and now he wishes to live with his grandaunt. We feel it's in his best interest to grant that wish."

Isla listened to the pair make excuses to why they wanted to get rid of the boy. They owned this wonderful shop, yet had no love for the child, a family member who deserved it. Had Liam met the same type of relatives when he moved to Wandsworth? Was he passed around from one home to the next, considered a bother?

She glanced towards the front door. Outside, across the street, that once-young-boy sat, hoping to find friends in a world where none existed. Mending his wounds and nourishing his body to return him to health was easy; healing his mind would be the challenge. Remembering the torture she'd endured accepting her deeds, she shivered. Kiefer had pulled her back from the threshold of a horrible fate and dulled the anguish.

"How old is he?"

"Fifteen," said Bess. "He's able; he won't slow you down."

"Does he have a horse?"

"Something as good as one," said Harry. "Better in my opinion."

"What is better than a horse?" asked Lyneth. "A pony?"

"A donkey."

"Does he know how to handle it?"

"He does."

"Will you provide his food?"

"Yes, and money to buy more on The Trail," said Bess.

"Or we could supply a week's ration to all," said Harry, "then you can buy the remaining meals. How many in your band?"

"Four, plus the boy."

"Perfect. It'd be to your advantage and ours. The packs will be ready for pick up at dusk."

"Today?" Lyneth glanced at Isla. "When do you expect us to leave?"

"That's the hitch." Harry adjusted his weight. "It's the reason we need complete secrecy."

"I don't understand."

Isla listened closely while the man explained in a low voice that the boy in question had been caught stealing a pair of boots earlier in the day and was currently entrapped in the village pillory. Their task was to rescue him from the contraption during the emptiness of night and escape with him under the cover of darkness. The theft was a minor crime, and Harry would make retribution in the morning, after the boy was discovered missing so no one would bother looking for him. It sounded simple except she detected fear in the man's voice. Perhaps it was fear for the safety of his grandnephew.

Regardless, Lyneth accepted the deal and said she'd return at dusk to gather the five food sacks and the donkey. As they prepared to leave, Isla picked up two of the purple fruit and handed Harry a coin.

"No charge." He waved away the money. "Enjoy."

"Thank you." She followed Lyneth outside and down the sidewalk to their predetermined destination. She glanced across the street and saw McGuigan and Liam sitting quietly, casually scanning the lane. The two men had little in common, yet she felt attracted to both, one as a friend and the other as... She didn't know anymore.

She faced forward, feeling more unsure of their relationship now than she had when she escaped Blackvale. Back then, she felt unworthy and didn't want to see him. After accepting life as it happened, she wanted to renew their friendship. She knew he'd change; he'd been a boy the last time they'd been together. However, she wasn't prepared for his unwillingness to communicate. When she'd accompanied him to the pool to bathe, he refused to let her touch him. She only wanted to remove his shirt and tend to his cuts and scrapes, but he had shoved her away forcefully. He regretted it immediately and apologised, yet he kept his distance. He wouldn't disrobe and get into the water until she left. Bashfulness was never a trait Liam possessed, so his reluctance baffled her.

"This way."

Lyneth's voice shook her from her thoughts, and she abruptly changed directions to follow her.

"Mind on task." She forced a smile. "You'll have time to think of him later."

She cleared her mind. The task at hand would net them much needed funds, more than she expected. If they performed well, she imagined it would lead to others. That suited her fine; she'd rather explore Ath-o'Lea than work in her aunts' shop where they held up frilly dresses and wondered out loud how they'd look on her. She rolled her eyes. Those dresses wouldn't stand a week where she went.

3

The Distance Between Them

LYNETH PROVIDED A LIFT with her knee and clasped hands for Liam to climb onto the roof of the low-sided shed that sat on the perimeter of the small grassy hill in the centre of the village. The man weighed so little, she hoisted him into position without straining a muscle. His strength, what remained after spending days entangled in the tree, had returned to his legs, and he walked swiftly. His ability to run any distance remained a mystery.

The condition of his body was that of someone who hadn't eaten a proper ration in months. He looked worse in McGuigan's clothes, and he faired little better in the proper-sized clothing Isla had bought for him at the keep. She'd gotten a size larger, knowing he'd grow into them eventually. When they shared the evening ration at the tavern, he hadn't wanted Isla to spend her money on him, but she insisted and bought him a bowl of soup and several biscuits. He ate slowly as if he didn't want to upset his belly with too much food.

After climbing onto the shed roof and crawling to the edge, she lay on her stomach facing the pillory situated on the small hill. The boy named Deaglan stood in the punishment contraption, his head and hands protruding out the opposite side of thick wood.

Liam rested a foot away, scanning the scene before them. His expression revealed his seriousness in the task of providing surveillance.

"Have you done this before?" she whispered.

"Remove a boy from a pillory? Can't say I have."

"How about being on watch? Staking out a location?"

He rested his chin on his folded arms and kept his eyes on the pillory. "I know what to do if you're asking."

"What other skills do you have that we can exploit?"

He cast her a glance. "You're direct. I like that."

"Out here, I often don't get a second chance to know my ally from my enemy."

"Rest assured; I'm your ally. I know how to watch for danger, cautiously sneak around and listen to a voice tone to learn the truth."

"Survival skills necessary for big cities like Wandsworth."

"You been there?"

"Once. Never wish to return."

"Neither do I."

"Weapons. Which can you use?"

"Daggers are my specialty, but I can swing a sword."

"Yet we found you with none."

"Lost my daggers last week when two men tackled me."

"That's where the beating came from?"

"That and a few other scraps. Mostly for food." He pointed to the right. "That's not where they're supposed to enter the clearing, but I spot movement."

She squinted to see the area better. "Couple of shadows."

"How well can you see in the dim light? Being part human."

"Not as good as you; that's why you're here. That and your excellent hearing."

"The shadows are small. Either women or boys or a race smaller than elf." He watched in silence a moment more. "Two boys, no three. The other is shorter. They carry something."

After a long pause, she asked, "What?"

"...buckets?" His eyes darted to the opposite side of the clearing. "Damn," he mumbled under his breath.

Lyneth looked in the direct from where McGuigan and Isla were to approach the pillory and saw two figures creeping closer. The two crept forward, unable to see the boys approaching from the other side of the hill. "We do nothing unless they can't handle it. We keep an eye on the big picture."

"That boy skilled enough to protect Isla?" His rough voice didn't hide his dislike for McGuigan.

"He'll do. He's young and has a lot to learn, but he's strong, eager." She huffed. "Don't worry about him not giving his all; he'd give his life for her." They locked eyes, and she sensed he knew that and part of him was envious. "She's made good friends since her escape from prison. Never forsake those who'll help you or the ones you love. Anyways, she's as deadly as he is and at times more so."

He raised an eyebrow. "With a sword?"

"Never seen her use one. Daggers."

"I'd have sworn a sword would have been her weapon of choice."

"Why?"

"Her das. He's a skilled swordsman. She emulated him. We used sticks; she'd beat me every time."

"Interesting. I've met Bronwyn. He's a good man. Never saw him in a fight. They're not blood related, yet she admires him more than most children do their parents."

"She always has." His expression darkened. "Him and his honour."

He spoke the last word as if foreign to his lips, giving the impression he didn't like Bronwyn. That wouldn't sit well with Isla. "I see the three kids. Teens. They're sneaking like they've something to hide." They approached the backside of the pillory to avoid detection by the boy trapped in the device.

Isla and McGuigan crept towards them. Isla paused, grasped McGuigan's arm and motioned him behind a bench. The light illuminating the space came from one lantern hanging on a pole ten feet from the pillory. The pair hid in the shadows, apparently waiting for the three teens to move closer.

The boy in the lead stood upright and strutted in front of the pillory. "Deaglan is a nit-head." He pulled something from the bucket and threw it at the pillory. It struck the boy's face, then splatted to the ground.

The other teens giggled and joined their friend.

"Moron!" One of them threw something, striking the wood. Then he threw another object.

"Great. They've come to enact childish revenge." Liam grunted. "Another twenty minutes and they'd have missed their chance."

"And now we have to wait until their done." She relaxed, hoping the escapades were short lived. A blinding flash exploded before her, and she turned away to shield her eyes. The light faded as quickly as it appeared, and she blinked to focus in the dim light. "Did you see what happened?"

"No. The light appeared out of nowhere, blinding me. What the...?" He leant forward. "What is she doing?"

Through blurred vision, Lyneth watched Isla pick up one of the buckets the teens had dropped, pluck an item from inside and throw it. It struck the half-blind teen in the face, and he screamed. She threw another, hitting a second teen. As they ran away, she threw the bucket at them.

"That wasn't in the plan." Lyneth wiped her eyes to clear her vision.

"Neither was that."

She stared, confused by Isla's actions. She'd taken something from another bucket and squished into Deaglan's face. Isla said something, but she was too far away to hear clearly. "What'd she say?"

"Whore's leaf?" He shrugged. "Horse thief?"

"I'll go with the second one."

Isla motioned McGuigan forward, and together they released the latches that held the pillory in place. When Deaglan was freed, Isla grabbed him by the ear and dragged him away. McGuigan stumbled after her, scanning the area behind and to the sides. They disappeared from view, and Lyneth waited.

"Five minutes," she whispered. "We wait. Make sure no one follows."

"That's overly cautious."

"If you stay with us, you'll learn it's worth a life to wait."

"You're leading the party, so I'll listen to your orders."

She fell silent to observe the scene before her. Although Liam spoke the words, did he believe them? His body language and his manner of speaking suggested his experience in life taught him to be wary of everyone and everything around him. That wasn't a horrible trait, but it was one to take cautiously.

ဆ ❖ ශ

Isla shoved the boy against the wall. He stood a foot taller than her, but he had no muscle to speak of. As soon as she had chased away the teens pummeling the pillory with rotten fruit, she realised Deaglan, the boy she was to rescue from the device, was the same elf who had stolen her horse that morning.

"You're a compulsive thief." She held him by the front of his shirt. "No wonder your aunt and uncle want to get rid of you."

"Take it easy." McGuigan put his hand on her shoulder. "He's the package."

"I can't believe our luck." She pushed her hand against his chest to hold him in place. "Listen, boy. You steal any of my stuff again, I'm removing fingers."

"Isla, calm down." Lyneth walked out of the shadows. "Don't damage the merchandise."

"He's the boy who stole my horse this morning."

"Looks like we have a project child." Lyneth removed Isla's hand from the boy's shirt. "Don't run, Deaglan. Your uncle Harry sent us." She stood eye-to-eye with him. "Listen carefully. In the morning, you're supposed to be given ten lashes for stealing those boots." His eyes widened, and fear twisted his face. "Your uncle Harry and aunt Bess don't want to see that, so they've sent us to rescue you."

"But I've stolen before," he whined. "They've always let me go."

"It appears you stole one too many things."

Isla quietly chuckled as Lyneth put the fear in him that'd make him agree to accompany them without arguing. This was the plan, and Deaglan was believing every word.

She glanced at Liam who had trailed Lyneth to the muster site. He silently stood back, watching the affair unfold. Their gaze connected for a few seconds, then he pulled his away and returned to the conversation before them. She continued to stare, wondering if he'd reconnect. Her guess proved correct and once again, his eyes fell upon her. His brow raised slowly, and a familiar quizzical expression crossed his face, the same he'd given her many times while they explored the woods around Maskil. Warm feelings stirred, and a smile creased her lips. A similar smile teased the corner of his mouth, and his face brightened. For a moment, everything around them disappeared, and she was left with only the distance between them.

She lifted her foot to step closer to him, but someone whacked her shoulder. Turning abruptly, she found McGuigan's tense face.

"I said get going."

She snapped back to her surroundings. Lyneth was leading away the boy, and McGuigan was pushing her forward, making her follow.

"After you." She gestured for Liam to go first, wanting to keep him in sight as they hurried away.

After several twists and turns, they came upon their horses and the donkey meant for Deaglan.

"I'm told you can ride this," said Lyneth, untying the donkey from the post.

"I can."

"Good. Get up. You follow behind me, okay?"

"Got it." He leapt onto the medium-sized donkey and gathered the reins.

Isla mounted her horse and helped Liam to climb up behind her. They wiggled into position, and she waited for him to hold on. "Do you still know how to ride?"

"I suppose. I haven't ridden since...you." He rested his hands on his lap. She stared at him, trying to read his expression in the dim light. "I haven't done a lot of things since you."

"Things you've missed?" She nudged her horse forward.

"Things I've craved as if life itself."

"Tomorrow, you ride again." She grinned and looked over her shoulder. "We'll start there. Hold on." She winked. "I never want to lose you again."

Several emotions battled for dominance on his face. Sadness won, and he pressed into her back and wrapped his arms around her waist. He stared into the darkness and fell silent.

Not knowing what to say to disperse the mood, she focussed on the task. She shadowed Deaglan and his donkey, and McGuigan took up the rear. They left Moonsface and followed the trail leading to Inglenook. Lyneth had shown her the paper with the aunt's name written on it: Valey Eldon, Caspar Lane. The assignment sounded easy, but she wondered what trouble this immature thief would cause on their journey.

Yet that was not the question dwelling on her mind. It was: What was her future with Liam?

4

We Followed our Hearts

THE ITCH ON LIAM'S shoulder intensified, and he stopped next to a tree and scraped the spot against the trunk. This made it worse. If rubbing the skin raw removed the curse, he'd do it, but the scar that blackened his shoulder deeply penetrated his body. Fighting the urge to scratch, he continued and returned to the camp they'd set up late yesternight, a few miles from Moonsface.

The quick bath had relieved the itch and removed the remaining dirt he hadn't had time to wash away the day before when their leader, Lyneth, had given him thirty minutes to rid himself of his wretched stench gathered from not washing for weeks and from wearing the same clothes since he'd left Wandsworth two moons earlier.

He slowed his pace, then stopped next to Isla. She looked up, and her beautiful eyes captivated him. Never had he gazed into such dark puddles that held his attention. When she had peered through the branches to see who had been caught in the tree, her eyes made his heart prance. Unbelieving what he had seen, his mind raced, trying to piece together an awkward puzzle. When she had spoken, he both dreaded and rejoiced the familiarity of her voice. He longed to find her, but he equally feared seeing her again in his condition.

"Thank you." He handed her the bar of soap she'd lent him. "It smells wonderful." Although lavender wasn't his preferred scent, it was hers.

"Any time. I'll let Alaura know you like it."

"Alaura? Is she still at Moon Meadow?" He knelt on his blanket and pulled his new-to-him rucksack near.

"She lives at Maskil." She leant close. "With das." A knowing smile blossomed across her face and if others weren't around, he'd have stolen a kiss from those beautiful lips.

"They are united?"

"Yes. Finally."

"What do you mean?" Then he remembered. "Your bashful das. How long did it take him to offer a pledge?" He bit down on the last word and hoped she wouldn't mention their pledge to unite made many years ago.

"That wasn't the problem, though Das avoids matters of the heart as if they are dragons beneath the table. Alaura was pledged to another, and then a duke got involved and..." An odd expression crossed her face. "They're united now, living happily at Maskil. They took the scenic path." She rested her hand on his, and her touch made him tremble. "That happens between even dedicated mates."

The longer her hand lingered, the hotter the fire grew within and the more the itch expanded on his shoulder. His past rushed forward, causing an ache in his heart that would never heal. It spread to his throat and threatened to sting his eyes. He forced his mind to think of other things, anything other than his inability to be with her. "And Farlan. How is he doing?" He cleared his throat and moved his hand away from her, pretending to gather his gear.

"He's like always." Her smile faded. "Except he's united and has three kids."

He stopped and stared. "Three? I've been gone only six years."

"He knew what he wanted, and he dove in heart first."

"Sanderson?" He rolled his blanket tightly and tied twine around it to keep it in place.

"Sandy has his hands full."

"In what way."

"Farlan is a sergeant, and that causes amusement, but my das is a lord, and the three of them together," she giggled, "provide interesting entertainment."

"Bronwyn is a lord?" His back stiffened. The Lords of Aruam Castle were his enemy; they had murdered his das. He'd never pledge allegiance to them. He'd rather kill them.

"Only recently." She exchanged a glance with McGuigan, and after they shared a secret message, she turned back to him. Her solemn expression revealed her reluctance to speak further.

"You know what I think about the lords."

"I do but trust das. He'd never treat you unfairly."

The man was incapable of treating anyone unfairly. He was too *honourable.* "I'll trust him, but the others..." He fastened the clip to his rucksack and glanced at Lyneth, who tacked up her horse. "We better get moving." The more distance he put between him and Moonsface the better. He lifted his pack to his shoulder.

"Here."

He turned and found her removing a dagger and sheathe from her waist. When she held it out to him, he hesitated.

"Take it. I have two others." When he didn't accept it, she stepped close and wrapped the leather around his waist. "You need a weapon to protect yourself on The Trail, and to protect the rest of us."

The excitement created when she tugged the belt securely around his waist expanded to his chest and flew to every limb. She worked quickly to fasten the end of the sheathe around his thigh, then tugged on it, making his blood overheat. Her scent filled his senses, and he melted under her gaze. What ever she asked, he'd do.

She stepped away. "You look ready for The Trail."

"More like La-la Land." McGuigan chuckled as he passed.

Liam composed himself quickly. Had he been that obvious? He didn't want to be. He wanted to... Pain flared up in his chest. What he wanted was impossible to obtain.

Isla tightened the girth and checked the stirrup straps. After adjusting the bridle, she secured their bedrolls behind the saddle. With the horse ready, she stood aside with reins in hand.

"Up. You're steering today."

Liam glanced warily at the saddle and over the horse. "Is it well trained?"

"Not exactly. It's a two-bit horse; the best my lack of quality coins could afford." She patted its neck. "Not sure what I'll name it yet. Any ideas?"

"Two-bit?"

"I was thinking of something more exciting like Raindancer or Winddodger."

"Or Sundry."

"I want him to grow into a good name, not stick him with something boring."

"Call him Spindrift."

Her mouth opened, then she remembered their days of watching wisps of snow fly into the air off the castle roof and her pointing out what it was called. She had been enthralled by the word and used it every chance she had. Considering the horse and the name, she nodded. "Spindrift it is. Climb up."

"Not well trained? Maybe I should wait."

"I'll be here to correct him if he misbehaves." When he didn't move, she added, "You were on him yesterday; he was fine."

He put his foot in the stirrup and hoisted himself up but failed to reach the saddle. His foot smacked onto the ground, and he fought to regain his balance.

"Let me help. When you're ready." She waited for him to gather strength for another leap. A sharp sound pierced the air, and she shot a glare towards the donkey. It squealed for an unknown reason. She remembered that's what donkeys did. The sound travelled far; the reason they weren't good for The Trail. They'd alert everyone within a mile of their location. Deaglan mounted, and the donkey settled.

She turned back to Liam and found him staring at her, his gaze fixed on her lips. It triggered her nerves, and her body warmed from their closeness. The urge to kiss him grew.

"Mount up." Lyneth rested on her horse, checking the path in front of them and behind.

"We'll try again." Liam grasped the saddle horn. He bounced on his foot to create momentum, then pushed himself into the air. She braced his leg and pushed on his butt to give him extra lift. He settled onto the leather seat, and she handed him the reins.

"Leave them slack until I'm up. Hand." She waited for him to offer his, then she used it to leap into the saddle. "Do you remember how to hold the reins?"

"Like this?" He grasped one in each hand and placed his thumbs on the leather strap.

"Can he ride?" Lyneth rode up beside them.

"Yes," said Isla. "But he hasn't ridden in a few years; I need to know he can handle my horse if necessary."

"We'll go slow at first for him to get reacquainted, then we'll pick up the pace." Lyneth guided her horse to lead the group. "McGuigan, you're in the rear."

"Use your leg to tell him to walk. Not too hard, but hard enough. This isn't Clover."

"If it was, we'd fly like the wind." He glanced over his shoulder, half smiling. "She was fast." He shrugged. "Or as kids, it felt fast."

"No, she was fast. And smart."

"She preferred you at the reins."

"She liked you."

"She threw me into the river." He frowned. "Then blew snot at me and trotted away as if she was the best horse in the land."

"She is the best horse in the land." She giggled and wrapped her arms around his waist. The warmth from his body enticed her to pull closer, and she rested her chin on the side of his left shoulder. "My hands are right here if I need to grab the reins." She held them out before him, then returned them to his stomach.

The horse moved beneath her. Unsure of what to do, it walked straight across the trail towards the trees. She put her hand on his and tugged the reins gently. "Like this."

He adjusted his hands, and the horse followed behind Deaglan and his donkey. Once it straightened, his leg pressed against its side, and it picked up the pace.

She relaxed against him and watched the trail ahead. Feeling his heartbeat against her chest, she counted the beats. It was faster than normal.

They travelled for almost an hour, heading northwest, through a forest of large trees that cast intense shade over the bushes growing below. The lack of thick underbrush allowed her to peer for a hundred feet or more into the woods between tree trunks. Birds, squirrels and the occasional larger wildlife crossed their path but otherwise, The Trail was quiet. The birds sang sweetly, telling her no unsavoury intruders tramped nearby.

When her horse reared, she latched onto Liam's shirt with one hand, and the reins with the other. He had quickly caught on to riding again, and she was more worried about the lack of training of her horse. "What was it?"

She leant around his arm with her hand resting on his back for balance.

"Fox," he said. "Darted from the bush. Spooked me and the horse."

The tips of her fingers felt an unusual heat permeating from his body, and she moved her right hand to his shoulder blade. She pressed her palm against his shirt, and negative energy shot into her arm, swirled around and withdrew. It shook her nerves and sent her heart racing. The energy shot out again, this time into her shoulder. Her muscles cramped, and she gasped for breath to absorb the pain.

Liam whirled, his eyes bulging in horror. "Don't touch me!" He tried to shove away her arm but failed to reach it.

Frozen by agonising pain, she lost her balance and tumbled with him when he flung himself out of the saddle. She slammed hard against the ground, and her vision darkened momentarily. He jumped and ran from her side to the edge of the forest.

"What in Knavesmire are you doing?" McGuigan caught the reins of the prancing horse.

Isla slowly rose, gripping her right arm, hoping the discomfort from the fall and the negative energy left quickly. "What was that?" She stared at Liam. His face twisted in agony, and his bottom lip trembled. "Why did you do that?" she yelled, trying to break him out of the spell that held him.

"I... Don't touch me." He searched the ground as if he'd find the answers hiding in the low shrubs growing along the trail.

"Why?" It wasn't the first time he'd avoided contact, but she thought he'd gotten over the discomfort from her riding behind him with her arms around his waist.

"I can't..." Tears welled, and his voice shook. "I've done you wrong. I've broken our pledge. Many times. I've been with other women. Hauflin women." His eyes pleaded with her. "My promise to you. I've broken it. We will never be..." He flinched and gripped his chest.

Isla's heart ached for him, and she took a step forward. "I've broken it, too. First with McGuigan, then with a man named Arthur. I've wanted to tell you, but I was afraid you'd hate me."

"I will never..." He choked on spit. "We're not mates; we're barely friends." Looking up, the saddest expression blanketed his face. "I release you from the pledge; you're free to choose another. We were foolish kids."

"We *are* friends." The lump in her throat made her eyes water. "We weren't foolish; we followed our hearts."

"We're not pledged!"

"I heard you the first time."

"Now that that's established, let's get moving." Lyneth sat with her arms crossed over her saddle horn.

Isla shoved her hands into her pockets. "Do you want me to ride with you?" When he didn't answer, the sting in her eyes increased.

"Ride with me," said McGuigan.

"Is that what you want?" She glared at Liam.

"It's for the best," Liam muttered.

"You'd give me to another man?" She threw herself up behind McGuigan. "Fine."

"I'll take her any day." McGuigan twisted and kissed her on the lips. Smirking, he gathered the reins.

She wrapped her arms around his waist and pulled closer. "It's easy to know who your friends are." She looked away, not wanting to see the man he'd become. He was weak of mind, cold and despicable.

"Liam, mount up," said Lyneth. "We're wasting daylight."

Isla heard footsteps, the creak of leather and her horse neigh. She pressed her forehead against McGuigan's back and as they rode away, tears came. He rested a hand on her thigh, but her numb body didn't feel his warmth. Instead, it felt the sting of reality. Liam had changed and was nothing like the boy she'd kissed in the bakery supply room, the one she'd pledged her love to. This man found trapped in a tree was not her Liam. If he had died there, she'd have never missed him.

The location Lyneth chose to camp was next to a babbling brook, one that flowed from the mountains in the distance. She'd stopped here a few years before with The Mercenaries when they visited the small village of Bannock. Morwen had suggested the spot because of its access to water and the small grassy clearing fifty feet from the road.

Lyneth dismounted and scanned the area. It hadn't changed much since she'd been here last. The Springan flowering bushes had shed their petals, and the grass grew long. Some areas were cut low, probably by travellers' horses. She released her mare to let it graze freely.

"You're doing it wrong."

She turned and saw Isla standing next to her horse talking loudly to Liam.

"I can help," he said, keeping his voice even.

"I don't need your help." She removed his bedroll and rucksack and shoved them into his arms. "Go. Get away from me!" She ignored him until he walked away, then she stared at his back.

Lyneth went to her side and patted the horse. "He gets the hint; you need not yell."

"His head lacks sense." Isla unfastened the cinch roughly.

"He has things on his mind."

She lowered her brow and frowned. "We all do."

"I recall another young hauflin struggling to make a new life in an unfamiliar world with strangers." Lyneth caught the saddle when it fell forward. "We tolerated her until she found her balance."

"It's not the same." Isla fell silent as if replaying those days in her mind. "I was in prison."

"You don't know where he escaped from."

"Do you?"

"No, I'm saying I think he escaped from horrible circumstances." She released the saddle into Isla's arms. "If you're patient, you might learn from where." She leant close. "The words were one thing; the kiss was cruel."

"McGuigan kissed me."

"You accepted it."

She twisted her lips to the side, then slowly released her tension, accepting the assessment of the action. "Fine. Not that it matters."

"It does if he matters." Lyneth walked away, leaving Isla to think about it. She approached Deaglan who removed the bit from the donkey's mouth. "I'm surprised it keeps up. I was told donkeys were stubborn, not trail worthy."

He released the animal to graze. "People ignorant of donkeys say that. I ride her everywhere."

"Except when you're stealing horses."

His face turned a light shade of pink. "I had walked too far. Was going to be late. First horse I ever stole."

"Tried to steal."

"You have me there. It was a wild ride, and I'd have gotten away if not for those men."

"I had forgotten about them. Isla said they were dangerous in appearance. How did you get away?"

"They weren't dangerous. Only travellers looking for a friend."

"Looking for a friend on the road?"

"A hauflin. They said they needed to give him something he had forgotten at home before he left to visit family up north."

"Did they describe him?" She glanced at Liam who spread his bedroll next to the fire.

"Not much. Brown eyes, brown hair. That's almost every hauflin I've met. And young." He shrugged. "That's usually the ones who pass through Moonsface." He picked up his rucksack and bedroll.

"Did they say where they were from?"

"Wandsworth."

The place name added a piece to the puzzle she'd been putting together since she'd met Liam. These men might not have been looking for him but if they were, she was glad to be on this trail and not the one headed towards Edgewood, where those men were headed. "I'm glad the donkey is working for you." The animal hee-hawed, piercing her ears. "Though I wish it were quieter."

"That means she's happy." He laughed. "She loves to eat."

She led him to the campsite where McGuigan and Isla had already started a fire. Seeing the large space around Liam, she tossed her bedroll next to him, then helped gather wood for fuel.

The evening went by quietly with only a few words passing between McGuigan and Isla and none between them and Liam. She asked him a few general questions to keep him involved, but then she lost interest and lay back to rest.

At ten o'clock the others settled in their bedrolls, and Lyneth sat against the thick trunk of a nearby tree to watch for the first shift. An hour passed, and the calmness of sleep deep in the forest settled upon the campsite. An owl hooted in the distance and peepers peeped along the brook.

The evening watch was less stressful than when she'd travelled with The Mercenaries. Many sought to find the group, and Elspeth had taken great care ensuring their safety while they slept. Since they'd distanced themselves from the Rothkin/Kintale feud, she felt safer. It helped knowing Tigh na Mare warriors weren't roaming Ath-o'Lea hunting for her. She and the others were not running to or away from anything.

Movement caught her eye, and she saw Liam pick up his boots and rucksack, and sneak from the campfire. He crept towards the trail, which put him a few feet away from her. She made no motion to stop him.

"If you're looking for forgiveness," she said in a hushed voice, "this is not where you'll find it."

He stopped, and a painful expression crossed his face.

"When she wakes and finds you gone, she'll either be glad and never think of you again, or her heart will ache, and she'll spend the next several years searching for you. Which do you think she'll do? Can you live with the decision you force her to make?"

He stared at Isla, who slept soundly. The dimness supplied by the gibbous moon highlighted the torment he endured. His hesitation and deep consideration of her words exposed his feelings even if he was incapable of admitting them.

"Her anger today was fuelled by a strong emotion. You're wise to know which one that was."

He stood upright and slouched his shoulders. For a long moment, he stood there as if arguing with himself on his best course of action.

Then, he walked slowly to his bedroll, released his boots and rucksack and lay down.

Lyneth checked her time piece; in another hour, she'd wake McGuigan. If he'd been on watch when Liam attempted to leave, he'd have encouraged him, causing a ripple that would have affected their future assignments. She held no doubt Isla wasn't finished with this man. In fact, if she was a foreteller, she'd predict Liam wasn't finished with her either. His daft smiles and goofy, lost expressions disclosed his feelings though he tried to hide them.

She half chuckled. Young love was crazy at best. When it involved true love, it increased the trouble and pleasure beyond any boundary. Her thoughts drifted to Rod; they were more mature, older than Isla and Liam when they had found each other, yet...her emotions swung wild in every direction. She would do anything for him; she had even begged to stay at Blackvale to be with him.

5

Deep, Forbidden Magic

THREE DAYS LATER, THEY entered the small village of Bannock. Isla smiled at the signpost created from stone and a thick, carved log: *Welcome to Bannock, the hubbery of Knollton Mountain Range; Population 2467.* She wondered what they meant by hubbery. This village wasn't large enough to be the central part of any area.

They passed the first dwelling. The land afore it was over-grown with lush gardens filled with colourful fruit and vegetable plants. The orange pumpkins were as large as caldrons. Cute wooden statues of turtles, large green moths and long-eared baby goats peeked between leaves of tasty squash and cucumbers, and a white pebble path winded its way throughout. A few benches provided seating for the gardener to relax and enjoy the sight and the sunshine.

She stretched her neck to see around McGuigan to the other side of the road. That dwelling also had interesting gardens in front. She gazed at it as they passed, and Liam rode into her line of sight. A stupid grin contorted his face.

"Do you still dream of a home surrounded by large gardens?" he asked.

"No. Dreams are for silly children." Since throwing her from the horse, she'd only spoken to him to educate him on how to saddle the two-bit animal. They exchanged many looks and sour faces, but she had nothing to say.

"What is that?" McGuigan pointed to a bright yellow sign next to a small dwelling. "Weslia's Wyrd." He glanced at Isla. "What do you make of it?"

She peered closer and read the fine print. "She reveals your destiny? Sounds like bad magic."

"Not exactly," said Lyneth over her shoulder. "She answers one question, and only one."

"Any question?" asked McGuigan.

"Yes. The answers aren't always what you want or expect."

"Have you visited her?" Isla scrutinised the front of the building. The bright purples, reds and gold conjured deep, forbidden magic.

"Yes."

"What question did you ask?"

"I'm not telling."

"Was the answer true?"

Lyneth was about to respond, then she looked at each of them and clamped her mouth shut.

"Well. Don't keep me in suspense."

"I believe it was." She turned to face forward and fell silent.

Isla huffed. "That's not answering my question."

"I'd ask the location of a treasure chest full of gold," said McGuigan. "Then I'd buy a faster horse. What would you ask?"

Her gaze fell upon Liam, and several questions came to mind. "Maybe, what is..." *that thing on his back?* His expression changed as he mentally finished the question. "No, I'd ask, Who is my..." *mate?* Again, she paused to allow his imagination to fill in the blank. His lips closed, and he tried to break eye contact but failed. A real question came to mind, and she sat up, wondering if Mystic Weslia had the answer. If she did, she'd visit as soon as they settled.

"Well?" McGuigan followed Lyneth onto a narrow lane.

"I'd ask for a cure for Kiefer. Where I'd find it? What to do to help him."

"You get one question."

"I'm thinking. We'll go. Tonight."

"I'll come with you."

"Who's Kiefer?" asked Liam.

"A friend. A best friend." She stared at the building, marking its location.

"You have two best friends?"

Her mind elsewhere, she stared at him, confused.

"You can have only one best friend," said Liam. "That's what best means."

"I have..." Her mind tried to unravel his words, but Kiefer and the mystical woman consumed her thoughts.

"Do you really think she tells the truth?" Deaglan lagged, staring at the entrance to Weslia's Wyrd.

"Probably not," said Liam. "These foretellers want your money."

"I'll wager if it doesn't cost much," said the boy. "I'd ask about enchanted staffs or maybe a golden orb. I'll ask for a magical horse. One with wings."

"You ask a question, not for something." Liam frowned. "You need to start thinking seriously. Don't waste time on foolishness."

"One man's foolishness is another's opportunity."

"I'm not sure you understand the sentiment of that statement."

Deaglan shrugged. "Doesn't matter."

Gold, magical horses and staffs didn't interest Isla. They couldn't heal Kiefer. Only powerful magic or a potent natural remedy held the means to rejuvenate his health. If she found a cure, it'd be worth all the coins in her pouch.

℠ ✦ ℟

McGuigan carried an armful of split logs towards their campsite. The wood was included in the price of the camping plot in Bannock's Gathering Grounds. Lyneth had explained that the few inns in the small village were often booked and were expensive. Most travellers rented a camping plot at the Gathering Grounds, where they were provided with water, wood, a place to hitch their horses and hay.

Scanning the faces of the others who camped in the area, he noticed Liam walking towards him and staring off into the distance. The man was on his way back to the wood pile for the third and final load they'd need to keep the fire going until they left in the morning.

"What are you looking at?" McGuigan paused but didn't stop. He had wanted the man to leave the day he pushed Isla from her horse. His actions were cruel and had left a severe bruise on her hip.

"I'm wonder where he's going." Liam pointed through the crowd of people gathered around a large fire. The sun had set, and twilight illuminated the land.

He followed his line of sight and saw Deaglan rushing towards the exit of the Gathering Grounds. "If he gets caught stealing, we'll have a real problem." He set the wood down by a pole. "I'm going after him."

Liam fell into step beside him. "The fool doesn't know when he's got it good."

"You don't have to come. I can handle the boy."

"You'll be faster with help. In case he goes behind one building and we don't know which way he'll turn."

Liam was right, but he didn't want to admit it. "He's running." He started to jog. "I'd rather deliver the donkey than this boy."

"Animals are easier to control." Liam ran beside him, already labouring for breath.

"This way." He ducked down a narrow lane. "We'll cut him off." They raced down the lane and between two small dwellings. "There he goes." They made several more turns, then ran in a straight line.

"He's going to that woman." Liam drew a ragged breath. "The one who answers questions."

McGuigan slowed to a walk, not wanting him to collapse before they reached Deaglan. Drawing a deep breath, he released it slowly to decrease his heart rate. "He's heading in that direction." Now that they travelled the road to the village entrance, he easily tracked the dark head bobbing in the distance.

"The fool is gone to throw away his money." He gulped a breath and dragged the back of his hand over his forehead.

"You going to make it?"

"I'll be fine."

"You're out of shape." More like too skinny. His complexion had returned to a degree of normalcy after several days of regular eating, but he needed muscle.

Liam smirked. "You'd be, too, if you hadn't a wholesome meal in weeks."

"Weeks?" He cringed. "I can't go two days."

"You could if you had to."

He doubted it. He loved food. "He's gone inside. You were right." They walked quickly to Weslia's Wyrd and stopped at the door. He tried the handle; it was locked, so he knocked and waited.

"She won't answer," said Liam and pointed to a sign on the exterior wall.

McGuigan squinted to read it in the dim light: *Door is locked while in session. Please, be patient.* "Great." He knocked again, louder this time.

"Let's try around back." Liam leant against the post holding up the roof over the doorway.

"He's probably paid his money. He might as well get his question answered." He gazed upon the front yard. "We'll give him five minutes. Then I'll check the back door while you guard this one."

A long silence followed before Liam spoke. "Thank you."

"For what?"

"Taking care of Isla. I may not be her friend, but it matters to me that she's in good hands." He looked away. "I see she is."

"You're lucky I didn't punch you. The fall gave her a large bruise."

"That was not my intention." He pressed his lips together. "Promise me something."

"No."

"Please. I trust you'll do right by Isla."

"More than you."

"Promise you'll keep her safe."

"I don't need a promise to do that."

"I mean, keep her...near."

He lowered his brow. "Beside me?"

"Yes." His face twisted. "Keep her from wandering off, chasing foolishness." His voice trembled. "I wish to spend a few days with her and at Inglenook, we'll part ways." He drew a long breath.

"I don't understand, but I'll keep her from following, if that's what you mean. You call this boy a fool, but a bigger one stands before me."

"I can't disagree."

A loud crashing sound echoed between the dwellings and grabbed their attention.

Liam leapt into the alleyway. "He's running."

McGuigan jumped off the step and followed him between the buildings. When he reached the back yard, he quickly scanned the area. A seasoned elf stopped abruptly beside him.

"That boy stole a special deck of cards. Do you know him?"

"Unfortunately. He's under our care." McGuigan stepped away, hoping to avoid an argument. "We'll get them back and return them."

"He knows not how to deal them," the man shouted after them. "Danger awaits!"

McGuigan cursed under his breath and chased after Liam who was already a hundred feet ahead of him. The hauflin was small and skinny but fast when rested. His problem was endurance. He tried to catch up, but after several twists and turns, he managed only to not lose ground.

A solid force struck him in the forehead, and he crashed to the ground. His vision blurred, and he scrambled to see what had hit him. A strong hand jerked him to his feet and rammed him against the wall. Blinking quickly, he stared into the faces of two young elves. One held a club, ready to strike.

"Got any coins?" The man scowled, revealing a gaping hole in his top row of teeth.

"I've got nothing." McGuigan swung his fist, but the club struck it down, sending stinging needles into his arm.

The man groped his shirt, then drove his hand into his trouser pocket. He jerked forward, and his eyes bulged from the sudden movement. A solid whack to the back of his head brought him to his knees where he collapsed to the ground.

The man with the club turned and faced Liam, who held a thick metal rod. A stupid grin plastered his face. He swung, missed, then tried again.

This gave Liam time to swing around and bring the bar across the man's back. A quick move delivered the bar to the man's forehead. The attacker snapped backwards and fell to the ground, motionless.

"Come on." Liam threw down the bar and jogged down the back alley.

McGuigan caught up easily now that Liam had exhausted his energy in running and fighting. "Where did you learn to do that?"

"There are plenty of thugs to practise on in the city."

"I'll see if I can catch him." He dug down and added strength to his legs, quickly out-pacing Liam.

"Left," shouted Liam.

McGuigan followed his command. When he turned the corner, he saw a shadow running up ahead. He had to be at least eight hundred feet away. While he ran at full speed, he failed to decrease the distance between them, and the boy quickly disappeared between two buildings. He stared at the location, so he wouldn't bypass it.

By the time he reached it, the boy was no where in sight. If Liam hadn't stopped to help him, he probably would have caught him. Now they were faced with the task of searching the back streets of Bannock for a careless young thief.

He stopped to let Liam catch up. The hauflin staggered towards him, then plopped down on a crate to rest.

"He's gone?" Liam gasped for breath and held his chest with his hand.

"I don't know which way he went."

"Give me a minute, then I'll see what I can find." He stretched out on the crate, gulping air. "He'll tire, too. He's probably eager to use those cards, so he'll find a place to hide."

"Let's hope not." He wiped what felt like blood from the side of his face and scanned the dark alley. Catching a glimpse of Liam, he forced words from his mouth. "Thank you."

"For what?"

"Coming back for me."

"We're on the same side."

"Still, you didn't have to."

"Because?" When he didn't answer, Liam supplied an answer. "You don't feel we're on the same side?"

"I don't know you."

"That's a fair answer. You don't trust me is probably a more accurate one."

"I won't lie; I don't."

"I don't expect you to." He jerked his head towards the alley. "Let's see if we can find this rascal before he causes more problems. We'll go slow. Listen for him. I've tracked sneakier teens in larger places. We'll find him."

"Lead the way." McGuigan fell into step behind him. Tucking his hair behind his ears, he listened to the sounds of the village.

Less than an hour later, they stopped near a half-open door leading into a small shed. Colourful lights spilt out, shining on the door and the ground.

"Let me," whispered Liam in cant. He moved silently to the shed, then slipped along the front. Before he reached the door, he glanced back with an odd expression. He shrugged, then moved forward.

Unable to read the body language, McGuigan waited. An odd sound touched his ears. It came from inside the shed. He'd heard it before, but the time and place eluded him.

Liam reached the doorway and peeked inside. He quickly withdrew and rested his back against the wall. His eyes darted across the ground. Withdrawing his dagger from the sheath, he gripped it tightly, then sprang into the shed.

McGuigan rushed forward with his sword drawn. The racket coming from inside didn't sound friendly. When he reached the door, he came to an abrupt stop and stared at the sight before him.

Deaglan sat cross-legged in a trance with several cards turned up in front of him. Brilliant lights shot out of the cards and danced on the ceiling and walls. On the other side of the cards, tentacles emerged from a hole in the floor. They wrapped around Liam and tossed him about like a flag in the wind. His dagger struck several times, but it didn't weaken the tentacles of the large octopus. Liam struck the ceiling, then was squished face-first into the wall. Blood dripped from numerous cuts, and the dagger flew from his hand.

Quickly assessing the situation, McGuigan sheathed his sword and dove for the cards. He scooped them up and quickly formed a deck. A solid thud behind him made him swing around. Liam lay on the floor, struggling to rise, and the tentacles oozed slowly into the hole. In less than a minute, the octopus and the hole vanished.

He grabbed the wooden box and shoved the cards inside. After ramming them into his pocket, he went to Liam, who gasped for breath on his hands and knees. "It's gone."

"I've never seen anything like it." Liam fell to his butt and rested his back against the wall. His face was battered and bruised, and blood ran into his eye and from his mouth.

"Octopus. Seen one once in Ellswire. Fishermen had caught it and brought it ashore."

He wiped his eyes with his sleeve. "I hope they ate it."

"That was the plan." He sneered at Deaglan, who stirred from his daze. "What was his plan? To be eaten?"

"Not sure. It was..." Liam swallowed and choked on spit, "singing to him. Strangest thing I've ever seen."

"What happened?" Deaglan appeared fuddled. "That thing. It was...huge."

McGuigan slapped the boy in the head. "That's for stealing the cards." He hit him again. "That's for almost getting us killed." He grabbed him by the back of the shirt and dragged him to his feet.

"Killed? I saw it. It was to bring me treasure."

"I think it planned on taking you to that treasure on the bottom of the sea." He dragged him to the door.

Liam stood but lost his balance and fell.

McGuigan reached out a hand. When Liam hesitated, he said, "Take it."

Liam grabbed it, and he hauled him to his feet. "Thank you."

"For what?" He raised an eyebrow. "We're on the same side." He shoved Deaglan out the door and down the alley, taking the shortest route to Weslia's Wyrd. Liam followed, a little shaky at first, then steadier on his feet. After returning the deck of cards, apologizing for the theft and promising to punish the boy for his actions, they walked back to Bannock's Gathering Grounds.

The sun had set several hours beforehand, and many of the travellers had turned in for the night. A few still chatted and sang around their campfires, providing a festive atmosphere. When they approached their site, Isla was the first to spot them and came running.

"Where have you been?" She stopped in front of McGuigan, who flung Deaglan towards the bedrolls prepared near the fire.

"Chasing this kid around Bannock. He was caught stealing, then found more trouble."

"You're hurt."

"Just a scratch." He jerked his finger over his shoulder. "Tend to him. He got the worse of it."

She looked past McGuigan and when she saw Liam, her mouth dropped open. "Is anything broken?"

"I'm okay. I'll take care of it."

"He lies. He needs help." McGuigan picked up a thick stump and set it near the fire. "Sit."

Liam stared at the seat and didn't move until Isla's fingers wrapped around his hand, and she led him to it.

"Where did he steal from?" Lyneth glared at Deaglan.

"Weslia's Wyrd." McGuigan rested on his bedroll and pulled a cloth from his rucksack to wipe his face. "A deck of cards that conjured an enormous octopus that threw Liam around like a leaf in a wind storm."

"Must I tie you every time we enter a settlement?" She leant into Deaglan's face. "I have no problem doing that, but I'd prefer to trust you. Can I?"

He nodded. "I don't ever want to see something like that again."

Isla poured warm water from the kettle hanging over the fire into a bowl and added more water to cool it. She tossed a cloth into it, then went to Liam.

"I can do this." Liam reached for the cloth.

"Let her." McGuigan lay near them. "She's skilled."

Isla knelt before Liam and removed the cloth from his hand. "If I can touch you." He nodded, and she gently wiped away the blood. "I'll need to stitch the one above your eye."

"Do what you must."

McGuigan watched him. The man never took his eyes from Isla as she cleaned his face, stitched the cut, applied ointment and bandaged spots that needed it most. By the end, Liam's expression had softened to that of a lover staring at his mate with the intentions of loving her a lifetime.

When she offered to mend the holes in his new shirt, he accepted and while he visited the latrine, changed out of it. He settled in his bedroll facing her with a peaceful smile on his battered face.

6

More Powerful than the Threat of Death

ISLA HALTED AT THE hitching rail and stared at the front door of Weslia's Wyrd. The early morning's bright light cast upon the wooden entrance diminished its magical appeal. Lyneth warned her this woman's answer wouldn't satisfy her. It had taken several years to please Lyneth; Kiefer didn't have that time.

"Have you changed your mind?" Liam sat behind her. He had offered to come while the others prepared to leave Bannock.

She glanced over her shoulder at his battered face and once again, a twinge of dread swept through her chest. He'd taken a bad beaten. One of his eyes was swollen shut, and the cut on the corner of his mouth had reopened.

"We can leave, and no one needs to know," he said.

"I'd know. I have to do this for Kiefer."

He slipped from the saddle and waited for her. When she dismounted, he held her waist and eased her to the ground as he'd done many times in the past when they rode Clover, Alaura's pony, at Moon Meadow. She fought against his act of gallantry changing how she felt about him, but...her heart fluttered.

"I'll stay by your side." He secured the horse to the pole and followed her.

She knocked once, and a seasoned elf answered. His stern expression made her step back and into Liam.

"You again." The man frowned. "Have you taught the boy a lesson?"

"We have, sir," said Liam. "We'll be taking him from your fair village today."

He huffed. "It appears you were taught a harder lesson."

"One I won't soon forget."

"What do you want?" The man folded his arms.

"My friend wishes to have a question answered."

"Is she a thief, too?"

"Far from it, good sir. She's an honourable woman."

Isla glanced at him. If he knew her past, he wouldn't have used that word.

"She may enter."

"May I accompany her."

"Only mates are permitted. Are you mates?"

"Yes," lied Isla.

"The cost of an answer is five bits?"

Isla handed him the coins, and he led her into a room dimly lit with half a dozen candles. A woman sat behind a table decorated with two candles, a small dish, a deck of cards and a bright-purple tablecloth. She was as seasoned as the man who had answered the door. Her long golden hair held pale-green streaks. The light brown, short-sleeve dress she wore exposed a fair amount of skin around her neck and the top of her bosom. A small round pendant inset with a flat, oval red stone hung from a gold necklace and rested above the dress line.

Weslia, she assumed. The one with mystic magic.

"Who has a question for Weslia?" She spoke as if she sang a slow song.

"I do." Isla stepped forward.

"Sit, dear." She gestured towards the chair directly across from her. "Your mate may..." Her mouth froze, and she tilted her head and became lost in deep thought. In the seconds that passed, her expression grew dark, and she stared at Liam. "You are forbidden at my table." She ushered him away. "Against the wall."

Isla glanced between Liam and Weslia. "Why?"

"It's okay. I'll sit here." He sat in the chair provided.

"His blood is...sour."

She tucked the comment away for later consideration and sat across from the foreteller. She'd never been to one before. The Mystic One at the Dukedom of Dunakan didn't count. That women didn't predict her future but almost destroyed it. When she'd returned the Rope of Entanglement to Merk Lindrum, he'd given her another pouch with the magical grey powder in case she encountered the deadly poyson again.

Mystic One... Mystic Magic... Certainly this woman was elf, not newlin. She peered closer to positively identify the race.

"You seek what you will not find." Weslia set the cards in the centre of the table.

"But..." She wanted to find a cure for Kiefer.

"I am pure elf."

Isla sat straighter. This woman sensed more than the obvious.

"Shuffle the deck."

She picked up the cards. The last time she had shuffled a deck, she ended up in bed with Arthur. He had taught her how to please a man; he also revealed his ability to drive her wild. Did Liam possess the same ability? Or would he generate a deeper response, one that made her crave him?

"You overflow with queries today."

"That's not the one I wish to ask."

"You'll find the answer to it soon. Please. Focus on the question you wish answered. Let other distractions leave your mind."

Isla thought of Kiefer and the injuries he had suffered at the hands of Orenda Nassen and the Tigh na Mare warriors. She thought of his internal wounds, the way they felt when the energy in her fingertips delved deep beneath the skin and how she had attempted to heal them. He had slept for six days in Catriona's bed before he finally woke. When he did, the true depth of his injuries revealed themselves. He had difficulty talking and breathing. He felt a heavy weight on his chest and weeks later, he still couldn't walk across the room without resting. His inability to consume regular food meant those caring for him had to cook and mash it as if he were an infant.

Alaura had tended to him and consulted Beathas, and their treatments had helped, but his abilities were limited. He'd never return to The Trail. For now, he and Catriona tolerated each other, and he remained at her dwelling, sleeping in a small bed shoved into the corner, but this arrangement was temporary.

"You love him dearly."

Her eyes had grown blurry with moisture. "I do."

"Surrender your life for his, you would." Weslia nodded sympathetically. "Your question is worthy. Prepare it, and I will answer exactly. Set one card upright before you." Once the card was down, she continued. "Set a second card beside it."

She obeyed, then laid down the remaining four cards where she was told to place them. The colours in the cards came alive and shone upward. They mingled together and glowed upon Weslia's face.

"You may ask one question. You may not change the words once said. Form the question in your mind, then speak it."

Isla considered the question. She was certain of it and spoke it. "Where will I find a cure to heal Kiefer's body?"

Weslia closed her eyes and moved her hands over the cards. The colours glowed brightly, making Isla raise her hand to block the glare. Dust sparkled in the air, settling on the table and its contents. When the lights dimmed, Weslia's concerned expression eased. "A worthy quest deserves a positive outcome. Find the cure in your mate's pocket."

Isla stared. That was no answer. She wanted to know the name of the place, the village, the mountain, the building where she'd find it, not the pocket of... She turned slowly and set her eyes on Liam. He had nothing in his pocket. All his clothes were recently bought. If he had a cure, why didn't he tell her?

"Thank you for visiting Weslia's Wyrd." She gathered the cards.

"But he doesn't have anything." She spun quickly. "Do you?"

"I have nothing."

She faced Weslia. "Where will he find it?"

"One question per person per moon." She placed the cards in a small wooden box.

"Liam, you ask. Please," she begged.

"No! He is unwelcome at my table." Weslia placed her hand over the box.

"But..." she turned back to the table, "I'm desperate."

"Your question has been answered." She rose. "Enjoy your day."

Isla's mouth hung open. Her question hadn't been answered. She'd been given a tease, a hint, but no real answer.

"This way, please." The man who answered the door gestured for them to leave the room.

Liam placed a comforting hand on the lower part of her back and guided her outside and to the horse. She stood frozen by the hitching rail, staring at the morning sun.

"Lyneth was right. She doesn't answer as expected. I don't think she answers at all." Her mind raced to solve the riddle, but there was nothing to grasp onto. "How can I find what I seek in a pocket I do not know?"

Liam cleared his throat. "Would this Kiefer be your mate? Your love for him was detected by the woman."

"Mate? Nonsense. He's like a brother to me."

"What about McGuigan?"

"A higgler's chance."

"Then maybe you'll soon meet him." His voice softened.

"I won't find him in time." She swallowed hard and tears moistened her eyes.

He slipped his hand farther across her back to rest upon her hip. "Maybe we misunderstood the answer."

She stared into his sympathetic eyes. "It could not be clearer. I'd find it in my mate's pocket. If she thought you were him and you have nothing, then we have nothing."

He deliberated a moment and his grip tightened, pulling her closer. "What if the answer revealed a truth unknown?"

"What?" The heat from his body warmed her.

"Did you not say you were afraid there was no cure?"

"I was told there was none."

"Then you have your answer."

"I don't understand."

"Weslia told you there was a cure."

Was he right? If he was, her search for the cure would uncover the identity of her mate. They'd be one and the same. She threw her arms around his neck. "Yes. That's it. There's a cure." She pulled away quickly. "And I'm going to find it."

"I'll look, too."

She felt awkward about the hug since he didn't want her to touch him. Yet, yesternight when she had tended his wounds, she allowed her full access to his face and hands. His eyes had never left her, and his expression suggested he wanted her to do more than clean his cuts. She was certain if she tried to remove his shirt, he'd have refused. Instead, he slipped away to change it, then gave it to her for repairs.

"We should get back to the others." He untied the reins from the post. "They'll wonder where we are." Once the leather straps were in place, he turned to her. "After you."

She mounted and helped him up behind her. His hands wrapped around her waist, and his chest pressed against her back. "Are you comfortable?"

"Yes. Are you?"

She glanced over her shoulder. "I am. You're not going to throw me off again, are you?"

He shook his head. "I'm sorry I hurt you. That was not my intention, but I know I did. For..." Words failed, and he looked away.

"Forgive you?"

"You don't have to."

"I know. Are you asking for it?"

Through the bruises, cuts and swollen eye, the worry shone through. "Will you forgive me?" His face twisted in anguish.

"Yes. I forgive you for throwing me off my horse."

"Thank you."

She turned forward and commanded the horse to walk. Liam settled behind her, pulling closer and holding her tightly. His closeness stirred feelings she'd rather not think about, but with his body rubbing against hers and his breath falling upon her neck, the fire racing through her blood burnt hotter.

Weslia had said Kiefer's cure was in her mate's pocket, yet...if Liam was him, where was it?

Two days later, Liam and the others entered the small village of Legover. The coach from here had passed them the previous afternoon, and the driver waved as he slowly went by. The elves of this area were more about business than much else. Occasionally, one would stop for small talk but for the most part, they hurried off to their destination. Liam didn't know if that was their nature, or they simply had no time for hauflins.

Though business was on the minds of the elves, they had time to overly-decorate their dwellings. Each one was unique and adorned with various paraphernalia. Liam would never spend such energy in creating the elaborate displays; he'd rather focus on creating a comfortable living space for him and his family.

His dreams evaporated. Family. It was something he had always dreamt of, but that future was branded out of him. He'd enjoy Isla's companionship until they reached Inglenook, and then he'd do as he'd promised.

"Disgraceful."

He followed the sound of the gruff voice. A mature dwarf riding in the direction they had come from scowled at him. The man was armed with a large sword and three daggers. In the saddle behind him sat a woman about the same age.

"You're a disgrace to men."

He touched his face to see if something was stuck on it. The cuts were scabbing over, and his eye was fully open. He found no reason why the man would make the comment. "Why is that?"

"Being dragged about like a sack of animal feed by a woman. A real man takes charge of his mount."

"You are truly luckier than I, fine sir. While you have the pleasure of holding cold, stiff leather, I must hold a warm, soft body."

The man recoiled. Riding away, his grumbling carried on the breeze.

McGuigan chuckled, and Isla looked over her shoulder. Her pleasant smile plucked his heart strings.

"I'd gladly ride behind you every day." He pulled her snuggly into his body, and one hand slipped into her armpit and a finger wiggled deeper.

She squirmed and released a spontaneous giggle. "Stop, you rascal." She slapped his arm.

He continued, wiggling his finger and dragging it across the pit of her arm. She had always been ticklish and when he wanted a turn riding in front, he'd tickle her until she surrendered. Today, he tickled her for fun.

She twisted and squirmed, trying to get away from his probing finger. Her giggles and then carefree laughter sounded like music to his ears. It felt like a lifetime since he'd last heard it. He'd give everything for the ability to hear it every day.

Her fingers grabbed the sensitive skin on the inside of his thigh and squeezed. A sharp pain shot down his leg, and he rose to escape it. She twisted the skin, and the pain became unbearable.

"Ouch! I surrender. Ow! Please, let go." He pulled his hand away from her arm and used it to protect his leg.

"You know I don't like tickling." She slapped his leg to reinforce the fact.

"But we agreed I was allowed to tickle you. I was to protect you from all other ticklers."

"On the day of your birth celebration. That's the only time."

"And when I feel sad." He made an unhappy face.

"You look anything but sad."

"But I've missed all those celebration days. I have six to make up for. This was only one."

She rolled her eyes, but a smile captured her lips before she turned away.

Lyneth had told them they'd stop at Legover to gather the needed supplies at the keep, then they'd travel a few more hours before making camp. The woman, in her late twenties or early thirties, probably felt like she tended to a herd of unruly teens. She was not far off the mark in some respects. Deaglan was the one to watch because he was impulsive and had no regard for authority. He reminded him of another boy the same age who roamed the streets of Wandsworth looking for excitement. That boy found more than he could handle, and then it enslaved him. Many teens had lost their freedom, several their lives, on the city streets, serving a man who controlled his gang with a weapon more powerful than the threat of death.

Legover Keep was a modest shop with a window on either side of the door. He swung his leg over the rump of the horse and dismounted. His hands caught Isla's hips as she descended, and he eased her to the ground. Taking the reins from her, he secured them to the hitch.

"Keep this up, and I might expect it always." She winked and walked towards the door.

While he was with her, he'd spoil her, do the little things other men failed to notice caught a woman's attention. Nothing he bought impressed her like the simple act of easing her to the ground from the saddle.

"Where are you going?" Lyneth paused by the door and shouted to McGuigan who jogged across the dirt lane.

He made a strange motion with his hands and kept going, right into a shop.

"A candy shop," said Isla.

"In a small village like this?" Lyneth grabbed Deaglan's arm to stop him from entering the keep.

"They are in the strangest places." Isla opened the door and held it for Liam.

"Deaglan, stay with me," ordered Lyneth. "Keep your hands where I can see them."

Liam followed Isla around the keep, fingering a few items, but not interested in buying anything. He had what he needed to survive on The Trail, much more than he had begun with when he'd left Wandsworth. He'd pick up a few food items and hoard the rest of the coins he had earned on this assignment. Initially, he refused payment, but Lyneth explained she had negotiated the deal for four escorts. They received half the payment when they left Moonsface and would receive the rest on arrival at Inglenook.

Seeing a slim sword, the perfect size for him, he picked it up. It was well crafted, and he admired the intricate design on the hilt. He balanced it on his finger; it was perfect. Stepping away from the table, he swung the weapon in a pattern, then drew it near. It came with a sturdy leather scabbard and belt. He checked the price, expecting it to be well out of his price range, but it wasn't. It'd take half his coins, leaving him plenty to buy food for several weeks. He sheathed the sword, wrapped the belt around it and carried it with him.

He paused next to Isla, who had stopped to read the cover of a book on display. Her eyes grew moist, and her breathing grew heavy. He placed a hand on her lower back and pressed against her.

"What's wrong?"

"This book." She blinked away the tears.

"*A Trail of Hope.* Sounds familiar."

She picked it up and opened it to the first page. "I was reading this when Kieron Ruckle stole me from Das."

"It was in your pouch." He remembered now. "And it reminds you of that time?" He held her tighter, wishing he'd been there for her.

She nodded. "It's about a girl who becomes lost, and she leaves pages behind for her das and brother to find her." She sucked in a quick breath. "That's what I did."

"You left a trail of pages from the book?"

"I did. Das followed them."

He cautiously kissed the side of her head and left his forehead pressed against it. "You were always a wise girl. I'd have never thought of that."

"You would have done something else. You're resourceful."

"Maybe. What happened to the book?"

"After I escaped prison, I..." She shivered. "I left it with a message for Das at the Glen Tosh keep."

"What was the message?"

"I told him to go home. To forget about me." She closed her eyes and tears squeezed through. "I broke his heart and mine."

He placed the sword on the shelf and cupped her face, wiping away the tears with his thumbs. "Why did you do that? He loves you more than anyone."

"I know." She stared into his eyes and gripped his wrists. "I was ashamed. I chose life over honour."

"There's no use being honourable and dead." He kissed her forehead and drew her into his arms. "What did your das say when you saw him?"

"He forgave me."

"As he should have."

"While living on The Trail, he did things he wasn't proud of."

"Really? A taste of reality." Lyneth and Deaglan approached the counter on the other end of the small keep. Lyneth glanced towards them, then talked with the keeper. Although Liam enjoyed the embrace, he had to release Isla and follow them. As they separated, he dried her tears with his sleeve. "There. As good as new." His thumb rubbed the last drop away, then slowly brushed her bottom lip. Dragonflies zipped through his stomach as if fighting to free themselves, and he fought the urge to draw that lip between his.

Before he gave in, he released her and picked up the sword. "Lyneth is at the counter."

She returned the book to its former resting place, grasped his hand and let him lead her away. Not wanting anything, she waited for him to pay for his purchase.

"That's more than a fair price for a well-crafted weapon," he said as he handed the keeper the coins.

"It's been here for years. Not many hauflins pass through, and it's too small for other races." The man took the coins and tucked them into the cash box.

"That's to my benefit. Thank you." Liam held Isla's hand and walked out the door. "I can't believe my luck. I'd pay ten times that for a sword like this elsewhere." When they reached the horse, he buckled the scabbard around his waist. "Fits perfect. What do you think?" He looked up and found her in deep thought. "What? You know swords better than I do. Is there something wrong?"

"It's fine." She climbed onto the horse.

He hadn't expected that reaction. She loved swords and had always went on about their construction and their fancy designs.

"Candy?" McGuigan held a paper sack in front of him.

He peeked into the bag. "Jelly mints?" When he nodded, he took one. "Thank you."

McGuigan held the bag up to Isla, but she shook her head. "More for me." He popped one into his mouth and stuffed the bag into the pouch on his belt.

Liam jumped into the saddle behind Isla, and they turned the horse and followed Lyneth from the small village. She was unusually quiet, and he rested his chin on her shoulder. "You can tell me anything," he whispered. "I won't judge but be the one to confide in to ease the pressure of a secret."

Her gaze swept over his face. "If I believed you, would you do the same and believe me?"

"I don't understand."

"That I would not judge you but be the person to confide in to ease the pressure of your secrets?" His long silence made her frown. "I didn't think so."

7

The Smell of Wood Smoke

BEFORE THE LIGHT FADED from the sky, Isla pulled her sewing kit and Liam's shirt from her rucksack. She'd sewn closed two holes the previous night and would mend the final one this evening. Her sewing skills weren't the greatest, and her aunts had reminded her of that fact during her time working at their dress shop. However, she was good enough to secure a button, mend a hole and close a cut. That's all she needed on The Trail. She had no plans to make an entire shirt at any time in her life. She'd leave that to Rhiannon, Loren and Alaura.

Liam stretched out on his bedroll next to her and rested his head on his rucksack. Lately, his actions confused her. His spell of pushing her away had ended, and now he acted as if he wanted to keep her near. He went out of his way to do small things for her without being asked. In the mornings, he'd roll up her blankets, tack-up her horse and fetch water for tea. In the evenings, he'd remove the saddle and carry her things to the campsite. His gentle manner of holding her hand and comforting her when terrible thoughts entered her mind warmed her heart. This was the way she'd imagined him to be when they reunited.

Yet, the nagging feeling he hid something horrible ate at her nerves. Although they rode on the same horse, he never wanted to ride in front.

When he held her, he ensured he knew where her hands were as if he feared she'd touch his shoulder again.

He pointed to the pouch next to her leg. "Is this the same one from years ago?"

"It is."

His face lit up. "Are there oatmeal raisin cookies inside?"

"I'm surprised you're not helping yourself to a peek."

"I haven't earned that right."

She tossed it onto his belly. "You won't find cookies, but there's a small sack of nuts."

He withdrew the sack and popped a few into his mouth. After digging deeper, he looked up. "You still carry them?"

"Yes. They're special." The stones beneath the false bottom reassured her. She'd gathered most of them in her youth, several before she was five years old. She had no reason to support the significance of the stones. It was as if they found her, not the other way around.

He touched the stone hanging around his neck. "This stone is special. I'm not sure the rocks you picked up near the pond are."

"You still carry that? It's just a rock I found along the Shulie River." She smiled mischievously.

He leant close, close enough to kiss. "Oh, it's special. I'm never taking it off."

The sparkle in his eyes danced, and she pushed him away. "You're distracting me. I need to finish this before the sun sets." She straightened the thread and dug the needle into the material.

A hand blocked her view, one with a single almond nut resting on the palm. She stared at him as she picked it up and put it into her mouth. The sentiment that he'd share his last morsel of food with her, as they had promised when they were children, made her heart skip. He was the same boy her blood burnt for many years ago. The years hadn't changed him.

She threw down the shirt and stood. "Come with me." She didn't wait for comment or to see if he followed. Her feet carried her down an animal trail along the stream they'd camped beside. When she'd gone far enough to ensure their voices wouldn't be heard by the others, she stopped.

Liam followed closely and when she turned, a quizzical expression crossed his face. "What? I meant nothing—"

She grabbed his shirt and jerked him forward, sealing her mouth onto his. His warm, moist lips sent lightning bolts through her blood, and the fire within exploded. The need to have him left her breathless, and she kissed deeper, feeling his excitement grow.

A strange flavour entered his mouth and splashed against her lips. The taste grew and made her flinch. Drawing back, she lightened her kiss while he eagerly pulled her near. His hands rubbed her shoulders, slipped across her back and grasped her buttock.

Her mouth filled with the horrible taste, and it made her body shiver. She gagged and pushed him away. "Stop." She gasped and wiped her mouth with her hand. Leaning to the side, she spit several times.

"What's wrong?" he asked, breathless. "Are you okay?"

She spit again and wiped her lips with her sleeve. "You taste horrible." She shivered. Seeing the stream, she hurried to it, dipped her lips into the water and drew up a mouthful. She spit it out, then repeated the action.

He knelt on the bank beside her and placed a hand on her shoulder. "Are you sick?"

"Sick? Not me." She took another drink. "That came from you."

He touched his mouth. "What did?"

"That horrible taste. It's like..." she thought hard, trying to think of something similar, "poyson." She stared at him. "You taste like poyson." She narrowed her eyes. "Why would that be?"

He stood. "You're being silly. No one tastes like poyson."

She stood to challenge him. "Except you."

"That's crazy."

"Is it? What's on your back?"

"Nothing." He walked away, and she grabbed his arm.

"Take off your shirt."

"I won't."

"Are you bashful?"

He rolled his eyes. "Don't ever confuse me with your das. We are nothing alike."

"You both have brown eyes."

"There's something."

"You were both born at Maskil."

"You've got me; we're twins."

"You both have a piece of my heart."

His mouth froze before a comment escaped.

"You both would risk your life for me." She grabbed his shirt and pulled him near. "You both love oatmeal raisin cookies." She rested her hand on the top of his right shoulder. "You both make me laugh, drive me crazy and...if I cried for help, you'd both drop everything and come running." She slipped her hand to the spot where negative energy had attacked her arm. The heat radiating from his skin triggered her nerves.

He grabbed her hand and ripped it from his body. "I am not Bronwyn!" His eyes, wild with anger, grew dark. He tossed her hand aside and marched away without looking back.

She wanted to chase him and rip off his shirt, but that wouldn't solve their biggest problem: his inability to trust her.

Several black spots dotting the ground caught her attention. She bent to examine them closer and found the weeds burnt and the ground scorched. Was this her spit? She stood back and imagined her reaction to experiencing the horrible taste in her mouth. These spots *were* her spit. Crazy. Was this poyson or something else?

Her head jerked forward, and she fell against the cool ground. She struggled to rise, and a solid force struck her. Her vision blurred, then went black. Footsteps rushing around her simmered in her ears as she lost consciousness.

ࠊ❖j

McGuigan popped a jelly mint into his mouth. Hearing movement in the bushes, he looked and saw Liam enter the campsite and settle on his bedroll. He stretched out like before and rested his head on his rucksack.

"Where's Isla?" He peered down the path they'd gone and didn't see her.

"She's coming." Liam rubbed his temple roughly.

"I don't see her."

"She's mad. Give her a minute."

"That was fast."

Liam glanced up. "In what way?"

He chuckled. "Not that way. I mean you're quick to arouse anger."

"I've got the knack." He stared at the branches hanging overhead.

"I'd call it dumb love." Deaglan laughed. "Damfool."

McGuigan chuckled and tossed another jelly mint into his mouth. "Wait. You'll be there one day."

"I kiss them and run."

"Until you want more than a kiss."

"If she doesn't return soon, McGuigan, take a walk." Lyneth stared down the path. "I'm not hearing her."

"She's really mad," said Liam. "She won't ride with me tomorrow."

"I'll go." Deaglan jumped up. "Is she crying? I'll make fun of her, then she'll be mad at me." He laughed. "Or I'll steal her horse."

Liam sat up. "Stay, kid. You're going to get yourself in real trouble one of these days."

"I'm too good, too fast." He plopped down next to the fire and poked a stick at the embers.

"That's what everyone thinks, and then they get trapped and they dig a bigger hole." Liam released a heavy sigh.

"McGuigan, go," said Lyneth.

He rose and walked down the trail, popping another jelly mint into his mouth. Tucking the bag into his pouch, he stretched his neck to see up ahead. There was no sign of Isla. The farther he went, the more his nerves stood on end. Two hundred feet from camp, he reduced his speed and drew his sword. Something wasn't right.

Glancing back at the camp, he thought about Liam leaving Isla out here. Why would he do that? Even if she was mad, she would have followed him back to the site. A horrible image entered his mind. He didn't know Liam; he didn't know what he was capable of doing. Would he have hurt Isla and...?

He shook the thought from his head. Isla was fine; she was up ahead pouting about the spat she had had with Liam. He was certain he'd find her soon. A moment later, he stopped at a small clearing next to the stream. Several dark spots dotted the ground. Some were black, others red. He touched a red one; the wetness stuck to his finger and he brought it to his nose: blood.

Standing quickly, he scanned the area. Nothing moved out there. Sneaking along the path, he watched for Isla and those who may have taken her. Or had Liam done this? His blood warmed. A minute later, he paused before entering the campsite. Everything was as he had left it. When he stepped into the clearing, Lyneth stood.

"Where is she?"

Liam sat up and stretched his neck to peer down the path.

"That's a question to ask him." McGuigan grabbed Liam by the shirt and jerked him to his feet. "Where is she?"

"I left her by the stream. She wouldn't wander off. I'm sure she's still there." His face bent with the possibilities.

"I saw the blood." He strengthened his grip and twisted the shirt to make it tight around his neck, hoping to squeeze the truth from him.

"Blood? Why would there be blood?" Liam tried to pull away. "Please, let me find her. I'm sure she's fine. She was mad at me. That's all." He squirmed under the pressure building around his neck. "I'd never hurt her; she's all I care about."

"McGuigan, let him go." Lyneth stood with her sword drawn, peering into the trees. "I believe him."

He thrust him backwards, and Liam tumbled across the ground. "If she's hurt, you'll pay."

Liam scrambled to his feet and shot down the path Isla had led him onto.

"Is he escaping?" McGuigan watched him disappear into the trees.

"I think he's checking the last place he saw her." Lyneth walked a larger circle. "This is the last thing we need."

"Travelling with a killer is never a good thing."

She whirled. "Do you know something I don't?"

"He doesn't say it but from his actions, he's a trained killer. Maybe an assassin. He took two men down with a pipe. He hit them only to knock them out, not kill, but I bet if he wanted to kill them, they'd have fallen faster."

"If he's on our side, he's an asset." She pulled her extra dagger from her rucksack. "If he's not, we've got a complicated problem."

Liam found the blood and squeezed it between his finger and thumb. Whatever or whoever had taken Isla had no idea what they were dealing with. He arched his back, fighting the poyson as it seeped from the brand. Containing it in the scar kept his body under his control, but it generated a maddening itch that made him want to rip his skin off. If he didn't calm his nerves, he'd lose all sense of his actions.

Blood. Maybe it wasn't Isla's blood. It might be that of an animal she killed, a person she'd wounded and then followed. The thought calmed his nerves, and the poyson settled.

He stood and searched the area for tracks. He found them leading into the bushes. They were footprints of an intelligent being, not an animal. The poyson grew excited; it hadn't killed for many weeks and it craved blood. It drew him forward, and he picked up the trail. He hadn't gone far before he found horse prints. Three of them. Three men. Three dead men.

His vision blurred, and the poyson spread into his chest, anticipating the fight. The benefit of the cursed brand was his increased ability to track and follow a scent, one of fear and sweat. He travelled faster, not caring about the wear on his body and the damage sustained as he crashed through bushes. His only ambition was finding the men who rode those horses. Nothing else mattered.

Oblivious to time and distance, he didn't slow until sounds that didn't belong to the forest touched his ears. The soft neighing of a horse, the gentle shake of their tack and heavy breathing of men who waited for death to claim them. He sniffed the air. A fire burnt. He followed the smell and soon found flames illuminating a campsite.

When he entered the small clearing, his ragged breath brought spit and foam to his mouth. He panted heavily and gripped the dagger as if an ogre tried to rip it from his hands.

"Get back!" shouted the man holding a rope that hung from a tree. "Don't move."

Liam scanned the area, searching for Isla and identifying his targets. Two men moved slowly towards him but stopped thirty feet away. One, a dwarf and a mix of some other race, stood with his mouth open, his scruffy beard making it appear like a black hole. He held his sword at the ready. The other, a human of large stature, had shaggy blonde hair, a scar across his chin and leather armour that would prove useless against the poyson.

The third, the one who had spoken, was a bag of races, mostly human. His dirty, dark hair matted to his face. He held a sword in one hand and the rope in the other.

His eyes followed the rope to a branch where it folded over and stretched to another tree, then went down to... His eyes worked to solve the puzzle. Why was the rope tied to a sword suspended in air and secured three feet off the ground? If the man released the rope, what would happen? He followed the tip of the sword and a wad of spit clogged his throat. The poyson surrounded his heart but didn't penetrate it. Sweat dripped into his eyes, and his fingers gripped his weapon.

Isla stood tied to a tree, her mouth gagged. She stared at him with the darkest brown eyes he'd ever had the pleasure of staring into. Blood oozed from a wound on her forehead.

His heart ached to hold her, to tell her she'd be okay, to tell her he was not a monster...to tell her he'd leave and take the danger with him. The warmth in his heart fought against the poyson, and his vision cleared. To kill these men and rescue Isla, he'd have to let the poyson take control, but shame of her seeing the killing machine he'd become made him fight the urge.

"We know what you are!" shouted the man holding the rope. "A rabid man with no conscience. You can kill us, but do you want her dead, too?" He held the rope in front of him. "If I release this rope, she dies."

"I am not the man you seek." Liam attempted a bargain.

"Lay down your weapon," ordered the bulky human. "We'll let her go once we have you secure."

"Who are you looking for?" asked Liam, sheathing his dagger.

"A Maverick."

"I am not him."

He glanced at the man holding the rope. "What if he's telling the truth?"

"It's him." He turned to Liam. "Take off your shirt."

Liam hesitated. They'd know for sure if they saw the scar. "If I go peacefully, you'll release her?"

"That's the deal. Now remove your shirt."

He slowly unfastened the buttons. Isla already suspected he had a past to hide; revealing it was better than exposing the monster. He tossed the shirt to the ground and turned to show the men the branded capital M that marked him as a Maverick. The itch in his right shoulder grew, but he maintained control over the poyson.

"Told you it was him. Now shackle him like the animal he is."

He stared timidly at Isla. The pain in her eyes jabbed his heart. Their last moments together would tell her everything she needed to know: he was a liar and a killer. The lump in his throat made swallowing difficult. He should have left that night when Lyneth had stopped him, sneaked away like the villain he was.

The two men tackled him and threw him to the ground. He let them do what they wanted, so they'd release Isla. The sound of steel and shackles clanked in his ears.

The dwarf of mixed races chuckled. "The sooner we cage this monster, the sooner I'll enjoy a sweet morsel."

Liam braced his jaw and stiffened his muscles. They'd not honour the deal. He released the poyson and groaned as the energy surged through his blood. It reached every limb and painted his vision red. He gave it free rein, and it lashed out, galloping around his body like a stallion let loose on fresh pasture. He drifted from his mind. The poyson had full control. Its first target was the man with the rope.

Before the man secured the first shackle, Liam jerked his hands free and leapt to his feet. He watched the scene playout as if an observer and at times, he saw nothing. The man at the rope fell under his blade, and Liam flew into the air, taking down the suspended sword before it made contact.

He rolled across the forest floor, smashed into a trunk, then raced forward. The men's attempt at defence failed quickly, and his sword sliced through them. The scene blurred, and the poyson rejoiced, dancing in his blood and seeking another victim. He hopped around the fire, celebrating and lashing out. When he saw the person tied to the tree, the poyson craved their blood. He rushed forward with dagger in hand, ready to slice their throat.

Dark eyes stared up at him. Fear pulsating in them stalled his weapon. His body twitched and fought for control. The poyson battled to hold its ground, and he slammed his hand against the tree until it released the dagger. He fell to his knees, gasping for breath and reclaiming what was his. The agony of squeezing the poyson back into the brand arched his back, and he cried out. Shivering from cooling sweat and from the warmth the poyson stole, he collapsed to the forest floor.

Tree branches swirled above, dancing in the moonlight. The smell of wood smoke permeated his senses. A fire. It drew his attention. Violent flames licked the sky and illuminated moist chunks of flesh scattered upon the ground. He staggered to his feet and beheld the scene. The three men who had attacked him lay in dozens of pieces across the forest floor. Blood splattered trees and rocks.

He closed his eyes. Memories of other kills flashed in his mind. The Maverick mark had created a monster, a feral, evil monster.

He released a guttural cry; he was better dead than forever bonded to a master. He'd never run far enough to escape. They'd hunt until they captured him, and the brand would reveal his identity.

Soft movement made him whirl. Isla. His body recoiled, and he stumbled backwards. She'd witnessed his malicious deeds; saw what he was. He recalled the terror in her eyes; of him. That was worse than death, worse than the scar and poyson combined.

Tears welled as she stared at him. He imagined what she thought, and it led to him leaving and never seeing her again. Long moments passed and when the realisation that she was still tied and bound struck, he jumped up. In his haste, he scared her, and she braced herself as if he attacked.

"No, no. Please." His trembling fingers gently pulled the gag from her mouth. "I'm not going to hurt you," he whispered, his throat sore from the strain of letting the poyson run wild.

"What was that?"

He pressed his lips together and untied the ropes, wishing to avoid the inevitable conversation.

"Please, be honest with me." Her fingertips gingerly touched his skin as if they'd release the monster within.

He longed to embrace her fully but hesitated, worried he'd invoke more horror. She grasped his hand and pulled him to face her. He searched her eyes for strength and found doubt.

"I can't be yours," he whimpered. "What lives inside owns me." Tears flowed like when he was a boy and his das had been killed. His meeme's arms had cradled him while he cried himself to sleep. Now, the arms he craved more than life itself feared him.

He fell to one knee, pressed his forehead against her stomach and sobbed uncontrollably. "I ruined our lives." He wrapped his arms around her and held tightly. "I can't undo it."

She cradled his head against her. "Where did it come from?"

"An evil man who brands his follows." The past invaded his mind like the smoke had devoured the room in Wandsworth where he left two of his victims. "It makes them follow without question. Poyson. It's a monster. A death grip. I want you," he wailed. "I've only ever wanted you."

He remembered their kiss, the reaction of the poyson, his inability to keep it locked away. It desired her warmth and had seeped through his blood until it found her mouth. He shuddered, knowing he'd never kiss her again, never feel her body against his, never enjoy the simple pleasures between mates. He'd live, yearning for sensations he'd find nowhere else.

She eased his arms from around her waist and slowly sank to his level. Cupping his face in her hands, she dried the tears. She kissed his cheek and then his chin. "Liam, I don't know what this is, but I know one thing."

He stared, wishing he'd die in her arms, giving him the only peace he'd find.

"I want you," she whispered. Her finger dried his lower lip, and she kissed it softly. "When I want something, I'll do whatever necessary to get it." She gripped him tightly. "Do you have control over it?"

"Yes; no. Sometimes." He shook his head. "But it has me."

She lowered her brow. "It can't have you."

"I don't want them to hurt you to get to me."

"They'd have to kill me to get to you." She stood and pulled him to his feet. "Secure your weapons. We're leaving. Dead bad men no longer bother me."

He gawked, unbelieving his ears. The Isla he'd known would be horrified by this sight.

She turned. "Are you coming?"

He followed without hesitation and scanned the area. "Where are the horses?"

"They spooked and tore off when you howled like a banshee."

His breath caught. He didn't remember that.

She picked up his shirt and held it open for him. After he slipped his arms inside, she fastened the buttons.

"I can do this."

"I know." She finished, then she grasped the material and pulled him near. "But I don't know everything. While we walk, you talk, or else."

He leant back; she gave that look Alaura had given Bronwyn many times. Witnessing it from the sidelines, it had entertained him, but having the look cast at him made his nerves jump.

8

A Pet that Never Ages

THE MORNING SUN PEEKED through the trees by the time Isla retraced her steps and walked into the small clearing where she had argued with Liam. The trail left by her captives' horses coupled with Liam's footsteps following them, led her directly here. She would have arrived sooner, but the poyson dwelling inside Liam had claimed his energy. He had said it would. Once the ecstasy of the kill subsided, his body hungered for rest. He wanted to stop and sleep, but she refused. She needed to return to the others as quickly as possible to alert them to the danger and to let them know she was well.

"A few hundred feet more." She gasped for breath. The strain of half carrying and half dragging him through the bush exhausted her body. She hoisted his arm higher onto her shoulder and re-established her grip around his waist. "We're almost there."

She hoped she was anyways. Lyneth may have moved camp to a more secure location when she and Liam didn't return. The path that had taken her two minutes to descend yesternight took her five this morning. When she reached the head, she saw the camp set up like she'd left it except no one was about. She pushed herself to complete the final steps to the bedrolls and fell upon Liam as she tried to ease him down slowly. He grunted when her knee struck the inside of his thigh.

"Isla."

She turned quickly. Lyneth, McGuigan and Deaglan emerged from the woods behind her.

"Are you wounded?" Lyneth knelt on the other side of Liam, who had already fallen asleep.

"Nothing to speak of."

"And Liam?" She saw blood and winced.

"He's exhausted." She unbuckled his scabbard and removed his sword, then his daggers. "He took a beating."

Lyneth pulled off his boots. "Where did the blood come from?"

"Men who had kidnapped me."

"They're dead?"

"As can be."

Lyneth glanced at the path. "How far?"

"About two miles."

"Good. Still, as soon as you're able, we'll leave."

Isla fell onto her bedroll and rubbed her tired eyes.

"So, he wasn't the one to blame." McGuigan stood over them.

"Why would you think he was?"

"He returned without you."

"He'd hurt me no more than you."

"I've proven myself; he hasn't."

"He has to me."

"I still don't trust him."

Her body relaxed and sleep beckoned. "Trust me." Her voice trailed off, and she closed her eyes. Aching muscles loosened, and her mind emptied.

Lyneth led the group into the village of Brador. It was similar to Legover except it was twice the size. At the entrance rested a communal gathering ground. This would be where they'd spend the night. As she made the turn onto the grounds, she watched Isla and Liam, who rode in front of McGuigan. They'd been relatively silent about their excursion the day before. Isla had assured her she'd know the full story. The girl had recovered quickly, but Liam still suffered from the rescue and was lethargic as he rode on the back of the horse. As soon as they stopped, he slept and didn't wake until they started again.

Inglenook was a week away. She'd be glad to reach it and unload her cargo. While her goal was final payment, the release from being responsible for the boy's life was equally welcomed. To ensure Deaglan's safety, she and McGuigan had hidden in the bushes near the campsite and waited for Isla and Liam to return. She was unsure of what she'd have done if they hadn't.

"Good day." A middle-aged elf stepped from the small building at the entrance. "Seeking a place for the evening?"

"Yes." Lyneth dismounted. "For the five of us."

"Step inside."

She followed him into the building, provided their names and paid for the site.

"Pick the site that best serves your needs. Firewood is in the centre of the grounds. Take what you require. Latrines are provided." The man slipped the coins into a cash box. "If you need extra supplies, we have a few essentials. For a more extensive selection, the Brador Keep is located two blocks away."

"Thank you."

"Will this be a one-night stay?"

"Yes. We're leaving in the morning."

"Enjoy your evening."

Lyneth left the building, mounted and rode on. Several travellers already camped on the grounds. These she bypassed and picked a quiet site on the edge.

Once the site was set up, the fire burning and a night's worth of wood stacked nearby, she pulled her food sack from her bag.

"Can I talk to you?"

She looked up. Isla stood next to her. "About?"

"In private."

"McGuigan, watch the boy."

"I'm not a nursemaid." He set three rolls on his tin plate and dug into his bag for more food.

"No, you're a guardian. Now guard."

"As the oldest, watch both boys." Isla smirked.

"I'm oldest?"

"You are," said Isla. "You're two seasons older than Liam."

"If either of them get out of hand," said Lyneth, "set them straight." She followed Isla to a wooden bench where they sat and watched over the gathering grounds.

"Liam has an infection," said Isla.

"Is it contagious?"

"No."

"You don't sound confident."

"If it was, I'd have gotten it by now. I tasted it, but I'm fine."

"Tasted it? Explain."

"Do you remember the Mystic One at the Dukedom of Dunakan? The one who gave me the duchess's affliction?"

"That was poyson, not an infection."

"It's the same."

"The same poyson?"

"It tastes the same."

"Lindrum's magic." Regardless of where she went, the evil wizard followed. "How is he awake and moving? The duchess had fallen into an endless sleep, and you were doing the same."

"I don't know." Isla played with her stone necklace as she gazed across the grounds. "You saw me. Was I going to lapse into a sleep, or did it look like I'd die?"

She thought back to that day. Everything had been in haste. Rhys had rushed into the inn with Isla in his arms. Morwen and the peculiar man named Arthur followed. Then she remembered the stench filling the room. "You say it's the same?"

"Yes. The bitterness is distinct."

"I thought you were going to die. I think everyone did. You had the cure, so we didn't have to find out."

"I've another dose."

"Where did you get it?"

"Merk."

"I don't understand your relationship with that man." She'd kill him if given the opportunity.

"He gave it to me because I'm supposed to be his saviour. He needs to keep me alive."

"Interesting." Lyneth considered the deal they had discussed at Maskil to free Rod. They planned to trade his life for a unique pet. She didn't think the plan would work, but Isla insisted the man adored pets and would do anything to have one no other possessed.

"I want to draw out the poyson, but I need you to administer the powder."

"Wait. I can't do that. I'm no healer. Morwen and Kiefer saved you. I watched." She'd be terrified to do something wrong. "No. We'll think of something else."

"If something bad happens and there's no other option, the powder is in this pouch." She put her hand over a small leather pouch attached to her belt. "McGuigan will help. He was there."

"It is the last of the very last option." It really wasn't an option. She'd never allow Isla to do it. "Where did he get this poyson?"

"That's another story. I'll tell you because I trust you, and I want you to hear the story from me." Worry blanketed her face. "Please, don't judge him. He was a boy when this began. A boy whose parents were murdered, who was sent to a strange city to live with family who didn't want him. You need to know because of the threat it brings to us. I'll understand if you turn him away, but I'll go with him."

This story would be easier to swallow if they weren't in charge of a fifteen-year-old boy and if they hadn't recently been hunted by Tigh na Mare warriors who killed four of their members, the strongest of the group.

Since the moment she'd met Isla, she had felt she'd be the one to help rescue Rod. After more than a year, they hadn't accomplished that goal, but they were closer today than they were then. Finding her mate had changed her world, changed her perspective; there was nothing better in life. If Isla was willing to help her reunite with Rod, she was willing to help her remain with Liam.

Isla rose early. Her mind was set on breaking the fast with bacon and eggs, one thing she missed while travelling The Trail. Bacon kept for two days and eggs often broke from the rough ride, so she didn't carry them. This morning, she'd jog to the market and pick up ample supply for today and tomorrow, risking the egg breakage.

"Where you going?" McGuigan knelt next to the fire with his food sack.

"The market."

He stood and licked his lips. "They'll have ham, sausages. I'm coming." He walked beside her.

"I hope they have biscuits." She jostled him, and he pushed back.

"Fresh beans."

"No! You're not allowed."

He laughed and clipped the back of her head.

She jerked forward and poked him in the ribs. Movement on her other side caught her eye. Liam walked beside her. Since the night the poyson had taken control of his body, he'd said little. His overly polite comments and gestures kept her guessing his thoughts. When he said sorry for no reason, she felt it was yet another apology for what the men had done to her because of him and for what he'd done that led to being branded.

She squeezed his hand, but he said nothing. She bumped his shoulder with hers and smiled. His seriousness remained. With her free hand, she poked his ribs. He flinched, and she kissed his cheek quickly. His expression softened, and he tightened his grip on her hand.

"Are you up for bacon?" she asked.

"I am."

"I'll get a pound. Maybe two." She scanned the campsites as they passed. Many were occupied with travellers who were waking up. The smell of wood smoke and food cooking filled the air. She breathed it in, and her stomach growled.

They left the gathering grounds and walked towards the market, a block away. Shop owners were turning signs, unlocking their doors and placing wares on the sidewalk. They greeted customers as they entered and waved at those who passed.

Isla scanned the signs over-hanging the shops, looking for anything interesting. The elaborate decorations filled her eyes, and she allowed Liam to guide her forward while she stared across the street. Only elves strolled the sidewalks, making her stand out, but she didn't mind. She'd been in all sorts of places where she was the only hauflin.

A taller pedestrian caught her attention, and she watched him pause outside a large display window. The longer she stared, the more the man appeared familiar. She slowed her pace and squinted. He was human, about six inches taller than the tallest elf. When he turned and she saw his face, she stopped.

"Are you coming?" McGuigan stopped.

"Who is it?" Liam followed her line of sight.

"Someone I haven't seen since the day I left Blackvale." An idea popped into her mind. "Stay here. Both of you." She released Liam and hurried across the street.

"Specks." She stepped into his path, startling the older man. "You said you'd see me again, and here I am. It is good to see you well." She needed to quickly establish their relationship on friendly terms, as it had been at the castle.

"Child, a surprise. Pleasant, it is." He adjusted the thick spectacles balanced on the bridge of his nose and inspected her. "Well, I see."

"I am." She stepped closer to the building to allow someone to pass, and he did the same. "Are you on..." she leant close and whispered, "an adventure?" This was the word they used instead of mission or quest.

He glanced about. "Indeed."

"I have something." She dug into a side pouch and withdrew a paperweight she had found at a keep many weeks ago. "Please, give this to Merk." She held it on her flattened palm. The glass weight was half an orb. Inside, preserved for a lifetime, rested a small crab. "It's a pet that never ages."

"Interesting." He held it up to the morning sun and strained to see it better through his spectacles. "He will like this."

The gift delivered, she prepared to ask the question. Scanning the area around them, she didn't see anyone close enough to hear, but she kept her voice low. "You are aware of the dark magic Merk spreads to individuals in Ath-o'Lea."

"I know it well."

"Not long ago, I withdrew it from a woman. It made me sick, but Merk had provided a powder to overcome it."

"He cares for you, child. I told you so."

She didn't believe that, but she'd play along. "Are you aware of a street gang that uses this magic, this poyson to control its members? They're located in Wandsworth."

He drew back. "It is a bad mix. He regrets it."

"Merk regrets giving them the poyson?"

"Regrets it all."

"Will the grey powder cure it?"

"No. It is a bad mix. Bad people."

"What will cure it?"

"Are you inflicted, child?" His worry lines deepened.

"No, but my friend is."

"It is best to end it quickly."

"How do I get it out of him quickly?"

"I'm sorry," he said sympathetically. "His end should come quickly. It is the only way to release him before he harms those he loves. He will regret that more than death."

"But I want him alive. What do I need to save him?"

"Colostrum from a green dragon."

"What's that?"

"The first milk. It renews life, conquers all infections. A full cup."

"Does a shop sell it?"

He tilted his head. "I have been to many places." He paused. "Only one place." He held up his finger and stared at the ground. "It is...Dougendun." His eyes brightened. "Yes. I'm certain. A shop that also sells magical fifes, if one interests you." He frowned. "A wily oracle, hauflin dwarf. He will charge double."

"I care not what he charges. I will buy it."

"No, child. Be not eager. Be wise. He will ask of you what you are unwilling to give, and that price may not be measured in coins."

"Thank you." She hugged him. "I wish you safe travels." Releasing him, she giggled at his odd expression. "I have something for you." She dug into her pouch past the false bottom and into her stash of stones, and extracted the clear stone she'd found along the castle wall. "This will aid in your adventures. Fashion a necklace with it or keep it in your pocket. It helps either way."

He gazed into it. "I believe it will." He tucked it into his pocket. "Thank you. And now, I must go. I dislike tardiness. Be well, Isla, and I will see you again."

"I don't doubt it." She stepped away and jogged across the street. When she glanced back, Specks was gone. She searched the full length of the boardwalk without seeing him. Where did he go?

"Who was that?" McGuigan pushed himself away from the building he leant against and walked towards the market.

"Not here." She grasped Liam's hand and pulled him along. "But I have good news. I know a cure."

Liam waited for more. When none came, he pulled her to face him. "For me?"

"Yes." She kissed his lips gently. If she didn't linger on his mouth, she didn't taste the poyson. It left her delivering many quick kisses throughout the day. "And I know where to get it."

His face brightened. "Are you certain? Can he be trusted?"

"Yes, and yes." She pulled him along the boardwalk. "Let's go. I'm eager to learn more about his place, and..." she winked, "eat a plateful of bacon."

His smile tickled her heart. Even with the lingering cuts and bruises, he was the handsomest man she'd met. She never wanted to leave his side again. Wherever he went, she'd go. Wherever he was, she was home.

9

Weaving Tales to Excite Readers

THE SNAP OF WOOD made McGuigan look towards the fire. The wood smouldered from the damp day, hissing as it dried over the flames. The mist they endured during the afternoon had moved on, leaving a damp, chilly night. He had hoped to be farther south by the end of Sumortide. Travelling to higher terrain meant cooler than normal nights, and the increased possibility they'd wake covered in snow.

He pulled his bedroll nearer the fire. Beside him, Deaglan sat cross-legged with playing cards. The bent corners and stains indicated the deck had seen better days.

"Know how to play?" The boy shuffled the deck.

"Not really. Simple kid games."

"Ancient Wizard?"

"Yes. Silly Sevens."

"I love Silly Sevens. Play you."

"Sure." He straightened his blankets, removed his boots and sat down. "You need a new deck."

"It's a new deck you want?" Deaglan snapped his fingers and blew on the cards. He flipped his hand over and revealed a shiny new deck, complete with brilliant colours.

"How did you do that?" McGuigan looked to the left and right, trying to find the old deck.

"Magic." Deaglan grinned.

"Wow. You didn't say you knew magic."

"I don't like to brag."

Isla rolled her eyes. "You only like to steal?"

"I don't steal anymore."

"From what I know, you don't steal any less," she said.

He laughed. "I'm trying."

"Try harder." Liam used a stick to move a log to a better location and sent sparks into the air. "You've been lucky so far, but it won't hold forever. You are fortunate your aunt wants to take you in. Be grateful and use it to better your life."

"You sound like my granduncle, an old man."

"We going to play or talk?" McGuigan flattened a place on his blanket to throw the cards. "Are you playing, Isla? It's better with three or four people."

"The last time I played cards, it didn't go as planned." Her face twisted into a gentle smile. "Not that it was horrible." She glanced at Liam. "But it won't happen again."

"Is that a yes?" asked McGuigan.

"Sure. Liam?"

"I don't play cards."

"You did with me." She slid down her bedroll. "Sit next to me. McGuigan, move back to give us room."

Liam reluctantly sat beside her. "Just one hand."

"Lyneth?" McGuigan held out his hand for the cards. He wanted to see the new deck.

"No, thanks. I'd rather read." She held up a book.

After several adjustments, the four teens gathered around a central smooth surface. McGuigan dealt seven cards to each player.

"Did you transform the old cards to new ones?" asked Isla. "Or are you making us think we're playing with new cards when we're really using the old deck?"

"That's my secret." Deaglan slapped down a card.

"What do you mean?" McGuigan picked up a card. "We *think* we're playing with a new deck?"

"It's an illusion." Isla laid a card on the pile.

"Is that what it is?" The truth disappointed him. He'd rather have a new deck. He flipped over the card and examined the back. It was perfect. He bent it between his fingers. It was crisp.

"Don't bend my cards," said Deaglan. "You going to play?"

Liam scanned the cards in his hand. "I don't have any clubs."

Isla leant over. "You can lay the five and change the suit."

"I didn't know that." He threw down the five of spades.

"Sevens are wild. You can play them at any time and call the suit you want to change it to."

"Got it." Liam adjusted his cards.

"Can you do other magic?" McGuigan waited for him to play, then laid down a duke.

"Lots." Deaglan played a card, snapped his fingers and waved his hand in the air.

McGuigan watched his hand closely to see what he'd create. When nothing happened, he frowned. "Maybe you're bragging."

Isla broke into laughter. "Fiery red hair. Cute!" She grabbed his cheek and squeezed it.

He pushed her away and felt his head. "My hair is red?"

"As red as flames, and just as lapping." She laughed so hard, she fell against Liam, who wore a big grin.

His hair felt high and rigid. He dragged his hand over the top and it felt like it stuck straight up. "What'd you do that for?"

"The giggles," said Deaglan. "Your turn."

He threw down a card. "Change it."

"Okay." He snapped his fingers and swooshed his hand in front of McGuigan.

"That's so much better!" Isla laughed harder.

He touched his head and to his horror found only skin. "Where did it go?" Only diseased dwarfs had no hair.

"I gave it to the bald man at Brador."

"Get it back."

Deaglan grinned widely. In a flash, the hair returned.

"What colour is it?"

Liam's eyes grew wide. "It's got a life of its own."

McGuigan reached up. His hair flowed like grass in changing winds. "That's enough. You've got lots. You can brag."

Deaglan kissed his palm and blew it into the air. "There. Back to normal. I mean back to shaggy, black and dirty."

"Thank you. Isla, your turn." He eyed the boy. "Can you do serious stuff, too. Wait. Don't do it, just let me know if you can."

"I'm working on more advanced magic. Something that will impress my aunt."

"Does she work magic?"

"Yes. She's the reason I want to be an illusionist."

"Ah, so these are the old cards looking like new." Isla picked up a card but couldn't lay one down.

"You have me." Deaglan grinned. "My aunt likes to help people with her magic. She's settled down now but before, she travelled everywhere to help people and to gather knowledge."

"Is that what you want to do?" asked Isla.

"Not really, but I want to learn more magic. It's fun. Exciting."

"That wears off fast," said McGuigan. "It must have a purpose because fun and exciting won't make you feel good for long." He had believed travelling The Trail would, but it quickly transformed into an experience he hadn't expected.

"I'll think of that when I'm older."

"Best to start thinking of it now, while you still have many opportunities." Liam laid down a card. "Last card."

"I still have four left." Isla frowned. "How can you win when you don't know how to play?"

"I had a great teacher." He kissed her cheek.

"You had an awesome teacher." She leant into him.

McGuigan watched the hauflins. Although Isla trusted Liam fully, he needed more time. Liam's past could ambush them at any moment, a dangerous past that had the potential to kill everyone in its path.

The low fog obscured Liam's view. Visibility was down to less than two hundred feet. Lyneth rode next to Deaglan in the lead, and McGuigan rode next to him and Isla. The dwarf was a peculiar fellow. For the most part, he was naïve, but there were times his maturity shone through. His dedication to Isla both pleased and annoyed him. Their former intimate relationship fertilized the seed of jealousy, and he had to suppress this history when he looked at him, or his mind filled with images of them together.

Despite this, McGuigan's readiness to defend Isla, along with his previous actions that saved her multiple times, made him feel indebted. If he couldn't be here, McGuigan would be, protecting her from the dangers on The Trail and comforting her when she needed it most.

"Heads up."

He peered forward at Lyneth's command. Through the fog, the shape of a dwelling formed. It was a small home, well-decorated on the front with a narrow, winding path leading to the door.

Movement caught his attention, and he saw a figure looming out of the fog. It stood bent over on the far end of the yard. Drawing nearer, he saw it was a female elf, seasoned, wearing trousers, an old flannel shirt and rubber boots. She held a weapon—no, a gardening implement in her hand. She was working the dirt with it.

A sign hung near the entrance to the garden: Lady Coraline of Maiden's Way - Fresh Vegetables and Delights.

"I wonder if she has potatoes." Isla stretched her neck. "I bet she does. Can we stop?"

Lyneth glanced back at her. "We'll stop for a short break." She rode to a grassy area with a pole for hitching horses that lay opposite the small cottage.

Liam spied on the woman in the garden. When they slowed and left the road, she gazed in their direction.

"I wonder what she means by delights," asked McGuigan. "Candy?"

"Biscuits," said Isla.

"That's not a treat."

"It is to me."

Liam waited until Isla halted the horse, then he dismounted. She slipped out of the saddle, and he eased her to the ground.

"You are spoiling me," she said. "I'll not know how to dismount fully with you catching me every time. What if you're not riding with me one day?"

"My wish is that day will never come." He caressed her cheek and ran his fingers through her long brown hair. His dreams filled with laying alongside her, claiming her as his mate, but he feared what he'd expose her to. The poyson seeped into her mouth when they kissed; what would enter her if they joined? He'd never risk it, so while his body ached for her, he'd keep his distance.

"I'll do everything in my power to make it so."

"I know you will, and I am indebted to you for trusting me, giving me a chance."

"You fail to understand." She gripped his belt buckle and pulled him forward. "I'm not giving you a chance; I'm giving you everything. There will never be a time when I will not want you. The love I have for you is unbreakable, unending. I know that in my heart."

He didn't deserve this unconditional love, yet he'd do anything to keep it. "Isla, I'm yours. Although we were far apart, I've always been yours. I broke our pledge..." he swallowed hard, "but I want to honour it now with all my heart. When I'm free of this curse, I'll offer again, and I beg you to accept it. You're my heart's desire and without you, I am nothing."

"I wish that offer to come quickly, yet I'd wait an eternity for it."

The strings in his heart played a sweet melody, and he drew her near to taste the moist sweetness of a kiss. Before the poyson reacted to the intimacy, he released her lips.

"Are we procuring potatoes or pleasure?" Lyneth poked her head around the rump of the horse.

"Yes. Potatoes." Liam released Isla. "Let us get enough for a few days. After you, my lady."

"Such formality." She slapped his bottom and sneaked away.

He watched her walk across the dirt road. She was pretty when she was twelve, but she was irresistible at eighteen. Her curves, though hidden beneath rugged trousers, captured his attention. On warm days, she left the top two buttons of her shirt unfastened, and he'd gazed into the dim cavity that dipped between her breasts, longing to trace those curves with a gentle finger. When she was twelve, his biggest desire was to impress her with his skill and wit. Now he wanted to ravish her body, exhaust it in every manner, making her sweat and scream in ecstasy. He wanted to lay with nothing between them and watch her face as he brought her wave upon wave of pleasures; he wanted to hold her while she slept and protect her from danger.

"What are you thinking about?" McGuigan walked beside him. "Do you love potatoes that much?"

He cleared his throat. "Yes. I've always loved potatoes."

"You're weird. I prefer meat, ham, a hefty slice of beef. I don't think this woman has that." His face brightened. "But she has delights. That might be candy."

"Candy and meat. That's quite a combination. Your meat would go better with potatoes."

"I'm thinking of dessert."

"Candy potatoes?"

"Do they make them?"

"These days, they're up to making anything." He followed Isla through the small gate and down the winding path that took her to a sheltered area with a table to the side.

"Greetings." The woman in the garden emerged from the greenery. "I am Lady Coraline of Maiden's Way. How may I help you today?"

"Potatoes," said Isla. "Do you have a small bag to sell?"

"Yes. It's been a good season for potatoes."

"Onions? I'd like to buy three."

"Anything else?"

"What delights do you have?" asked McGuigan.

"They're inside. You may browse while I gather the vegetables." She picked up a basket from near the table. "Weston will answer any questions."

McGuigan hopped onto the stoop and opened the door.

"Shall we see what she means by delights?" Liam gestured for Isla to proceed before him.

"Yes. She might mean candy, or she might mean something more delightful." She followed McGuigan inside.

Liam held the door open for her, Lyneth and Deaglan. He'd keep an eye on the boy to ensure he didn't steal anything. The last thing they needed was to make trouble for the friendly shop keeper.

Bright light inside the cottage entered through many large windows, including one in the roof. Liam had never seen a window in a roof and marvelled at the design. If he had a dwelling, he'd put one in his bedroom and watch the stars while laying in bed. Regardless of the weather, it'd feel like he was outside.

"No candy." McGuigan's voice lost its excitement. "Just books, bread and..." he glanced at Isla, "biscuits."

"Yes." She stood in front of the shelf, gazing at the delights.

Liam nodded at the man sitting at the small table reading a stack of papers. He was as seasoned as the woman outside. He imagined they were mates, living in an isolated location, doing what they loved, spending both days and nights together. He longed for that life with Isla. He didn't like to garden, but she did, or at least she used to. What he'd do was a mystery. Before he lived on the streets of Wandsworth, he had an interest in making things from wood, but that disappeared with his freedom.

He glanced at the titles and the author's name: Caroline Eldlow. The author and the woman outside in the garden were probably one and the same. *A Trail of Hope*. He picked up the book and read the title again. It was the same book Isla had showed him at Legover Keep, the same one she tore pages from to leave a trail for Bronwyn.

"Is it a good book?" Isla leant over his shoulder. Seeing the title, a twinge of sadness crossed her face.

"The woman outside is the author."

"You're certain?"

"Her name is Coraline and the author's name is Coraline Eldlow. The rest of the books are written by the same person."

"I wonder..."

"Will you tell her you read the book?"

"I don't know."

"More delights." McGuigan entered another room, and Deaglan followed him.

Liam spoke in a low voice. "She might like to hear you enjoyed reading the book." He saw Lyneth indulging in the bookshelf, leaving McGuigan to watch Deaglan. "Think about it. I'm going to *mind* the boy, make sure he doesn't... You know." She nodded, and he entered the adjacent room.

McGuigan examined a small wooden case. "Cards." He turned to Deaglan. "A real new deck. I might get them. You can teach me a few games. I've seen others play by themselves. Do you know any?"

"I know Singleton but not Lone Star." Deaglan walked farther into the room and stopped at a closet with a black curtain covering the opening.

Liam scanned the room. It was dimmer than the first with one small oval window to emit light. The colour of the walls was rich brown, and the thick drapes were dark green, making the room appear darker. Small clay bowls, wooden spoons and trinkets occupied the shelves. On one rested small sacks tied up with twine. Another had bottles filled with colourful liquids. He prepared to ask the man, Weston, the contents of the sacks and liquids when he saw Deaglan reach for the black curtain over the closet.

"Real delights?" McGuigan reached for one of the sacks and held it to his nose. "Candy. I'm certain."

"Deaglan, that's closed-off for a reason." Liam walked towards him.

"I only want a peek." He pulled the curtain aside and gazed into a dark-green space.

"What is that?" McGuigan stepped towards him.

"Not of our business," said Liam. A slight breeze blew from the closet; it smelt of fragrant blossoms. It must have had a window open to the garden, or the owners were drying flowers inside. He reached for Deaglan to pull him back, but the boy poked his head into the closet.

"Incredible," said Deaglan excitedly. "I've never seen anything like this."

"What is it?" McGuigan pushed forward, bumping Deaglan.

"You shouldn't be in there." Liam grasped the dwarf's arm to pull him out but when he touched him, he felt a strong tug. He tried to release him, but his feet skidded across the floor. In one strong jerk, he flew through the opening in the curtain and crashed into McGuigan. They tumbled over an uneven surface and rolled to a stop.

He jumped to his feet and stared in shock. The inside of the closet appeared like the middle of the forest, complete with a bird flying in the sky. A river flowed a short distance away.

"This is the best magic ever?" Deaglan spun around.

"Only one problem." Liam scanned the area, ducked to see beneath branches and took several steps back from where he came. Not seeing the doorway, he gripped the book in his hand tightly and jogged up the hill. "How do we get out of here?"

ঙ ❖ ೮೪

Isla pushed open the door and walked out to the garden. The woman named Coraline was digging potatoes.

"I'll add a few more to the basket." Coraline smiled up at her. "Have you journeyed over this land before?"

"No. First time." Isla put her hands into her pockets and admired the garden. It was well organised with grey-pebble paths separating beds and meandering around benches and large fruit trees. Clumps of late-blooming flowers, vegetables and berry bushes dotted the property. "You have apples."

"Yes. They won't be ready for another five weeks."

"If I pass through at that time, I'll stop." She watched the woman lift mounds of soft soil and extract potatoes with brown skin. Although she wanted to tell her she had read the book, she feared it would lead to things she didn't want to discuss.

"That on the mind which fails to reach the tongue often creates regret." She looked up, the shovel half dug into the dirt. "What is it, child?"

"You're an author."

"Yes, I delight in weaving tales to excite readers and to entice them into thinking in ways they've not in the past."

"I read one of your books."

"Which one?"

"*A Trail of Hope.*"

Coraline released the shovel and sat on the wooden edge of the raised garden plot. "I'm sorry, but I'm happy to see you well."

"Why would you be sorry I read it?"

"That book is special." She gestured for her to sit, and she did. "I was a girl when I became lost. My father and older brother searched for a long time before they found me."

"It's a true story?" She replayed the events in the book in her mind. There were fairies and mischievous brownies. They weren't real, only imaginary.

"It is based on my true story, and ..." her expression transformed, "that book finds its way into the hands of those who need it most. I'm guessing you shared a similar experience."

"How do you know?"

"I've had many readers who have written and visited, who have told me their lost story. How did my story help you?"

She thought of that day long ago when Alaura had given her the book. When Kieron Ruckle kidnapped her, she was almost finished reading it. "It inspired me to leave my own trail to help Das find me."

"Did he?"

"Yes."

"That's why I write. The wisdom I impart through the written word has helped many."

"Thank you."

"Your book is no more? It has been torn and scattered through a forest?"

"It's in pieces. My das saved the pages he found and returned them to the book."

"He is a conscientious man." She stood. "When I'm finished gathering potatoes, I'll give you a complimentary copy. I encourage you to reread it; it'll help heal the wound. I assume you enjoyed it."

"I did. The fairies, naughty brownies. They were real?"

"Mostly." She winked. "I've always had a vivid imagination."

"I would like to read it again." She saw the basket half full of potatoes. "Would you like help? I've harvested potatoes before."

"Certainly. Digging in the dirt is good for the soul."

Isla worked alongside Coraline, pulling potatoes from the ground to fill the basket. Then they dug up three onions. Back at the table, they rubbed off most of the dirt and placed the potatoes and the onions in a sack. Isla paid her for them and jogged across the road to store them in her saddle bag.

Returning to the cottage, she found Coraline and Weston in deep conversation in the front room. Lyneth stood by with a queer expression.

"Didn't they go outside?" asked Lyneth.

"Who?" Isla glanced around the room, looking for Liam. He, McGuigan and Deaglan were not there.

"The boys. They're gone." Lyneth went into the adjacent room, and Isla, Coraline and Weston followed. "In there?" she asked the owners of the home and pointed to a curtain draped over the doorway of a wardrobe.

"Yes. It appears they went on an adventure." Weston commiserated. "They did not make a request, but I felt a vibration in the energy and when I entered to identify the disturbance, I found the room empty."

"If they're behind the curtain, why not draw it back?" Isla grabbed the thick material and dragged it across the black metal rod. A small closet with a pair of large rubber boots rested on the floor. Nothing else occupied the space. "They're not in here."

"That is a magical closet, open to one adventure in turn." Coraline cast a worried glance at Weston. "Do you know which book they carried?"

He shook his head. "I saw no book."

"Without a book, they couldn't enter."

Isla gulped. What book did Deaglan have tucked beneath his jacket, preparing to steal?

"I'm confused." Lyneth peeked inside the closet, then withdrew her head. "You say they went in there and now they're on an adventure. How is that possible?"

"Magic," said Coraline. "Those wishing to experience the worlds in my books will do so by entering this magic doorway."

"How do they get out?" asked Isla.

"Ideally, they'd receive instructions on how to exit when they so desired. However, since this was an unplanned adventure, they'll have to either experience the full story to the end or stumble upon the exit. Depending on the book, it will be a few days or several months."

"Several months?" Isla stared at Lyneth. "They can't be gone that long." She turned back to Coraline. "Can we enter the story to help them?"

"We know not which story they entered, and there is one adventure at a given time."

"What are we to do while we wait?" Her mind raced, thinking of other ways to reach them.

"Under the circumstances, I suggest bringing your horses to the stable. You can stay in the cottage in the garden until they return."

"This isn't good," said Lyneth. "We're expected in Inglenook in a few days."

"It's unfortunate, but there is nothing we can do." Coraline walked towards the door. "My offer stands. If you wish help with the horses,

Weston will show you the stable. I must return to the garden." She paused. "We share the ration at seven o'clock. You are welcome at our table."

Isla stared into the closet. While men from Wandsworth would never find Liam in the story of a book, the poyson was always with him. If his life was threatened, it may take control, and that thought filled her with fear. Liam had stopped on the brink of taking her life; McGuigan and Deaglan might not be that lucky.

10

An Elf for a Day

MCGUIGAN TOOK SEVERAL STEPS forward. "What's that? Singing?" He walked onto a path, searching for the source.

"We shouldn't leave this location." Liam stood on the small hill they had tumbled down. "If they search for us, they'll come here first."

"Where are they coming from? The sky?" Deaglan followed McGuigan.

"The same place we came from." Liam didn't move. "Come on. We can't wander through the forest. They'll never find us."

"Maybe we'll find them," said Deaglan.

McGuigan stopped. "What if we fell through a trap door and the cottage is over there." He pointed into the trees. "I'd feel silly waiting for them to find me."

Liam made a face but remained where he stood.

"We'll look over there to see where we are. We won't go far."

"Only a short distance." Liam followed.

Sweet voices sang on the breeze, and McGuigan had to learn whose they were. They sounded like women. He hurried down the path and one hundred feet away, he came upon a small lake with water that sparkled in the sunshine. His eyes widened, and he gazed upon the sight before him.

Three beautiful women with long blond hair stood waist-deep in the water. Their hair flowed over their shoulders, cascaded across their bare breasts and floated on top of the water. They twisted thin strands around their finger and rubbed water over their skin.

"Whoa!" Liam turned. "We need to go."

The girls stopped singing and giggled.

"We're sorry," said McGuigan. "We didn't know you were bathing." He turned his head, but he still saw their image out of the corner of his eye. "We shall leave you in privacy."

"Please, don't go." One of the women waved him forward. "We will enjoy the company."

He hesitated to move one way or the other. These women were not dwarf, not human, not hauflin. From the information he'd gathered in his quick observation, they appeared to be a mixture of elf and something else; something delicate. Yet, they were beautiful, and his nerves stood on end. "We do not wish to disturb you."

"No disturb," said the woman. "Willingly received." She moved towards the shore, revealing a mesh pair of shorts that clung to her skin and revealed her sensual curves. She picked up a towel from the grass and wrapped it around her. "My sisters and I love company."

"Sisters. You are all so pretty, it's not hard to believe you're related." He turned, and the other two emerged from the water. They each picked up a towel and wrapped it around their mid-section.

"I am Leigh. This is Beigh and Deigh."

"It's a pleasure to meet you." McGuigan flinched when she ran her finger down his arm.

"We should go." Liam kept his distance.

"No, no, don't." Beigh slid to his side as if gliding on air. "You will make me happy if you stay."

Deigh placed her hand upon Deaglan's shoulder. "You are strong. Handsome." She brushed his cheek with her finger. "Will you stay and talk with me?"

"This is a bad idea," said Liam. He stepped away from Beigh.

"Not a bad idea." She reached out to him, but he moved away. "I wish to make you happy." She hummed a soft song.

"That's enchanting." Deaglan's face lit up, and he gazed at the woman. "I've never heard a voice like that."

"I can sing, too." Deigh held onto his arm to keep him from walking to Beigh. She opened her mouth and a magnificent sound escaped.

"Beautiful women with beautiful voices." McGuigan's senses danced, and his head became light. "We should stay. Rest."

"Yes. Rest with me." Leigh joined her sisters and sang a sweet song. She wrapped her fingers around his and danced before him.

His head swooned while she twirled and flung her hair into the air. When she held her body against him, his thoughts went to other, more intimate activities. Then her towel was on the ground, and his eyes filled with a delightful sight; delights. These were the delights indicated on the sign. This was better than candy.

Leigh led him by the hand, swaying in front of him and tugging on his jacket buttons. She giggled as one popped open.

He'd never been enticed like this by any woman, and he delighted in the attention she bestowed upon him. When a second button unfastened, he giggled, too. Before thought progressed past the jacket, it was on the ground, and her hand was on his chest, poking her finger between the buttons of his shirt and caressing his skin.

Beigh touched his shoulder and smiled. "We will make you happy."

"I am happy." When she kissed his cheek, his blood warmed. She wanted him, too, but which one would he have? They were both beautiful, both wearing a skimpy pair of shorts and both tempting him to be with them.

"No." Leigh slapped Beigh. "He is mine. You have the short one." She scowled at her sister.

"The short one refuses." Beigh grabbed McGuigan's arm.

"Make him not refuse, silly girl."

"He has another."

"And you are weak. Make him."

"I want this one."

"You can't have him." Leigh pushed Beigh away.

"I pick him."

"I picked him."

"Me! I want him!"

"Can't have. Mine!"

Beigh shoved Leigh to the ground and threw a net that appeared instantly upon her.

"This is no way to act," said McGuigan. "You are sisters. Be happy." He helped Leigh to stand and to remove the netting. "It's not nice to push your sister."

"I picked you," said Leigh. "You will be with me."

"I will take him," said Beigh.

"Take the short one."

"The short one," said McGuigan, "has a mate. He is not interested."

"We have our ways to ensure he is," said Leigh sweetly. Her expression turned. "Except Beigh is horrible. She gives up too easily."

"No woman will persuade him. He is dedicated to his mate."

"No woman?" Leigh spoke in a soft voice.

"None."

"We shall see about that." She skipped to Liam's side. He backed away. "I wish to make you happy."

"I am happy. Stay away." Liam held his hands out in front of him.

Leigh sang sweeter than before, and she danced, swaying her body back and forth, moving her hips to entice him to watch.

"I'm not interested. I love my mate." He blocked his view with the book he'd picked from the cottage shelf. Stepping away, he lost his balance, stumbled, then regained it again.

The sweet song filled the air, kissing McGuigan's ears and sending marvellous sensations throughout his body. He unfastened the top button of his shirt and ran his hand over his neck. His heartbeat slowed, and an overwhelming feeling of wanting to lay down made him fall to his knees. Leigh continued to sing, and Liam dropped the book and a goofy expression crossed his face.

Deaglan lay back on the grass, shirtless, and allowed Deigh to remove his boots. He appeared half asleep, dreaming a fantastical dream.

Leigh wrapped her arms around Liam's neck and rubbed her cheek against his.

Impossible. Liam would never betray Isla. Through sleepy eyes, McGuigan's mind fumbled to make sense of it. How could Leigh entice Liam to be with her? There was no magic powerful enough... Or was there?

He slapped his face and yanked hard on his beard, bringing his senses to life and disturbing the magic the women possessed. Stumbling to his feet, he grabbed a chunk of his hair and pulled himself forward, ensuring he yanked hard to cause pain. His mind snapped back, and the song, though sweet, did not control him. Not knowing any other way to break the spell, he clenched his fist and struck Liam hard in the jaw. The hauflin slammed into the ground, shook his head and leered at him.

McGuigan put up his hands. "Sorry, pal. It was the only way."

Liam rubbed his jaw and grumbled under his breath. Then he considered the woman. "She's a wicked water wench."

He peered closer. "But she's beautiful."

Leigh let a tear slip down her cheek. "That was harsh. I wish to make you happy." She touched McGuigan's arm, and he pulled back. "Do you not want to be happy?"

"I'm quite happy. I don't need to pretend." He walked to his jacket, picked it up and slipped it on. "Deaglan, get up." He shook his head in disbelief. "Get dressed." The boy was down to his shorts, and the woman had her fingers on the band, ready to remove them. He marched over and slapped the boy.

"What?" Deaglan put his hand over his cheek. "I'm busy."

"Get dressed." He clipped him in the back of the head. "Grab those clothes and let's go."

Deaglan jumped up, ready to fight until he realised he stood in bare feet. "What the...?" His arms went over his front. "Where are my clothes?"

He rolled his eyes. "Behind you."

Deigh scowled at McGuigan. "Leave. You are not welcome. He is my honey pot." She held tightly to Deaglan's arm.

"He's not yours. He's a boy, too young for such things." He yanked Deaglan from her grip.

Deigh's face turned red, and her eyes bulged. She lurched forward and in doing so, transformed into a short creature with over-sized eyes and large mouth. Sharp teeth glistened in the sunlight.

He back-handed the woman, and she slammed into the ground with a solid thud. "Grab your clothes and run." He drew his sword and stood ready to defend the boy. "Go!"

Deaglan scrambled to gathering his belongings, then raced towards the path.

As McGuigan backed away, he glanced at Liam; the man followed with his sword drawn. The women hissed at him, grabbing his attention much the same as they had done when they first arrived. However, now he was repulsed by their ugliness. The women had transformed into stout creatures with light brown skin, wisps of hair shooting from the top of their head and twisted legs with knobby knees. Their thin luscious bodies were disfigured by rounded bellies and deep belly buttons adorned with sprigs of dark hair.

"Ever see anything like this?" He asked Liam.

"Can't say I have. You?"

"Fortunately, no." He waved him onto the path. "Lead the way."

Liam pushed Deaglan forward, in the opposite direction from where they came.

The creatures stopped in a row. They scowled and hissed, and their long fingers clawed the air in front of them.

"What's the chances they can't leave the water's edge?" McGuigan hurried his footsteps.

"I'd say a good one," said Liam. "They're not following."

"They're sneaky. They might be fooling us."

"We'll know soon." Liam turned. "Let's go."

McGuigan sheathed his sword and hurried after them. They jogged for several minutes before stopping in a meadow overgrown with wildflowers to gather in a circle and discuss the ordeal.

"I remember where I've seen creatures like that," he said.

"Where?" Deaglan pulled on his trousers.

"Books I read as a child."

Liam stared in the direction they had come. "Brownies," he said slowly. "Naughty brownies."

"More like crazy brownies," said McGuigan.

"No, the book." He pulled *A Trail of Hope* from his jacket pocket. "Isla read this. She said there were naughty brownies and friendly fairies in it."

"What was it about?"

"A young girl became lost, and her das and brother searched for her. What if..." he stared at the cover, "we're living in the story?"

"I'd say you're crazier than the brownies."

"I'm with him." Deaglan buttoned his shirt.

"From the boy who was about to lose his last piece of clothing to one of those creatures," said Liam. "You create illusions. Tell me this is impossible."

Deaglan tucked in his shirt. "Okay. All right. Maybe. But if we're in the story, who's creating the illusion?"

"Maybe that's the delight mentioned on the sign, and..." he thought about it, "it's the author. She's elf. Perhaps an experienced illusionist."

"Possibly." Deaglan pulled on his boots and picked up his jacket. "But why send us here?"

"As I said, it might be the treat, and we weren't supposed to enter without permission." Liam crossed his arms and glared at the boy. "But someone didn't listen."

"Now what?" McGuigan surveyed the terrain around them. "How do we get out of here?"

"Maybe we follow the story." Liam pointed down the trail. "I bet if we go this way, we'll find the das and his son."

"And do what?"

"I don't know. I didn't read the book. Maybe if we help them find the girl, the story will end, and we'll escape."

"Sounds crazy, but it might work." McGuigan adjusted his scabbard belt and walked past Deaglan. "Next time, when he says stop, stop, and when a woman wants you out of your pants..." he grinned, "make sure she's the race you think she is."

"Better yet, run to the nearest adult and hide behind them." Liam smirked.

"I'm sixteen next week. I'm old enough." Deaglan followed them, buttoning his jacket as he walked fast to keep up.

"Great," said McGuigan. "A sixteen party. I'm getting you so wrecked, you'll fall out of your pants." He laughed, remembering his sixteenth. His buddies had him flat on the floor before noon. Then he recalled his mum's anger. For the first five minutes, he had shaken with fear. Then he passed out, and it became a happy memory.

Isla dragged the hoe over the soil, keeping clear of the onion spikes growing from the ground. The warm temperature had forced her to strip to her singlet as she toiled in the garden. The past two days had reminded her of times she'd worked with Alaura in the garden at Moon Meadow. Back then, it was a game for fun, and she'd be rewarded with a delicious snack from the garden or a ride on Clover.

Now, the work made her back ache, embedded dirt under her nails and created a blister between her thumb and index finger. However, she enjoyed the harvested food when breaking the fast and sharing the evening ration. Coraline and Weston graciously allowed her and Lyneth to join them; the couple treated them to delicious home-cooking and intriguing conversation.

"Stay low," whispered Lyneth, and she dipped close to the ground.

"Why?" Isla mimicked her movement.

"Strangers approach."

"They're in the garden?"

"No, they've stopped to talk to Coraline. They haven't seen us."

"Who are they?"

Lyneth stared at her. "I think it's the men you met on the road to Moonsface."

"The four large humans searching for a young hauflin man?"

"Yes. They are dressed in dark clothing and are heavily armed."

She crept to the end of the onion patch and peeked through a leafy bush. The top of the men's heads emerged as she rose higher. She stopped the moment she positively identified them as the same men. They had to be from Wandsworth and searching for Liam. Thankfully, he wasn't here, yet a twinge of fear nibbled her nerves as Coraline talked with them.

Precious moments slipped by. These men had followed two days behind them. If not for the storyteller's cottage, the men never would have caught up to them before they reached Inglenook. Then what? If they had backtracked, they'd have encountered them.

If Dougendun was in the opposite direction, she'd have gone there but after searching her map, she still didn't know where it was located. No one in their small group had heard of it. The woman who had mentioned it in Blackvale Castle's prison was long gone. This mysterious place was their next destination, but she had no idea how to get there.

The men rode away, and Coraline watched. Then, as she'd done several times after travellers stopped, she resumed her gardening activities.

Isla crept back to Lyneth. "They're leaving."

"Was it them?"

"It was."

"They look formidable. Four men their size with those weapons are ready to attack someone of similar size, not a small hauflin."

"Yet, they'd have trouble capturing him." She remembered the way Liam attacked the three men in the forest. They were seasoned fighters, yet he took them down with ease. Or, she thought, the poyson had killed them as if they were young men new to The Trail.

"You sound serious, yet I struggle to believe you."

"Don't. The poyson inside Liam is deadly. Never doubt it."

Lyneth winced. "The sooner we rid him of it, the better I'll feel."

"You and me both. Right now, I'm concerned with what Coraline told those men."

"You shouldn't be."

Isla jerked her head around and found Coraline admiring the blueberry bush and plucking a dead leaf from a branch. "We are not the ones to fear. I hope you trust me."

"Trust you, child? I trust my instincts, and they tell me those men bring nothing but nasty trouble. They search for your young friend. They insisted you passed as other travellers identified you."

"What did you say to them?"

"The truth." She turned to another bush behind her, never looking at them. "I told them I did not see you pass as I don't sit by the road watching for travellers. And I told them I didn't know the location of the young hauflin they sought."

Isla settled on the edge of the garden bed, still hidden from the road. Coraline had spoken the truth. If they had the ability to detect lies, they'd not have been alerted to one.

"It appears your friend, your mate, has gotten himself into more trouble than he has the ability to overcome."

"It is unfortunately and, yes, it is trouble that makes me fear for his safety."

"Perhaps I can help."

Isla stared up at her. How could this stranger help Liam? "I have no way to repay you."

Coraline chuckled. "You are paying it off as we speak...if you return to your chores now that the men have travelled out of sight and around the bend."

Isla grasped the hoe. "I'll weed your entire garden if you can help him."

"Surely, you jest, child. My garden extends to many acres. You'd spend the next two months weeding, well into Harvest when it won't be necessary."

"I will do what I can."

"I know you will; that is why my offer is made." Coraline moved away, returning to the carrot patch.

Isla shrugged at Lyneth. "We are here anyways. We might as well accomplish something."

"Promising we'll weed the entire garden is a little much." She leant forward. "I'm far from happy in the dirt."

"I know, but just this once. Please."

"This once. For you."

"Thanks." Isla drove the hoe into the dirt and ripped out a weed. If Coraline saved Liam from those men, she'd weed the entire garden, spending night and day doing it. Afterwards, she'd reap the reward. Afterwards. Once he was free of poyson, she'd spend all night reaping the reward. The notion put a smile on her face and made the work enjoyable. It also made her blood warm, and the butterflies in her belly take flight.

ओ ❖ ः

Liam put up his hand to stop McGuigan and Deaglan. "Shhh," he whispered. "I hear something."

"Singing?" McGuigan pressed against him.

"It's my stomach." Deaglan put his hand over his belly.

Liam understood the need for food. He was hungry, too, after spending two days wandering through the forest with nothing to eat. Still, he ignored the boy. "No. More like...struggling." He lifted his ear to the wind and listened intently. Grunting mixed with moaning. Thoughts went to another activity, one more intimate between a man and a woman, but this was a youth novel. Certainly, it didn't include such things. Alaura wouldn't have bought the book for Isla when she was that young if it had; the woman was almost as bashful as Bronwyn.

"Are we going to sit around, hoping something will happen?" asked Deaglan.

"We'll sneak closer, get a glimpse at what's happening." He considered the boy. "Sneak. That means move slowly, quietly. Stay out of sight. Can you do that?"

"I'm a pro."

Liam groaned. The boy was over-confident. "Stay behind McGuigan," he whispered. "Do as we do." He crept off the path and onto a small rise. Staying low, he peeked between the branches. What he saw before him confused him more than the three half-naked women in the water.

In front of an ancient stone cottage stood a bedraggled woman near a small fire. The short human poked burning logs with a stick. In her heavy state, when she moved, she moaned and groaned; the source of the sound he had heard. She appeared happy with her day until sounds erupted from a small cage nearby. She waddled over and poked the stick between the rungs.

Liam strained his eyes to see inside the cage. Small figures cowered in the corner until the stick pulled away, and then they threw themselves at the rungs, hissing and calling the woman names. They had wings. He rubbed his eyes. The friendly fairies. If he hadn't seen it himself, he would not have believed it. Fairies were stuff of tales, stories to tell small children. But this was a story. They didn't exist in real life. Still, the three small figures inside the cage captured his attention. Were they to save them from this woman? He wished he'd paid more attention to Isla when she spoke about the story instead of stealing her oatmeal raisin cookies. Then again, the cookies were delicious.

"What does she have in the cage?" McGuigan rested beside him on the bank.

"Fairies. The friendly fairies."

"You're kidding me." He peered harder to see for himself.

"Fairies? The hag caught fairies?" Deaglan's face lit up. "I'd love to have a fairy for a pet. It'd grant me wishes."

"Fairies are not pets," said Liam. "No more than I am."

"Still, imagine having your own fairy." He fell silent for a moment, then spoke louder than he should have. "If we catch one here, can we take it back with us?"

The old women looked in their direction.

"Shhh." Liam ducked and pulled Deaglan with him. "Stupid," he whispered. He waited for the woman to resume her activity, then slowly peeked over the small rise. The wretched face he met gawking back made him tumble down the hill.

"Men!" Her raspy voice reached the leaves in the tallest of trees. She raised her stick and swatted the ground.

McGuigan scrambled, pulling Deaglan with him.

"Get them! Get them!" The hag hooted and gave chase.

Liam glanced over his shoulder. On her knobby knees, she was running as fast as he was. While he planned to run up the path, Deaglan leapt into the bushes. McGuigan saw him and gave chase. The hag let out a hoot and followed them, leaving Liam to run from nothing. He stopped, paused to give her space, then raced after them.

Deaglan sprinted into the clearing, past the fire and snatched the cage with the fairies. He leapt over a small bench and dashed into the bushes.

McGuigan struggled to keep up. As he raced across the empty space in front of the cottage, his feet came out from under him, and he slammed against the ground. After rolling several times, he smashed into the small bench and came to a sudden stop.

Liam sped towards him, but the woman reached him first. She lifted her poker stick and slapped him several times across the back. He fell forward and tried to crawl away. The hag lifted the stick and poked him in his left butt cheek.

"Ah!" screamed McGuigan and rolled to his side, gripping his butt where the stick had struck. "Stay away!"

Liam tackled the woman and pinned her to the ground. "Can you get up?"

McGuigan rose to his knees. He held onto his butt as he forced himself to stand. "I'm up. I'm going. Damn that hurts." He stumbled towards the bushes.

Liam was about to follow when the hag beneath him hurdled herself into the air, spun and held the poker out in front of her as if she wielded a sword. "Stop!" he said, his hands up. "We'll go. Stay calm." He tried to reason with her. He didn't want to hurt her, but he wasn't staying.

"Thief! Thief!" she screeched. "You are mine!" She launched into the air, tackled him and pinning him on his back. "Mine! I claim ye!" Puckering her lips, she pressed them to his mouth.

He fought against her, but... His muscles relaxed, and images of a warm fireplace and a hearty meal devoured his thoughts. Lips moved upon his, and he did nothing but dream of hot food, his cosy surroundings and a long nap. His eyes opened slowly, and the hideous woman was upon him, yet he remained still. He tried to throw the bedraggled woman aside, but his strength failed. Feeling her fingers on his shirt buttons, he called for help, but her lips blocked his mouth. Thoughts of joining with this ugly hag sent an icy shiver down his spine.

Then she was gone. Incapable of moving his head, he searched the area with his eyes.

McGuigan came into view and stared down at him. "What are you doing? Get up."

He thrust his body upward, yet he remained on the ground in the same position. "Help." His voice, a whisper, came with a gasp.

"Is she your type?" McGuigan smirked. "Do you need a moment?"

Liam lowered his brow and hoped he frowned. "Help up." Again, his voice was barely a murmur.

McGuigan reached out a hand. "Grab it." Not seeing a response, he knelt and examined his eyes. "Can you move?"

"No."

"What did you say?"

"No." He made a face to go with the word.

"Damn." He stood, grabbed Liam's arms and threw him over his shoulder.

Liam tried to brace his ribs against the bouncing on boney shoulder but had no control over his body. He saw the woman unconscious on the ground.

McGuigan rushed through the bushes. "Deaglan, wait up!"

The forest floor passed quickly beneath Liam. His arms dangled in front of him, slapping McGuigan's back. He tried to gather spit and remove the woman's foul flavour from his mouth, but his tongue barely moved.

"Is she following," asked Deaglan.

"No, she's out cold," said McGuigan. He slowed his pace. "She put Liam under a spell."

"Is he dead?"

"No, just can't move."

"An illusion?"

"Don't think so."

Liam considered this. Was it an illusion? He imagined his hand moving. Nothing. He imagined his mouth saying, *No*. Nothing. He groaned in frustration but made no sound.

"You have rescued us."

The small voice touched his ears. The friendly fairies.

"You are our heroes," said another fairy.

"She's a horrible old hag," said the third. "Nasty."

"Deaglan, stop," said McGuigan.

"Why?"

"So we can set them free."

"What part of having a fairy of my own didn't you understand? Now I have three!"

"Please, let us out," cried the first fairy. "Do not be as horrible as the hag."

"We will release you," said McGuigan. "Deaglan, stop."

"This isn't fair."

But the boy must have stopped because McGuigan did and Liam hung still, waiting for something to happen. A door creaked open and wings fluttered.

"Thank you, thank you!" said the first fairy.

"Yes, double thank you," said the second fairy.

"Triple thank yous," said the third fairy.

McGuigan jerked his shoulder and moved Liam forward, then eased him onto the forest floor to examine his eyes. "Can you hear me?"

"Yes."

"What was that?" He leant forward.

"Yes."

"We can help!" The fairy with the brown hair flew close to his face. The soft wind from her wings brushed his skin. "I'm Daisy. These are my friends, Pansy and Rose. That old hag cast a vile spell, but we can break it."

"How?" asked McGuigan.

"With a kiss." She flew in front of Liam's face and hovered. "You're sweet. I shall call you Sweetie." Steadying herself with her tiny hands resting on his chin, she bent forward and kissed his bottom lip. She giggled and flew away.

Liam felt a warm sensation travel from his lips to the muscles in his face, then it shot down his neck and into his core. "I feel it."

"And we hear you," said McGuigan.

"Incredible. Thank you."

"Thank you," said Daisy. "You saved us. That hag wanted to sell us to the pedlar. He'd take us to the great city, and we'd never find our way home."

"She's the meanest hag in the forest," said Pansy. "We dislike her, so we play tricks on her."

"Yesterday, she tricked us," said Rose.

"You're safe to return home," said McGuigan.

"Without a wish?" asked Deaglan.

Pansy giggled. "We don't give wishes."

"We give gifts." Daisy returned to Liam. "I will give you two gifts for saving us." She stood on his chest and opened his shirt pocket. "This will give you the ability to be an elf for a day." She walked to the other pocket, held out her hand and a dark bottle appeared. A blue cloth magically wrapped around it. "This will restore your youth and your vitality." She secured it inside the pocket and fastened the button.

Pansy flew in front of McGuigan. "I bear gifts for you." A dark rock materialized in her hand. "This will ignite into fire on command." She slipped into his breast pocket. "And this wee stick will grow to ten feet long when you say *Pansy Please*." She placed the two-inch stick inside his other pocket.

"With this pill," said Rose, "you will steal a voice." She placed it inside Deaglan's pocket. "This will turn night into day." A small brown sack appeared, and she placed it into the other pocket.

Liam pushed himself to a seated position. "Thank you for the gifts. We will use them wisely."

"Wisely?" Deaglan laughed. "You mean mischievously."

"Waste them if you will, but I'll use mine when I need them."
McGuigan patted his pockets. "They may save my life or the life of
someone I love." He reached out a hand to Liam. "Can you stand?"

Liam grasped the hand and pulled himself to his feet. "A little shaky
but I'll manage."

The three fairies fluttered in the air beside each other.

"We must be home," said Daisy.

"Our families will be worried," said Pansy.

"And we should not worry those we love," said Rose. "Thank you,
and safe travels." She flew away.

"Thank you," said Pansy. She zipped through the air after Rose.

"Thank you." Daisy smiled, waved and followed her friends.

"Incredible," said Deaglan. "No one will believe me."

"Except us." McGuigan slapped him on the back. "And we will
never confirm your story." He laughed.

"Great. I'll look like a fool."

"Not a fool." Liam shook his legs to restore the feeling. "A child."
He smirked. "Shall we continue?"

"After you, Sweetie." McGuigan gestured for him to walk first.

He groaned and stepped onto the path, hoping to find the end of
the trail and the book soon. They'd met the nasty brownies and the
friendly fairies. What was left for them to find? The girl. Surely her das
and brother searched for her but if they didn't, it was up to them to
rescue her. If they failed, would she be lost forever?

„ ❖ ”

The next day, McGuigan found a patch of blueberries and fell to his
knees to eat. He'd have to consume the entire field to satisfy his hunger.
When Deaglan knelt beside him, he pushed him away.

"Get your own patch." He picked several berries and shoved them
into his mouth.

Deaglan moved a few feet away and began picking.

"What I need is meat." McGuigan shoved another handful of
berries into his mouth. He didn't care if they were in the blue, purple or
white stage.

"Food of more substance would remove the grumbling faster." Liam
knelt several feet away, eating the berries and scanning the large field.

~ 113 ~

Something caught his eye, and he walked deeper into the blueberry patch.

"What did you find? Food?"

"A piece of paper."

"I can't eat that." He continued to pick.

"It's a page from a book." Liam stared into the distance. "She came this way."

"Who?"

"The girl in the story."

McGuigan stretched up and scanned the area. "Do you see her?"

"No." He examined the ground. "Her footprints. She went that way."

He continued to pick and shove berries into his mouth. This was the first food they'd stumbled upon since the raspberry patch late yesterday evening.

"We'll follow her." Liam put the page down.

"You're leaving it behind?" Deaglan stood.

"If her das and brother are following, they'll need to see it." Liam followed the footprints. "Come on. The sooner we find her, the sooner we get out of here."

"You hope." McGuigan picked quickly, filling his hand.

"That's what we're following." Liam grinned. "*A Trail of Hope.*"

"Oh, Sweetie, you're a funny one."

He leered back at him. "Please, stop, or I'll start."

"You ain't got nothin'."

"Pip-pip, young man."

"She didn't." He slapped his forehead. "I'm going to get her."

Liam laughed. "She did."

"I don't get it," said Deaglan. "How is that funny?"

"It's not." McGuigan followed Liam onto the trail. "Now being a wicked water witch's honey pot is." He clicked his tongue on the side of his mouth. "Let's go, Honey Pot."

"Shut up. Just...shut up." Deaglan frowned. "That woman was ugly; she gives me nightmares. I want to forget about it."

"Oh, that won't happen. I've got a good memory."

They travelled across the field and into a thick forest. The sun indicated it was late afternoon.

"Why is this girl walking through here again?" asked McGuigan.

"She's lost," said Liam.

"Why wouldn't she turn around and go home?"

"That's what I said to Isla."

"What was her response?"

"I can't remember. I was too busy eating her cookies."

"Maybe we should stop and read the book," said Deaglan.

Liam rushed forward. "Another page." He turned to the others. "We're on the right path." He gazed ahead. "I wonder if this was how Bronwyn felt when he searched for Isla; every found page renewed his hope, kept pushing him onward." He set the page on the ground where he had found it.

"Are you sure her family searches for her?" McGuigan yawned and stretched his back.

"I don't know," said Liam. "We might be playing the roles of her family."

"That would make me the das." He frowned. "Because I'm oldest."

"Sure thing, old man." Liam walked on. "When we stop for the night, I'll read more of the book."

"Skip to the end. We'll get there faster."

"You'll avoid all the boring parts," said Deaglan.

"Sounds like a plan." McGuigan spotted something up ahead. "What's that?"

Liam followed his pointing finger. "Looks like...a lighthouse? What would that be doing here? There's no water."

"Not that we can see. I bet the girl went there."

"In that case, I hope they're friendly like fairies, not nasty like half-naked women."

They approached the stone structure cautiously. The closer they came, the more confused McGuigan grew. The round tower, at least five hundred feet high and two hundred feet in diameter, had at least four levels to it: bottom, two mid-floors and the roof. The two large windows marking the two mid-floors were rounded on the top. The roof was trimmed with low merlons. In the centre of the roof was a square structure, similar to that of a lighthouse. The four sides consisted mostly of glass, and a dark object rested in the middle of it. If it did possess a lighting apparatus, it wasn't lit, and it needn't be given the sunny weather.

The immense size of the windows and merlons suggested a large being lived here, but who larger than a human would build such a structure in the middle of the forest, far from water? Troglodytes were larger. He slowed his pace. So were ogres. Both were unfriendly creatures he didn't want to encounter in a real or fictional story. Fictional. That meant what lived inside the tower was a fantastical creature the author conjured up. It might be green with six legs, large fangs and three eyes.

A large symbol came into view. It rested on the stone wall ten feet above the ground. Straining his eyes to see clearer, he saw out-stretched wings. Harpies? They were hideous creatures.

Liam stopped and gazed up to the top of the tower. "I remember the third creature Isla mentioned was in the book."

"What is it?" McGuigan stood beside him.

"Dragons."

He stepped back. "Are you serious?"

Liam pulled the book from his pocket and flipped to the back. McGuigan and Deaglan hung over his shoulder, scanning the pages as he turned them.

"That's it." He pointed to the words. "Green dragons."

"Damn. We are in serious trouble." McGuigan backed up farther. "That means they're home."

"Maybe we sneak by without meeting them," said Deaglan. "Let's go around. Or go back." His voice squeaked.

"It says, the dragons appear menacing but do not attack the girl."

"What about the das and son?" asked McGuigan. "Were they attacked?"

Liam flipped through several pages. "No. I don't think so."

"Could you be more affirmative?"

"I have to read more."

"We'll sit and wait."

Liam sighed and sat on a fallen log. After a few minutes, he said, "The dragon is friendly to the girl. To the man and boy, it asks a question."

"What question?"

"What do you have for me?"

"It wants payment?"

"No, a gift."

"What did they offer the dragon?"

"A staff with a brilliant light on the end," said Liam. "A light that can never be doused."

"That would be perfect for their lighthouse." McGuigan stared up at the roof. From this angle, it appeared empty.

"Perfect; fantastic."

He spun around and gawked into the snout of a large green dragon. It stood twelve feet, at least, and peered down at him with large yellow eyes.

"What gift do you offer for trespassing?"

"I've got...nothing," stammered McGuigan.

The dragon opened its mouth and blew, tossing him into the nearby bushes. "You?" He leered at Liam. "Your offering?"

"A book." Liam held it up.

"I've no purpose for books scripted in your tongue." He huffed and blew him into the bushes.

McGuigan up-righted himself and stared in awe. The dragon didn't harm them, only sent them out of his way.

"Boy, the gift you bear?"

"I have..." Deaglan searched his trouser pockets, "a jackknife, a piece of string, two buttons and a silver coin."

"Worthless." The dragon blew him into the bushes. "Does no trespasser have an object I desire?"

"What do you desire?" asked Liam, stepping from the bushes and brushing the leaves from his jacket.

"A gift I do not possess."

"What is that?" McGuigan stood a foot behind Liam.

The dragon peered closer. "What my heart desires."

"A mate?" asked Liam.

Tilting his head, the dragon considered this. "A mate? A companion?"

"Yes, if that is what you call the female you desire most."

"A companion I possess."

"Congratulations, ...? What is your name?"

"Falkor."

"And your mate?"

"Magon."

"Congratulations, Falkor, and to your mate Magon." Liam bowed slightly. "Finding one's heart's desire makes one happy."

"But..." he dipped his head lower, "happiness is greater if..."

"You had offspring?"

Falkor retracted his head. "Precisely."

"If I may ask, sir dragon," said Deaglan, "why didn't you scorch my bottom with fire?"

"Do we really want to start this conversation?" asked McGuigan.

Falkor hung his head. "The eternal fire has been snuffed, dousing our ability to belch and to breed."

"You need fire to have offspring?" asked Liam.

"How is fire involved?" McGuigan's imagination conjured up several scenarios but none made sense.

"Fire energizes our ritual."

"What if you swallowed a stone that made fire?" asked Deaglan.

Falkor tilted his head. "A sizzling ember? Fails to work."

"No, a stone that ignites upon command."

McGuigan put his hand over his chest pocket. Inside was the stone the fairy had given him.

"Conceivably." Falkor leant close to Deaglan. "Does one have such a stone?"

"No, but he does."

McGuigan stood straight when the dragon swung his snout in his direction. "Well, I might..."

"Might?" His bright yellow eyes widened.

"A fairy gave it to me."

"May I gaze upon it?" His hopeful expression illumed his face.

McGuigan withdrew the stone. "I've never tried it. I don't know if it works."

"Will you gift it to Falkor?" He rubbed his claws together.

"Only if you promise you won't use your fiery breath on innocent victims, like us."

"Promise. Promise. We are allies."

He held out the stone and waited for the forceful snatch, but Falkor plucked it from his hand gently. The dragon stretched his neck and pointed his mouth to the sky, then he dropped the stone inside. He shook, shivered, then burped. "Fire ignite!" His eyes grew wide, and he drew a large breath. Wind escaped his lips, followed by a rush of flames. It scorched the nearby bushes, leaving them smouldering with grey smoke rising from them.

Falkor grinned at McGuigan. Then he pounced on him, knocking him down and placing his front claws on his chest. He roared, and then breathed fire over his head and into the bushes. The leaves and twigs burst into flames, crackling and spewing smoke.

McGuigan trembled from the inevitable. The next breath would singe his hair and head. He wiggled to free himself, but the dragon was too heavy.

Falkor leapt to the ground. "Fire!" He laughed, and his chest shook. "I possess fire!"

"You enjoy the gift?" Liam held back.

The dragon veered towards him. "Enjoy? No! Adore it. Love it! The best gift received. You may trespass, but not before..." he half closed his eyes, "I mark you." His large front claw struck Liam's chest and pinned him to the forest floor.

"Please, don't hurt me." He put his hands up to protect his face, but the dragon pinned his right arm to the ground.

"Open your hand," ordered Falkor.

Liam cowered but opened his hands. Falkor leant close to his right palm and breathed gently. A puff of smoke escaped his mouth.

"Ow! Ow!" Liam wiggled his fingers. "What did you do?"

"Left my mark." The dragon stood and released him, and Liam examined his palm. A one-inch wide dark ring blackened his skin. "Remain friendly to my kin, and they will welcome you. Show your mark and trespass freely." He turned to McGuigan. "Raise your right hand."

He hesitated, not wanting to be burnt or marked with anything. Yet, the dark-yellow eyes left no room for discussion. He opened his hand slowly. Falkor grasped it, held it close to his snout and breathed on it. A surging pain erupted in his skin and travelled through his nerves. He wanted to cry out but absorbed the pain with clenched teeth. The dragon released him and reached for Deaglan.

"Wait. I'm not sure." Deaglan backed away.

"Be sure." Falkor snatched his arm and held it to his snout. "Open." When the hand opened, he repeated the action.

"Ouch! Ow! Damn it! I'm going to die!" Deaglan fell to his knees and gripped his hand.

McGuigan stepped forward to help the boy and found the same ring singed into his skin. "Really. You're going to die?"

"It felt like it." Deaglan gripped his arm and pushed himself to his feet. "That hurt."

McGuigan turned to the dragon. "Did a young girl pass?"

"Indeed."

"When?"

"Earlier."

"Around what time?"

Falkor tilted his head. "We do not mark time."

"Was it today?"

"Indeed."

"Great. This morning?"

"No."

Scratching his head, McGuigan tried another tactic. "How far are we behind her?"

"Behind her? Not far."

"She's close."

Falkor looked around. "Not close."

"Which way did she go?"

"South of Blueston."

"Blueston? Is that the tower?"

"Indeed."

"Great. We are trying to find her."

"You will fail."

McGuigan paused. "We won't find her? Who will?"

"Kin."

"Did they already pass?"

"Indeed."

"That's great news," said Liam. "We need to catch up and end the story."

"May we pass?" asked McGuigan.

Falkor bowed his head slightly. "You may trespass, my allies."

He hadn't considered the dragon a friend, but... he stuck out his hand. "Thank you. I am happy we met."

The dragon eyed the hand curiously, then stuck his large claw into it. "I am happy you trespassed." He shook the finger, then released it.

"Falkor, thank you." Liam held out his hand and shook the large claw. "I am happy to call you friend."

"I'm not going to be left out." Deaglan reached for the claw. "I'd have a dragon as friend before enemy every day." When the dragon accepted his hand, he giggled. "No one is going to believe me."

"Dragons will." Falkor stretched his wings. "My companion awaits, and I wish to share your gift with her." In seconds, he was air borne and flying towards the tower.

"Unbelievable." Deaglan's mouth hung open. "A real dragon."

"A real fake dragon in a story," said McGuigan. "Unbelievable."

Deaglan stared at him. "He was real. I have the mark to prove it." He held up his hand to expose the ring.

"Bet it will fade when we get out of this book," said Liam. "Let's go." He hiked through the trail. "The girl, her das and brother are up ahead. We don't want to miss this."

"If we do, are we stuck in the story?" McGuigan hurried after him.

"Let's not think of that."

As they travelled past the looming tower, McGuigan gazed up to its top and searched for Falkor, but he was nowhere in sight. The trail continued through low bushes and into hilly terrain. "Did you hear that?" He stopped and listened.

"Sounds like voices." Liam grinned. "Maybe they found her."

"I don't want to interrupt the reunion." He hiked up an incline and entered thick trees. "Let's watch from above."

"Good idea." Liam followed.

McGuigan walked parallel to the path they had followed. When he reached a break in the trees, he stopped to peek below. "It's them." He lay on his stomach to observe the scene. Liam and Deaglan lay on either side of him.

The girl, an elf, had fallen, and a man rushed towards her with a young man trailing him. No sooner had he reached her when a small creature leapt from the bushes and grabbed the boy. It drove him to the ground and dragged him away.

"What the...?" McGuigan prepared to rise.

"Wait. I'm certain there's a happy ending," said Liam.

"Read the last page," said Deaglan, "to see if they all live."

Liam flipped the book over and opened the back cover. His finger moved down the page, scanning the text. "Yes. They all live."

Another creature jumped out and tried to capture the girl. The father drew his sword and killed it. She screamed as the first creature pulled away her brother.

"Are you sure they all live?" asked McGuigan.

"Yes. You know books. They make you fear someone is going to die at the end, then..." he shrugged, "it all ends well." His brow furrowed. "But if that doesn't happen, we help them."

The father rushed towards his son, killing a third creature on the way. He tripped, rolled to his feet and continued. The girl ran after him, screaming. He caught up to his son and killed the mysterious creature. The boy scrambled to his feet, and the girl jumped into her father's arms. The three hugged for a long time.

A robust wind whirled overhead, and McGuigan lifted off the ground. He tried to grab a branch to anchor him, but he missed it. Seeing Liam and Deaglan also rising, he grabbed them around the waist and pulled them close.

"Hold on!" His grip tightened. Wherever they'd go, they'd go together. The wind increased in strength, and the sky darkened. The forest floor and the trees disappeared, making him fear the fall if it came. He closed his eyes and waited for fate to take its course.

11

Those Who Travel the Land

ISLA DRAGGED HER TONGUE over her top teeth. She never tired of eating biscuits, and she wanted to ensure she extracted every crumb. If she were home, she'd take another, but three was her limit as a guest. The steaming bowl of pea soup in front of her smelt delicious. She'd wash down the biscuits with it.

Lyneth, who sat beside her, was already half finished her soup and spreading butter on her first biscuit. Coraline and Weston sat on the opposite side of the table. The mates were excellent hosts, generous with their home and their knowledge. Coraline offered advice on how to reach Inglenook and avoid most travellers, including the four men searching for Liam. She also provided a contact who could furnish safe lodging while they stayed in the town, as well as an exit plan.

The cloak Coraline gave her was similar to the one she had taken from the Dukedom of Dunakan. However, the Cloak of Glogyn, as it was called, didn't conceal the wearer; it created the illusion he was another race. In this instance, it would visually transform Liam into an elf. There was one condition; Isla had to return it after Liam was freed from the curse. She made the deal without hesitation.

With a spoonful of soup halfway to her mouth, the sound of strong winds perked her ears. "What's that?"

Coraline smiled. "They return." She pushed her chair from the table. "Shall we greet them?"

Isla jumped up. The boys had been gone five days, and she worried they'd never return. She followed Coraline to the small room off the treat shop. Lyneth and Weston did the same.

Coraline drew the dark curtain and looped it on a hook. She peered into the closet containing the pair of boots and waited. "Any moment. Stand away."

Isla pressed her back against the wall. A fierce gust of wind battered her face, whipped her hair and hurled dust into her eyes. She shielded her face from flying debris. A solid thud landed near her feet and fearing injury, she retreated to the doorway. Scanning for the source of the sound, she saw Liam and Deaglan on the floor beneath McGuigan. They clung to one another as if best friends.

Lyneth chuckled. "You boys have grown attached while you were away."

"Get off me." Liam pushed McGuigan.

"Give me time." McGuigan used his arms to push himself onto his knees, then he scrambled to his feet.

Isla reached for Liam and pulled him up and into her arms. "Missed you." She kissed him, then hugged him tightly.

"And me?" McGuigan stood with arms open.

"You, too." She kissed his cheek and pulled him into their embrace.

"Hey, my girl." Liam slapped his arm.

"And me." Deaglan wrapped his arms around all three.

"We're not that close." Liam pushed the other two away.

"Do you feel you're tending to young ones?" Coraline asked Lyneth.

"Every day," said Lyneth. "That makes me the nursemaid."

"Nursemaid?" McGuigan marched over to her. "We've travelled together for almost two years, facing every challenge, and you think of me as a child?" He gawked at the biscuit in her hand. "Can I have a bite?"

She pushed it into his mouth.

"Do you have more?" he mumbled over the food. "I'm hungry enough to eat a pan of biscuits followed by a pot of soup."

"Food." Deaglan rubbed his belly. "I've not gone this long without eating in my life. Please, feed me."

"Let us return to the evening ration." Coraline gestured for them to follow.

Isla held onto Liam, waiting until the others left the room before she spoke. "I was worried. You were gone so long."

"I worried for you, wondered where you'd search for us?" He caressed her cheek. "We didn't know how to escape the story."

"We learnt where you were but didn't know exactly. Coraline said you carried one of her books, and that's the story you entered."

"I did. *A Trail of Hope*."

"There was nothing we could do but wait," she said. His stomach grumbled. "Hungry?"

"Starved. We've not eaten anything but berries."

She kissed his chin. "Then I shall stuff you." Grasping his hand, she dragged him to the kitchen and sat him in her seat in front of the bowl of pea soup. "Eat."

"Is this yours?"

"I am full of biscuits. Eat."

Two extra chairs were added around the table for McGuigan and Deaglan, and bowls of soup had been placed in front of them.

"This is a homecoming." Coraline held the basket of biscuits out to Liam, and he took one. "It is always pleasant when travellers return. We shall share the ration and the tale. Isla, no hovering. Grab a seat and join us. And another bowel of soup."

She found a chair and squeezed it between Liam and McGuigan, then scooped out another helping of soup. Catching Liam's eye, she placed her hand on his lap, then dipped the wooden spoon into the warm mixture of vegetables and peas. They exchanged grins and for the first time in five days, her muscles relaxed.

"Please, share with us your story within the story." Coraline took a drink of fruity-flavoured water. "Which book did you take with you?"

"*A Trail of Hope*," said Liam.

"You encountered the naughty brownies?"

McGuigan laughed the loudest. "We did, and they were very naughty, right, Honey Pot?" He snickered.

"You understood their intentions?" asked Coraline.

"Yes, but we weren't interested," he said, "though they insisted." "Their magic worked on Liam, and I was certain he'd not be tricked into wanting another woman."

"You wanted another woman?" Isla raised an eyebrow.

"No. Never." He placed a gentle hand on her forearm. "They used magic."

"And they didn't want you in that way." Coraline's soft voice settled the laughter. "Once you were disarmed and disrobed, they'd have led you to the water's edge, then dragged you to the depths of the lake."

"We'd have drowned?" Deaglan's mouth dropped open.

"Yes. You would become one of many victims claimed through the centuries."

"I should thank you for punching me in the face," said Liam. "If not for you solving the mystery, we'd all be dead."

"Any time." McGuigan shovelled soup into his mouth.

"Why did you punch him?" asked Isla.

"Pain broke the spell."

"And the dragons," said Coraline, "what gift did you give them to trespass their lighthouse?"

"The gift of fire breath," said Deaglan, snatching another biscuit from the basket.

"What?" Coraline shared a worried glance with Weston. "That creates unexpected dangers to those who travel the land."

"Falkor is a nice dragon." Liam took a drink. "Reasonable."

"Fire may change his disposition."

"He'll never harm us," said Deaglan. "Neither will other green dragons."

"I'm doubtful." Coraline eyed him. "Dragons are unpredictable creatures; they're not to be trusted."

"Falkor is grateful for our gift." McGuigan put another spoonful of soup into his mouth. "He and his companion can now have offspring."

"Explain for I'm becoming more confused as you speak."

"Without fire," said Liam, "dragons can't perform the mating ritual, which means no conception."

"Interesting. And you say you don't fear being attacked by green dragons. Why?"

He held up his hand to reveal the dark ring.

"I've got one, too." McGuigan revealed his mark.

"And me." Deaglan held up his hand.

"Incredible." Coraline shook her head. "This was not part of the story."

"I'm more confused by your ability to give the dragon fire breath," said Isla.

"I didn't," said Liam. "McGuigan did."

"But how?" She stared at her friend and waited while he chewed.

"The stone," said McGuigan. "It had the power to ignite fire on command."

"Where did you get it?"

"The friendly fairies."

"Why did they give it to you?" asked Coraline.

"For rescuing them."

She exchanged glances with Weston. "My father and brother received no gifts. The fairies were not in need of rescuing; they were happened upon, and they showed Father which way to go."

McGuigan shrugged. "We rescued them from the horrible hag who lived in the little cottage."

"Was this woman short? Haggard?"

"Yes. She was quite a sight."

"She was fast," said Liam. "And she knew magic."

"She paralyzed Liam with a kiss," said McGuigan.

Isla playfully glared at Liam. "You were kissing her because...?"

He chuckled and flicked her nose. "Because she tackled me. I was saving this young man from her stick."

McGuigan groaned. "That still hurts. I think she broke skin."

"This woman, you say she captured the three fairies?" Coraline appeared puzzled.

"Yes," said Liam. "In a cage."

"And the fairies gave you a gift?"

"They gave each of us two gifts."

"What were the other gifts?

Liam reached into his chest pocket and extracted a small sack. He withdrew the pill from inside and held it between his finger and thumb. "This will transform me into an elf for a day."

McGuigan withdrew the two-inch stick. "This will grow ten feet long when I command it to do so."

Deaglan presented his own pill. "This steals a voice, and this powder," he pulled it from his other pocket, "will turn night into day."

Isla reached into Liam's second pocket and removed a small dark bottle wrapped in cloth. "What does this do?"

"That..." he shrugged, "will restore my youth and my vitality." He laughed. "How young do you want me to be?"

"You found it!" She threw her arms around his neck and planted a quick kiss on his lips. Tears welled in her eyes as she gripped the bottle tightly.

"Found what?"

"The cure for Kiefer. I need to put it in a safe place, guard it against damage." Her eyes widened. "And find a portal to get it to him."

"Are you certain?"

"No, but... It must be it. I found it in your pocket, and you are my mate." She stared at the bottle. It was a precious item that had to be guarded.

"I hope it is what you seek."

"We won't know until he drinks it." She whirled. "Coraline, are there portals at Inglenook?"

"Indeed. Where do you need to go?"

"Maskil."

"I'm unsure but check with the contact I've given you."

"I will."

"I see you have a pass."

She smiled. "I do. Given to me by a special man."

"Use it wisely. It is a gift not given to many." She rose from the table. "I have the perfect vessel to protect the bottle." She left the room and returned a short time later with a small box lined with silk. "This will shield it from the harshest of strikes and from freezing."

Isla placed the bottle inside, closed the lid and secured the latch. She squished the small sack containing the grey powder to the side of her pouch and wedged the box next to it. Fastening the flap securely, she placed her hand over it and sent a wish to the Welkin nymphs for it to reach Kiefer safely.

Beside her, Liam dug into his soup eagerly. His lack of food consumption showed on his face. He had begun to add weight, and now that had been set back. Still, if this was a cure for Kiefer, it was worth it. She'd nurse him back to full health and rid him of the curse. Then he was hers for the taking.

Tomorrow, she'd tell him about the four men who searched for him but tonight, they'd enjoy being together, reunited again.

ಬಿ ❖ ಚ

Lyneth centred the dark brown blanket onto the back of her horse, then heaved up the saddle and wiggled it into place. They were leaving Lady Coraline of Maiden's Way and Weston this morning and heading for Copper Ridge by the path behind the cottage. They'd not see the main road again until they reached Inglenook in three days.

They each had a five-day supply of food, including a sack of scroggin, for the journey. Weston had dried the fruits and nuts during the warmer months and stored them for Forstig provisions.

A few feet away, McGuigan tacked up his horse. The boy, only nineteen, had his moments of maturity, but he was still innocent in many ways. Now that he felt comfortable on The Trail, he was prone to joking more. His witty comments often lightened the mood and made her laugh. Although she teased him and his stubbornness annoyed her, she'd become fond of having him around.

"How's your butt wound?"

He made a face. "Sore. Bruised. The stick broke skin."

"Did you disinfect it?"

He scrunched his nose. "Yeah."

"Did Isla help?"

"She was busy with Liam."

"Do you want me to look?"

"No!" He shook his head. "It'll be fine."

"No need to be shy where a wound is concerned."

"Well,... I... It's not..." He grumbled. "Can you? It's going to be awfully sore in the saddle."

No one else was in the stable, so she ushered him towards the light. "Where is it?"

He removed his scabbard, then unfastened his belt. "Right here." He lowered the back of his trousers halfway down his butt. The inflamed bright red skin around the puncture wound measured four inches across.

"Good grief. She stabbed you hard." Lyneth returned to her saddlebag and removed a pouch.

"It's not that bad, is it?" He stretched his neck to see the wound.

"It's infected." She pulled a bottle of clear liquid from the pouch and removed the cap. "This will hurt."

"Not too much. Right?"

"You tell me." She held a rag beneath the wound and poured the clear liquid over the broken skin and large red area. It bubbled and hissed as it sunk into the laceration.

"Owwww. Ohhh. That stings bad." McGuigan gripped the wooden rail with one hand and clung to his trousers with the other as he sucked in a deep breath and clenching his teeth to absorb the pain.

"Give it a moment." The redness around the puncture wound concerned her most. It should have been disinfected the night before, and it wouldn't have progressed this far. It would need daily care until the redness faded. She dabbed the area to remove the puss, then poured more cleansing solution on it.

"No more." He bent forward in pain. "That's plenty."

"Stop whining. You know it's unavoidable. If the infection spreads, I'd have to remove your leg to the...butt cheek."

"Not funny."

"Neither is this. If you could see it, you'd understand."

"What's that supposed to mean?" He twisted again in an attempt to see his rear end. "There's nothing wrong with my butt."

"The wound is badly infected." She considered his behind. "Your butt looks fine."

"And this is where a mate comes in handy."

She chuckled and dabbed more of the puss away. "Won't I do when in dire need?"

"Only in dire need."

She applied a healing cream, then withdrew a large bandage. "I'm... Let's..." She stood and considered the wound. "Do you wear shorts?" She hadn't seen any beneath the trousers.

"Yes." He pulled them over the rim.

"Good. Let's get those up, and we'll tuck the bandage inside them. It will cushion the wound against the saddle." She held the bandage in place and helped him slide up the shorts to secure it.

He pulled up his ·trousers and fastened them, then grabbed his scabbard. "It feels like it will stay."

"Good. I'll check it again tonight and apply more cream."

He looked up awkwardly. "I suppose."

"It's important it's kept clean and treated."

"I know." He crossed his arms. "Thanks. You didn't have to."

"I know, but I've got to keep you in fighting shape, *young man.*" She placed a hand on his shoulder, and his expression from the nickname made her laugh. "I mean it in fun. You and I are the most experienced in this group. We must tend to each other and them."

His face brightened. "That's what I was thinking."

She stuck out her hand. "Teamwork?"

He grasped the hand and shook it firmly. "Teamwork."

Footsteps sounded on the dirt, and Isla, Liam and Deaglan entered the stable.

"There's the rest of the gang." She returned to her horse to finish tacking up.

Within thirty minutes, they were bidding farewell to Coraline and Weston. The brisk morning made Lyneth button her jacket to the top and don gloves. Travelling in the shadows of tall trees made it cooler than if they rode in the bright sunshine.

"I've not felt this cold since I lived in Maskil." Liam pulled closer to Isla. He wore his jacket, gloves and the unique cloak Coraline had lent them. His hauflin form had been altered to that of an elf.

"Yet this is warmer than Maskil," said Isla, "warmer than Blackvale Castle in Forstig."

"I agree to that." Lyneth led the way through the trees. The narrow path accommodated one horse at a time. She'd be warier if this trail was not as exclusive as it was. Coraline had said few knew about it and fewer travelled it. It was the long way to Inglenook, the off-the-beaten-path trail.

A few hours into their journey, and the scenery distracted her eyes. Large trees with dark-green, thick leaves and intricate brown and grey bark, leafy bushes with colourful blossoms and sharp rock outcrops lined the path. When the forest opened to overlook the valley, the view below captivated her.

As each hour passed, they climbed higher onto the side of the mountain. By noon tomorrow, according to Coraline, they'd reach Copper Ridge, then they'd descend slowly into the valley with Knollton Mountain to their north. Another day and a half of travelling would deliver them to Inglenook.

The men who searched for Liam would have reached the town yesterday. They had probably already asked many people about seeing Liam and those he travelled with. Under the circumstances, she and the others would enter Inglenook as The Mercenaries had entered many places: in two groups. One question remained: who would go with who?

The men sought hauflins, so ideally, Liam, disguised as an elf, would travel with her and Deaglan; two young elves travelling with an older woman of elf and human lineage wouldn't draw attention. They'd deliver Deaglan to his aunt, regroup with Isla and McGuigan and head north.

However, Isla would disagree. She'd argue to remain at Liam's side. Except she had to understand her presence gave his away. The four men had seen her on the road to Moonsface, and they might stop to question her. They wouldn't give a second glance at two elves and a half-elf in an elf settlement.

She planned to have this difficult conversation tonight before they reached Inglenook. As the oldest of the group, she hoped she had sway, but Isla was emotionally charged. She remembered Elspeth handling deep emotions during discussions; maturity always won. Except her former leader hadn't had four teenagers with over-excited feelings to deal with. This was either going to end quickly or not end until they departed Inglenook.

12

Part of The Mercenaries

THE SHOPS IN INGLENOOK were much like those in Bannock. The owners took great care in decorating the fronts, appealing to customers and enticing them to enter and to buy their products. However, Isla wasn't interested in buying anything; she had all she needed except a small supply of food to add to her rucksack. What she searched for, many wouldn't recognise, but miniature shells carved into wood and stone meant one thing to her: portals. She needed to find one and get the cure to Kiefer. She'd take Liam with her, far away from the men who hunted him. By the time they returned to Inglenook, she hoped they'd be long gone.

"Up ahead," said McGuigan.

She peered past the shops and boardwalk and read the street sign: Flint Street. They trotted the horses to the corner and turned down it. She glanced at him and sighed. Between him and Liam, they had convinced her this was the better plan, but she disliked it. She wanted Liam with her, not with Lyneth and Deaglan. Although he was disguised as an elf, she feared the four men would see through it. It did make sense that he'd blend in, given this was an elf settlement, but the goal was to get him off the streets as quickly as possible.

She reflected on the other fact: the men would recognise her and ask again if she'd seen a young hauflin male. If Liam was on the back of her horse, she might stumble her words. Still, she didn't willingly agree to this plan.

"Stop scheming," said McGuigan. "We've done this before. Remain calm. All will work out."

"I know, but..." Her shoulders slumped forward.

"Are you thinking of the reason you're here? Keep it in mind, think of it, live it. If asked, you'll say it automatically."

His maturity and reasoning at this moment irritated her. She wanted him to agree with her, to be irrational and follow her without question. Lyneth had told her she was in Inglenook to attend the Grain Moon Festival. The two-day celebration marked the end of Sumortide and the beginning of Harvest. The colourful decorations of late-blooming flowers, stalks of grain and images of the moon touched every shop. There was no doubt a big event was planned for the town, and signs proclaimed items to help celebrate the festivities.

Isla didn't care about celebrating the end of the warm season. She'd be heading north once business was done, and that meant cold weather. Coraline didn't know exactly where Dougendun was located, but she was certain it was farther north, somewhere between Pogwa Mountains and a hauflin settlement called Titterton. Ideally, they'd wait until Springan, but she wanted the poyson out of Liam as soon as possible.

As it was, by the time they reached Pogwa Mountains, they'd already be well into Forstig with Wintertide on the threshold. It'd be the worst time of year to explore the area.

"Excuse me. Why are you visiting Inglenook?"

The voice shattered her concentration, and she searched to learn who had spoken. She saw only McGuigan, who grinned mischievously. "Really?"

"Just keeping you alert." He rode close and playfully slapped her knee. "You're so deep in thought, you're not taking in your surroundings. You might miss something you're looking for."

She glanced behind her. Had she passed a carved shell, one that indicated a portal? Damn. She turned forward. "Okay. I see your point. I'm paying attention."

"Do you want to take a walk after we get the horses settled?"

"Aren't we supposed to stay put?"

"Sort of." He grinned. "I can't see any harm walking along this street to window shop and stretch our legs."

"You saw a candy shop, didn't you?"

"I may have."

"Good. I'm looking for candy."

"You are?"

"Yes. A sweet treat is on my mind." Her treat would be the scallop shell...and maybe a wedge of chocolate.

The strange horse beneath Liam was more difficult to ride than Isla's, but he managed to reach Caspar Lane in a controlled manner with Lyneth's guidance. She had more experience riding than he'd ever have. He had suggested she ride in front, but she insisted it would draw less attention if the man took the reins and *his woman* rode in the rear. Deaglan followed beside them on his donkey.

Lyneth stretched her neck around him. "I see a hitching pole on the side of the dwelling."

He slowed the horse and steered it in that direction.

"Are you excited to see your aunt after all these years?" Lyneth asked Deaglan.

"I suppose." He gazed upon the home with a peculiar expression. "It was more exciting getting here." His face lit up. "Travelling is thrilling; it's what I want to do."

"When you get older, you can go on adventures. Go wherever you want."

"I'll be sixteen in a few days; I'll be old enough."

"You need to be more than sixteen," said Lyneth. "You need experience with a weapon, knowledge of surviving in harsh conditions and a few friends to go with you."

"That's why I'd go with you."

"We're not friends," said Liam. "We're your escort."

"But we've become friends, *Sweetie*." He smirked.

Liam groaned. With the boy gone, that left only McGuigan to tease him with that name.

"I think your aunt will have other plans for you," said Lyneth. "Have you finished your lessons?"

It was Deaglan's turn to groan. "Boring. I can't sit in a class for hours each day. My soul will die." He halted the donkey and dismounted. "I'm sure Aunt Valey will understand. After all, she travelled Ath-o'Lea for years. She knows how exciting it is."

Lyneth slipped from the horse and secured the reins to the wooden pole. "Your aunt sounds like a wise person, one who knows The Trail is both exciting and dangerous. I'm sure she left Inglenook after her formal lessons were completed and after she possessed knowledge and skill to ensure her survival."

"She did, but that's old fashion."

Liam had no defence against the boy's stance. He'd dropped out of class studies with three years remaining because the system wasn't designed to educate homeless boys.

He followed them onto the path leading to the front door. His long elfin legs felt strange and fooled his eyes. He had stumbled many times the first day in disguise. Although he still occasionally tripped, he walked fairly confidently. He stopped behind them and waited while they knocked.

A woman, he presumed was Aunt Valey, opened the door, and her pleasant face brightening at the sight of her nephew. She drew him into her arms and cooed. Then she looked at the two who had accompanied the boy, and her mouth froze open in shock. Deep emotions criss-crossed her face, and she slowly released Deaglan.

A man appeared from behind her, spotted Deaglan and limped quickly to him. He embraced the boy with one healthy arm and one arm severed at the elbow. "It's a joy to see your arrival. Valey has near driven me crazy waiting for you."

Liam turned back to the aunt, who still gawked in bewilderment at her visitors, then he noticed tears in Lyneth's eyes. They knew each other. Lyneth stepped over the threshold and wrapped her arms around the aunt's neck, and they hugged tightly, sobbing softly with the man, presumably Deaglan's uncle, watching curiously.

"I thought... Oh, you don't want to hear it," said Valey.

"I thought you were dead." Lyneth choked on the words. "We searched for you, but..." Sobs claimed her voice.

"Lyneth?" The uncle released the boy. "It can't be." He stepped closer.

"Rhys?" She released Valey and gave him a warm hug.

"We believed you were caught in the explosion." He gripped her shoulder with his only hand. "We left believing she'd taken everyone with her."

Lyneth wiped her eyes. "We escaped."

"And the others?" Valey slipped an arm around her waist. "Who was in the stone shack?"

"Elspeth. She ordered us out." She sniffed back moisture and tried to contain the tears. "She was... We couldn't save her. The wounds were fatal." She drew a deep breath. "She killed Orenda in the explosion; it's what she wanted."

"McGuigan?"

"Safe."

"Isla?"

"She concealed us after we escaped. Her bubble kept the debris from hitting us."

Valey wiped her eyes. "She's a keen one. Kiefer? He was hit by a blast." Her face contorted. "He wouldn't have survived."

"We took him with us." She sniffed. "He's...not well. I fear he'll die within the year."

"He survived?" Her mouth hung open.

"Isla wouldn't leave him. We said his wounds were fatal, but she tried to drag him out. McGuigan carried him, so she'd leave. He'll never be the same. He's weak, in constant pain. He can't even bend to tie his boots. He'd have suffered less if..." she glanced at Liam, "Isla had let him die." Pain racing across her face revealed that truth.

Liam broke eye contact; he hadn't known this. Why had Isla saved the man for him to suffer?

"Her dedication to those she loves blinds her to reality," said Valey. "And this young elf? Where did you find him?"

"That's Liam," said Deaglan. He crossed his arms and lowered his brow. "How do you all know each other?"

"Liam?" Valey approached him. "*The* Liam? The one Isla spoke of?" She peered closer. "You're supposed to—"

"Yes. He is him," said Lyneth quickly. "The elf she sought."

"Isla must be ecstatic." She held out a hand. "It's great to meet you. I'm Valey Morwen Eldon. This is my mate, Doran Rhys Eldon."

Morwen? Liam quickly put the pieces together. These two were part of The Mercenaries. Isla believed they were dead. He accepted the hand and shook it. "It's good to meet you. I've heard many good things about you."

"From Isla?" She chuckled and wiped a stray tear. "She is too kind. I'm sure you've been on the receiving end of her dedication."

"I have." He grinned and released her hand.

"How did you both escape?" asked Lyneth.

"By the most unexpected means." Valey wrapped her arm around Doran. "A man we once thought of as an ally, then as a traitor: Arthur."

Liam stared, wanting to hear more.

She glanced at him. "If she's told you, then you know of him. It is the same man."

"But he can't be trusted," said Lyneth.

"Trustworthy or not, I had no choice. Doran was in no position to fight or run. He'd have died without Arthur's help." She cleared her throat. "He delivered us to safety and when he left, his long face revealed his regret in his betrayal of our trust. His biggest regret was Isla. He'd lost her, and I believe his act was in some way to help mend the riff between them. When the shack blew and he believed her inside, he wept like a babe."

Liam swallowed hard. The man had loved Isla deeply. She had told him she'd never trust him. Yet, what would be their relationship if she did learn to trust him again and if Arthur discovered she was alive?

"You're avoiding my question," said Deaglan. "How do you know each other, and if you can't answer, I'll make something up. I believe, you went on adventures together."

Valey laughed. "You've always been sharp." She placed a hand on Lyneth's shoulder. "Has he been entertaining you with his wit?"

"He's been entertaining us all right. Keeping us chasing him through alleys, down roads and into closets."

"I've stories to tell, too," he said, seriously. "I've been seduced by a naughty brownie, spoken with a dragon, captured fairies and been attacked by an octopus."

"He certainly has a grand imagination." Valey guided Lyneth down the hall. "Stay for tea, and we'll catch up. I want to hear how you escaped."

"The stories are all true." Deaglan scrambled after them.

"As they were when you were ten."

"Actually," said Lyneth, "they are."

Valey stared at her. "You joke."

"No, he finds trouble everywhere he goes. You'll have your hands full keeping up with him."

"We'll put a stop to that."

"Good luck," said Deaglan.

Valey cast him a deep frown.

"He means it," said Liam to Doran who ushered him to follow. "You'll need luck to tame him."

"If not for me, *Sweetie*, you'd not have found the cure for Kiefer."

While he was right, Liam wasn't going to admit it.

"Is McGuigan and Isla waiting outside?" asked Valey.

"No, they're making contact with the place we'll stay tonight," said Lyneth. "It was to be a simple drop-off of a mischievous boy, not a reunion with old friends."

"There's been a change of plans; you're staying here tonight." She held tightly to Lyneth. "I miss so much; please, shine light on the shadows in my heart."

Liam grimaced. He was uncertain if that was a safe option for these two who survived The Trail but wore deep scars. Missing the adventure of travelling was one thing; missing good friends who died by your side was another.

಄ ❖ ಜ

The candy shop McGuigan had spotted on the way into Inglenook had strange and unusual candy varieties and chocolates filled with exquisite flavours. Isla bought two filled with cherry cream and two filled with caramel. She'd give one of each to Liam to enjoy. At the threshold, she stopped and turned around.

"May I have two with the white filling? The mint ones?"

The lady behind the counter placed two in a bag and accepted payment. "Enjoy."

"Who are they for?" asked McGuigan when they reached the boardwalk.

"Kiefer."

"They'll be rotten by the time you see him."

"Not if I have anything to do about it." She pointed to the shops on the other side of Flint Street. "Let's explore a little this way." The woman welcoming them into her inn was also their contact. She knew of two locations in Inglenook with portals. One was located on Drafton Lane, the other on Wapenshaw Way.

"We can't stay away too long. You heard what Lyneth said."

"I forgot my time piece."

"Good thing I brought mine."

She frowned. "It won't take long to find these streets."

Fifteen minutes later, she stopped and ask for directions and learnt the closest street, Wapenshaw Way, was located ten minutes from their location.

"That's going to make us late," said McGuigan.

"We'll hurry." She tapped his elbow. "Pip-pip." Her walk changed into a trot, and she moved off the boardwalk to avoid slower moving pedestrians. Craning her neck, she searched for the street name. After five minutes, she found it. "Here we go." She turned left and slowed her pace. "Look for the shop that sells shoes. What did she call it?"

"Minder's Shoe Shop?"

She tapped his arm and grabbed his hand. "We can't stop now even if we are late." She danced in front of him and lifted their hands together."

"Whoa!" He pulled her close, and she stumbled into his arms.

"What did you do that for?" She was about to lecture him, but the expression on his face told her not to."

"The pretty hauflin who ventured to Moonsface for the first time."

The rough voice made her turn, and she pressed backwards into McGuigan's arms. The man she'd met on the road when Deaglan had stolen her horse, the one whose scar ran from his left eye to his cheek, stood in front of the three other men who travelled with him.

"I see you made it to Inglenook." His face remained stern.

"I did. We did. My mate and I. We're here for the festival."

"Mate, you say." He eyed McGuigan. "Interesting. I was under the impression hauflins were interested in their own kind."

"Obviously, you don't travel far."

He chuckled, though he didn't appear amused. "On your travels, did you happen to see the young man we seek? He is dearly missed by family and friends, and we wish to reunite him."

"Why doesn't he go home then?" She gripped McGuigan's hand, hoping it would calm her nerves.

"He suffers from a head injury and doesn't remember where to go."

"He should be in an infirmary. Maybe that's where he is."

"Did you see him?"

She shook her head. "Mostly, I see elves." She scanned the area. Almost everyone was elf. "There's a hauflin over there. Way over there. He's got brown hair."

The man looked to where she pointed. "He's too old. The one we search for is your age. We thought you might be able to help since travellers along the way said they'd seen a young man travelling with a pretty hauflin girl." He peered closer. "You're a pretty hauflin girl." He stared, and his breath fell upon her forehead.

She pressed harder against McGuigan, trying to put space between her and the man. "Thank you, but I already have a mate."

McGuigan wrapped his arms around her. "And I don't plan on giving her up." He took a step back. "We have to go."

"Where are you rushing off to?"

"We're exploring," said Isla.

"You should slow down. You'll see the sights better."

She pulled McGuigan with her as she made a wide circle around the men.

"Who's that?" asked McGuigan when they were a few feet away.

"An odd stranger I met on the road when that boy stole my horse," she said loud enough for the men to hear. Her nerves rattled under her skin, and she hoped by holding tightly to him and getting away from the men would calm them. She didn't dare look back. Instead, she guided him to the boardwalk and strolled with pedestrians to the corner. Once she rounded the corner, she stopped abruptly. "I want to see if they stopped," she whispered, "but I'm afraid they'll see me."

He pulled her along. "Let's do the duck and spy."

She searched for an out-of-the-way place to hide and spy on the men who followed. "Here." She pulled him into a teashop that opened to the street. "We can see the corner from that table."

"Sit. I'll get a drink."

She sat with her back to the wall and her eyes on the sidewalk and the opposite side of the street. A minute later, McGuigan joined her. He set a drink between them and gave her a straw.

"What's this?" Green foam rested on top of the liquid.

"They called it Mystic Mango."

"What's a mango?"

"Something mystic. See anything?" he whispered.

"Nothing yet." She took a sip. "Tangy." She dragged her tongue across the roof of her mouth.

He drew the liquid up the straw and made a face. "Strong." He shivered and took another drink. "Better the second time."

She tasted it again. "Not much." Her eyes widened. "Stay still." She gathered energy with her fingers and created the Bubble Spell. "They're walking on the other side of the street. They stand out like black horses in snow."

"I see them." His eyes remained glued on the men while he slurped the drink. "This isn't half bad when you get used to the taste."

"Would you buy another?"

"It's not that good."

"Should we follow?" She didn't want to, but then she did. She'd rather be the one following than the one being followed. The men stayed together, so two didn't lag to follow the followers. She groaned. That sounded confusing, yet the Rothkin Clan practised the technique. They had taught her that lesson the hard way.

"If we do, we'll know where they are." He took another drink. "But we know where they are. Let's slip away to warn Lyneth and Liam."

"So, we watch them leave?"

"Maybe." He sucked on the straw, creating noise in the bottom of the cup.

"It's gone?" She peeked inside. "Are you sure you'd not buy another?"

He grinned. "Not at this time."

"Let's watch to see which direction they go, then return to Wapenshaw Way and find the shoe shop."

"We're going to be exceptionally late."

"At least we have a good excuse."

"We went shopping for shoes?"

"That's it." She released the Bubble Spell. "They're at the end of the street." She craned her neck to spy. "They're turning left. They're gone. Let's go." She moved to the edge of the café and paused. "They're still gone." Holding onto his hand, she hustled along the street, heading for Wapenshaw Way. She spied on the corner of the building where the men disappeared, letting McGuigan guide her along the boardwalk.

"Crossing the street," he said.

"Okay. Guide me." She kept her eyes glued to the corner of the building, looking for any sign of a human in dark clothing to emerge. None did, and she passed through the door of Minder's Shoe Shop.

"Nothing?"

"Nothing." She scanned the interior of the shop. It was small with shelves on either side laden with shoes and boots, most made of leather, some tall and others short. Some had laces while others had straps, and still others were pull on. They came in various colours, but mostly black and brown. Straight ahead was a short counter, and beyond that was the workshop. Two customers were in the shop.

"I'll be with you in a moment." A man wearing a leather apron knelt before a lady dressed in a modest green dress and helped her try on a shoe.

"Thank you." Isla scanned the shelves near the front window, keeping an eye on the street where the men had gone. She picked up a shoe and flipped it over. It was well made, but it was better worn with a dress, not a pair of trousers that sat on a horse.

A few minutes later, the keeper placed the shoes inside the lady's carry sack, and she departed with the man who had stood next to her during the fitting. This left the shop empty.

"How may I help you." The man tucked a stray lock of hair behind his ear. His blond hair streaked with green highlights rested above his ear lobes.

Isla stepped closer. "We seek a portal. I am told one is located in this shop."

The man strode to the front door, locked it and flipped the sign around. "It's not something I make public knowledge. How did you learn of it?"

"The owner of Wurley Inn informed us. We were sent to her by a good friend."

He nodded. "Follow me."

"Where does it go?" She walked behind him.

"One goes to Moonsface, the other to Sky Glen."

"Wait. We don't want to go there." She turned to McGuigan. "Where is Sky Glen?"

The keeper answered instead. "It's a six-day travel west of Wandsworth."

Her heart sunk. Moonsface was closest, but from there she'd still have weeks of travel before she reached Maskil. "Are you discreet?"

"I don't understand."

"If someone walked in here and asked what we were looking for, what would you tell them?"

He glanced at her feet. "A size 4 boot."

Relief washed over her. "The portal on Drafton Lane. Where would that deliver us?"

"There are two: Castle Oaktree and Maskil."

Isla stuck out her hand. He accepted and shook it. "Thank you. That's the direction I prefer. Please, tell me where I'll find Drafton Lane."

"Take a right out the front door, then the first right and keep going until you reach Mazer Street. Take that, and you'll find Drafton, second on the left."

"One more question, and I will bid you farewell. Can we, please, leave out the back door?"

"You wouldn't be the first." He turned. "And you won't be the last. This way." He led them through the workshop, down a short hallway and to a window-less door. He opened it, glanced outside and ushered them through. "Enjoy your day."

13

Hope with All My Heart

ISLA SAT DUMBFOUNDED, LISTENING to Lyneth. The fact Morwen and Rhys had survived the battle with Orenda Nassen and her Tigh na Mare warriors was unbelievable. She had seen Rhys get hit and go down. When McGuigan asked if they had help escaping the scene, her ears perked up. Had the Rothkin clan helped them, too?

"Arthur." Lyneth caught her eye and held it.

"Arthur?" Isla's mouth froze on the end of the word. "But..." Pieces of a much larger puzzle fell into place. The man had been there, like she had imagined. He had left the note in her shirt pocket, the one Alaura had found that read, *My door is always open.* He was the one, not Matteo, who had taken her to safety, concealed her in a hole beneath boughs and kissed her before leaving. Her fingertips touched her bottom lip, remembering the soft kiss he had delivered.

"He took them to safety," said Lyneth. "He believes you died when the shack exploded. He was devastated."

Her gaze fell to the floor. There was still good in that man and like it or not, he still owned a piece of her heart. She didn't want him thinking of her as dead. Her next trip to Ellswire, she'd... She released a sigh. She wanted to see him, hear his side of the story, but she didn't want to resume their relationship.

When she looked up, she found Liam watching her. She had told him about Arthur; he knew she'd loved him, that they shared more than an evening ration. She'd also told him the story of Arthur rescuing her when she'd broken into an Ellswire shop, and her rescue of him when a man had torn his gut with a dagger. Liam knew about her healing hands and that she had used them to save Arthur's life.

Arthur had also known about Liam, and that caused a pause in their relationship. He had suspected she thought of another, so was not surprised by her story of *lost love, love unresolved*.

She held no doubt Liam was her mate, though they had yet to share a night of passion. As others had said, she just knew, as her das had when he'd met Alaura. Given this situation, how would Arthur fit into her life? Would he accept a friendship?

"Morwen is Deaglan's grandaunt?" McGuigan scratched his head. "Did she change her name so others wouldn't find her?"

"That's her middle name," said Lyneth. "Her full name is Valey Morwen Eldon, and his is Doran Rhys Eldon."

"Wow. I'm..." He chuckled. "They'll have fun with Deaglan. Can I meet them?"

"They're eager to see you both. They've invited us to stay in their home."

"But..." Isla focussed on the task. She wanted to see Morwen and Rhys, but she had to reach Maskil as soon as possible. Kiefer needed the medicine, and Liam had to put distance between him and the men from Wandsworth. "I'll see them when I return. Tell them, I couldn't be happier to know they live. Explain I have a cure for Kiefer."

"They are aware of it." Lyneth paused. "Morwen said for you to not get your hopes up. She's never known anyone to recover from such an injury."

"I'll hope with all my heart." She stood. "It's dark; we must go."

"When you return," said Lyneth, "find us at Caspar Lane. How long will you stay?"

"Two nights. I doubt I'll escape family before then."

McGuigan hugged her. "I hope it works. Tell him I'm sending wishes to the Welkin nymphs for his recovery."

"I will." She slung her bag over her shoulder with the few items she'd need for a short stay, nodded a good-bye and went for the door.

Liam followed close behind in the magical cape that transformed him into an elf.

They walked in silence for many blocks. Her mind rolled over the news of her friends' survival, Arthur and the cure she carried in her belt pouch. Images of home mixed in, making her thoughts tumble together. She needed to focus on the directions the man at the shoe shop had given her, but she'd no sooner think of the street name when another thought barged into her head.

"Pole." Liam pulled her towards him so she wouldn't walk into a pole with a lantern hanging from it. "Watch where you're going." He cast a sideways glance at her. "Who..." he cleared his throat, "are you thinking of?"

She wanted to grasp his hand, but she'd already established McGuigan as her mate in this town. "Everyone."

"Including Arthur?"

"Yes. Morwen. Rhys. Kiefer." She swallowed hard and tears welled. "Elspeth and Brac. Home." She wiped moisture from her cheek. "I'd like to see them. See they are well with my own eyes."

"We could postpone this trip."

"No. I need to get this to Kiefer. I've believed them dead this long, seeing them well can wait two more days. Knowing they're well is satisfying news."

"And Arthur? He thinks you're dead."

"I should write him a letter." That sounded foolish. What would she say? "Or..." Since he associated with the Rothkin clan and was on scene with them, then he'd quickly learn she was alive. "I'll say nothing. If my hunch is correct, he knows I survived."

"Do you trust him?"

"I don't know. I'll reserve judgement on that." She pointed to a street sign. "Mazer." They walked down it, and she searched for Drafton Lane, second on the left.

"Do you think...?" He stared at the ground. "I would understand if..." He shoved his hands into his pockets. "We can talk about this later."

She glanced at him curiously and tried to read his expression in the dim light cast by the lanterns lining the boardwalk. "Talk about what later? Trust?" The softness of his voice triggered the meaning behind his words, or lack of them. "Wait." She pulled him near a shop window, away from the occasional pedestrian that passed. "Are you worried about Arthur?"

He shook his head but didn't make eye contact.

"Liar." The urge to touch him grew. Although he appeared as an elf, the sad expression in his eyes was all Liam. "We've talked about this. I thought it was settled, that you understood." She crossed her arms to entrap her hands. "Please, don't doubt my words."

"I thought... Maybe where he... I know you..." His cheek pinched. "I'd understand. Under the circumstances."

"You might understand, but I wouldn't." She booted him softly in the shin. "We'll discuss this more thoroughly later. Apparently, I have to paint you a picture." She motioned him onward. "Let's go."

He followed in silence, not giving her any indication he had taken her words to heart. She'd deal with him in Maskil in private. A smile caught her lips and her belly warmed with thoughts of spending time alone with him.

They found Drafton Lane and Nat's Pergola and as they approached, a seasoned elf carried a decorative wooden frame into the shop. It reminded her of the trellises she'd seen in gardens. He returned for a wooden box, then closed the door. She rushed forward and knocked.

He opened the door a crack. "I'm sorry. We're closed for the day. Open again at seven."

"Please, let me in." She forced a sad expression. "We can't wait 'til morning. I am in need of..." she glanced about and seeing no one near, she whispered, "a portal to Maskil. Please, can you help?"

The shop keeper scanned left and right. "Hurry." He stood aside and let them enter, then closed and locked the door. "You have payment?"

"He does, and I have this." She pointed to the scallop shell fastened to the front of her jacket.

"This way." He led them through the shop and to a narrow hallway. He unlocked a plain, wooden door on the right and gestured for them to enter.

Isla descended a short flight of stairs, ducked her head to avoid a beam and entered a room no larger than a horse stall. On the opposite wall were two jail cells big enough to accommodate three average-size humans. Each held a portal.

"What's this?" Liam backed away from the cells. "He's going to lock us up?" Colour drained from his face.

"No." She held onto his arm. "This is the way portals are set up. It's to guard against someone entering without permission. Calm down."

"Why would I lock you up?" The man's face wore a curious expression.

"No reason. He's a nervous fellow." She peered into Liam's face and smiled reassuringly. "Have you ever made a portal leap?" He shook his head. "First rule: you can only make three a day." She had learnt this rule the hard way. "Don't be tempted to do more than three, or you'll get sick. Too many, and you will die. Understand?" He nodded. "When you enter, you'll feel a tug; don't fight it. When you've crossed the centre, you'll be jerked forward. I'll hold onto you. Maybe you'll stay on your feet."

"Where to?" asked the keeper. "Castle Oaktree or Maskil?"

"Maskil, please." She pulled a coin from her pocket. "This is for his passage." A large sign on the wall next to the door gave instructions to those arriving through the portals: Pull Rope for Service. The rope hung in one cell and was easily reached through the steal bars from the other.

The keeper walked to the cage on the right and unlocked it.

"Are you Nat?" asked Isla.

"I am. Nathan to be exact."

She stuck out her hand. "Thank you, Nathan. I appreciate the service."

"You're welcome." He shook her hand, then stepped aside.

Isla walked inside the cage, and a cold chill swept over her. Cages reminded her of Blackvale, and she didn't want to think of the days and nights locked in a cell before discovering how to escape them. She stood in front of the portal, and a warm breeze drew her forward. It'd been many moons since she'd made a leap. The door clanked shut behind her, and Liam jumped. She reached for his hand and held it tightly. "The first time is always unnerving, but you'll get used to it."

"Lead the way. I trust you'll keep me safe."

"Always." She stepped forward, felt the drag and continued walking. The strong force tugged her into the darkness, and Liam gasped and tightened his grip. When they came out the other side, he lost his balance and fell to the stone floor. His cape flew up over his head, and he struggled to get it back into place.

"We're here." She pulled him to his feet.

"Incredible." He stared at the shimmering black space in the wall.

"I never tire of it. But remember," she pointed a finger at his chest, "only three a day, the most."

"I heard you the first time."

"Good. Just making sure."

"How do we get out of this cell?"

The room was similar to the one they'd left except the wall colour was different. The same instructional sign greeted them, so she grasped the rope hanging from the ceiling and tugged. A distant sound of a bell kissed her ear.

"We wait," she said. "Someone will come."

"The shell you carry. Where did you get it?"

"From a man who watches the stars. Only worthy, trusting travellers have them."

"You've made interesting friends and have visited fascinating places."

"You were enticed by naught brownies, treated by friendly fairies and spoke to a dragon. I've done none of those."

He chuckled. "I can do without the brownies."

"Unless they have raspberries in them." She winked. "We'll get a few to take back with us."

"I haven't had one of those since you."

"Look at all the things you're doing since me." She hugged into his side. He stood at least a foot and a half taller than her, making it awkward to kiss him unless he stooped. Hearing footsteps on the stairs, they turned towards the cell door.

A mature elf entered the room. He wore a sword on one hip and a dagger on the other. His long hair was pulled back in a single braid, and he dressed in thick pants and a woollen shirt.

"Welcome to Maskil." He unlocked the door and released them.

"What street are we on?" she asked.

"Elsin Lane."

"Elf Quarter."

He closed the door and stared at her. "Yes, that's what my father called this area."

"We should call it that again."

He shrugged. "Those not of elfkin will be offended."

"Too bad for them. They can move."

He half nodded and gestured towards the stairs. "You're familiar with the area?"

"I was born here."

"Visiting family?"

"Yes." She climbed the stairs and opened the door at the top. The room she entered smelt strongly of wood smoke. It contained crates of unidentifiable items, and heavy-duty tools hung on the wall. She walked to the front of the building and arrived in a large shop, open to the evening air and heated with an elaborate oven. She offered her hand to the keeper. "Thank you."

"Pleasure doing business." He shook her hand.

She stepped onto the boardwalk and looked up at the sign over the door: Everard Blacksmith. She'd ridden by the shop before but had never stopped in.

"This way." She tugged on Liam and led him behind a building. "You should remove the cape before we go farther. No one is looking for you here, and it'd be difficult to explain you. To be honest, I'd slip up faster than if I encountered shiny ice."

"I agree." He pulled the cape from his shoulders and tucked it into his rucksack.

She smiled as he returned to his natural self and normal height. "Now, I can do this without standing on a chair." She grabbed the front of his jacket and pulled him to her lips. "Yes. This is much better." She giggled on his lips and felt his smile.

"I'm not complaining." He grasped her hand. "Lead the way, my lady."

"As you wish, Sweetie." When he groaned, she added, "I'm allowed to call you sweetie."

"Yes, but only if you are referring to me as *your sweetie*, not as a fairy's sweetie."

"You will be sweetie to no other." She led him down the alley and onto a familiar street. "This way. Towards the Human Quarter."

"Catriona's?"

"Yes. I'm sure she'll remember you."

"I'm sure she will, too. Is she still a little off?"

"That's what makes her special."

When they arrived at Catriona's dwelling on Horizon Lane, thick drapes hung closed over the front window. The edges glowed from bright light inside. Isla knocked and waited, and in short time the trap door for the peephole opened.

"Who is it?"

"It's Isla. May I come in, Catriona?"

The trap door closed, and the large door opened. "Isla, it's good to see you." As soon as the visitors crossed the threshold, the door was shut and locked.

Isla scanned the room, looking for Kiefer. When she didn't see him immediately, her smile slipped. Where was he? Not in his bed. Not in Catriona's bed. Nor the comfortable chair in the corner or at the small table. Her heart beat faster. She'd been gone for three moons. When she left, his progress had stalled, and Alaura feared he'd remain in the woeful condition.

A thud and a soft groan from the back of the dwelling, near the water closet door, caught her attention. "Kiefer?"

"He's fallen." Catriona scuttled in his direction. "Help me."

Isla rushed after her. When she saw Kiefer, a sharp pain struck her heart and expanded into her chest. The once strong and vibrant man, the one who had talked her out of hurting herself, the one who had tended to her through several illnesses, lay sprawled on the floor, unable to rise. He'd lost a considerable amount of weight, making his face gaunt. His skin was pale in some areas, purple in others. Sores dotted his arms and neck, and his dark brown hair had lost its shine and had thinned to reveal sections of scalp.

Catriona grasped Kiefer's arm and tried to lift him.

Liam pushed past Isla and braced his other arm. "Does this hurt?"

Kiefer huffed. "It's bearable." His red, cracked lips stumbled over the words.

"Slowly," said Catriona.

Isla stood frozen, unable to help or offer encouragement. They dragged him to Catriona's bed and eased him onto the blankets. His toes were twisted and blue, and he groaned in pain when his bare feet lay flat on the floor. Lyneth was right; Kiefer would have been better off dying with Elspeth. Saving him had prolonged his death, made him feel every inch of it as it stole away. But she had loved him too much to let him go, to lose hope he'd survive and recover.

Spit caught in her throat, and she fought tears that seeped from her eyes. Liam wrapped his arms around her and led her to the bedside. She clung to him, regretting she'd came, regretting she'd saved him.

"Who is it?" Kiefer reached out, and Catriona caught his hand.

"It's Isla. She's come to visit you." She tucked a blanket over him and patted his chest.

"Isla? Is it really you?"

She wiped the tears away and sat on the bed. "Can't you see?"

"Shadows." He coughed. "Too dark in here."

She laid her head against his chest, and the tears came.

"Isla, please, don't cry. I've cried for both of us." He patted her head, then clutched her with arms that failed to hold strength.

"I'm sorry," she sobbed. "So, so sorry for doing this to you."

"Sorry for..." he cleared his throat, "having hope? Don't ever be. You did not cause this."

"We have a cure." Liam wiped the corner of his eye and grinned awkwardly.

"We've tried all the cures," said Catriona. "Now, we wait."

"Not this one."

"Who is this?" Kiefer's finger twisted in his direction.

"It's Liam," said Isla.

Kiefer's haggard face brightened. "You found him?"

"I did."

"And is he... You know?"

"Yes. You were right."

He patted her cheek. "I'm always right."

"Liam, the boy you played with as a child?" Catriona considered him, and her brow creased.

"The same." Isla unclipped the pouch on her belt and removed the special box Coraline had given her to carry the potion the friendly fairies had gifted Liam. She hesitated, not wanting to give false hope, but... She sighed. All she had was hope. "I am told this liquid will restore youth and vitality. You are to drink it all."

"Where did you get it?" Kiefer grasped the bottle and her small hand.

"Fairies."

"Gosh, we're believing in fairies now." Catriona folded her arms.

"Does it taste good?" asked Kiefer.

"I don't know. It's for you, not me."

"Restore my youth, you say?"

"Yes." She sniffed. His youth had faded with his health.

"Can you remove the cap?"

"You're not going to drink that." Catriona reached for it, but Isla blocked her hand. "What if it's poyson?"

"Then the end will be quicker," said Kiefer.

Isla twisted off the cap and held the bottle in the air. "May the wood fairies and Welkin nymphs make this the cure we seek." She lowered the bottle to his lips. "Drink it all."

He pushed it up and swallowed hard. A little settled on the corner of his mouth, and he licked it up. "Not bad. Tastes like maple syrup. I should have saved it for my pancakes." He chuckled. "The expression on your face is priceless. Thank you."

Isla rolled her eyes. "If you weren't in this condition, I'd push you in a lake."

"Can you stay a while? Entertain me with tales of The Trail?"

"Are you writing a book?" She kicked off her boots and folded her feet beneath her.

"It'd be a short one." He clipped her chin with his fore finger. "Tell me, where did you find Liam?"

"In a tree that was trying eat him."

Liam chuckled, grabbed a chair and sat down. "I hadn't thought the tree was doing that."

"You were a man being consumed by a tree?" Catriona gawked at him. "Was the tree large? Thick branches? Was it alive?"

Isla stared at her. "Yes. Why do you ask?"

"I had a dream. I didn't know it was you, only a small man. It was really an image. It was long ago." She plopped down in a chair.

"What other dreams are you having?"

She looked up. "I won't talk about them."

"I have news." Isla poked Kiefer gently in the ribs. "An incredible story about who we found at Inglenook. It will brighten your day."

"Tell it then. I'm always looking for a brighter day."

Isla smiled though her insides churned. The news about Morwen and Rhys would make him happy, but... Why wasn't the fairy potion working? Kiefer showed no signs of improvement. Magic was supposed to work fast; minutes had passed, and his raspy voice hadn't changed. The colour in his face was as pale as when she walked in. His greenish-blue eyes, the ones that danced when they were excited, were dull and barely moving. It was as if his life slipped away before her.

By the time they left Catriona's dwelling, Kiefer was exhausted and had fallen asleep. Liam wiped away Isla's fresh tears and held her tightly as they walked on the street.

"Maybe the potion works slow because the damage is extensive," he said.

"But it's magic."

"I know, but... Can't we give it time to work?" He tried to smile but failed. Her sadness made him sad.

"By morning?" Her face twisted in anguish. "We should see improvement by morning, right?"

"Let's hope." He read the sign of the street they turned onto: Saunter Lane. Isla's parents lived here, and she insisted they spend the night with them. "Maybe we should get a room at the inn."

"You've already suggested that."

"But it's late. Almost ten o'clock."

"My parents won't mind. They'll be happy to see us, to see you. They'll be surprised." After a short pause, she spoke again. "Did the fairy give you instructions? I mean, was all he supposed to do was drink it?"

"No instructions. She didn't say to drink it."

"What?" She whirled. "What if we were supposed to rub it on his chest? His whole body. Maybe pour it in his ear, or... Or... I don't know. Maybe mix it with something."

"Isla, calm down." He pulled her into his arms. "I'm certain it was a drinkable potion."

"But there was nothing on the bottle. I should have consulted Meeme first or Beathas." She dragged her hand down her cheek. "I'm so stupid."

"You are not stupid." He followed her as she turned onto a narrow walkway that led to a front porch. This was it. He'd have to face Bronwyn Darrow tonight. A light was on inside. They were up.

"I'll show Meeme the bottle. Maybe she'll know what we did wrong." She opened the front door and walked in.

"You're not knocking?" He reluctantly entered.

"I live here." She pulled him inside and closed the door.

The pleasant aroma of a warm meal lingered in the air, and memories of the place he had called home long ago rushed into his mind and calmed his nerves. Soft candle light illuminated the small sitting room in the front of the house, and harsher, lantern light, lit up the small room off it that appeared to be the kitchen. A fit dwarf exited the sitting room to see who had entered his dwelling. The short mustache made him look older, and the years had made him leaner, more rugged, and far from the naïve, well-fed guard who had worked at the castle years ago.

"Isla." He shouted over his shoulder. "It's Isla." His eyes left his daughter and settled on the man beside her.

Liam's feet felt like they were stuck in frozen mud. The happy welcome Isla had promised he'd receive when Bronwyn saw him didn't appear. However, she was correct on one thing; he was surprised.

"Das, it feels good to be home." She hugged him, then turned to Liam. "Guess who I found?"

"I see. Liam Jenkins." Bronwyn's mouth moved but words didn't escape. His attempt at smiling contorted his face.

The longer he stared, the more Liam felt as though his entire life with all his horrible deeds was being laid out before him. Bronwyn Darrow, the most honourable man he knew, was scrutinizing every aspect of it, judging him unfit for his daughter. If he knew what he'd done in the previous moons before leaving Wandsworth, he'd have thrown him out of his house without hesitation.

"Liam?" Alaura froze ten feet away. "It is. Well, this is a surprise."

"I knew it would be." Isla hugged Alaura. "We came because we found–I mean, Liam found a cure for Kiefer." Her face twisted. "But I'm afraid we didn't administer it correctly. Can you help?"

"Of course. Come to the kitchen." She put an arm around Isla's shoulder. "We'll let Bronwyn and Liam talk."

Liam was about to say he'd like to hear the conversation about the potion, but the expression on Bronwyn's face silenced him. "Bronwyn." He stood rigid, wanting to be anywhere but here.

"Hang your weapons in the closet behind the door."

That was not a suggestion but an order and Liam obeyed, removing his sword and daggers and storing them in the closet. Bronwyn didn't wear his sword in the house either. That had to be an Alaura rule.

"Sit." He pointed to a chair.

Liam sat upright, feeling too uncomfortable to press his back against the soft cushion.

"You and Isla; you're friends again?" Bronwyn sat in the chair opposite him with a round, low table between them. On it rested three books and a lit candle.

"We always have been." His neck grew warm, and he unfastened his jacket.

"Just friends."

"Best friends."

"You should remain just friends."

"Good friends."

"And that's all." He rubbed his chin. "Are you leaving tomorrow?"

"We plan to leave the following morning."

"Isla will stay. Harvest is no season for her to be on The Trail."

"I doubt she will agree."

"As a good friend, convince her."

He rested his elbows on his knees and clasped his hands. "I'll try, but I feel my words will be wasted."

"How is life in Wandsworth?"

"Not what I expected." He pressed his lips together. It wasn't as if Bronwyn knew what he'd done and that he carried the brand on his shoulder. The man knew only the thirteen-year-old boy who had left Maskil. All he had to do was answer the questions and provide no details.

"Your aunt and uncle. Did you like living with them?"

"Not really." That was the truth.

"Your aunt was your meeme's sister, was she not?"

"Yes. Older sister."

"Did she have children?"

"No. They couldn't."

"Couldn't?"

"Apparently."

"As the only child in the home, did they shower you with attention?"

"Not exactly."

"When did you leave them?"

"A few years ago."

"Where have you lived since?"

He rubbed his forehead. "Why all the questions? I disliked Wandsworth. I didn't like the people. I missed Isla and—"

"Isla doesn't need you. She has good friends."

"Am I missing something? I'm not anyone special but—"

"Far from it."

His mouth froze. Whatever this man thought of him, it was blinding him from reason.

"Meeme said we did it right." Isla walked into the room. "She's never heard of this potion, so she can't speak of its effectiveness." She tapped Liam's knee. "Push back, so I can sit."

As he moved to accommodate her on the chair in front of him, he glanced at Bronwyn. The man appeared ready to curse, but honourable men didn't swear.

"Das, did you hear of such a potion in your travels?" Isla's hands rested on his knees, and she eased herself against his chest, but he didn't dare put his arms around her.

"What?" Bronwyn's attention snapped to the conversation, yet his eyes remained on her hands. "What potion?"

"Liam." Alaura nodded her head towards the kitchen. "Let's allow them to talk. I'll get you a drink of water."

He lifted Isla by the hips and squeezed past her to follow Alaura down the short hall. The compact, eat-in kitchen was perfect for a small family: two parents, two kids. It was similar to his dwelling when he was young. It even had a pot of herbs on the windowsill. He pushed the memories from his mind; he didn't want to think about that time.

Alaura poured a glass of water from a pitcher kept near the back door and offered it to him.

"Thank you." He took a sip and remembered the flavour of Maskil water. It tasted sweet compared to that in Wandsworth.

"It's good to see you well." She leant against the countertop, and her gaze swept around the kitchen.

"I was surprised when Isla told me you were living here." He took another drink. "I thought you'd have moved to Petra or another place."

"I like Maskil."

"And Bronwyn."

"I can't deny that."

"I thought you were only friends, but Isla knew. She told me so, but I didn't believe her. I mean, you pushed him into the lake."

She laughed. "She's perceptive, and that was an accident."

"She is. It's like she can read my mind."

"She knows your history?"

He shrugged. "She knows me. She trusts me."

"She still likes you?"

"I still like her."

"Perhaps you should explore other opportunities. You're young."

Her words hit low, taking the wind from his lungs. Fumbling to express his feelings, he spoke without considering his options. "I'm confused. I've always thought you wonderful. You're like Meeme..." A stubborn lump swelled in his throat, stirring unwanted tears, unwanted images from when he was thirteen. He coughed to clear his throat and wiped away his tears. "I don't want to..." He drew a deep breath. The pain he'd buried long ago renewed. His horrible path in life had started in Maskil; he hated this town and couldn't wait to leave.

"I'm so sorry about your meeme." She stood in front of him, tears in her eyes. "She was a wonderful woman."

Anger tried to surface, but his broken heart snuffed it. "I don't understand." He swallowed hard. "What did I do to lose Meeme and Das. Was I a bad boy?"

"Goodness, Liam. You were a good boy. This was not your fault." She pulled him into her embrace as if he was her child. "Don't ever think you caused their deaths."

"My aunt said Meeme wouldn't have been killed..." he choked on the word, "if not for me." Tears flowed freely as he recalled that horrible day.

"Nonsense." She held him tighter. "Your aunt is wrong. She should have better sense than to blame a child."

"I hated her," he muttered. The years before he escaped to the streets were horrible, and his thoughts blew over them, not wanting to stop to remember anything specific.

Alaura kissed the side of his head. "You deserved better."

"I didn't believe I did."

"Never think that." She sniffed back the moisture and wiped her eyes. "You can't ever stop believing in yourself."

"Alaura!"

She pulled away but didn't let go.

"What are you doing?" Bronwyn's face twisted in confusion.

"Reliving horrible memories."

"I should go." Liam inched towards the back door. "Tell Isla I'll be back in the morning."

"Good," said Bronwyn. "There's the door."

"Nonsense. He stays." She held tightly to Liam.

"But...he shouldn't."

"He will." She lowered her brow and gave him *that look.*

Liam would have smiled if not for the circumstances. As he had buckled under Isla's *look,* Bronwyn did under Alaura's.

"He sleeps down here on the chesterfield." Bronwyn put his hands on his hips.

"I'll make up a comfortable bed for him." She grabbed a cloth near the sink and dabbed Liam's face. "Go sit with Isla and don't leave. Do you hear me?"

She cast him the same look, and he cowered. If she and Isla had a *look* contest, he didn't know who'd win. "Did you teach that to Isla?"

"What?"

"How to give *that look.* It's powerful. If Isla told me to jump off a bridge and gave me *that look,* I'd be over the rail without question."

"Women come by it naturally."

"I've never met another." He looked at Bronwyn. "You?"

He frowned and shook his head.

"Then you boys are fortunate to have women who do." Alaura lowered her brow. "I expect you to obey it. Now go to Isla."

"Yes, ma'am." He sneaked by Bronwyn and entered the sitting room. Isla sat in the same chair, and he slipped behind her and gave her a hug.

She caressed his cheek. "What did Das say to make you cry?"

"He didn't." He braced his jaw, not wanting a repeat of what had happened in the kitchen. "Alaura and I were talking about...before."

She gently kissed his lips.

All he wanted to do was relax in this cosy warm room and hold her in his arms but when he looked up, he saw Bronwyn and Alaura watching them with uncertain expressions. He hadn't had a place to call home since he was thirteen and while this inviting place teased him and made him yearn for a home, this would never be it.

14

A Second Chance

ISLA STARED INTO EYES that were more blue than green this morning. They were not as dull as they were yesternight. A spark lived within each. Or was she imagining it because of the bright sunshine streaming in the window? His pale skin cried for the sun. Maybe if he got a little, he'd feel better.

"Are you done?" Kiefer placed his index finger between her eyes and pushed her away.

"Do you feel better?" She rested on the edge of the bed. He appeared to have not moved from the night before, which meant Catriona slept in his bed or... Perhaps the woman was welcoming men into her bed after all.

"Yes. The chocolate mints made me feel great. They were delicious. Do you have more?"

She tilted her head and frowned. "You know what I mean." She ran her finger along his chin, examining his skin.

"I feel better because you're here."

"Catriona becoming too much? I'll find another place for you to stay."

"I feel better because you're here regardless of where I am." He grasped her hand. "I'm happy Rhys and Morwen are safe. That makes my heart beat faster." He glanced at Liam relaxing in the soft chair in the corner. "And that you found him. Your heart's desire."

"Perhaps I should find yours, then she'll nurse you back to health and kick your butt when you stall."

He laughed. "Catriona's good to me. A little..." he rolled his eyes, "unpredictable, but she has a good heart for taking care of an invalid who landed in her bed uninvited. Her addiction to clutter is a slight irritation. Bags hanging on bed posts disturb my sleep."

"I'll put them in the closet."

"She'd complain when she returned." He coughed, and his face turned red. Hacking to clear his throat, he settled into the warm, soft mattress and sighed. "Where are you off to next? Some place warm? I know that's where I'd go."

"Unfortunately, somewhere colder."

"Sounds horrible. Where?"

"Dougendun."

He stared at the ceiling, lost in thought. "I've heard of it, but..."

"It's somewhere between Pogwa Mountains and Titterton."

He shivered. "Can't you wait until Springan?"

"No, we have business there."

"What sort of business can't wait?"

She cast a glance at Liam. "I trust him completely. He may have information that can help us."

Liam picked at the fluff on the soft chair. "I'd rather you didn't."

Kiefer grasped her hand. "Sorry, pal, but we don't keep secrets from each other. Do we, Isla?"

She winced. "We don't. Have you heard of a street gang in Wandsworth named Mavericks?"

His eyes widened, and he sat up straighter. "Tell me more."

"You've heard of them?" He nodded, and she told him about Liam's involvement with them, and the scar he wore on his shoulder.

"You were branded? When?" He gawked at Isla. "While we were on our way to Wirksworth? That's when he reached out to you."

"Yes. The reason he has some control is because I took half the poyson."

"You left it on the side of the road." He rubbed his forehead roughly. "This will baffle the Mavericks. Branding ensures a member remains loyal, under their control and deadly. Are they hunting you?"

"Yes." Liam cleared his throat. "I feel they will until I'm dead."

"I can arrange that." Kiefer laughed at his surprise. "We can fake your death to get them off your trail."

"Right now, we're concerned with getting the rest of the poyson out of his body. Specks told me the first milk of a green dragon will kill the infection."

His chuckle transformed into laughter, then a cough. He lay back and caught his breath. "Has to be a green dragon, not red or yellow?" He smirked.

"Now you're making fun. But we're going in search of it at Dougendun. The only place that sells it."

"Sells it? Are you correct on this?"

"That's what Specks said, and he's been everywhere."

"But what about the decline in green dragon offspring?"

"Tell me more."

"Part of this dwarf curse involves green dragons. Their numbers are dropping because females can't conceive."

She looked at Liam. "Didn't McGuigan give the dragon a stone that created fire to aid in conception?"

"Yes. The dragon's fire was out."

Kiefer squeezed her hand. "Tell *me* more."

"Remember the friendly fairies? That's where they met the dragon, where they got the mark."

Liam held up his right hand. "It's fading, so the protection doesn't last forever."

Isla saw the ring, but it was much lighter than when he had arrived out of the book.

"Part of me wants this cure to work, only so I can travel The Trail again," said Kiefer. "Your adventures sound more exciting than those with Elspeth. Hers was a good cause, but there were too many principles and philosophies involved."

"You get on your feet, Kipper, and I'll drag you onto The Trail."

He grinned. "Promise me."

"Promise. Now rest. Eat well. Lots of fatty foods. Nothing sweet. Alaura's orders."

"Says the one who brought me chocolates." He pointed to the closet. "My rucksack should be there, buried under a mound of stuff. Get it."

She dug into the pile of belongs and found his well-used leather pack. "You're not well enough to leave yet." She sat next to him and forced a smile. By the time she returned from Dougendun, he'd either be well or...

He unfastened the top and withdrew his map. "Spread this out for me." His arms lay by his side, and he drew a deep breath. "It's past my nap time."

"We won't stay much longer." She didn't want to exhaust him. "What am I looking for?"

"Dougendun."

She stared at him, and her mind emptied. "You know where it is?"

"Never been there but Jack, a man I met on The Trail, drew it on my map. He said I'd need to know its location one day."

"Strange." She searched the map. "What was he? Human?"

"No. He might look like one, but he had traces of dwarf and hauflin. He had a peculiar way of speaking. Hair almost black. Thin dark beard. Slender frame. A few inches shorter than me."

A familiar image took shape, and her eyes settled on Kiefer. "Was he newlin under disguise? Like that woman we saw on the side of The Trail?" She hesitated to say Willow's name.

His face twisted from one memory to another. "Yes. He resembled Nyx, too."

"That's why he knows where Dougendun is. Why did he believe you'd need to know this information?"

"To give to you?"

"Maybe. Regardless, I'll use it to find Liam's cure." She withdrew her map from her shoulder sack and copied down the location of the mysterious place.

The front door opened, and Catriona entered. She carried a sack in each arm. "You're still here?" Her gaze fell upon Kiefer. "You're still awake?" She checked the clock on the wall. "You should be napping."

"I was settling to do that."

Isla folded the maps and returned them to their respective sacks, then put Kiefer's in the spot in the closet where she'd found it.

"He won't wake until around five," said Catriona. "You can visit him again then."

"He sleeps away the day?" Isla went to the bedside.

"He sleeps more and more *each* day."

She hovered over her friend, adjusting his pillow and tidying his blankets. "We'll visit before the evening ration." She kissed his forehead and caressed his cheek. "Rest well, Kipper. My thoughts will be with you, hoping for the best."

"Be well, Isla, and whatever happens, I know you've done everything within your power. No regrets."

She kissed his forehead again. "No regrets. I would hang onto you even if the odds were horribly against me." She released him and followed Liam out the door without looking back. His relaxed image was what she'd remember, not his broken body confined to bed.

Isla and Liam spent the early part of the day roaming the city of their birth, then they travelled out the front gates and explored the road to Moon Meadow. On the way there, she guided him through a narrow path off the road to a small mound of stones in a peaceful meadow overlooking Shulie River. In the distance were the Pogwa Mountains.

"What's this?"

She held tightly to his hand. "The day you left Maskil, Das and Farlan brought me here." The lump in her throat forced her to draw a deep breath. "That day, we buried your das."

His face turned red, and he sucked in his cheeks.

"Das told me to bring you here to show you he had a respectable burial, that we did care about what happened to him." She kept her grip on him when he fell to his knees and sobbed. "He won't be forgotten, Liam. His death burnt his memory in the hearts of many."

"The lords killed him." Spit flew from his mouth. "They should be dead, buried where no one can find them."

She knelt beside him. "Your das is found. See the dried flowers secured with a ribbon? Farlan and I brought them. He comes often; he can't let it go. He tried desperately to save him. When you see Farlan, know his heart bleeds for you."

"And your das?" He wiped away his tears.

"Das wasn't there to witness the death, so while he feels horrible about it, it's not the same as Farlan, who fought to reach him but failed. He blames himself. We'll visit him tomorrow before we leave."

"I don't know. I can't..." His body slumped. "My heart aches, and I feel I will break apart."

She cradled him in her arms. "We'll go slow. Remember there are many who love you; you are not suffering alone."

"Many?" He laughed sarcastically. "No one loves me but you."

"Nonsense. Farlan does. Meeme, Das, his family."

He snorted. "Your das hates me."

"If he hated you, he'd have never allowed you to stay in his home."

"I stayed because Alaura insisted."

"Das has always been fond of you. There's no reason for him to change his mind." She stroked his head, dragging her fingers through his hair.

They remained at the grave for a long time, then walked to the road and strolled to Moon Meadow where they sat by the pool to view the waterfalls.

On the way to the Darrow dwelling to share the evening ration, they stopped to see Kiefer. He was sitting at the table eating soup and bread. Catriona complained that he hadn't slept as long as he should have and would be exhausted by the end of his meal. She recommended not returning until morning to ensure he had sufficient rest.

"She's overly fussy about him," said Liam as they walked away from Catriona's dwelling.

"I was thinking the same." Isla held his hand and gazed up at the stars. "She's always been obsessive, but she's annoying him with her fussiness." She found Archer in the sky and marvelled at the three stars on his belt. "Did you know the stars moved?"

He looked up. "Yes. I've been watching while on The Trail. You can't see them in Wandsworth. Too many lights."

"Crazy. I'd not live in a place like that."

"I never will again."

"We don't have to live anywhere." She swung his arm. "We always have a place to sleep when we visit Maskil, but I like travelling The Trail."

"It's exciting now, but..." he grinned, "we might want to settle somewhere one day." He poked her belly.

"What does my belly have to do with it?" She kissed him and released his hand. "If I settle anywhere, it will be here. Our family and friends are here." She whirled and flung her arms in the air. "There's nothing like knowing your home as a kid."

A dark force struck her, and stars filled her eyes. Her feet left the ground, and she was thrown across a large body. The ground sped beneath her while she struggled to gather her senses. She was on a horse with a heavy blunt object driven into her back. The pounding of hooves flowed up the horse's legs and into her gut, mixing with the pain of the force on her back.

"Stay still, pretty girl." The rough voice grated against her ear drums.

She reached for her dagger, but... Alaura had made her put her weapons in the closet. The only thing she had was a pocketknife. She kicked and twisted her body until the pain in her back grew. Arching her shoulders, she tried to absorb most of it.

"Sit still!"

The horse halted and turned, giving her time to scan the area. They were in an alley behind... She stretched her neck to see. She didn't recognise the neighbourhood. A shadow ran into the alley towards them.

"Stop there!" ordered the man holding her.

Liam stopped before them, out of breath from running.

"Let these men shackle you, and I'll release the woman."

Three men came out of hiding, and she strained to see their faces. They were large humans, dressed in dark clothing and heavily... Men from Wandsworth. They had followed them through the portal.

A strong arm gripped her waist, and thick rope wrapped around her neck. "Stay still." The rope tightened, restricting air flow.

"Please, don't do this." Isla gasped as the rope tightened. "The poyson will claim him, and he'll kill you."

"Not if he wants to see you set free." His hot breath fell upon her cheek.

"That's what the other men thought, and they're dead." Her fingers wrapped around the rope with the hope of bracing it from her skin. "If he feels I'm threatened, he will kill an army. You know this. Walk away."

"Shut up. We're taking him back to where he belongs." He raised his voice. "Toss the sword aside and get to your knees, and I'll let this fair maiden go."

Liam fell to his knees.

"The sword!"

He unfastened the scabbard and dropped it and the sword beside him. "Let her go."

"Shackle him."

"Let me go first." Isla struggled to free herself. "He won't surrender if you still have me.

"Shut up." He pulled on the rope, making her gag.

On his knees, Liam stretched to see her. "Let her go!" His voice deepened. "Or no deal."

The three men surrounded him, each carried chains and shackles.

"Please." Isla gasped. "The poyson is taking over. Let me go and save yourself." She gripped the rope with all her might.

"Stay on your knees. When you are shackled, I'll release her."

"Now." Liam growled, and his brow lowered over his darkened eyes. "Release her!"

"Liam, no!"

But it was too late. He rolled quickly to the sword and snatched it from the ground. One of the men swung a chain around his foot and jerked it, slamming him to the dirt. Liam jumped up, grabbed the chain and flung it around the attacker's neck. One quick tug, and the man was on the ground, and Liam's sword was in his back, slashing it several times before turning on the other two.

"He will kill us all." Isla drove her elbows backwards into the man's gut. She had to get away before Liam reached them.

"Kill him!" ordered the man behind her. "It is dead or alive."

The men attacked from two angles, but they were large, encumbered by heavy weapons and were no match for Liam's speed and agility.

Isla looked away. This was not Liam, but the horrible poyson within, and if she didn't escape soon, it would claim her. She wiggled and swung her limbs like crazy, throwing her weight from one side to the other and ignoring the pain increasing around her neck. Finally, she found a weakness and pushed through it. The hard thud on the ground dazed her for a second, then she leapt to her feet and raced down the alley searching for cover.

A stranger ran from the shadows and grabbed her. "Are you okay?"

"Get out of here. It's not safe. Please! Go!" She pushed him towards the street while she hid behind crates, waiting for the last victim to fall. It didn't take long. All four men and the horse she'd been on were cut down, shredded into many pieces.

Liam stood in the middle of the bloody chaos, his chest heaving and his breath rattling loud enough to fill the narrow alleyway. He grabbed his scabbard, strapped it on and sheathed his sword. A noise sounded farther up the alley, and he squatted low to listen. Then as slowly as the poyson had claimed him, it slipped back into his shoulder, and he fell to his knees, gripping his hands as if he wanted to rip them off. His wail shook her heart and though she wanted to go to him, she feared the poyson still controlled his mind.

Heavy feet struck the cobblestones, and several dark figures emerged from the shadows. They were guards from Aruam Castle, and they paused to assess the battle scene before them. They'd blame Liam, but he hadn't done this. Staggering to her feet, she raced forward.

"Stay where you are." One of the guards, one she didn't recognise, held out his hand. "Don't move." He slowly approached Liam.

"Wait." Isla rushed to the guard's side.

"Stand back, miss."

"Give him a minute. Please. Let him regain control."

"Isla?" She whirled and saw her das standing behind her with another guard and Tam.

"Das. Give me a chance to explain."

"The report from Wandsworth explains everything."

"What report?"

"The one on him." He jerked his chin towards Liam. "Arrest that man."

"No." Isla tried to run, but the guard caught her arm.

"Give her to me." Bronwyn grabbed her by the shoulders. "You have to let him go. He's a cold-blooded killer."

"No, he's not," she cried. "He's got an infection."

"You're blinded by love. You can't save him."

She struggled to break free, but he wouldn't let go. "I will save him. He's my mate!"

"No! He will never be your mate. He'll be locked in the dungeon where he'll be put down like the animal he is."

"Das, don't say such things. Please, believe me."

"Tam." He shoved Isla into his arms. "Take her away. I don't want her to see this."

Tam held her with both arms. "It's for the best," he whispered in her ear.

"No! Don't do this! Das!" Through the dim light of the moon and sporadically-placed glowing lantern, she watched Liam scurry down the alley. Das and the two guards chased after him. "Das!" she screamed long and hard. "I've got to save him."

"You can't save a man like that," said Tam.

"I saved you."

He baulked, and his eyes swept over her face.

"I gave you a second chance because there was good in you. There's good in Liam. He's infected with poyson from the Maverick brand. These men tried to capture him." She squirmed in his arms, hoping to break free.

"Maverick brand." He held her so tightly, she gasped for breath. "He's branded?" When she nodded, he loosened his grip. "How can he..." He rolled his lips over one another. "That poyson controls completely."

"I absorbed half of it."

"You're infected, too?"

"I expelled my half. He couldn't."

"That leaves him in control?"

"Unless he's threatened, then the poyson takes over." She gazed down the alley. "Right now, he's a scared boy running for his life, feeling everyone is against him." She looked up. "Please, help me find him. He deserves better than this. His das was murdered by the lords, and his meeme was killed in front of him while on their way to Wandsworth. He needs our help."

"Killed in front of him?" Pain tore across Tam's face as he stared down the alley. "Do you know where he'll hide?"

"I think so."

He released her. "Take me there."

She sprinted from the alley, over the street and to a lane that entered the Hauflin Quarter. She spotted the former Jenkins' dwelling and raced behind it. Slowing her pace, she listened carefully and heard sobbing. Tucked inside a crate, huddled in the corner, Liam rocked back and forth with his arms gripping his bent legs.

"It's okay. We're here to help." She spoke softly and approached slowly with an outreached hand. When she touched his shoulder, he jumped.

Tam peeked into the crate. "Can he walk?"

"Probably not. He shuts down after an episode." She caressed his wet cheek, and he pushed her hand away.

"Leave me." His body shook uncontrollably.

"I'm never leaving you." She touched his arm, first with a finger, then her entire hand. "We're going to take you somewhere safe. Do you hear me?"

He shook his head. "Leave me. Let them kill me." He buried his face in his knees and cried.

She wrapped her arms around his neck and rested her head against his. "Come with me, please." Her voice caught. "We'll go somewhere warm. Safe."

She eased him forward, and he allowed her to help him up, but his legs gave way, and he fell. Tam reached in and touched his arm, and Liam recoiled into the corner.

"Who is he?"

"Shhh. It's okay. This is Tam. McGuigan's uncle." She caressed his cheek. "Remember, pip-pip, young man?"

He nodded. "His uncle?"

"Yes. He's going to help." She slid him forward and out of the crate. "Up." She grasped under his arms and lifted him. He staggered backwards, and Tam caught him.

"He's shaking like a leaf in a nor'easter." Tam scooped him into his arms. "Is sweating normal?"

"It is. He's cold from the inside out."

"Does it last long?"

"About a day."

Tam puffed, then marched away.

She trotted beside him as he weaved in and out of lanes and alleys. When he stopped at a fenced-in back yard with a large garden, she hesitated. Was he taking him to her parents' home? Or his, the adjacent dwelling? If Das knew Liam was next door, he'd cut a hole through the wall to reach him.

Tam climbed the single step to the back door. "Key. Behind the wreath."

She reached behind the evergreen decoration, found a key on a hook, unlocked the door and held it open for him to pass. He marched through the kitchen and up the stairs to the small room, which in the adjacent dwelling was her room. He found his way in the dark and laid Liam on a bed.

"I'll get light." He soon returned with a lit lantern and after hanging it on a hook, went to the bedside. "What can we do?"

"Warm water, so I can wash him."

He went downstairs again.

Isla sat on the edge of the bed, holding Liam's hand. "Can you hear me?"

He mumbled a few words but didn't open his eyes.

She removed the scabbard and slipped it with the sword beneath the bed. Then she took off his jacket and drenched shirt. He'd hide if he knew she exposed his scar, but he slept like an old man in a rocker.

Footsteps and voices on the stairs made her turn. Her hands shook as she stood to greet the person accompanying Tam. When Rhiannon's head peeked around the corner, she was both terrified and relieved. She was her das' sister and would feel obligated to tell him about Liam, but she was also a reasonable person, who followed her own philosophy.

"Put the basin on the table." She directed Tam. "Can you get us another light?"

Tam set the water by the bed and left the room.

"Isla, this is unexpected."

"I understand. If you want us to leave, we'll go."

"He appears in poor shape for travel. Let's get him rested first." She grimaced. "Instead, let's get him clean." She picked up the wet cloth from the basin and wrung it out.

"I can do it." She reached for the cloth. Once in her hand, she gently wiped Liam's face, washing off the dirt, sweat and blood. He had suffered a few cuts but nothing serious. His face clean, she washed his chest and arms.

Tam returned with a second lantern and set it on the dresser. "How's he doing?"

"As expected." Isla washed his stomach and above the rim of his trousers.

"We'll take them off." Rhiannon unfasted the button.

Isla placed her hand over hers. "I should do this. He's shy, and he's not wearing shorts."

"Oh. Of course. We'll use a blanket." She draped a blanket over his mid-section and blocked the view while Isla wiggled his pants off his hips.

Tam stepped up and removed the boots, then helped slide the trousers the rest of the way.

"That will need stitches." Rhiannon pointed to a bad wound above the left knee. "I'll get my sewing kit."

While she was gone, Isla finished washing Liam's legs and feet. She spread the blanket over him up to his chin and left the leg that needed treatment exposed.

Rhiannon returned and prepared the needle and thread.

"I'll do it," said Isla.

"You can't hem a skirt."

"But I can stitch a cut."

"You've done it before?"

"I have."

"Let's see if your handiwork passes inspection." Rhiannon handed her the needle and thread.

"This isn't a dress."

"Precisely. He can't change his skin if you mangle it."

"But he'll still love me." She leant over the leg and prepared to make the first stitch. On The Trail, she'd not think twice about where to put it or the angle but here, under her aunt's scrutiny, it had to be perfect.

"It's bleeding well. You should not dally." Rhiannon dabbed the excess blood.

She stuck the needle into the skin. Liam's leg twitched, but he remained sleeping. The stitch went directly across, sealing the skin together. The next stitch was almost as important as the first, but the third stitch had to be the same width from number two as between number one and number two. This was the hard part. She had a problem judging distances between stitches.

"Should have been a little closer with that one." Rhiannon hung over her shoulder. "Let's do better on the fourth stitch."

If this was a dress, she'd zoom through, purposefully making a mess, so her aunt would send her onto a different task, but sewing up a wound was important. She'd take her time and do her best.

"That one's better."

"Only five more," said Isla.

"You can squeeze in six for a proper closure."

"Five will do."

"Six is better."

"You're making me feel incompetent."

"Your lack of confidence is not my concern. Your skill with a needle is, and it needs improving." She placed a hand on her shoulder. "Striving to be better is not a weakness but–"

"A show of character and courage." Isla finished the quote she'd heard several times while working at the dress shop for her aunts. "I'm better now than before."

"And that is who you compare yourself to. Now finish up, and I'll get the cleansing solution."

Isla focussed on the task, judging the stitches and poking the skin in the perfect spot. When she finished, she had added six neater stitches that held the wound almost perfectly together.

Rhiannon reached over and snipped the thread and took the needle from her hand. Holding a cloth beneath the wound to catch the excess, she poured clear liquid over the cut. It sizzled and created yellow foam. She dabbed it away and added more solution. "We'll leave it open to the air while he rests and bandage it in the morning."

"Thank you." She stared into her aunt's face. "I know the position this puts you in, and I am truly grateful."

"Liam was always a good boy, sweet on you. I believe everyone deserves a chance to redeem themselves. If this is what you say, and I trust you'd not bring an unworthy man into my home, then he is a victim, not a criminal."

"He is worthy. He's proven that to me. I will never give up hope. As a wise man once told me..." she glanced at Tam, "a good man isn't down until everyone who matters has lost hope."

"That be the truth," mumbled Tam.

Rhiannon stood. "I'll prepare a ration. Will he wake to eat?"

"No, he'll sleep until mid-day."

"Then there will be three at our table." She left the room and descended the stairs, taking the wash basin with her.

Isla covered Liam's leg and tucked in the blankets. Seeing his hair displaced, she combed it into place with her fingers, then arranged the blankets with a perfect fold beneath his chin. She kissed his forehead and caressed his cheek. A bruise developed under his eye. She kissed it, then tucked a stray hair behind his ear.

"You're like your meeme."

She looked up at Tam.

"You fuss and pamper as if he were a helpless child."

She remembered the fussing and pampering she'd given him when he suffered an arrow wound to the chest. He had grumbled throughout it, but he had survived because of her stern actions. "It's how we keep our worthy men surviving under dire circumstances." She stood in front of him and placed her hand on his chest where the arrow had entered. "We give our all willingly, so they will live, and we regret none of it. All we desire is the same in return if we fall."

He pulled her into his arms. "You would get that and more."

"That's what fuels us." She wrapped her arms around him, resting her head against his chest. Finding this man on The Trail amongst ruthless bandits had changed both of their lives. It had taken much wheedling to learn his story and to gain his trust and loyalty but now that she had it, no one could break it, not even her das.

Tam signed the official report, then handed the ink pen to Kellyn for her to sign as witness. When she was done, he gave it to the clerk. "Send notification to the authorities at Wandsworth for their records so they can close the case."

"Yes, sir." The clerk took the document and walked into an adjacent room.

Tam led Kellyn out the door and to the courtyard in front of the main Aruam Castle gates where he stopped.

"Are you certain this was the right action to take?" she asked.

His sister's demeanour had changed drastically since they'd returned to Maskil. Her appointment as corporal to lead the first women's division of castle guard was part of it, but her finding her mate had been the biggest influence. She no longer made an ass of herself, though she still liked to make one of him when the opportunity arose. He chalked it up to the price of being her younger brother.

"It was." He considered the many reasons to support this answer but chose the one that would be his future philosophy. "When I first served the castle, I followed the book and those in authority without question, though my gut sometimes sharply disagreed; look where it got me. This time, I serve by my gut, and it tells me this is the right action."

"How long will you be?"

He grunted. "How long does it take to change the mindset of a stubborn honourable man?"

"Depends on your method of persuasion. Personally, I'd grab him by the scabbard belt and get into his face." She chuckled. "He might take offence to you doing that. If that failed, I'd punch him the mouth."

"That's all you've got? You're wearing that uniform because you did the impossible and convinced that man a women's unit was necessary. How did you do that?"

"Sat on his lap and played with his mustache, after I whacked him across the knee with a hot poker."

"Not an option."

"Hit him low."

"No."

"I mean sucker punch him with emotion. He may be a lord, but he's the same boy who got his ear pulled by Beathas, the same one who danced in a field creating a light spell." She pointed towards the castle. "There goes the baby of the family now."

Tam turned and saw Bronwyn walking with a private towards the guardhouse. "Give me thirty minutes."

Kellyn slapped him in the shoulder. "That's the spirit. It's more than enough time to convince Alaura."

He marched across the courtyard, making a bee-line for the guardhouse entrance to intercept Bronwyn. "Private." Both men looked, and the irony of his friend's rank triggered a grin on the corner of his mouth. "You." He pointed a finger. "Follow me." He walked away, not waiting to see if he followed, and didn't slow until he reached the castle wall. Then he did so to keep the same pace of the men on duty to not stir suspicion.

"Where are we going?" Bronwyn walked next to him.

He pointed up ahead to the North Tower.

"What's this about?" His haggard appearance suggested he'd been up half the night searching for a boy in the alleys of Maskil. His clean uniform indicated he'd returned home, changed and broke the fast with Alaura.

They walked the final three hundred feet in silence. Tam entered the tower, allowed Bronwyn to pass, then secured the door.

"Is this about the raid the other night?" Bronwyn leant against one of the thick windowsills.

Tam settled against an adjacent sill and folded his arms. He rolled a wad of spit around his mouth and formed the sentences to convince this man he was wrong. When he was ready, he swallowed.

"I completed the official report for yesternight's incident and closed the file. Guards have been ordered to call off the search for the boy."

"Why?" Bronwyn's mouth dropped open. "We didn't find him."

"We found his body, and Isla, Kellyn and I buried him beside his das this morning."

"What?"

"You're disappointed?"

"I'm...saddened. It's a tragedy." He rubbed his forehead roughly. "I was fond of him, even considered a visit to Wandsworth to bring him here to provide a home with us. Isla... My heart breaks for her."

He formed his words carefully. "His life was tragic. His das was murdered, then he witnessed his meeme's murder." He swallowed hard as memories he buried long ago flashed before him. It had happened so quickly. No one was supposed to die; they were to take the contents of the steel chest on the stagecoach and release the horses to stall the travellers' progress. Kieron Ruckle had other plans.

Muscles tightened in his stomach and shot a pain into his chest, where the scar from an arrow wound throbbed. He had grabbed the boy, hoping to protect him from seeing further mutilation of his meeme, when Keiron gave the order: kill him. Instead, after dragging the boy away, he shoved him into the bushes. He had growled and in the meanest voice he could muster told him to run. Terrified, the boy bolted and didn't look back.

"Horrible," said Bronwyn, "but that didn't make him a cold-blooded killer."

"Keiron slit his meeme's throat from here to here." His finger went from one ear lobe to the other. "Then that despicable gnome claimed her soul."

"You were there?" His eyes grew wide.

"Kieron ordered me to kill Liam. Instead, I helped him escape." He gritted his teeth. "How would you feel if someone killed your mum like that in front of you?"

Bronwyn stared out the window. His eyes grew glossy, and he sucked in a quick breath. "I'd have killed him without mercy or died trying. Mums are precious beyond measure."

"As a boy, he was helpless, and then he was delivered to his aunt and uncle's home, where he was beaten routinely."

"For what?" His face twisted in confusion.

"Minor offences: being a few minutes late, eating cookies when he was told not to, spilling a drink... The usual stuff."

"But that's what kids do."

"He endured two years of abuse before he left to live on the street. He begged for food and slept in crates. He started to steal to survive. By the time he was seventeen, he was recruited by the local street gang, the Mavericks." He paused. "Ever hear of them?"

He shook his head. "You?"

"I encountered them when I passed through Wandsworth after the failed quest. Their leader, a stalky human, tried to recruit me; said I'd be set for life. I declined; set for life meant slave for life."

"How so?"

"They brand valuable members to ensure their allegiance."

"A hot iron like they do with cattle?"

"Exactly, except this iron delivers a shot of poyson into the blood. You become a slave to it; you can't escape it. It makes you into a killing monster... Exactly like Liam."

"He'd been branded?"

Tam allowed the information to sink deep and to churn emotions. He'd remain silent until it ripened.

"Branded?" said Bronwyn. "Did it make him a better killer?"

"According to the report, when did he first kill?"

"Springan. This year."

"Exactly the time he was branded against his will. He wasn't a killer before then."

"How do you know?"

"The branding is a life-altering experience, and Liam reached out to the only person he believed cared: Isla. She was travelling to Wirksworth."

"How did she get to Wandsworth?"

"She didn't. They connected through..." He shrugged. "You and Alaura, you have that connection."

"They're transfer joined?"

"No. Their connection isn't created by magic but by...love? Their hearts connected, and Isla absorbed half the poyson."

"She's the same?" He rose off the sill.

"She expelled her portion. Because Liam carried half a dose, he somewhat controlled it. When those men threatened Isla's life yesternight, the poyson took over and killed them to save her." He paused. "You say Liam's life was tragic; I say it was worse for a boy his age. What is your assessment of him now?"

He released a helpless sigh. "He was an innocent victim."

"Yes." Exactly the word Rhiannon had used.

Bronwyn fell against the sill. "What is done is done, and..." a whimper escaped, "Isla will never forgive me. She's lost her mate, and I've..." He stood and wiped the corner of his eye with the back of his hand. "Where is she? I need to see her. I can't take away the pain, but I've got to do something."

"Follow me." Tam led him out the door. He'd know soon if his plan worked. If it hadn't, he'd resort to Kellyn's solution and punch him in the face.

ಬಿ ❖ ೞ

The room grew warm, and Rhiannon opened the window. The cool breeze blew across the bed, delivering much needed fresh air. Isla sat next to Liam's bottom with her arm resting on his hip while her meeme examined the brand. Alaura and Kellyn had arrived ten minutes earlier and after quick introductions, her meeme insisted on seeing the scar.

"Don't touch it." Isla grasped Alaura's hand. "It will leap into your arm."

Alaura recoiled. "Will it stay?"

"No. It lashes out as if to sample, then returns to his body."

She placed her hand in the centre of Liam's back. "I feel it." She closed her eyes. "It simmers like a lurking monster, one that will pounce when given a chance. It is a life of its own, and it craves blood." She opened her eyes. "Evil magic, worse than that which infected you at the castle, yet the same."

"The grey powder can't kill it. It's a bad mix."

"It's incredible he can control it as he does."

"May I turn around?" Liam asked over his shoulder.

"Of course." Alaura removed her hand, and he rolled to his back. "We must treat it as a wound, an infection, as you call it, Isla." She touched Liam's chin. "Do you understand? This is something beyond your control."

"It feels like it's my fault." He sunk into the mattress and pulled the blankets over his upper body, hiding the scar.

"Did you ask for the brand?" He shook his head, and she placed a hand over his. "Then this is not your fault."

Footsteps on the stairs made Isla stare at the door. She moved into a position to block the view of the visitor from seeing Liam. Her meeme sat beside her, doing the same thing.

Rhiannon stepped out of the room. "Remove your sword."

"I'm on duty." It was her das' voice.

"While you're in my home, you'll not wear it. Hand it over." Her stern voice left no room for discussion. The sound of unbuckling drifted through the doorway. Rhiannon walked past the door with the scabbard and sword in her hand.

Tam entered the room and stood off to the side. Bronwyn came in next and when his eyes settled on Isla, his expression softened.

"Bronwyn," said Tam, "how would you feel if your mate was killed and you were left to live life alone?"

He stared at Alaura. "That's enough, Tam."

"How would you feel if someone saved her?"

"Stop. I already feel horrible." His sad eyes fell upon Isla. "I'm sorry. I wasn't able to... I wish I had known."

"I was," said Tam.

"You were what?"

"Able to save him."

"Save who?"

Isla and Alaura parted, exposing Liam behind them. The expression on Bronwyn's face shifted with the flickering sunlight shining in the window. He adjusted his stance and stared at the boy.

"You said he was dead; that you buried him."

"That was the turkey bones from the ration two nights ago." Rhiannon stood beside her brother. "And the clothing he wore."

He frowned at her, then scanned the room. "Am I the last to know?"

"Those not here are the last to know," said Kellyn. "You know because we trust you to do what's right. Don't prove us wrong."

He glared at her. "You made a false report."

"I witnessed Tam bury a body."

"Tam?"

"I buried remains and will swear to it."

He huffed. "This is wrong."

"This boy has been running alone and scared for too long. He needs our help and while you may refuse him, I will not." Tam lowered his brow. "What say you? Would you forsake a citizen of Maskil and deprive your daughter of her mate?"

He retreated, his eyes darting from Tam to Isla. "Can we trust him?"

"Yes." Isla stood. "I trust him with my life."

Bronwyn cautiously stepped forward and grasped his daughter's face with both hands. "Do you say this out of love or because you truly believe it to be so?"

"Both. Das, I tried to tell you of the infection; you ignored me. He's a good boy, the best. He is worthy of my love."

He drew her into his arms and kissed the top of her head. "Show me this brand. I need to see what is responsible for the horrendous sight I saw yesternight."

She led him to the bed, and Liam pushed against the wall, pulling the blanket with him. "Das, tell him you won't hurt him."

"I won't hurt you. Now show it to me."

Isla held Liam's hand. "It'll be okay."

"I can't." His bottom lip trembled, and he gripped the blankets so tightly, his knuckles turned white. "I'm unfit to be your mate."

She knelt on the bed in front of him. "I will never love another like I love you." She caressed his cheek. "Please, trust me. Trust Das. Trust everyone in this room. We want to help."

"She speaks the truth, Liam." Rhiannon sat on the foot of the bed. "There is no bond stronger than that of a mate." She glanced at Tam. "It doesn't matter what obstacles you must overcome; you will overcome them to be together. My brother may be mulish and excessively honourable, but he understands the unstoppable power of love. Don't you, little brother?"

"I do," said Bronwyn, "and if Isla and everyone here has put their faith in you, then I am no one to say otherwise. Please, show me what we are up against."

Liam slowly moved from the wall. "I didn't ask for it." Deep lines etched his young face. "They forced it upon me." He twisted to reveal the large M branded on his shoulder and buried his face in his bent knees and sobbed.

Isla wrapped her arm around him. "Shhh. You are safe here." She gave her das *that look*, the one Alaura had taught her to give to those she loved when in need of enforcing what she believed in.

Bronwyn held back, staring at her. "You are exactly like your meeme in more ways than I can describe." He sat on the bed side. "This brand, it is deep?"

"Connected to his blood."

He hovered his hand over it.

"Don't touch it."

"Why?"

"It will poke you."

He lowered his palm over the brand, and his face went blank. Ripping his hand away, he gripped his wrist and gasped in pain.

She grabbed his hand. "It will pass. Breathe slowly."

"It... It jabbed me."

"Yes. It's as if it takes a taste."

He moaned, and his face turned red from the strain of withstanding the pain. "How long?" He gritted his teeth.

"A minute or so. I told you not to touch it."

"I won't do it again."

"Do you feel the strength of it?"

"I do."

"He cannot fight it; it's too strong."

"How do we get rid of it?"

"There's one cure and tomorrow, we leave in search of it."

"We?"

"Me, Liam, McGuigan and Lyneth."

He shook his arm and flexed his fingers. "Beathas?"

"She cannot cure this."

He glanced at Alaura. "We have nothing that will undo it?"

She slid her hand over his shoulder. "Nothing, or we would have used it by now."

"Liam." Bronwyn reached out to him. "Give me your hand." Liam kept his hands tucked close to his body. "Am I to trust you with Isla's safety?" When he nodded, Bronwyn flexed his hand. "Grab it."

Liam slowly reached for it and when Bronwyn grasped him, the boy shook.

"Do you promise to keep Isla safe?"

"I promise."

"Is her life more important than yours?"

"It is."

"She may go with you. Keep her safe. Bring her home."

"It is my greatest desire."

Isla watched the two most important men in her life make a deal, one she'd ensure was met. She'd help Liam find a cure for his infection, and she'd return home to bring that news to her family.

15

Mixture of Fear and Curiosity

THE TRAIL NORTHEAST OF Inglenook took them to higher ground and colder temperatures. Lyneth dreaded the idea of trekking through a mountain pass this late in the season but if snow didn't fall and impede their progress, they'd reduce their travel time by two weeks. This path put them on a direct course to Allestree, a small town near Edgewood. From there, they'd travel the main trail to Maskil and into Pogwa Mountains.

She glanced back at Isla, who steered her horse around a boulder on the edge of the trail. She and Liam had returned eight days ago. They'd spent the night at Morwen and Rhys' dwelling, sharing the story of their visit to Maskil, including the attack of the four men from Wandsworth. The elimination of those men meant no one pursued them. This put her mind at ease, yet others hunting Liam might still be out there. For now, the boy travelled as himself, a hauflin. However, his name became Liam Fetyplace. Liam Jenkins was dead and buried, hopefully eliminating the threat to his life.

An hour later, she halted near a mountain spring. It was tucked into the mountain side and faced east. Although they were shrouded in shadows now, when the sun rose, they'd be kissed first by its heat when embers glowed in their firepit.

"It's pretty." Isla stood on a rock to see over the treetops and gaze at the valley below.

"It'd be prettier if it was warmer." McGuigan pulled the saddle off his horse.

"Don't become a Brac."

He stopped, saddle in hand. "Why would you say that?"

"The colder it got, the grumpier Brac became. Don't be like that."

"I mean, why would you say his name?"

"Why shouldn't I? Can't we remember him?"

"Yes, but...in a friendly way."

"With all the sass he threw your way?"

"He didn't mean it."

"I know. He was making fun." She went to her horse and helped Liam remove the tack. "He liked you. That's why he said them."

He huffed. "He liked a warm meal, and lots of it."

"See. That's good. Let's remember him in fond ways."

"It feels strange."

"It will pass," said Lyneth. "I understand what Isla's doing. We should talk of him. It makes us feel better; it's as if they live on through our verbal memories."

"Maybe." He set down the saddle and pulled off the blanket. "But...it doesn't feel good to talk of the dead."

"It doesn't now because it's raw." Lyneth removed his horse's bridle and handed it to him. "Give it time, especially with your dad."

He fingered the leather of the reins, avoiding eye contact. "I won't live that long." He walked away.

She understood. Loosing a friend was not comparable to losing a family member. She'd give him time and offer a shoulder if needed.

"Shhh!" Liam crouched low to the ground and unsheathed his sword. "Someone's out there."

Lyneth drew her sword. "Where?"

He pointed down the trail from where they came.

"You and Isla, that way. McGuigan." She jerked her chin in the opposite direction. He fell into step behind her, and they sneaked into the bushes.

She strained to hear what Liam had heard. As a hauflin, he'd hear softer sounds than her, so she'd depend on McGuigan, who had better hearing. Elspeth's method of assigning partners had proven beneficial; she'd take the best at hearing and seeing and pair them with someone with lesser abilities. That's why Kiefer, a human, and Isla made a good team; she spied and listened for him. While dwarfs had better hearing than humans, they were inferior to a full-blooded elf, and hauflins beat them all. Given the members of their small group, the hauflins would need to accept the fact they'd be separated often to provide each team the benefits of their skills.

Then there was the mate factor. Elspeth honoured it, and she felt she should, too. Mates were permitted to remain together unless they agreed to part. Morwen and Rhys went on almost every mission together.

Lyneth pressed closer to McGuigan and made eye contact. "Do you hear anything?" she mouthed.

He shook his head and leant his ear towards their target. A twig snapped, and he pointed in that direction. She went to move, and he placed a hand on her knee and shook his finger. He leant near her ear and whispered. "Horse hoofs."

"How many?" She stared into the deepest blue eyes in all Ath-o'Lea. When they'd first met, his eyes seized and held her attention. They revealed excitement and sadness as if a gateway into his heart. At the moment, a mixture of fear and curiosity danced within them.

He listened further and held up one finger.

She nodded, then moved forward in the direction of the road, planning to rest in the bushes along it and spy on the person who travelled it. Finding a well-hidden location, she squatted and waited, directing McGuigan to find a similar spot nearby. He crept six feet away and settled into position.

She tilted her head into the wind and listened. The distinct sound of a horse walking touched her ears. McGuigan was right; there was only one, and it approached slowly. Moments ticked by, and the sound grew louder, then it stopped. Clanking of metal and squeaking of leather drifted down the narrow path. The person dismounted and walked next to the horse. The nearer the footsteps came, the faster her heart beat. Personally, she had no enemies, but The Mercenaries had many, and then there was those who hunted Liam.

The horse came into view: a chestnut brown mare with a long blaze on its nose. She didn't recognise it. The rider stood on the opposite side, near the horse's head and wore a cloak. The person was too short to be human, too tall to be hauflin. Her guess was an elf, which would be common given the area they travelled. The question was, what would the person do when they spotted the campsite?

The stranger passed at a casual pace as if they were out for a stroll. Or they were tired. Movement caught her eye. Isla emerged from the opposite side of the trail and crept behind the stranger. She didn't carry a dagger, and she wore an odd expression. What was she doing?

Liam also emerged from the bushes and stood on the trail watching her, confused by her actions.

Isla quickly reached the traveller and... Lyneth's jaw dropped. Isla kicked the stranger in the rump. The person whirled, ripping the hood off their head. Deaglan!

She left the security of the bushes and stomped onto the path. "I'm not believing my eyes. You are this foolish."

The boy rubbed his butt and grinned. "I missed you, too."

She folded her arms. "Your aunt will be worried. Why did you do this to her?"

"It was easy after I learnt she travelled with you."

"What do we do with him?" McGuigan stood beside her.

She huffed. "Right now? Make him gather wood and build a fire. Later? Give me time to think of more chores."

"Great!" Deaglan rubbed his hands together. "I haven't been warm in days."

"No fire?"

"It'd give me away."

"And walking into our camp wouldn't?"

He shrugged. "We're far from Inglenook; it doesn't make sense to return me."

She wanted to smack the confident smirk off his face, but he was right; returning him would put them behind by more than three weeks. They'd end up taking the main road instead of risking the pass. "We'll find another way to return you." She walked towards the camp. "Firewood, Deaglan, and lots of it."

"Yes, ma'am." He hopped into action and followed her. "It's great to be back with the gang."

"Gang?" asked Isla. "We're not a gang."

"Sure we are; we're a group of friends travelling together."

"Gang indicates a group of criminals. We're not criminals."

"You'd rather the Friendly Travellers?"

"Why would we call ourselves that?"

"It's what Lyneth called you."

Isla cast a frown in Lyneth's direction. "Why?"

"I didn't want to use The Mercenaries. That name died with Elspeth. We don't need enemies because of a name."

"The Friendly Travellers? It sounds like we're a theatre group looking to put on a play."

"We don't sound threatening; no one will trouble us."

"No, they'll expect entertainment." She jerked her thumb towards Deaglan. "We've got that, but I'm not into performing."

"Let's call ourselves The Good Guys," said Deaglan.

"Good guys don't steal horses." Isla pointed to the horse Deaglan led. "Where'd you get that?"

"I borrowed it."

"Great. We've a chronic horse thief with us. Where's your donkey?"

"My aunt locked it up, fearing I'd run off on it."

"What about the Avengers." McGuigan walked beside Deaglan. "That's an awesome name."

"What are we avenging?" asked Isla. "How about..." she thought for a moment, "the Warriors."

"What are you trying to do?" asked Lyneth. "Challenge the best fighters in town?"

"The Fighting Bandits?" offered McGuigan.

"There's a name that would get noticed." Isla lifted the saddle from where it was dropped, and Liam took it from her. "We'd be chased out of every settlement."

"Young Troopers," said Deaglan.

Isla unclipped the bridle. "Why don't we cut to the quick and call ourselves the Easy to Kill Band?"

"Lyneth and Her Misbehaving Brats." Lyneth pulled the saddle bags from the horse and walked to the centre of camp.

McGuigan blocked her path. "Who appointed you leader?"

"I'm oldest."

"By a few years."

"I'm more experienced."

"By a few years."

"I'm tallest."

"Only by a few inches. I say we call a vote."

"I vote for Lyneth." Isla carried her bedroll to the firepit. "She's the most mature."

"I agree," said Liam as he followed Isla. "We need someone as a spokesperson to make the final decision, but why do we need a name? Can't we be friends travelling together?"

"A name provides distance." Lyneth poked McGuigan in the ribs, then moved past him. "Instead of leaving our names for others to quickly identify us, we use a group name. It provides a blanket of protection. You wouldn't want your name spread around, but no one would know you were a member of our group."

Liam placed his saddle bags near the fire. "Makes sense. Let's pick a name."

"The Rowdy Rustlers." Deaglan carried a few sticks to the firepit and tossed them onto the ground.

"You're not a member, so you can't give suggestions." Isla spread out her bedroll. "And we'll need a lot more wood than that."

"I am a member. I'm here long term."

Lyneth groaned. "Short term."

"I don't want a name that describes us today," said Isla. "We won't be the same five years from now. Heck, we may not be the same this time tomorrow. The Warriors is a name we can grow into. A warrior isn't only a fighter; he wasn't born a fighter. He didn't become a warrior because of a fancy sword. Along the road of life, he grew into a warrior. He travelled. He fought. He drew blood and gave blood. He got dirty and, yes, sometimes he fell. But he got back up and carried on. Through it all, he never gave up, and the battle scars he earned are his medals of honour.

"Our goal is the same. We want to be warriors–fighters who don't go down easily and always rise. It will take time to live up to the name, but it's a name worth striving for. We'll grow into in. In the journey, we will become warriors."

"I like it," said McGuigan.

"Lyneth's Warriors," said Lyneth out loud.

"No!" He frowned. "Just The Warriors."

She chuckled. "We'll try it on; see how it fits."

"Don't I have a say in this?" Deaglan crossed his arms.

"You're not a member." She pointed to the forest. "More wood."

He kicked a stick and went towards the trees. "I am, too."

"What are we going to do with him?" Liam watched the boy go off for firewood. "He shouldn't be with us; it's too dangerous."

"We could send him home by coach when we reach Edgewood," said Lyneth.

"He'd never stay on it." Isla arranged a few sticks in the firepit.

"That's not a good idea," said Liam. "It's too dangerous."

Isla locked eyes with him. "I agree with Liam. If we have to, we'll suffer it out until we pass this way again."

"That might not be until Sumortide." McGuigan dropped his rucksack on his bedroll. "We might be arrested by then; guilty by association. You'll have to lecture him, keep him under control."

"Why are you looking at me?" Lyneth gripped her rucksack. "I'm not his mother."

"You're the closest we've got to one."

"That would make you the father, given you're the oldest man."

He clenched his teeth and sucked air quickly. "I'm too young for this."

"So am I."

"But you're our leader." He smirked.

"I tend to butt wounds," she said. "I'm not a nursemaid."

"I don't need a nursemaid." Deaglan dropped an armful of sticks near the fire. "I'm a Warrior." He went off to gather more.

"Liam, maybe you could give guidance." Isla rested her hand on his forearm. "You know better than us what should be said to keep a young, worthy boy out of trouble. Deaglan isn't a bad person; he's curious, eager, full of mischief. A little butt kicking will keep him on the right track."

"I'll see if I can talk sense into him."

"It's settled then." McGuigan pulled out his flint kit. "Lyneth is mother and Mr. Fetyplace is father."

Lyneth unfastened the top button of her jacket. "This can't be happening."

"Congratulations!" He grinned. "You're a mum."

She walked by and smacked his head playfully. "This isn't over." Joking aside, she felt responsible for Deaglan. He was Morwen and Rhys' nephew. She'd feel horrible if anything happened to him. At the next settlement, she'd send a message to let them know where he was and to tell them she'd watch over him until they returned to Inglenook.

Snow blew off the evergreen trees onto the path and swirled in circles in front of Isla before whooshing into the undergrowth and adding to the growing white mounds. It sent a shiver down her spine and across her shoulders. The temperature had dropped two days ago, and her bones slowly took on a constant chill even when she stood near the fire. The snow had held off until noon, then what started as flakes gently falling, transformed into a steady downfall by late afternoon, stealing the Forstig wonderland she'd admired. Lyneth recommended they press on, traverse the pass to reach lower ground where she hoped there'd be no snow and warmer temperatures.

Liam pulled his cloak around her and held it closed with his hands. Pressing closer to share his body heat, he half chuckled in her ear. "Didn't know that would happen."

She felt taller, and Liam felt shorter. Looking over her shoulder, she stared into his eyes, the only part of his face exposed. Snow clung to his eyebrows and eyelashes, and the wind had transformed his light-green skin to patches of red. "Why do I feel strange?" The thick woollen scarf over her mouth muffled her voice.

His smiling eyes stared back. "You are now like me."

"An elf?" She'd look at her hands to confirm his claim, but they were well covered beneath gloves and his cape.

"Yes, and..." he winked, "you are still beautiful."

"You have eyes to see through clothing?"

"Now, that would be magical." He squeezed her.

She turned, settling into his warm arms. In front of her, McGuigan slumped forward, doing his best to block the snow and wind from biting him. He, too, wore a cape over his overcoat and thick trousers, but it held no magic unless the warmth was considered magical. Snow slid down the cape and onto the ground. Yes, that cape was magical. With

Liam pressed against her, she imagined she was warmer than the rest, and she was half frozen, which meant they were more so.

McGuigan halted, and she stopped her horse. What was he waiting for? Leaning to the left, she peered past him. Deaglan and Lyneth had also stopped. Squinting through the flying snow and the dim evening light, she saw a soft glow up ahead. She reined the horse to the left and craned her neck.

"What is it?" Liam leant over her shoulder.

She listened but the howling wind and squeaking of cold leather vibrated inside her head. Except... She strained her ears and sniffed the air: fire. Someone camped up ahead and had a fire raging in the storm. Her first thought was warming up beside it; her second was concern for who had made the fire.

"A large fire." She glanced at him. "I hope its maker is friendly." His eyes darted from her face to the trail up ahead.

Lyneth remained still, so Isla squeezed past McGuigan and Deaglan and stopped beside their appointed leader.

"What do we do?" She scanned the ground between her and the camp. The warm glow coaxed her to proceed.

"I'm unsure."

"We can't stay here, and we can't go back."

"I know."

"Let me go first."

Lyneth stared at her silently.

"Hang back." Isla nudged her horse forward. "Ready?" she said over her shoulder to Liam.

"I'm right behind you."

She'd have rolled her eyes, but she was afraid they'd freeze in the upward position. The glow from the fire appeared odd. It didn't dissolve slowly into the night air and send sparks flying; its edges were sharp as if a large bubble contained the firelight. Bubbles couldn't do that without entrapping smoke and suffocating the people inside, but no smoke accumulated beneath this half sphere that appeared to be made of glass.

She examined the rim and saw energy trapping the heat and light. The sides had oval openings tall and wide enough for a dwarf to walk beneath without bumping his head. Incredible. That's why smoke didn't gather. Its four corners touched the ground, securing the shelter.

At forty feet away, she saw one bedroll, a rucksack and other camping items. One traveller, not a gang. However, the camper was nowhere in sight. She scanned the edge of the forest, searching for footsteps in the snow leading away from the fire. Seeing half covered holes in the correct pattern, she guided the horse alongside them. They went into the woods and stopped. Sensing she was being watched, she stared at that spot. Snow and wind played with the energy, making it impossible to know if a second bubble concealed the traveller.

She sat straight and settled. "I see you," she lied. "Please, don't feel threatened. We mean you no harm." After a moment of silence, she tried again, speaking louder this time to ensure her voice was heard over the wind. "My name is Isla. May we share your fire?"

A form shimmered and transformed into a man, a small human no larger than Kiefer. His long thick coat concealed most of his body, and the snow-covered hood hid much of his head. He held up his hand to block snow from striking his face.

"Isla?" He called out against the wind. "Isla of Maura?"

She ran his face through her memory; she didn't know him. "Yes. And you?"

"Jack Somerled."

That name. Her das had spoken it. He said she could trust Jack if she encountered him on The Trail. She lifted her foot over the horn, straining against the heavy boot, thick pants and half-frozen leg muscles. "Grab the reins," she said to Liam.

"Do you trust him?" He held tightly, not letting her go.

"If he is who he says he is, yes." She removed the cloak from her shoulders and jumped from the horse. When her feet hit the ground, sharp pain shot up her ankles and into her cold legs, bringing her to her knees. She grunted as if it'd help absorb the pain, then sucked in a breath between her teeth. Looking up, she saw an open gloved hand. She accepted Jack's offer and rose with his help. "Thank you. Jack Somerled. You know my das."

"Bronwyn."

"That's him."

He pointed to the fire. "Come. Get warm. Bring your friends."

She walked beside him towards the transparent canopy that created a warm, cosy and snow-free zone to spend the night. When she stepped over the barrier, warmth kissed her skin. "How do you make this? Can you teach me?"

Jack removed his hood and unfastened the top button of his jacket. "It appears you have the talent needed. First an elf. Now hauflin."

"I can make a bubble, strong as stone, but not like this." She examined the design. A hole in the roof above the fire channelled the smoke up and out of the shelter. The ground within the canopy was dry and thawed as if Sumortide. It measured about fifteen feet square; it'd be tight with everyone inside but cosy and warm.

"You are more than halfway there," said Jack casting a glance around the shelter. "Creating the bubble is the first step."

"Jack?" Lyneth walked into the shelter and lowered the scarf to reveal her face.

"Lyneth? It's good to see you well. And McGuigan? This is unexpected news. Rumours speak of a horrible fate." He shook their hands. "Move your gear inside. I have shelter for the horses. But after you introduce these two young elves so we are all friends."

"This is Deaglan." Lyneth pulled the boy forward. "A runaway who believed life was an adventure on The Trail until he froze to death."

"Near froze," corrected Jack. "One word can make all the difference." He addressed Isla. "And this young man who shares your saddle?"

"Liam Fetyplace. My mate." Isla's tongue tripped over the sire name. She'd never heard it before. Alaura had insisted on it being Liam's new name yet under question, she wouldn't say why only that it was special. Isla believed it was a name in Alaura's family.

Alaura had trimmed Liam's hair, so it was two inches at its longest, and shaved his face. The makeover took years off his appearance, and even her das stared in disbelief as if he was seeing the innocent boy from six years earlier. Isla had a mixed opinion on his new image. She adored his rugged appearance more than his baby face, but she preferred this hair length. Alaura gave him a new jacket, to replace the one they buried, two new shirts, two pairs of trousers, socks and shorts.

When he stepped out of her das and meeme's dwelling to leave Maskil, it was as if a new man walked away. No one would identify him as the wild killer who had stood in the middle of the bloody alley scene two nights earlier, and that's what her parents wanted.

"Interesting." Jack waved them onward. "Come, we shall share stories when we are settled."

They removed the gear and placed it inside the shelter, then led the horses to a small clearing secured with a similar bubble. Inside was a mound of hay for the horses. Isla slid her hand into the dried grass and found it warm and smelling as if it was freshly cut from the field. It instantly made her feel as if it was Sumortide. Incredible. The frigid trip from the horse shelter to the campfire reminded her she was far from warmer weather.

"I won't lie, Jack, you are a life saver." Lyneth unfastened her jacket and held it open to the fire to gather much-needed heat. "I was starting to have my doubts we'd make it through the pass and into fairer weather."

"Never doubt. Just do." He added water to the tea pot hanging over the fire. His eyes shifted to Liam, who had removed his cape and shook the snow off it. "A truth reveals itself."

"We used it to keep the snow and cold away," said Isla. "Not to intentionally fool you."

"Indeed, or he'd still wear it." He stirred the pan containing his evening ration of potatoes, onion and small chunks of meat. "A pleasant evening awaits. Sharing a ration with good people instead of the loneliness of howling winds." He caught Isla's attention. "Bronwyn and his companions are well?"

"More than well. Meeme and Das are united."

"United? When?" His fork paused.

"Sumortide."

"Wonderful news. And his companions?"

"Tam and Kellyn?"

"They are the ones."

"Both are well at Maskil. Both have found mates and are united."

His brow bent, and he leant forward. "You fool this old man."

She studied his face. His dark complexion was like Kiefer's when he'd been baked regularly under the sun, as was his dark hair and thin beard. Jack's dark chocolate-brown eyes were unlike any she'd seen before; they were warm and stirred with deep emotions. Peering closer, she saw something else. The slight contours of his features hinted at a race other than human, and the energy dancing on the surface of his skin concealed an image she'd seen before. He was newlin.

He pulled back and poked at the food in the pan.

"I'd not fool you. Das told me to trust you. Tam united Bronwyn's sister, and Kellyn, as unbelievable as it sounds, united his brother."

"Incredible. Share my joy the next you see them."

"And your surprise?"

"If you must." He tasted the ration, then scraped it into a bowl. "I have mail for you."

"You're a messenger?"

"No, but Bronwyn and Kellyn have made me one."

"A note from them? When did they write it?"

"Shortly after you escaped Tigh na Mare."

"I'm interested in reading them." She spread her bedroll next to his. Seeing the tight quarters, she moved it closer to accommodate Liam's on her other side.

"She was with us at that time." McGuigan flopped onto his bedroll and dug into his food sack. "I rescued her from the dungeon."

"You, young McGuigan?" Jack placed the pan on a rock near the fire. "Use it if you please."

"I did. Best thing I've ever rescued."

"Impressive. Snatched her right out from under her das' rescue."

"We didn't know he was behind us."

"It was for the best." Isla laid a large piece of frozen meat in the pan. The bonus of cooler temperatures was the ability to keep meat from going bad on The Trail. She'd saved this piece for when they'd need the energy most; today was that day. It was large enough for her and Liam. She set the pan over the fire, then pulled out a few potatoes.

"I believe it was." Jack poked a potato and put it into his mouth.

"I met loyal friends along the way."

"And a mate."

She grinned. "That was the best meeting." An object struck her, and she jumped back. A wet glove rested near her knee.

"I thought I was," said McGuigan. "If I hadn't saved you, you'd never have reunited with Liam."

She picked up the glove and threw it back at him. "You're not happy being second best meeting?"

"That's Kiefer."

"You want me to bump Liam down to third?"

He shrugged. "Sure."

"Kiefer," interrupted Jack, "he is..." His dark eyes probed her for the answer.

"Alive."

"Yet, he's not here."

"He suffered greatly and is unable to travel." She poked the meat with the fork and flipped it slowly. She'd paid a quick visit to Catriona's dwelling before leaving Maskil, and her already battered heart took another hit. Kiefer hadn't slept through the night and by morning, exhaustion confined him to bed. Catriona had said he'd tossed and turned, and his legs twitched, flinging blankets aside and onto the floor. He'd climbed out of bed countless times to pace the floor to ease the itch in his limbs, only to return to bed because of the ache caused by standing.

When she sat on the edge of the bed and held his hand, his long face and weary eyes tugged her heart strings. She'd give half her health to cure him even if he fought against it. Her hope of the cure working its magic slipped away as she rested her head upon his chest. She tried to be strong, but tears came anyways, and he wiped them away with a brave smile. After kissing him good-bye, she glanced back, holding her breath to stall the tears and ease the ache in her throat. Outside the door, she cried openly, knowing it'd be the last time she'd see him. If not for retrieving the first milk of a dragon to rid Liam of the curse, she'd have stayed by his side to comfort him during his final days.

Jack grasped her hand, and the heat from his touch sent soft energy through her blood. "Child, the strength of your hope may be all he needs to carry him through. Let us make a wish."

"To the Welkin nymphs? I've sent many."

The strength of his touch increased. "Your surprises multiply. We will send one to a special nymph named Ailsa. Close your eyes." He closed his, and she did the same. "Wise and kind, Ailsa, please, see to this man, our friend Kiefer of South Nova. He is a worthy spirit, one who deserves a chance to resume his journey. As a favour to me, as a favour to this child whose life intertwines with all that is good, let it be done if it can be done. Diolch." He squeezed her hand and opened his eyes. "We will not lose hope."

"Thank you. I will hold it as tightly as I can."

"I know you will." He released her and resumed eating.

Liam held the handle of the pan and flipped the meat and added onions. It sizzled and sent aromatic steam into the air.

She remembered the potatoes and quickly peeled them. They were cold, almost frozen, but they'd cook up fine beside the meat and onions. Not an hour ago, she was worried about freezing to death and now, her hope renewed for Kiefer, she prepared to enjoy an interesting evening with a man her das had spoken highly of. Although her das didn't know what a newlin was, unbeknownst to him, he was already friends with one.

16

A Sprinkle of Fairy Dust for Mischief

BRILLIANT SUNSHINE OF A cold, mountain-side mid-Harvest morning cascaded upon the land, releasing the magical sparkle of individual snowflakes resting on top of white mounds, making them appear as polished diamonds on goose down. Soft hues of pink and blue painted the horizon and lingering clouds journeyed onto new destinations towards the east. Low lying fog in the distance highlighted evergreens and bare branches of deciduous trees and deepened their colours, creating a magical Forstig wonderland. The snow and wind had erased the tracks made on The Trail by the Warriors the previous day, leaving a virgin landscape, wild and untouched.

With a warm breakfast settling in Isla's belly, she gazed upon this scene as she left the protective canopy over the fire and walked to the shelter to check the horses and to spend a moment with her two-bit Spindrift to increase the bond she had with it. She wasn't there long before Jack entered and, after checking his mount, came to stand beside her. She sensed he had something to say, perhaps sage advice for her journey.

"Isla, I know not where you gather your wisdom, but I suspect it a worthy source." He drew his hand down the mare's neck and scratched its withers. "I am tempted to ask, but..." his eyes locked with hers, "I fear the response. Perhaps I will not hesitate one day. However, there is one question of which I'm determined to know the answer. It is because I fear for you and your new-found friends."

"You tease my curiosity." She stepped closer. "Ask."

He scanned the surrounding forest, then rubbed his fingers against his thumb. "Your mate."

After a long pause with him searching her face for a would-be answer to an unasked question, she asked, "Is?"

He moistened his lips and softened his expression. "I wish not unhappy thoughts, but I sense veiled spite."

"Explain."

He released a sigh. "In your presence, I experience an abundance of positive energy. I assume you know of what I speak." She nodded, and he continued. "Your positive energy invites me closer, reassures me, ignites trust. You have this sixth sense, do you not?"

"I do. I feel the same with you."

"Good. Explaining will be easier. Your mate discharges negative energy, energy that incites my nerves to clamber for relief. I believe I should fear him, yet you instill confidence I am safe. If I had met him on The Trail alone, I'd have avoided him and not shared my fire. Do you not sense this?"

"I do, but it's not as strong as your detection."

"Perhaps your powers are underdeveloped."

"Perhaps, or they are buffered by love."

"Possibly. Do you know the cause?"

"Yes."

Surprised, he twisted his head. "It causes no concerns?"

"It's not him but what lives within him. We search for the cure."

"Please, enlighten me; reassure me."

She explained Liam's curse, where it came from and how they planned to remove it.

"Dougendun?"

"Yes, I am told it is the only place I'll find it, and..." she poked his chest, "because of you, I know the area where Dougendun is located."

"Kiefer."

"The one and only."

"Yet, it's an immense region. You'll not find it easily, and travelling will be challenging in Wintertide."

"I'll go anyways."

"What if I said you can get there faster?"

"You'd have my full attention."

"Only one portal travels to Dougendun."

"One? I had planned to seek a portal in every settlement we passed. Where is it?"

"Inishmore."

"That's a place shrouded in mystery, too."

"Yet I know it's location."

"Please, take us there."

"I am not a guide."

"Or a messenger."

A gentle smile creased Jack's lips, and highlights danced in his eyes. "You are much like your das, yet more like your meeme with a sprinkle of fairy dust for mischief."

"Is that a yes? On the way, you can teach me how to create that incredible shelter.

"Destiny has delivered me here; answer I will."

"Is *that* a yes?"

He nodded. "With pleasure."

"Good. One day, I'll take you to a second portal to Dougendun."

His brow lowered. "Is it closer?"

"No, much farther, and it only happens one day a year."

"Intriguing. I look forward to it."

Her das had told her he had travelled with Jack on several occasions, but their excursions lasted only a week or two before they'd part on their own journey. Their last adventure took them deep inside a mountain where her das and Kellyn had become lost. Her meeme spoke highly of Jack and said he had shared his expertise in magic to help strengthen her abilities. She'd accept the same offer, giving her a better ability to protect herself, Liam and friends while on The Trail.

ಬು ❖ ೞ

The next day, they rode down the side of the mountain and into a lush valley still green and free of snow. The last sprigs of life fighting for survival against the cold still bloomed, dotting the landscape with bursts of pink and red flowers. The sudden change as snowscape changed into grassy ground and leafy bushes still amazed Lyneth though she'd see it most of her life, and her eyes drank in the scene before her. They'd have had to travel two more hours the previous night before reaching the edge of the storm and finding pleasant temperatures that wouldn't threatened their lives. Although she was certain they'd have made it, the slither of doubt made her grateful for stumbling upon Jack when they had.

The trail they travelled headed more east than north and put them on a direct route to Allestree, a fair-size town on the edge of Skeenie Lake. Once they left the mountainous area, they'd enter thick forest with trees that reached for the clouds and blocked the sun. The trees growing in Yikker Wood were the largest she'd seen, so large that even if everyone in the group joined hands, they'd still not encircle a trunk.

She'd journeyed through the area several times, including a few occasions on her own when she was younger and aspired to seek adventure on The Trail as a lone mercenary. She'd never felt fearful of the area though rumours abound about strange noises disturbing campers at night. Although she'd heard them firsthand, she attributed them to the creatures that lived there, just as she'd heard animals in all areas she'd travelled in Ath-o'Lea.

However, her last solo trip through Yikker Wood was the one that instilled terror in her bones. She'd camped trailside at a firepit that had been used many times by travellers. The evening had been like many others, and she enjoyed the tranquility of the forest and her evening ration. Shortly after she settled in her bedroll, on the cusp of sleep, bandits swept in and bound her. The four men delivered her to a stronghold where she was then delivered to Blackvale Castle.

Thinking about travelling through Yikker Wood didn't ignite the terror it had when she'd first travelled it with The Mercenaries shortly after escaping prison. If not for Kiefer, she was unsure how she'd have faired. Sensing her discomfort yet not knowing why, he had provided encouraging words and remained by her side, not once asking why she felt as she had. At that time, if she'd not been committed to Rod, she'd have fallen for Kiefer. His kindness and gentle manner had touched her heart. The night he kissed her had driven an awkward wedge between them as she didn't trust him enough to tell him about Rod, still a prisoner of Blackvale. He sensed the mistrust and didn't pursue a more meaningful relationship. She felt bad given his personal attention to her well-being and while she wanted to remain close friends, he gave her space and returned to his role of travelling companion as a Mercenary.

At mid-day, they entered Yikker Wood and as she had many times before, she gazed up at the beautiful giants, admiring the intricate designs of their rugged bark and lush evergreen branches high above. Once under the full canopy of the trees, it felt like travelling within an expansive tree house with a smooth floor of dried yellow needles and random limbs that had broken from high above and crashed to the ground. Signs of other growth, short bushes, clumps of flowerless greenery and mushrooms, dotted the area.

"I...am...amazed."

Lyneth glanced over her shoulder at Isla. The young hauflin stared up at the trees, mouth open and eyes gawking.

"I've never seen anything like this."

"It's beautiful, isn't it?" said Lyneth.

"Not the word I'd use. Fascinating. Unbelievable. Captivating."

"True. It is the most amazing forest I've been in."

"If I grew up here, I'd have to climb every tree. I'd build a fort. Two of them."

The sound of rushing wings snapped Lyneth's head around to the front. A large bird flew in her path, startling her horse and making it lurch sideways.

"That was an owl!" cried Isla.

"You've never seen an owl before?" Deaglan rode on the horse behind Isla. "I've seen many with my uncle while hunting."

"Seen one? Yes." She stared at the grey owl as it disappeared into the distance. "Had one pass before me? No. That's a premonition."

"For what?" Lyneth hadn't heard of such a thing.

"A warning something unpleasant is going to happen."

"Nonsense," said McGuigan. "I've had owls fly in front of me before and nothing happened."

"Fly in front of you like that?" asked Isla.

"Not exactly. They flew higher."

"How much higher?"

"Twenty feet or so."

"That doesn't count."

"Someone's spooked." Deaglan laughed. "I hear opportunity knocking."

"Ignore that opportunity's arrival." Jack's mature voice left no room for foolishness.

Lyneth grinned and focussed on the trail. Having Jack along meant she wasn't the only mature adult in the group. He'd correct the teens' behaviour before it got out of hand, and the boys might listen to him more than her. She also felt safer with him. He provided an expertise none of them had, the same Elspeth had provided as they travelled The Trail: powerful magic.

Late in the afternoon with the sun sinking low and casting brilliant colours across the sky, they stopped at a campsite that appeared to have been vacant for awhile. Tall grass grew in the small clearing, concealing the rocks around the firepit. It provided a grazing area for the horses, but it meant flattening it to spread the bedrolls.

Lyneth bent the grass in a way it provided a thin cushion between her and the hard ground, then weighed it down with her blankets and gear. Deaglan copied what she was doing. The boy was eager, witty and learnt quickly. That would prove useful while he was with them on The Trail, but he had no skill with a weapon. That needed to change.

"Comfy." He lay on the bedroll and wiggled his butt into the blankets. "Thanks."

"Later, you and I. Weapons training. What do you prefer? Sword? Dagger?"

He propped himself up on one elbow. "Dagger. Two at a time."

"Let's go with one first." She might regret the training, but she hoped to protect him against minor threats without adding to the danger. Patience. That's what she'd need, or the lesson would end before it began. "You said you hunted with your uncle. The same uncle who owns the shop?"

"Uncle Harry has no stomach for hunting."

"What did you use on the hunt?"

"Short bow."

"Are you any good."

"Undeniably."

"How good are you?" That was a loaded question.

"Uncle Granger taught me everything he knew, so I spied on the masters. Learnt from them, then practised every day."

"Interesting." She loved the confidence of teenage boys even if it was misplaced. "Unfortunately, none of us carry a bow." So he couldn't prove or disprove his claim. "Is that your weapon of choice?"

"Without doubt."

"We'll work on the basics with a dagger tonight."

More than an hour later, she rested against her rucksack, letting her ration settle and enjoying the peaceful sounds of the massive forest. Jack sat next to her, cleaning his bridle. Deaglan played a game of Singleton on his bedroll, and McGuigan lay next to him on his belly, watching and learning how to play. Isla and Liam sat together about a hundred feet away on a fallen log staring into the forest and having a private conversation.

She'd wait before rousing Deaglan from his game to give him his first weapon's lesson. After a meal, she preferred to rest, let her stomach work the food through her system. Soon, she'd have the energy and patience to deal with a sixteen-year-old and his eagerness to use a dagger.

Isla and Liam walked back to the campsite, and Isla straddled McGuigan and sat on his lower back. He grunted as her weight settled but didn't say anything. He pulled a green jelly candy from his rucksack, and she leant over his shoulder to watch him eat it.

"Where did you get that?" she asked.

"I saved it. It's my last one." He bit it in half.

She eyed the remaining half of the candy and gave him a pitiful look. "Would you not share the last bite of food with me if I were starving?"

"Without hesitation." He plopped the remaining candy into his mouth. "But you aren't starving."

Isla slapped his shoulder playfully and rolled off his back to lean against Liam on his blankets. He dragged his rucksack near, withdrew a small paper bag and removed a chocolate from within.

"That's from the chocolate shop in Inglenook." She leant closer. "It's the cherry cream filled. Why didn't you eat it?"

"I saved it for a special treat." He bit off half of it.

She lay her head on his blanket beside his hand and peered up at him with sad eyes. "Would you share your last bite of food with me?"

"No," he said bluntly and pushed the chocolate into her mouth. "I'd give it all to you."

McGuigan groaned. "He's just saying that. If he was really starving, he'd want half."

"I'd make him take it." Isla chewed slowly.

"Let's have a game." McGuigan sat up and spread the blanket flat. "Come on, Deaglan. You playing?" He picked his new deck of cards from his pack and shuffled them.

"I'm in." He gathered his old, battered cards in a pile.

"Isla? Liam?" When they both agreed, he slid back to accommodate them.

"They're card players?" Jack dipped the rag into the cup of water and rubbed the leather strap of the reins.

"Deaglan got them started." Lyneth stared into the treetops. From here, it felt as if she sat in a bowl surrounded by the mammoth trees. Campsites open to the stars were rare in Yikker Wood, so she'd enjoy the starlight and the glowing moon. It'd take five days to traverse the forest and most of that time, the sky would be obscured from view.

"You don't play?" asked Jack.

"Haven't for a while."

"But you have played."

"Long ago in a different place." She and Rod had spent many evenings playing cards and now playing without him felt strange.

He set down the rag and leather reins. "I believe it's time you renewed your interest. Come." He stood. "Children, deal us in the next hand."

"Children?" Isla picked up a card. "We are far from children."

"I'm a man," said Deaglan.

"So am I." McGuigan laid a card.

"*Young* man," snapped Deaglan.

McGuigan shoved him, making room for Lyneth to sit between them.

"Last card." Liam moved over and allowed Jack on his blankets between him and the fire.

"Last card?" Isla tried to peek at it, but he held it against his chest. "I have five left. Are you hiding them in your sock?" She pulled at his sock and ripped it off his foot. His four toes wiggled in her face, and she slapped the sole.

"What do you call this game?" Jack observed the cards being played, mesmerized by the actions.

"Silly Sevens." Isla picked up a card. "Sevens are wild."

"Kinda like you." McGuigan poked her ribs, and she slapped him.

"What does that mean?" asked Jack.

"You can put it down at any time and change the suit to whatever you want." Isla fell backwards from McGuigan's hard shove, and her cards flew into the air.

"Suits are the designs?" Jack rubbed his forehead. "There are four, right?"

"Have you never seen cards before?" Deaglan slapped down a card. "Last card."

"I've never studied them. Where did you learn to play?"

Deaglan's eyes lit up. "Well, there was this girl, and she wanted to learn. I told her I'd teach her." He chuckled. "I stayed up all night playing with men at the tavern, and they taught me. My uncle found me and locked me in the house for a week. Never did get a chance to teach her."

"If you were my son, you'd have gotten worse treatment than that." Jack pointed to his card. "Why do you say last card?"

"If you don't, you have to pick up two."

"And the object of the game is to throw away all your cards?"

"Yes. Or, if you're Isla, you gather as many as you can." Deaglan laughed. "She's horrible at this game."

"I won!" Liam laid his last card.

"Are you serious?" Isla threw her cards on the pile.

"Given her luck," said Jack to Liam, "I request your coaching skill. I may be successful with your tutoring."

Lyneth gathered her seven cards and sorted them. Silly Sevens was Rod's favourite game; he had taught her how to play. Given the company she kept, she doubted the game would be played silently as she and Rod had played. With four young players vying for a laugh, she might regret agreeing to joining them.

৪০ ❖ ৫৪

A sharp squeal interrupted Liam's sleep. He pulled the blankets over his head and resettled. It shrieked again, and he slowed his breathing to listen closer. It sounded far away. There it was again. He poked his head from beneath the blankets and searched the campsite. Everyone lay sleeping except Lyneth, who sat on a nearby log on watch. She searched the trees and the sky for the source of the sound, and when she saw him sit up, she raised her hands to indicate she didn't know what it was.

The sound came again and this time, there was a sequence of sharp squeals before the forest fell silent. This disturbed Jack, whose bedroll was next to his.

"What is it?" whispered Jack.

"I don't know. Sounds far off."

"I've not heard that sound before." He focussed on the blankets and lifted his ear to the wind.

Liam waited. An owl hooted several times and the sharp squeal followed. "A type of owl?"

"Maybe, but none I've heard."

They listened for several long minutes, but the only sounds in the forest were the familiar ones of insects, evening birds, the occasional hoot of the owl and the gentle flow of the nearby stream. Jack settled again but didn't close his eyes immediately.

Liam peeked at Isla sleeping soundly on the bedroll next to his. She lay half on her stomach, her arm stretched out before her and her face in peaceful slumber. He sniffed the air and caught her scent. Leaning closer, her aroma filled his senses, enticing him to plant a kiss, but he didn't want to disturb her. If they'd been alone and he was free of this curse, he'd wake her slowly and join with her. The thought made him shudder, and he sank into his blankets watching her.

The chorus of the night animals soothed his nerves, and he slowly drifted off to sleep, dreaming of pressing his body against his mate's and exploring parts of her he'd never touched, never kissed.

Morning found him face down, hugging his makeshift pillow. A hand ruffled his hair, and he worked his mouth to form spit.

"Morning, sleepy head." Isla kissed his temple and left his side.

He blinked away the sleep, yawned, then pushed himself to a seated position. Everyone was already up, getting dressed and preparing to break the fast. The early sun, hidden behind the massive trees, shone brightly, sending its light across the sky and highlighting the tops of the trees in the west. Morning birds sang, mosquitoes buzzed and a woodpecker slammed its beak against a trunk high in a tree. He rubbed his face roughly with his hands to wake the rest of his senses. When he had settled after the strange sounds disappeared, he had fallen into a deep sleep, one filled with warm images of Isla. Her scent had consumed his every breath, and he drank it in as if he'd never again smell her.

She walked past him and left her scent lingering in the air. He knew her scent well and had locked it into his memory many years ago, yet this stronger version of it overwhelmed his senses and compelled him to be next to her. She was already washed, dressed and had their food out near the fire. Walking by again, he wanted to grab her arm and pull her down with him, but he stopped himself. She knelt next to the fire with a pan and potatoes.

"Are you okay?" She glanced over at him, and her smile sent his nerves dancing.

"Yes. I'm..." He shook his head. The sleep had made him silly.

"You are?" She leant over and kissed his mouth. "Tired? Hungry? Cute?"

"Late." He rose and went towards the stream, taking his rucksack with him. The cool water brought his senses around, and he splashed more onto his neck. A large grey squirrel raced down the trunk of a tree and perched on a rock on the other side of the stream to watch. Its beady eyes glared at him as if he intruded on a personal activity, and its nose twitched incessantly. It nattered nonstop and rubbed its front paws together. By the time he picked up his rucksack, the squirrel was irate. "It's all yours." He waved his hand over the water and returned to camp.

Isla had potatoes frying with onions and mushrooms. He wasn't fond of mushrooms, but Jack had picked them yesterday and assured him they'd add an interesting taste to the meal. Five days from the nearest keep, they'd have to ration what they had and maybe hunt to carry them through.

No sooner had he settled near the fire, and Isla's scent once again caught his attention. He stared at her, trying to figure out why. "Are you using different soap?"

She looked up from the pan. "No." She squished up her face to indicate he'd know if she was.

"Did you pick up a unique plant yesterday? A flower?"

"No. Did you see any interesting ones?"

"No."

She added water to the pan and steam rose in a cloud.

"Maybe it's the mushrooms." He leant over the pan and breathed in the warm steam. It smelt pungent. Moving away from the fire, her scent returned, and he gazed into her eyes. They sparkled and danced for him.

"You're being silly." She moved the food around in the pan.

"You're probably smelling her stink." McGuigan dipped his hard bread into the hot bowl of food in his hand. "She needs a bath."

"Like you don't." She slapped his leg. "I'm not soaking in freezing water. I'll wait until we get to an inn."

Liam sat back, not wanting to continue the conversation. Although he tried to keep his mind on other things, Isla's smell kept him thinking of her and her soft skin. When she handed him a plate of food, his voice came out softer than he wanted. "Thank you."

She smiled. "You're welcome." She sat next to him to eat her portion. "Lyneth said there were strange noises yesternight."

He cleared his throat. "I heard them."

"She said this forest is known for them. Rumours speak of strange and unnerving sounds that wake campers, and I slept right through it." She put a potato into her mouth and grinned.

"I was going to wake you, but I didn't want to disturb you." He ate slowly, watching her stab a mushroom and put it into her mouth. Her moist lips were especially rosy this morning.

"Wake me tonight if you hear them. I want to see if I can identify the source. Could you tell what it was?"

"No. I'd never heard anything like it."

"I've heard them before," said Lyneth. "It's nothing to worry about."

"Do travellers venture a guess at what it might be?" asked Jack. "They were peculiar."

"Some say owls, others say larger birds." Lyneth took a drink. "The birds I've seen wouldn't make that sound."

"Maybe we can catch it!" Deaglan shoved a mushroom into his mouth. "I can trap."

"Is there anything you can't do?" Lyneth smirked.

"He can't follow orders." McGuigan pointed a fork at him. "Or he wouldn't be here."

"Let's leave whatever it is making that sound be," said Lyneth. "We won't bother it, and it won't bother us."

"Sound advice." Jack poked his potatoes. "Let's stick to it."

Liam ate the rest of his meal in silence. When he finished, he waited for Isla to eat her last bite, then reached for her plate. "I'll wash them." He piled the forks and knives on the plates, rose to his feet and took the pan with him to the stream. The squirrel was gone, and he washed the dishes in silence. Here, away from Isla, his nerves settled, and he laughed at himself for being foolish.

On returning to the campfire, he packed the dishes into their rucksacks and rolled up his blankets. Isla was tending to her horse, so when he was done, he rolled up her blankets and secured them in a bundle. The odour in the material tickled his nose, and he leant towards the ground and smelt it. The thick green grass hadn't caused the smell.

"Lose something?" McGuigan organised his rucksack.

"No. I thought I saw something," he lied. Heat rose in his neck, and he stood with the bundles in his arms. As he approached the horse, he saw Isla had wandered towards a large tree. She placed a hand upon it, felt it and gazed up into its branches. Moving farther away from him, she walked between two great trees, their trunks large enough to carve a dwelling into.

He set the bundles next to the saddle and followed her. "Incredible, isn't it?"

"They are. Imagine if we had these to play in when we were kids."

"Alaura and Bronwyn would never let us climb them. They're too tall."

"As if that would have stopped us." She walked on. "If you laid this tree on its side, a woodsman could carve dwellings for five families."

"I wonder if anyone has done that." He grasped her hand gently.

She squeezed his fingers and led him farther. "I'd love to spend a day exploring. To see what and possibly who lives here."

He tugged her closer, and her scent filled his air passages. Glancing over his shoulder, he guided her behind a tree, one that blocked the view from everyone in camp.

"Thank you for washing the dishes," she said.

"You're welcome." He slowly backed her against the tree trunk. "I'm happy to serve you."

"Serve me?" She touched his cheek. "Kiss me."

He'd already made up his mind he would. Hesitantly, he touched his mouth to hers. He didn't want to arouse the poyson in his shoulder, so planted tiny kisses on and around her lips. She wrapped her arms around his neck and drew him nearer, latching her lips onto his and kissing him deeply. He ended the kiss before he wanted to, keeping the poyson at bay.

"Since I woke, I've wanted you. I can't explain it." He kissed her cheek tenderly.

"I thought you had always wanted me." She giggled.

"I do but today, I crave you. Your scent seduces me." He kissed her and held it until the poyson stirred. "It's like nothing I've felt before." His breath came quickly, and fire raced through his blood.

"Alaura said during the moons of Spring of Leaf and Harvest, a woman will attract her mate, making him silly and unable to control his urges. I'm sure she's telling tales."

"I'm sure she's not." He kissed her chin.

"She called it moon scent. She knew when Das would gather the courage to ask her to accompany him for the evening. It was on those days. Certainly, she's making it up."

"I doubt it." He kissed her again, lingering on her lips until the poyson moved. Unzipping her jacket, he slid his hands inside and grasped her back. Fearing he had teased the poyson too much, he avoided her mouth and kissed her chin, her cheek and her neck. He fumbled with the top buttons of her shirt, then while his hands removed her shirt tails from her trousers, his mouth explored the soft skin between her breasts. His legs shook as his bottom lip caressed smooth curves of one and then the other.

Her fingers combed his hair, pulling him nearer as she planted kisses on the top of his head.

Lost in her overpowering scent and delicate skin, the heat in his groin grew with his need to join with her. "The things I'd do to you here and now if I didn't have this curse." His breath fell heavy on her neck.

"Would be equal to what I'd do to you." She pulled him to her lips and kissed him hard.

He gave in, allowing the sensations to run rampant through his blood. A sudden rush of poyson forced them apart. "No," he gasped from shortness of breath. "I don't want you to taste it." He wiped his mouth, then grasped her head in his hands. "I'll do whatever it takes to protect you from it."

She fell into his arms. "Hold me until the excitement fades."

"Gladly." He held her tightly, knowing the excitement would fade for her, but it would linger with him until her moon scent ended. Their heavy breathing pressed their chests together, and he felt her heart pounding from the exertion and thrill.

"Has any other woman made you feel like this?"

The question stung his ears. He hadn't revealed the women he'd joined with, though she had told him about her previous relationships. The one difference between the women he had bedded and the men she had was she'd never meet those women, whereas he had already met one old flame of hers: McGuigan. Every day he had to look into the face of the man who tasted her pleasures. He felt he'd eventually meet Arthur, too, and that might be a harder relationship to accept given he was hauflin and she'd enjoy him more than McGuigan. Her lingering feelings for these men meant more than the dozens of women he'd taken between the sheets; those women meant nothing to him. He didn't even know all their names.

Yet the question she asked was easy to answer. "No woman has made me feel like you do."

She pulled away to stare into his face. "None?"

He shook his head. "Has any man...?" he hesitated, fearing Arthur's influence on her.

"No. If he had, I'd be with him."

Her matter-of-fact tone left no room for doubt, and his heart sang with her song. "We are mates, Isla. One and only. There will never be another for me. I don't need confirmation from joining; I know it in my heart."

"As do I." She fastened the buttons.

"Hey! Let's go!" McGuigan shouted.

Liam helped tuck in her shirt and they returned to where their horse waited and found it already saddled.

"You're welcome." Lyneth walked by. "Your saddle bags and rucksacks are near the firepit."

"Thanks." He retrieved the saddle bags and fastened them in place, leaving Isla to finish packing her rucksack.

The sound of large flapping wings reached his ears and he turned, expecting to see the large grey owl they'd seen before. Instead, a large shadow fell over the clearing, and the rush of wings stirred up dirt and made the grass sway. The horses neighed loudly and stomped their feet.

"Calm down. Whoa!" McGuigan stood beside his horse and fought to keep control of it by pulling the reins down.

"Scatter for cover!" Jack dragged his horse with him into the shelter of the trees.

Liam untied the reins from the branch. "Isla!" he called without turning. "Get over here!" The reins free, he spun to get her when a set of wings blew him over. Feathers slapped him and kept him pinned on the ground. "Isla!" He screamed so loud his throat burnt.

He rolled from beneath the feathers and jumped to his feet. What he saw made him stumble backwards. The creature was as large as a draft horse with a wingspan that measured more than thirty feet. Its large head was shaped like that of a majestic bird with a threatening beak. The hind legs were the same as a large cat, but the front legs ended in large talons made for ripping meat from bones.

His heart skipped when he saw what the creature grasped in those talons: Isla. Before he drew a dagger, the creature lifted off the ground, and the wind from its wings tossed him into the air. He landed with a thud and rolled several times before slamming into a tree. Scrambling to his feet, he raced after the creature that flew higher into the air, carrying its precious cargo. He ran until he lost sight of it, then fell to his knees, screaming her name. His heart erupted and tears streaming down his cheeks.

The poyson in his shoulder shrank as if fearful for its survival. It gathered in a small pool, then lay still.

Movement on his shoulder braced him, yet he felt numb to the touch. Jack stood before him in a fighting stance, sword in hand, peering in the direction the creature had flown. Then he stared back at him, his face long and his eyes wild.

"What was that?" McGuigan rested on a knee beside Liam with a hand on his shoulder.

"I'm uncertain." Jack sucked in a breath. "I fear a griffin."

"They are myth only." Lyneth stood on the other side of Liam.

"Many o' myth have their bases in truth." Jack sheathed his sword. "Come. Gather the horses. Our time is limited. We must find the nest in haste."

"Nest?" Liam stumbled along, guided by Lyneth. "She's going to be chick food?" He coughed on the pain in his throat.

"Tell me," asked Jack, "how much of a fighter is Isla? Will she succumb quickly, or will she make that griffin regret he snatched her?"

"Regret." McGuigan walked quickly beside him. "She's deadly with a dagger. Sneaky. Tricky."

"She can sweet talk her enemy into giving her food, gifts, letting her go," said Lyneth. "I've never seen anyone work like her."

"It can talk?" Liam stood stronger on his legs.

"I believe so. That will be to Isla's advantage." Jack caught his horse that jogged on the trail. "Sweet-talking women have saved themselves more than sword-wielding men. She has a chance."

A chance. A slim chance, but Liam would take it, hold on to it, let it feed his hope. He'd find the nest and rescue Isla. Another thought crossed his mind. If he wasn't quick, she'd rescue herself.

৪০ ❖ ৪০

The wind rushed by Isla, blowing her hair from her face and making her half-buttoned jacket billow. When the great creature had snatched her, she struggled to reach her daggers but its large, thick claws had pinned her weapons to her body, making it impossible to pull them free. Once she reached the top of the mammoth trees, she clung to the claws and sent wishes to the Welkin nymphs, hoping the large bird wouldn't drop her.

They sailed over the treetops and towards a mountain range. Which direction did they go? She considered the sun. Northwest. She'd have to travel southeast to find Liam and the others.

She scanned the area below. Never had she seen the land like this, not even from the highest tower at Blackvale Castle. The trees didn't look so large from up here, and the rivers appeared like streams meandering through the landscape. Brilliant Harvest colours painted the ground, making it more beautiful than fearful though she'd be terrified if the bird dropped her. She'd never survive the fall.

They flew over Yikker Wood and a small valley, then the bird circled, slowed and returned to the valley. It travelled northerly between a sharp cliff face and a hilly bank covered in trees. Flapping its great wings stalled its progress, and she spotted a large nest on an outcrop of rocks high above the ground. Before the beast set down, she studied the cliff, looking for a way to escape and saw a thin ledge that ended abruptly, then another ledge below it. She'd never make it. She stilled her nerves and prepared to snatch her dagger and defend herself.

The rough landing threw her into the bottom of the nest where she rolled until striking the side. Fearful she'd tumble out, she spread her arms to stop. Gathering her senses, she shook the dizziness away, jumped to her feet and reached for her dagger.

"Remain still." The whispering voice sounded female. "Leave the dagger."

She gripped the dagger but didn't draw it. Backing up against the coarse side of the nest, she scanned the area for the source of the voice and found an elf crouching low with her arms over her head.

She turned to the creature that had captured her, and its immense size and oddity forced her to press harder against the side of the nest. Her first impression was of a large horse that worked in the woods hauling logs. She'd never seen a horse with wings, but this one had large ones the size of a dragon's in a story book. The front legs were thick and scaly and ended with sharp claws. Its hind legs were that of a beast she couldn't identify, but resembled those of a barn cat except much larger. The heavily feathered neck and head was like a falcon, but its ears resembled a wolf. The mixed bag of animal parts came together as one massive creature that exhibited strength, wisdom and dexterity.

It rested on the opposite end of the nest and watched her with large, dark eyes. Her heart pounded and sweat gathered around the dagger handle. One dagger wouldn't bring down this monster, nor would the three she carried with her. She'd need another weapon to kill it.

The beast leant forward, and her grip on the weapon tightened while solutions tumbled through her mind in a jumbled mess, not knowing what to do to save her life.

"Don't move," whispered the elf. "Let it smell you."

The sharp beak neared her neck, and her muscles tightened. It moved down her shoulder, sniffing her like she was fresh meat. In one quick twist, the beak could break her in two or gouge out her chest. It drew slow, deep breaths, and its eyes glazed as if it became intoxicated with her odour.

"What do you want?" Her voice shook, and she clenched her fists to steady her nerves.

It pulled back and stared with its head tilted. "You."

It spoke. She blinked, unbelieving her ears. "Me? I am hauflin."

"Hauflin. Mine." It turned, perched on the edge of the nest and roared, sending a chilly energy bolt down her spine. Then it leapt into the air and flew away.

She raced to the edge of the nest and scrambled up the side, grasping thick branches to help her climb faster. Reaching the rim, she gazed onto the valley far below and observed the great beast soar over it as if it was its kingdom. It moved gracefully for its size. It made two loops around the valley, then perched on the rocky cliff near a magnificent waterfall to watch the land below and its nest.

Feeling movement beside her, she saw the elf clinging to a branch next to her. The girl was younger with an innocent face that suggested she'd never travelled The Trail. Her long blonde hair streaked with dark-green highlights was pulled into a single braid that hung halfway down her back. Deep-green eyes peered over the ridge, searching for the beast. She wore a thin jacket over a lose shirt and scarf, and the tight pants covering her legs was topped off with a skirt that went to her knees. At least she wore sensible boots that covered her calves. A leather pouch hung at her side, but more interesting was the short bow and sack of arrows hanging on her shoulder.

"Who are you?" She spied on the monster perched on the cliff.

"Cabela. You?"

"Isla. When did he capture you?"

"Yesterday. Before sunset."

"And he hasn't eaten you. Why?"

"I don't believe that's his intention."

'What is?" Isla peered farther over the edge, looking for a way to escape.

"He said he wants companions."

"And he chose an elf and a hauflin? Why wouldn't he seek it from his own kind?"

"There are no others."

She stared at the girl. The beast was either the last of its kind or the only one created. She'd seen many weird and unusual creatures in Merk's dungeon but nothing close to this. "How old are you?"

"Sixteen. You?"

"Eighteen. Any idea on how to escape?"

She shook her head. "We're too high. We'd fall to our death."

"So we have to convince him to take us to safety." She assessed the steep hill; it was near impossible to scale, and if she slipped...

"I've been trying. He's stubborn."

"He knows what he wants, but why us?"

"Because we're young females?"

"Of the wrong species. He'd have better luck with a mare."

"But they don't speak."

"There's that." She reconsidered the hill. If she climbed down and fell along the way, she'd be closer to the bottom. Gazing at the first place she'd land, several hundred feet below, she shivered. "Have you tried to escape? Did it try to stop you?"

"I didn't try. There's no where to go but down."

"Are your travelling companions searching for you?"

"I travel alone."

"Seriously?"

She nodded. "You?"

"My mate and friends will find me and attempt a rescue."

"If they are no match, they will be killed."

"That's my fear, and why I hope to escape before they arrive." She rubbed her chin and schemed her escape. "Why did you tell me to stay still and not fight?"

"The one he brought yesternight attacked him, and he killed her without mercy and threw her over the side." She pointed to the edge. "Her body lies near the valley floor."

Isla searched the area, and when she saw the body sprawled in an awkward position, she reconsidered her next plan.

"Mandaggio wants passive companions."

"It has a name?"

"He does. He's intelligent. Don't let his speech fool you."

"He's moving." She crouched low as he flew down the valley, then veered east. "Where's he going?"

"Hunting."

"For another?"

"Probably."

That gave her time to plan and consider the items in her pouches; none of them would get her off the side of this steep hill. Her best option was to conceal herself from the creature with an impenetrable bubble. The Levitation Spell came to mind, but Cabela was heavier than a boot, and she'd yet to learn how to lift herself.

ঙ ❖ ଔ

For the past hour, Lyneth followed Deaglan through the trees, giving him the task of tracking the griffin. He'd said he wasn't certain of the trail to follow because it left no tracks, but his uncle had versed him on the way birds travelled, giving him a better idea on the great beast's destination than the rest, who had no idea. She understood the position she placed herself in: she was allowing a boy, who bragged nonstop of his abilities, to guide them to save the life of one of their members. If he failed, everyone failed, and Liam lost his mate. Those were high stakes, but ones the rest had agreed to, including Jack, who knew little about the mythical creature.

They were travelling, as Deaglan had described it, as the crow flies. In his language, that meant slightly more north than northwest due to the prevailing winds. He explained the crow, or in this case the griffin, would fly slightly to the left of where he wanted to go because the wind pushed him right, which at the end of the journey would leave the griffin in the exact position he wanted to be. However, since they were travelling over ground and not affected by the wind, they'd travel northwest. If the winds increased, they might deviate slightly.

After he had explained his reasoning, he apologised to Liam for not knowing more but hoped his gained knowledge would rescue Isla. The boy had his moments when he wasn't stealing horses and tarot cards.

The forest thinned ahead, and Lyneth noted the trees grew shorter. Stretching her neck around Deaglan and his horse, she saw blue sky, a clearing in the trees. The opening grew larger and less than half a mile later, they rested on the edge of a rugged valley that in some places resembled a canyon with its high rocky cliffs.

Lush forest of average-size trees and bushes blanketed the forest floor with vibrant Harvest colours of orange, red and yellow. Exposed red and brown rocks lined the opposite side, much of it going straight up from the floor to heights where a feather would take minutes to descend. To the right, the valley snaked its way between this solid wall and a less menacing hill that consisted of several landings covered with foliage. From this, a waterfall spilt forth, crashing into a large pool one hundred feet below. To the left, the valley spread out into endless forest.

Lyneth scanned the cliffs, looking for sign of the griffin. Many of the ledges and landings on both sides where the valley narrowed could accommodate a nest. She ended her search in one direction, then started it in the other, straining her eyes to find either the nest, the griffin or Isla.

Beside her, Jack pulled out a monocle and spied on the opposite side. Liam dismounted and went closer to the edge to search from that vantage point.

"Get to cover." McGuigan turned his horse sharply and raced it across the short clearing.

The rest followed, not questioning the reason until they were well hidden in the trees.

"The griffin?" asked Jack. He secured his horse to a branch and sneaked towards the clearing.

"Yes. From the west." McGuigan followed him.

Lyneth stayed close, scanning the sky for the beast as she ran. She saw it and squinted; something dangled from its talons. Was it Isla or another victim? She stopped beside Jack who had the monocle pressed to his eye.

"It's not Isla. A human woman." He pointed to a line of bushes. "Take cover there. We'll watch where it goes."

The five slipped beneath the bushes quickly. The great bird creature flew along the valley to a ragged edge on the cliff.

"That's high." McGuigan pressed close to Lyneth. "Four hundred feet?"

"At least," she said. "It won't be an easy climb."

"We'll never reach it," said Deaglan.

She stared at him. He was probably right, but she wouldn't admit it. One way or another, they had to learn Isla's fate.

"What's it doing?" Jack half mumbled to himself as he stared through the monocle. "He's...dropped the human inside the nest, and... Isla climbed onto the edge."

"She's alive?" Liam reached for the monocle. "Please."

Jack let him have it. "A quick look."

He pressed the tool to his eye and watched. "Why is it...? He's stroking her, preening her? Tasting her? She's talking to it."

"Sweet talking it," said Lyneth, itching to hold the monocle, but not willing to rob Liam from seeing his mate.

"Let me see." Deaglan held out his hand. He stared through it, and his mouth opened.

"He's collecting females?" McGuigan glanced at Jack.

"That's the obvious answer, but the question is why?"

"Is Isla in heat?"

Everyone stared at Deaglan.

"She's not a goat," said McGuigan.

"Females of all species have heat cycles."

"But not the same."

Deaglan removed the monocle from his eye. "Uncle Granger explained it this way. All mature females enter a heat cycle. During this time, their mate is hyper-sensitive to their condition, and other males can fall prey to their charm. It's what we call the mating season. For rabbits, that's every two months. For intelligent beings, that's Harvest and Spring of Leaf. That thing is mauling Isla like she's in heat, and he wants attention."

"Damn," Jack mumbled under his breath.

"That's a crazy notion," said McGuigan. "That thing is not going to mate with Isla."

"She's lucky he's not more aggressive. He must be supersensitive to heats of other species."

"Inconceivable," said Lyneth. "Do you have proof of this?"

Deaglan hesitated.

"He doesn't," said McGuigan. "He's making it up."

"I'm not." His voice lost its confidence. "Uncle Granger warned Mother, but she didn't listen." A sharp pain crossed his face. "She insisted she was safe hunting at all times at every moon regardless of season, but..." he stared over the valley, "he said it was only a matter of time. She went anyways." His voice cracked. "He found her torn to pieces by male wolves who had tracked her scent."

Lyneth's mouth went dry. She felt the pain in the young man's voice, and it struck a chord in her heart, making her eyes water.

"She is, isn't she?" Jack grabbed Liam's arm. "I sensed it. She had my attention more than normal this morning, and I cannot explain it otherwise."

"She is." Liam wiped the corner of his eye. "But this thing... It's nothing like us."

"It may have a powerful nose," said Deaglan. "That's all it needs."

"He collects women because they are in heat and he's in rut?" Lyneth had no better word for the male's action other than what she'd heard family and friends use when speaking of male goats and deer.

"The once-a-year male cycle for most animals lasts from seven to ten days," said Deaglan. "If that's his intention, then it's a short window for rescue."

"I still don't believe it." McGuigan gave Lyneth a serious look. "What are the chances of him finding two women in heat within a short distance from his nest, and why does he need two? He wants them for another purpose."

"Regardless of the reason," said Lyneth, "he's going to fight to keep Isla."

"If he wants a mate, I'll give him one," mumbled Deaglan.

"I admit, I've got nothing," said Lyneth. "I've never dealt with a creature like this, and I've got no rope to reach her. Anyone?"

"It's a steep climb." McGuigan gazed over the valley. "Getting to her is the impossible part."

"I think I can climb it." Liam's voice sounded uncertain. "I'll try it anyways."

"Wait. There's another." Jack pointed to the far side of the valley.

"This isn't good." Lyneth rose on her elbows. "It might be an offering."

"Except..." Jack stared through the monocle, switching from one griffin to the other. "The hind feet on this new one has hooves not cat-like feet."

"Whoops." Deaglan stared at the new griffin on the scene.

"Now it possesses cat-like feet." Jack removed the monocle from his eye and glared at the boy. "Is this mirage of your imagination?"

"He can only make old cards appear new," said McGuigan.

"You create illusions?" asked Jack.

"I'm working on perfecting them."

"This is far from perfection." He placed the monocle to his eye. "And it may cause more harm than good."

"I'll try harder."

Lyneth watched the griffin at his nest. It caught sight of the second griffin and launched itself into the air. From its actions, it didn't appear to accept the new arrival. It flew straight for the illusion, and a short distance away, it positioned its body for an attack. It smashed through the imitation, shattering it. The griffin reared and screeched, flapping its wings vigorously.

"Now he's angry." Jack lowered his brow at Deaglan. "Don't try another trick without consulting us. Isla's life is in grave danger."

"Yes, sir."

The griffin circled the area where the image once flew, then returned to the nest. With one strong talon, it shoved Isla into the nest, and she disappeared.

"Now what?" asked McGuigan. "She's alive. We have to rescue her."

His face was so close to Lyneth's, she heard his quick breath. The emotions crossing his face were a mixture of fear and worry. He loved Isla; he'd never give up on her regardless of the odds. The young woman had gathered many allies in her lifetime, some powerful, many poor.

They were of all races and some mixed. If they gathered here today, she'd be freed within the hour. Even Merk Lindrum would aid in her rescue, along with half the enemies to the Kintale Clan and half the Kintale Clan. Was it her youth and innocence that worked her magical charm on these people, or did the girl possess another power?

She had her own reasons for wanting Isla alive. Helping her to free Rod was one, but it wasn't the most important reason. Isla's genuine openness, the brightness in her smile that lit her entire face and her eagerness to help those in need made a life worth saving. She'd do what needed to be done to ensure the girl was rescued.

17

Light as a Feather

THE FOUL ODOUR OF the beast before Isla made her dread breathing from her nose but even when she inhaled through her mouth, the stench lingered on her tongue. The newly captured woman, a human, was also young, appearing to be no more than twenty. She came ill-dressed for the cool weather, wore no shoes, as if she'd been plucked from sleep, and carried no weapons. She cowered against the nest, shivering from fear and the cold. When Mandaggio had approached the nest with the prisoner, Cabela had pulled Isla down in a low position, warning her to remain still and quiet, and to not attack.

Once the new arrival was settled, Isla had climbed onto the rim of the nest and started a conversation with Mandaggio, trying to understand why he needed three young women in his midst, but the talk was short lived. A similar creature, smaller in size, had approached from the valley, and Mandaggio flew out to intercept it. When it turned out to be an illusion, he flew back in no mood to discuss the situation and knocked her onto the bottom of the nest. Now he perched on the edge, staring south towards the wide-open valley.

Isla had searched for the source of the illusion and while she saw no one, she strongly believed it was one of Deaglan's creations, which meant they'd found her. Under the circumstances, she'd hoped they had taken longer to reach her location because Mandaggio was too powerful to defeated. She needed time to wheedle him into letting her go or find a way to escape the nest.

Mandaggio lifted off and flew a circle over the valley, passing the waterfall twice before he screeched loudly, his beak reaching out before him to send his call forth.

Isla climbed to the rim of the nest and watched him perform the action three times, then he perched on the rocky ledge near the waterfall to gaze upon the valley. His stolid posture made her feel as if he waited for something or someone, yet what visited a creature like him?

She moved nearer the cliff face, gazed over the edge and studied the crag to find a secure surface to place her foot. Her eyes mapped a dangerous route to a ledge fifty feet below. From there, a four-foot wide grassy strip skirted the cliff, then the route dropped ten feet to another level that appeared safer to travel. If she reached it, the terrain would not impede her escape further. That first fifty feet from the nest to the ledge bothered her most.

She shifted to the other side of the nest and assessed her escape route from this angle. Her eyes followed a narrow ledge with a low incline that appeared to provide footing to descend twenty feet. That left a thirty-foot drop to reach the escape route. Stretching her neck farther, she saw another course, an easier one that led closer to the ledge fifty feet below. However, there was a twenty-foot drop from one to the other. It wasn't impossible, but a hard, awkward landing might break bones.

She studied it further, committed it to memory, considered other routes, then returned to the other side of the nest and repeated the exercise.

Cabela climbed up beside her. "You've been up here a long time. What are you watching?"

"I'm studying?"

"The rocks?" She gazed over the edge, then crouched back. "It's too high."

"Not fond of heights?"

"No, and these are the highest I've been."

The constant natter she believed were birds in the trees below grew louder and drew her attention. She scanned the opposite ridge, then her eyes swept through the valley and into the forest below. Not finding the source, she looked to the horizon and saw a large flock of birds flying in a confusing clump. The dark spot grew, and she slowly realised it wasn't a flock of small birds but a small group of large birds. She strained to see if they were the same as Mandaggio, but they flew differently and... She pulled her neck back. They were characters ripped from the story books of her youth, horrid creatures that snatched children from meemes. She'd had nightmares of harpies, and her das removed the books from her shelf and told his sisters not to give her anymore with those *vile creatures*. It took a long time to forget their nasty deeds and to feel safe again in her bed.

Mandaggio flew into her line of sight and met the harpies over the valley. He screeched in his high-pitched voice, then travelled past the vile creatures towards the south and the endless land of trees. Why was he leaving? Were those creatures going with him? Her question was answered in a heartbeat: no. The harpies flew directly for the nest. There were six of them, more than enough to control three young females trapped on a cliff.

"What are they?" Cabela squeezed between Isla and the cliff face.

"Vile creatures we must fight." She withdrew a dagger. At this moment, she wished she carried ten, but she owned only three. "Get your bow ready."

"What is it?" The human woman poked her head from beneath her arms. "Is someone coming to rescue us?"

Isla gazed down at her. "Don't think so. Do you have weapons?"

"I don't carry any."

"Grab a stick from the nest wall. Something long, something solid you can swing." She tucked her feet firmly between two thick branches. She'd need all the strength she could muster to ensure the dagger drove deep into the chest of her attacker.

☙ ✦ ☘

Liam stopped walking and put his hand out to block Jack, who followed close behind him. "Look." He pointed at an obscure form on the horizon. "That's not a flock of birds."

Jack removed his monocle from the pouch and peered at the dark mass. "It's six..." he pressed his thin lips together, making his dark mustache flop over his bottom lip, "creatures. Not griffins." He stared longer. "Concerning."

"What?" Lyneth, who led the group by foot through the low-growing trees and bushes, stopped and peered back.

"Womenfolk, of sorts," said Jack. "Winged wenches with talon feet and feathered chests." He removed the monocle and stared at the rest. "I've seen them in books only; more mythical than griffins."

"What are they?" McGuigan stood next to Lyneth.

"Incredible. Unbelievable."

"Tell us," said Lyneth.

"Harpies."

Liam had read about them as a child. He had pretended to be one and captured Isla in his *claws*, but he regretted it when he saw her reaction. The terror in her eyes made him feel horrible, and he stumbled over himself to make it up to her. For weeks afterwards, she wouldn't enter the woods unless Bronwyn or Farlan was with her. Even then, she was wary and didn't want to linger. He'd promised to never speak of them again. Now, her nightmare was coming true, and he wasn't there to shield her from it.

"Let's go," he said. "We need to reach Isla quickly."

"The griffin is in the air." Deaglan stood between McGuigan and Liam. "He's going to attack them and protect the nest."

Liam watched the great beast fly over the valley. "Let's keep going. Maybe they'll kill each other, and our challenge will be scaling dangerous heights."

"That's positive thinking." Jack slipped the monocle into the pouch and followed. "However, I feel we will not be that fortunate."

The griffin screeched loudly, paused near the harpies, then flew south over the valley. The harpies continued to the nest.

"This doesn't make sense." Deaglan picked up a heavy stick. "Why did he abandon the nest?"

"I believe this was an offering, not a personal endeavour." Lyneth walked faster, pushing the bushes from the trail with little thought for the sound she made.

Liam needed to reach Isla and protect her from her worst nightmare. If anything happened to her, he didn't know where he'd go, what he'd do or who he'd become. He knew only his life would be more worthless than it was today.

The sound of Isla's heart thumping against her chest pulsated in her ears and drowned out the whoosh of large feathers. The vile creatures drew near, and she pressed her body against the stone and anchored her feet on two solid branches on the inside of the nest. The brawny human females soared through the air gracefully. Either of them could easily out muscle her, yet... She searched their sides and waists... They brought no weapons. She stood straighter and strained her eyes. They wore no scabbards or sheathes to carry swords or daggers; their upper body was covered in yellow and brown feathers that gleamed in the sunshine, and their bare legs ended in deadly talons. A flimsy skirt that flapped in the wind concealed their midsection.

No weapons. It was Isla's only advantage. Then she remembered the horrible stories from her childhood: sometimes they knew magic. She was doomed. She gripped her dagger tightly as the harpies slowed their pace, then came to hover ten feet from the nest.

"Three young prodigies." A blonde woman with red streaks in her long hair spoke in a raspy voice.

"I have first choice." Another blonde, this one with no streaks, flew closer, her eyes wide and assessing the three prisoners. "I've waited immensely for my gift."

"I am second." A dark-haired harpy clutched her hands in front of her chin. "I know which I desire. My prodigy; my apprentice."

"Me first!" The blonde came closer. "Pretty girls. One of each. Must choose."

Sweat gathered on Isla's palm and dripped along the dagger handle. The harpies appeared to not want to kill but enslave them. Returning to prison was far from what she desired and this time, she was old enough and strong enough to fight for freedom. Yet, the sight of these vile creatures and the images of them poking sticks into their victim's eyes and removing toes to feed to lizards paralysed her. Their current appearance was frightening but when they grew angry, they'd transform into beasts with menacing faces, large teeth and shrieking voices that stopped hearts.

Her mouth, void of spit, made her voice sound odd. "I don't choose any of you." She clenched her teeth to steel her nerves and forced her body to stand tall. "You're all ugly."

The blonde with the glimmering hair hissed. "Don't want that one; too mouthy."

"Me either." The second to choose crossed her arms.

A harpy with yellow hair peered closer at Isla. "Dirty hauflin. Hate hauflins."

"You're stuck with her," said the blonde. "Third picker."

"I don't want either of you," said Isla. "I'm leaving." She swung her leg over the side of the nest as if she was about to walk away.

The harpies laughed in unison.

"Mandaggio said I could leave," she lied.

The shimmering blonde settled on the edge of the nest. "He fibbed. You are ours for eternity."

"He lied to you." Isla glanced at the next step out of the nest, then back at the harpies. Defeating them all was impossible, but she'd take a few with her. A breeze swept across the sweat pooling around the dagger handle and sent a chill down her back. She'd not surrender. Her hand shot out, and her middle finger pointed to the harpy's chest, the path the dagger took. A solid thud was followed by a cloud of yellow and brown feathers flying into the air.

The blonde with shimmering hair swayed forward, her eyes wide with hate and her mouth open in a roar that never made it to her lips. She clutched the dagger, wiggled it but never freed it as she tumbled backwards and over the edge of the nest.

The remaining five harpies wore various expressions of horror and anger, and when they focussed on Isla, their intent was clear. Before they advanced, an arrow struck the chest of one. She hovered precariously, her wings losing strength as blood trickled from her chest and dripped down her yellow feathers.

"Sister!" The yellow-haired harpy caught her, and they both fell below the rim of the nest and from Isla's sight.

Three. That left three to deal with. Isla gripped her second dagger and prepared for the attack. When it came, she whipped her dagger at the one in the lead, the one with the blonde hair and red streaks. The dagger struck her wing, and the harpy fell into the nest. The remaining two were upon Isla before she drew her third dagger, beating her with their fists and pulling her hair.

She tried to regain control and squirm away, but they held her firmly, driving their long claw-like fingernails up her nose and into her ears until sharp pain made her scream. One of them slapped her face so hard, it left ringing in her soar ears. Each grabbed an arm and pulled in the opposite direction as if they intended to tear them from her body. Then they slammed her face down onto the rim of the nest and flipped her over. The dark-haired harpy put her talon upon her chest and held her in place with the full weight of her body pressing down. A claw rested on either side of her neck.

Isla gasped for breath, but the weight on her chest made it near impossible. She gripped the talon and tried to push it away.

"No one's choice," cried the harpy.

A scream from deep in the nest touched her throbbing ears. The second harpy had snatched one of the other prisoners. An arrow flew across her line of sight, missing its target, and a shadow crossed her face. It was the yellow-haired harpy, returning from tending to her sister, who was either dead or dying.

Isla drew quick breaths, but the dizziness increased. Sounds of scuffling, slaps and grunts rose from the nest, but her vision grew dim, and she saw nothing. If she didn't break free, she'd pass out. Gathering her strength, she thrust her legs into the air and wrapped them around the front of the talon. She locked them together and pushed with all her might, hoping to knock the harpy off balance.

A bright light flashed, and relief washed over her when the weight on her chest disappeared. She gasped for air and struggled to rise, but her aching bones resisted. The horrible sounds of skin being slapped and punched reached her ears, followed by the unmistakable crunch of a bone breaking.

Fighting the pain, she pushed herself up and the dizziness threatened to send her toppling. She wiped her eyes with the back of her sleeve, and it came away blood stained.

"Help!" cried Cabela. She was pinned to the floor under the weight of a harpy and was being struck nonstop with fists.

The young human prisoner had fallen, yet the harpy continued to attack her with a large stick.

Isla gripped her dagger and prepared to jump but when someone called her name, she searched for the source. Several hundred feet away, on a piece of land that poked into the valley stood five figures. Her friends had found the nest, and the harpy that had pinned her to the rim was heading their way.

A piercing scream made her whirl. The human prisoner had been tossed against the wall, and the harpy had her talons around her arms and was rising slowly. The large flapping wings stirred dust and debris, creating a small cloud that flung particles into Isla's eyes. Shielding her face, she leapt into the air and grabbed the girl's legs, hoping to pull her from the harpy's grip. Her hunch proved wrong, and she rose into the air.

ᔰ ❖ ᔱ

Liam gripped the dagger tightly and crouched low as the harpy approached at full speed. He feared the creature knew magic and was armed with a spear. She didn't appear to be carrying a spear, but magic was a hidden weapon.

"She's beautiful," said Deaglan softly as he gazed at the approaching harpy.

"And deadly." Jack pulled him beneath the tree and slapped his cheek lightly. "Don't fall under her spell."

Lyneth shoved a dagger into Deaglan's hand. "Use it for protection only."

He spun the weapon in his grip, then held it ready for the attack.

The dark-haired harpy thrust her hands forward and a breath later, a brutal force struck the centre of the group, sending them flying in different directions.

Liam soared twenty feet into the air and as he descended, the ground disappeared below. He scrambled to grab hold of a tree limb, but his hands slipped. In desperation, he latched onto the rocky edge and held tightly while his legs dangling in the air four hundred feet above the ground. His breath came quickly, swelling his ears. Glancing down, his mind wavered. He had to get his other hand on secure ground. Easing the dagger into the sheath, he cautiously reached up, but the soil crumbled under his grip.

A face popped over the side, and Jack quickly extended a hand. "Grab it!"

He gathered his energy and pulled his body up to latch onto Jack, but the grip wasn't secure. "Don't let me go."

"Fear not, son; it is my last desire." Jack clutched his fingers so tightly, they ached. "I need a better hold." He called over his shoulder. "McGuigan, grab my belt! Steady me."

"I can't," Liam breathed between clenched teeth. Feeling his fingers slip from the rock, he made a desperate plea. "Hold on."

A scream filled the valley. His head turned, and he saw a body sail from the nest and plummet to the rocks below. His struggling to get a better view to identify the person made his hand slip off the rock and left him dangling by Jack's death-like grip.

"Hold on! Don't let go." Jack reached with his other hand.

"Was that Isla?" The question burnt his throat. If that was Isla, then it didn't matter if he fell.

"No." Jack's face reddened as he strained to reach him. "Grant me slack," he called over his shoulder.

"Was it Isla?" he cried, not believing him.

"I don't know." He reached farther with his other hand. "Don't let go, son. Grab it now!"

Liam lunged for the hand, but he failed to go high enough, and his fingers brushed Jack's skin. The force of his weight descending severed the grip. His heart leapt as his arms flailed, searching for something to grasp onto. The rush of air filled his ears, and his eyes darted across the landscape, seeing the nest but nothing else as he braced himself for impact.

"Grab my hand!"

The voice shook him, and his eyes grew wide seeing Jack fall towards him.

"Grab it!" ordered Jack.

He seized his wrist. They'd die together.

Jack pulled him into his arms and tucked him close to his body. "Light as a feather; light as a feather; light as a feather," he said quickly. "Say it!"

But he was as heavy as a rock.

"Light as a feather." Jack continued to mumble the phrase and hold Liam as if he were a baby, covering his body with his own.

Light as a feather thought Liam. "Light as a feather." As Jack mumbled it, he cried it. "Light as a feather!" The air slowed, but they still moved fast. "Light as a feather!"

The sudden impact knocked the air from Liam's lungs, and he rolled in darkness, deep in Jack's arms. They came to a sudden stop, and he waited to regain his breath and for his heart to slow.

"Jack." He wanted to push aside the man's arm but hesitated. "Jack?" With his head pressed into his chest, he heard his heart beat grow faint. "Jack!" He gently removed the arm and slipped from his embrace.

Jack lay unconscious, cuts and bruises dotting his face. The shoulder of his jacket was torn.

"Jack?" He hovered close to his face, looking for a sign of life. "Please, don't." He shook him, but the man remained still. "Wake up!" Laying his head onto his chest, he heard a faint heartbeat; he was still alive. He needed Isla to heal him with her hands, but... He stared in the direction of the woman, who had been tossed from the nest, and his mouth went dry.

He closed his eyes but tears seeped through. He'd brought trouble into the lives of those he loved. His aunt had told him, screamed it at him, that he was the reason his meeme was murdered. If he hadn't been born, she'd have remained in Maskil but because she wanted him to have a better life, she travelled the dangerous trail to Wandsworth.

If he hadn't made stupid decisions at Wandsworth, he wouldn't have this curse on his shoulder, and his friends wouldn't need to go to Dougendun. They wouldn't have to travel the back trails to avoid those looking for him.

And Isla. She deserved a good man, an honourable one who'd make a safe home for her.

He touched Jack's face gently, and the cool skin made him flinch. He knew no magic, didn't have healing hands and had no knowledge to distinguish a healing weed from a poysonous one. All he could do was make Jack comfortable.

He scrambled to his feet but collapsed from shaky legs. Bracing his muscles, he rose again and carefully dragged Jack to a patch of grass bathed in sunshine near the base of the cliff. He removed his jacket and spread it over the unconscious man's chest, then he laid Jack's head on his lap. Leaning against the stone wall, he let his body deflate. He'd stay with Jack until the end.

ဢ ❖ ဨ

Isla leapt onto the back of the harpy she'd wounded in the wing. The vile creature had flung the human prisoner over the side of the nest and planned to do the same to her. She drove the dagger into the wretched woman's neck. The dreadful scream that followed made the yellow-haired harpy cease her assault on Cabela and glare in her direction. The menacing scowl shot fear to her core. She stumbled to the farthest part of the nest, then waited for the imminent attack.

The harpy hissed and grabbed Cabela's arm. She parted her legs to increase her upper body strength, then hurled the young girl into the air. Sensing her intent, Isla sprang up, caught the girl's foot and dragged her into the nest. A sharp sound in the distance made her search for the source.

The harpy's upper lip curled as she glared at the scene below. She twisted her fingers until they turned red, and then spat at the girls. "I'll be back to finish you." She spread her mammoth wings and flew off.

Isla raced to the side of the nest and scrambled onto the top. The dark-haired harpy was tormenting her friends, and the yellow-haired one was rushing to help the revolting creature.

"Let's go." She blinked away sweat, dirt and blood. "We can't wait." She scrambled over the side and dug her toes into a secure crevice. With the back of her sleeve, she wiped her forehead and eyes to improve her vision.

"Where?" Cabela peered over the side, then closed her eyes. "I can't."

"If you don't, you'll die." She grabbed her hand. "I'll guide you." The girl refused to budge. "There's no other way to escape."

"I don't want to." Cabela moved closer.

"Neither do I." She guided her over the side. "Don't look down."

"Great. That's what they all say, and now I'm looking down."

"Then look up at the red rocks." She moved her foot to start the journey, then sought the next step. "Better yet, look straight ahead. It feels better. Put your foot here." She moved Cabela's foot to the first stepping stone.

They inched their way down onto a narrow ledge with a gentle slope that took them twenty feet beneath the nest. Then Isla guided the way along a criss-crossing patch of short ledges and narrow foot holds. They passed beneath the nest on a lip no wider than the length of her foot, then travelled another thirty feet clinging to the side of the cliff.

"A bit farther." Isla breathed hard from the exertion and the ache in her arms and head. "You're doing great."

"I feel as if I will fall to my death at any moment; that's not doing great." Cabela's eyebrows were bent in a permanent V.

"Watch what I do." Isla rested on her knees. "I'm going to hang off the edge, then drop to the landing below. It's about ten feet, but stretched out, it'll be half that. It's grassy. It won't be a hard landing. I'll go first." She found a solid grip on two rocks and lowered herself over the edge. Stretched out, she held her breath and released the rocks. She hit the grass, rolled, then got to her feet. "Your turn. Remember to roll."

"I don't like heights." She peered over the side. "I can't do it."

"You'd rather stay on that ledge for eternity?"

Grumbling floated over the edge, then a pair of feet appeared. "I can't let go. I want to go back up."

"I'll wait. Your arms will eventually get tired and..."

Cabela dropped to the grass in front of her.

"That didn't take long. You should work on your arm muscles."

"I am not happy about this."

"But you're alive." Isla led her quickly along the grassy edge to the point where they had to make the twenty-foot drop to safety. She hunted for a secure place to hold onto while she dangled over the edge. Once she found it, she fell to her knees. "Last one."

Cabela stepped back. "I can't. Too far. I'll die." She brushed stray hairs soaked in blood from her battered face.

Someone screamed, and Isla whirled to watch the scene in the distance. Lyneth and McGuigan used their swords to defend against the two harpies. Rocks flew from beneath a tree, and she strained to see who threw them, but the person was concealed well by bushes.

"Come on," she said to Cabela. "If the harpies notice us, they'll attack and on this ledge, we have little hope of fighting them off." Cabela sat on the edge beside her, and she used a softer voice to entice her to jump. "When you let go, relax your body; let it flow. When you hit the ground, let if crumble naturally and roll across the grass. Watch how I do it."

"Did you use relax and jump off a twenty-foot cliff in the same sentence?"

"Possibly." Isla clung to the rocks and hoisted herself over the side. This fall was going to hurt. The alternative wasn't better, so she released the rock and let herself free fall. The ground came quicker than she anticipated, and she allowed her body to fall, then roll to the side. Taking a moment to let her muscles relax, she assessed the damage. Her knee hurt, but it wasn't too painful. She rose slowly, putting weight on both feet and found them uninjured. Gazing up at Cabela, she forced a smile. "Your turn." She'd give the girl a moment; fear of heights wasn't overcome easily. She had conquered them in the towers of Blackvale Castle.

"I'm going to die." Cabela sat on the edge.

"Okay. I'm waiting."

"You are a horrible girl. I will slap you when I'm able." She tossed her bow and quiver of arrows to the ground below.

Isla picked them up. "If you're slapping me, you're not dead."

She grumbled as she positioned herself to fall the twenty feet. "I don't like you."

Now that she was hanging on the edge, it wouldn't be long. Isla counted the seconds: five. The girl dropped, landed on her feet and fell flat. A deep groan escaped her mouth.

"You didn't roll," said Isla. "But I'm sure you're not dead."

Cabela gritted her teeth. "I think I broke my leg."

Isla fell to her knees and straightened the injured leg with care. "Where does it hurt?"

"Everywhere." She slapped her. "That's for making me jump."

The slap was to make a point and didn't carry much strength, or Isla would have slapped her back. Her face was already so sore, one more bruise didn't matter. "Here?" She pressed on the knee, and when Cabela shook her head, she moved to her ankle.

"Ouch. That's it."

"Twisted ankle." Isla stood. "Let's get off this ledge and under cover." She helped her stand and braced her weight on her shoulder.

They stumbled along the five-foot wide ledge towards the forest. The slight incline made the going slower, but they soon reached the cover of the trees where they stopped to rest.

"Once you get your wind," said Isla, "we'll get to a safer location." She stared in the direction of the fight, wanting to reach her friends quickly but not wanting to make the ankle injury worse.

Lyneth rolled and came up with a dagger in her hand. She flung it quickly, striking the dark-haired harpy in the arm. The strange creature flinched but didn't fall. Instead, she held up her hand and shot another gust of wind. Besides their powerful talons, the strong gust appeared to be the harpies only weapon.

McGuigan cursed from being blown over again and jumped to his feet, sword in hand to defend himself against the second harpy that had arrived from the nest. This one had yellow hair and was as menacing as the first.

Deaglan remained half hidden, pelting the harpies with rocks. He'd made several solid hits, but this only made them angry.

Lyneth glanced at the ledge where Jack had once stood. She hadn't seen Liam go over, but Jack had tried to pull him up. A twinge of pain erupted in her chest, and she pushed the thought aside. She had to focus on the wretched beasts before her and once they were defeated, she'd gather her team and assess the damage.

The dark-haired harpy dove for Deaglan who came out to gather more rocks. Seeing her chance, Lyneth rushed forward and struck the woman's wing, slicing it off at the elbow. Sharp cries erupted before she drove the sword home, silencing the despicable woman for good.

McGuigan grunted and stumbled backwards, wiping his eyes vigorously. The harpy knocked the sword from his hand, and he swung his fists at her, connecting with a solid punch and sending her to the ground.

Lyneth raced forward but didn't reach him before he ran into the grassy clearing with the harpy on his heels. The creature knocked him to the ground and grabbed hold of his leg with her sharp talon. She dragged him along the grass as she struggled to lift him into the air.

Lyneth ran faster, her heart pounding, fear of losing him clouding her mind. She sheathed the sword and put all her effort into running, closing the distance between them slowly.

McGuigan thrashed about, but this didn't deter the harpy, and she lifted him off the ground. He hovered three feet in the air for several seconds before the harpy gathered more wind beneath her wings and lifted him higher.

Seeing her chance fading quickly, Lyneth leapt up and caught hold of McGuigan's arms to weigh him down. The harpy flapped its wings harder, slowly regaining the height it had lost.

A quick buzz was followed by a solid thud, then another round of buzz and thud. The harpy lurched, then released McGuigan.

Lyneth crashed to the ground with McGuigan in her arms. Regaining her balance, she embraced him, relieved he had escaped. His arms wrapped around her and held tightly. She stared into his face, one young and still innocent. Over the two years they'd travelled together, she'd grown accustom to his presence, and she didn't want to think about travelling without him. The emotions confused her and, lost for words, she kissed the top of his head and cradled him while she caught her breath.

"Thank you." His voice shook.

"You're welcome." She patted his shoulder and released him. "We better see to the rest." Rising to her feet, she reached down to help him up. The harpy lay in a heap a short distance away with two arrows sticking out of its back. She glanced in the direction the arrows had travelled from and saw Deaglan standing with Isla and a young female elf. "We have company." One who has an excellent shot with a bow.

Isla was accounted for; that left Jack and Liam, and their prognoses wasn't good.

18

Memories Stirred from Another Place

ISLA FORCED HER HORSE to navigate the treacherous path faster, not wanting to take more time than necessary to reach Liam and Jack. When she learnt they had gone over the cliff, she had run to the edge, searched the ground below and found nothing at the bottom of the four-hundred-foot drop. That meant one of two things: they were alive and moving, or they lay hidden amongst the rocks and dirt. She put her mind on the first reason, understanding both were injured and in need of immediate assistance.

"Slow down." Lyneth trailed her but had fallen behind. "Don't wreck your horse."

She fought against the urge to push harder and slowed her pace, stretching her neck to find a sign of the men. All she saw was endless bushes, rocks and grass that stretched into the valley.

Traversing the rough terrain at a steady pace, she approached the location she believed lay beneath the cliff they'd tumbled over. From below, the land high above looked the same. She had mentally marked the spot with a large boulder, but she'd already past two similar large stones since reaching the valley.

Her eyes constantly swept the area, but Liam or Jack were nowhere in sight. That was a good sign. From the height of the horse, she peered around small grassy hills, over low-lying rocks and into the shadows where they might have fallen. Where had they gone? She increased her search area and scanned the land towards the valley and along the rocky wall. Where were they?

"Spread out!" She called over her shoulder. "They aren't here." She gazed up at the ledge again. Her eyes ached from the strain, and the swelling from the cut above her left brow made it difficult to use that eye fully.

Lyneth stopped beside her. "Are you certain this is the location?"

"Yes." But part of her second-guessed her answer.

McGuigan stopped twenty feet away. "It's the same spot. I remember that tree." He pointed to a large oak, its leaves turning yellow from the short days. "Over there." He moved his horse towards the rock wall. "It's them." His voice came quick.

Isla followed. Tucked beneath a small overhang on a grassy bank, she saw two figures: one upright, the other laying down. She wiped sweat and dried blood from her eyes to see clearer. It *was* them.

McGuigan reached them first, and he jumped from the horse and ran to them, stumbling over the uneven ground.

By the time she arrived by his side, he'd already made a quick assessment.

"Both are unconscious." He called over his shoulder to Lyneth, Deaglan and Cabela, who rode on the back of the boy's horse. "Quickly!"

Isla dropped to her knees and placed a hand on Liam's cheek. He hadn't looked up or acknowledged their presence. She dipped to see if his eyes were open; they weren't. His skin felt cold, and he visibly shivered. He'd given his coat to Jack and with the low temperature, his body had chilled. He appeared to be in the early stages of quavers.

"Is he...?" Impatient, McGuigan grabbed Liam by the shoulder and shook him.

Liam woke with a start, grabbed McGuigan's arm and stared as if blind.

"Liam." Isla grabbed his other shoulder, and his dark eyes turned to her. "Can you hear me?" His eyes darted from her face to Jack, then back again. "Liam." She caressed his cheek. "Can you hear?" He nodded slowly. "Are you injured?" He shook his head, but she doubted his response.

"Jack." His voice cracked, and his face twisted in anguish. "Help him, please."

"Is he dead?" Deaglan hovered over them.

"Alive," said McGuigan.

"He looks barely so." Lyneth placed a hand under Jack's nose. "Let's get him assessed, and if we can move him, we'll do it." She glanced around the valley. "I feel exposed here."

Isla slipped her hand beneath the layers of clothing and spread it over Jack's chest. His skin was warm with excited energy, making her fingertips tingle. A finger touched a solid object: his stone. She placed her hand over it, and it pulsated. Leaving it for later consideration, she spread her fingers over his chest and searched for damage: it was extensive.

Her nerves tensed, and memories stirred from another place and time when a similar situation made her save a life, one that was better left to drift away. Kiefer suffered his final days because of her. Would she commit Jack to the same painful end?

"Isla? What do you say?" Lyneth leant close. "Can we move him?"

Her lips froze, not knowing what was best for Jack, not knowing if he'd survive transport. Then she felt something else: the same positive energy she'd felt in his stone travelled his blood and sent pulsating signals to her fingers.

"Isla?" Liam cupped her face in his hands and gawked into her eyes. "You're alive." His lips trembled. "I thought you died; left me here."

"I'd never leave you." She kissed him, lingering on his mouth so he'd feel her warmth.

"Jack." His eyes pleaded with her. "Can you help him? Please. Save him."

"We will; we'll help you both." She turned to Lyneth. "We can transport him to a safer location."

Lyneth stood. "McGuigan, get your horse. Deaglan and... What's your name again?"

"Cabela."

"Help get this man on McGuigan's horse." She removed the jacket from Jack's chest. "Put your arm out."

"Jack needs it," said Liam quickly. "He'll freeze." He held his arms close to his chest.

"Jack will be fine, but you won't be if you don't warm soon. Give me your arm. That's an order." She grasped his wrist, and he let her have it. Once the jacket was on, she helped him button it, then spoke to McGuigan. "Mount and push back. We'll prop him up into your arms side saddle."

McGuigan did as he was told, then waited with open arms to receive Jack. Being taller and stronger than the older man, he easily held him once he got him into position.

Isla helped Liam to stand, but he'd been in the same position for so long and was so cold, he collapsed. "Deaglan. Help me."

The young elf grabbed one of Liam's hands and pulled him to his feet, then he heaved him off the ground and into his arms.

"I didn't expect that," said Isla.

"I'm no weak Wilma. Where do you want him?"

"The back of my horse." She mounted, then helped Liam get into position behind her. "Will you be okay?" She glanced over her shoulder. He nodded, and she guided her horse into a gentle walk.

The small group rode to the edge of the valley, then cut into the forest and set a path to intercept the trail through Yikker Wood. After travelling a mile into the cover of the mammoth trees, Lyneth chose a camping spot.

"McGuigan, Deaglan, Cabela make a fire and be quick about it. I've got the horses." She eased Jack from the saddle and carried him to where the fire would be constructed.

Isla held onto Liam as he slid from the saddle, but he still fell when he hit the ground. She jumped down and tried to help him to his feet.

He pushed her away. "Forget me." His voice was low and rough. "Bury Jack."

She grabbed the front of his coat and jerked him forward. "I'll never forget you. Now get up, or I'll drag you to the firepit." He accepted her help, and she sat him next to Jack.

"I'll get the blankets." Lyneth removed bedrolls from the back of horses, spread one near the fire and moved Jack to it. She wrapped several blankets around Liam, who curled into a ball and closed his eyes.

While the others worked to build the fire and set up camp, Isla removed Jack's boots, scabbard and daggers, then tucked him beneath the blankets. She unfastened the top five buttons of his shirt to gain access to his chest but left his stone covered to keep this secret between them. As she assessed the damage from the fall, her curiosity piqued, and she sneaked a glimpse of the stone; it was blue, the same colour as Willow's stone. Jack was no picket like Nyx.

She again evaluated the damage inflicted from the fall and found slight improvements since she'd first found him at the bottom of the cliff. Agitated energy still travelled through his blood, zipping from one injury to the next. What was it doing? She rested her head against his chest, closed her eyes and listened, letting her fingertips follow the pulsing energy. After a long silence, she knew. Incredible.

"How's he doing?" McGuigan set a rock in place for the firepit.

"Good. I think... Yes, he'll be fine."

"Great." His face brightened, and he went off to gather more rocks.

She searched Jack for additional injuries and found his right shoulder had taken the impact of the fall. His jacket was torn in the same location. She removed the jacket and stretched her hands over the wound. Mending tissues came easy, but bones were another matter, so she lay still and focussed on the large bone in the upper arm and the fleshy pieces connecting it to the body. Slowing her breathing, she fell into a tranquil state and thought of Jack's smile and all the good memories her das had shared with her. Her hands warmed, and the energy within his body danced to her song, mending the cracks in the bones and the disconnection from the body. She'd never felt this in anyone she'd mended, and it left her feeling as if the healing had been a celebration of sorts.

"Your face."

The solemn voice disturbed her, and she looked up to find Liam staring at her with the saddest of expressions.

"You are injured," he said softly and clutched the blanket tightly. "I cannot help you."

"Liam, I don't expect you to help." She forced a smile. "Are you warming up?"

"It doesn't matter."

"It matters to me." She buttoned Jack's shirt, then examined the rest of his body. His right hip was as bad as his shoulder. "McGuigan, can you help me?"

"Sure." He set the load of sticks next to Lyneth, who had the fire started, and went to her.

"Help me remove his trousers. He's wearing shorts." She winked. "It'd be awkward if he wasn't."

"A man on The Trail who wears shorts." He grinned. "A rare find."

"You wear them."

"I'm a rare find." He lifted Jack's midsection while Isla pulled off the trousers. "You can explain to him why he's not wearing pants." He pulled her into his arms and kissed the side of her head. "You had me worried." He gently wiped her cheek with the end of his sleeve. "It looks like they poked you with nails."

"Fingernails. Horrible witches."

He released her and went for more firewood.

She slipped her hand into Jack's shorts and rested it on his hip. In all her healing sessions, this was the most awkward, and she tried to think of it as just another skin surface. She spread her four fingers wide, covering his hip and a small section of his buttocks. The hip bone had been fractured, and severe bruising above it had caused minor internal bleeding.

No sooner had her fingers set to weaving together the damaged tissue than Jack's energy once again answered her call and aided in the healing. Her magic danced with his in smooth rhythm and together, they efficiently mended the bone and the tissues.

"Drink it." Lyneth knelt in front of Liam with a cup of tea.

"Give it to Isla."

"I made this for you." She peered into his downward face. "You need it more than she does."

"I don't need anything." He pulled his bent legs against his chest and rested his head upon his knees.

"He's still in shock." Isla removed her hand and pulled the blankets up to Jack's neck, tucking them in at the side to preserve heat. "Let me have it." She took the tea and sat next to Liam. Lyneth returned to the fire, and Isla took a sip of the warm liquid. "Mmm, you'll love this. She made a great cup." She wrapped her arm around his shoulder and kissed his ear. It was cold. He sat on the cold ground several feet from the fire. "It's your turn to get my attention." She set the tea on a flat rock and knelt in front of him. "I'm not leaving you." She slowly lifted his head from his knees. "You don't plan on leaving me, do you?"

His brow bent, and his lips pressed together.

"Once you get warm, you'll feel better." She cupped his trembling face and kissed his cold lips. "Take a sip. It will help." She reached for the tea and held it to his mouth.

"You should drink it."

"I'm not cold."

He touched her cheek. "Your face is horrible."

"Flattery. Please, don't write a love letter in this state. Drink." She pressed the cup to his lip and tipped it. He sipped and spied on her over the rim.

"Jack died because of me."

"He's not dead."

Tears pooled in his eyes. "He died in my arms."

She set down the tea, pulled back the blankets and put Liam's hand on Jack's chest. "He lives."

His eyes widened and he leant over Jack, peering into his face and pressing his hands against his chest. "But...he died. I felt it. But...he is hot." He pressed his ear against Jack's chest. "I hear his heart. Impossible."

"Not impossible. And now that he is resting peacefully—"

"He *is* dead?"

"Not that peacefully. He sleeps in dreamland." She tucked in Jack and removed the blankets from Liam's shoulders. "I'll make up your bed, so you can get warm."

"I want to stay here." He clung to Jack. "Keep him safe. He gave his life for mine. No one's ever done that."

Her heart skipped, and she couldn't deny him the security of knowing their friend was alive and healing. "Let me make up your bed next to him."

"No, I'll stay here."

"As cute as that is, I'm doubting you'll survive the night." She put her arm around his shoulder. "Drink your tea and eat your ration, warm up and then I'll tuck you inside Jack's blankets, so you can both stay warm. You'll be pillow pals."

"I am warm."

"You are far from warm." She grabbed his hand and held it in front of his face; it shook. "You think Jack is hot because you are freezing."

"Give me the tea."

"That's what I like to hear." She handed him the tea. "I'll get the food ready." But first, she spread a folded blanket beside Jack and got Liam to sit on it facing the fire. Then she wrapped the blankets around him and position them to gather heat streaming from the flames.

By the time the sun rested on the horizon, Isla had Liam fed, warm and tucked beside Jack, where he quickly fell asleep. His demeanor had softened and was less self-destructive by the time he settled, and his usual pleasantness had returned somewhat.

She glanced at Cabela sitting between her and Deaglan. The girl had tended to her own injuries with Deaglan showering her with constant attention. What ever she needed, he jumped to get. He'd also given her two of his blankets after she declined his offer of sharing his bedroll with her. The two elves played a game of 'let's see what he'll do for me' and 'what will she let me do for her'. She smiled at the antics, knowing it would wear off in a few days.

Cabela's campsite was somewhere towards Allestree. She had agreed to travel with them until that point, then she'd relieve them of her company. Deaglan had protested, feeling it would be safer if she travelled with them due to her sprained ankle. She assured him she'd be fine.

"Where did you learn to shoot like that?" Lyneth popped a piece of dried fruit into her mouth.

"That wasn't me." Cabela pulled her blanket tighter over her shoulders.

"Who shot the arrows?"

"Me." Deaglan grinned.

Lyneth stopped chewing and stared at him. "You weren't bragging?"

"I don't brag."

Lyneth almost choked on her food, and Isla and McGuigan laughed.

"With a shot like that," said Isla, "we should pick him up a bow."

"I agree. It would have been handy today." Lyneth ate a mixture of nuts. "When we reach Allestree."

Isla yawned. Although it wasn't late, her body felt tired. She gazed at the full moon in the clear sky; it was going to be a cold night. Those on watch would feed the fire as needed, which would keep the worst of the chill off. She yawned again, bringing tears to her eyes. She gave Cabela her blanket. "You need this more than I do."

"What are you?" asked Cabela. "Invincible to the cold like you are to height?"

"I'll be plenty warm beneath that mound of blankets." She'd lay beside Jack on the opposite side of Liam. "In fact, this is one too many." She removed a blanket and gave it to her.

"Thank you."

"It's compensation for forcing you to climb a cliff to save your life."

"Right." Her comment hinted at sarcasm.

Isla removed her boots and set them near the fire before she crawled under the blankets and tucked herself into Jack's side. Both he and Liam were toasty warm. Feeling sleep move in quickly, she rested her head on his chest and took a deep breath. Dizziness overtook her, and slumber claimed the sounds around her.

Movement tugged on Isla's mind but sleep held fast, not wanting her to stir. She yearned to remain lost in the emptiness of slumber. Sound pricked her ear, and her body drew nearer the anchor that secured her in dreamland though no dreams had played while she'd slept. Wiggling touched her nerves, prying a wedge between sleep and awake, and she released a low moan. Her body craved rest, and it fought every disturbance from the outside.

"Isla."

That was her name, but she refused to respond. Instead, she tumbled back into the darkness and released the muscle she'd disturbed to acknowledge the sounds and movement.

"Isla, I need to move."

The words tumbled through her brain, and she clenched her muscles. More wiggling resulted in her senses awakening further. She groaned and stretched her legs. Sunshine burnt her eyes as she slowly opened them, making her squeeze them shut several times before she focussed on the mound of blankets before her. She peeked across Jack's chest and found Liam also stirring from sleep. His handsome face in slumber made her smile.

"Isla?"

She raised her head; Jack stared back at her.

"Good," he said. "You *are* alive."

"As much as you." She rolled her tongue around her mouth to gather spit.

He wiggled his right arm from between them, grasped her wrist and removed her hand from his gemstone. "Inappropriate." He tossed her hand aside.

She remembered dwarfs broke fingers if someone other than their mate touched their union stone, so she curled her fingers and held her hand against her chest. But Nyx had said the stone wasn't a union stone. "Sorry. I didn't know where my hand was."

He wiggled his legs. "Where are my trousers?"

"We removed them, so I... Your hip was badly damaged."

He gave her a peculiar look. "I see. Your mate was thinking heavy as a rock, not light as a feather."

Liam lifted his head. "I tried."

"Try sooner next time."

"Yes, sir."

"My hip was heavily damaged, yet..."

"As was your shoulder," she said.

"Yet..." He rolled his shoulder. "It feels miraculously healed."

"Your body is amazing." A sly smile creased her lips.

"It is, but this is unprecedented. Either I did not sustain severe damage as you claim or..." he raised an eyebrow, "other forces achieved the desired outcome."

"You may never know."

He rested a hand on her shoulder, wiggled his other arm free and put it on Liam's shoulder. "I feel..."

"Warm?" she offered.

"Yes, but..."

"Cosy?"

"Not the word I seek."

"Loved?"

He glanced between the two hauflins. "That. Also squished, crowded, encumbered. What do I owe this...attention?"

"You died," said Liam.

"Almost," she said.

"No, he died."

She stared. He had been in no condition to know Jack was alive but hanging on.

"I couldn't hear his heart."

"I truly was on the brink of death." Jack patted their heads. "But now, I must move. Scoot and fetch my trousers." They slipped from beneath the blankets, and he sat up and groaned. "My body disagrees." He sunk into the soft mound.

"Give it time." Isla pulled the blankets over his chest. "You suffered greatly." She took his trousers from near the fire and stretched them along his side beneath the blankets. "You can keep them warm and when you're ready to rise, you'll have them."

"Thank you." He moved his shoulder slowly, stretching it one way then the other. "It appears I owe more than I can repay."

Halfway to her feet, she stopped and knelt beside him. "Consider it paid in full. You saved Liam without thought for your safety. A truer friend I will not find." She grasped his hand and held it between both of hers. "The Trail offers many surprises and has exposed me to horrible people, but it has also delivered many wonderful folk who have touched my heart deeply, those I'm thankful to know who've made me a better person, and those who I would suffer greatly if I had to live without. I'm happy to have met you, Jack. My parents' stories of praise have not done you justice."

She released his hand and stood. "I will fix you something warm to eat while you stretch and get those muscles working."

The rest had already risen from their bedroll and were in various stages of their morning routine. She joined in, taking care of the washing first, then prepared the meal for her, Liam and Jack. By this time, Jack was hobbling and favouring his right leg. Liam kept watch over him and if he anticipated his need, he'd jump to get it.

By mid-morning, the horses were saddled, and the gear was packed. Isla mounted and waited for Liam, who held Jack's horse steady while he got into the saddle. Once the man was up and settled, Liam left his side and walked slowly towards her.

"Ride in front of us," said Liam.

"I'll be fine." Jack adjusted the reins.

"And you'll ride in front of us."

Isla grinned at Jack's expression. "Liam, come on, or we'll have no one to follow." Lyneth, Deaglan and Cabela had already started on the trail. McGuigan waited for them and would take up the rear.

Liam jumped into the saddle behind her, settled in close and wrapped his arms around her waist. His eyes remained on Jack.

"I've been on the end of this attention," she said over her shoulder. "I enjoyed it, but I sense Jack likes his independence and doesn't want you fussing over him."

"Fussing? I'm helping."

"When the helping turns to fussing, I'll tell you."

"It won't."

All morning, his attention had been on Jack; he not once looked at her unless it was in passing. "Is my face still horrible?"

"Horrible?" His eyes were glued on the rider in front of them.

"Yesterday you said I looked horrible."

"Impossible." He regarded her. "You have bruises, slight swelling, odd pick marks, but... What are they from?"

"Sharp fingernails."

He winced. "Despite the marks, you are beautiful to me."

She raised an eyebrow. "Not horrible?"

He pulled closer. "Never." He snuggled into her neck. "I feared I had lost you and that made life not worth continuing."

"Did you let go?" This hadn't occurred to her.

"No. I slipped."

"Unless you hold my lifeless body in your hands, never give up on me; never give up hope." She pressed into him. "I will hold out the same hope for you."

"I hope that won't be until we're 350, and then we can rest together."

"That's a long time for us to ride The Trail."

He kissed her neck. "I'll have you home safe long before then. I told your das I would, and I'll not break that promise."

Home. It was in Maskil for her, a place he had said he hated. She hoped time changed that and when they settled, it'd be somewhere near her parents or in the Hauflin Quarter. But that wouldn't be for a long time. At the moment, she preferred The Trail.

The day passed quickly, and night found them camped under the protection of the great trees with a fire glowing in the centre of the group. Feeling tired from the journey, Isla settled into her bedroll soon after eating and snuggled into her blankets to find a comfortable position. Her body hungered for sleep, and she let it claim her.

Deep in dreamland, movement behind her chafed a nerve, but she didn't acknowledge it. A cool breeze followed by warmth touched her senses, then a force tightened around her waist and pressed against her back. The familiar scent stirred her blood and made her heart skip. Sound of quick breathing filled her ear and warm moist breath flowed and ebbed across her neck.

She woke with a start and lifted her head, disturbing Jack who lay on the bedroll near hers. He looked at her in the fire light, saw the source of the disturbance, then turned to his other side.

Without looking, she knew who had crawled beneath her blankets, but she didn't know why. Liam whimpered softly and strengthened his embrace. Kissing her neck gently, he rested his cheek against her head.

"What's wrong?" she whispered.

"I'm sorry."

"You've said that."

"I didn't mean to wake you; I wanted to..." he swallowed, "hold you like this. Feel you next to me." He rubbed his chin against her and kissed her neck again. "I fear I'll never have the pleasure of being with you."

"Nonsense." She turned and pulled him near. "We will always be together."

"Can I stay?" he pleaded, the dancing firelight highlighting his misty eyes. "Here? With you?"

"You'd not be able to escape now that I have you." She kissed him, lingering on his lips. "Stay with me always."

"It's my greatest wish, and my greatest fear is not surviving to see it through." He caressed her cheek. "Please, let me hold you as if...as if we've shared more than a kiss. I want to know the feeling in case—"

She placed her fingers over his lips. "Hold me to know what to anticipate without fear."

He tucked her head against his chest and laid his bent leg on her hip. "You deserve better."

"Better than a loyal man, one my blood burns for hotter than an inferno drenched in dragon spit?" She spanked his bottom playfully. "Now shush and let me sleep in your arms."

19

Gabardine at Dusk

MCGUIGAN STRETCHED HIS NECK to see why the horses walking in front of him slowed. For two days, they'd travelled the trail through Yikker Wood, steering clear of open areas void of gigantic trees to ensure the griffin didn't return to recapture Isla or Cabela. The weather had turned colder but no snow fell.

The girl named Cabela was pretty and self-sufficient. Deaglan had jumped to assist her before McGuigan had a chance, and now she rode without question on the back of his horse. When she spread her bedroll beside Lyneth or Isla, the boy immediately grabbed the spot next to her, giving him no chance to learn about her. Every conversation he started, Deaglan butt in and listened. He'd bide his time, smile at her, be overly polite and when he found the right moment, he'd talk to her.

The group gathered on the edge of a clearing and secured their horses beneath the cover of large trees. He scanned the grassy area and saw camping equipment, but there was no one about.

Cabela slid from the horse. "Nothing's been touched."

It was her camp, the place where the griffin had captured her. He ducked and searched the sky for the beast; it was no where in sight. Riding his horse deeper into the woods, he dismounted and tied it to a tree. If this was her camp, then she'd part ways with them. He cursed at

Deaglan under his breath for not giving him a chance to get to know her better.

"You had a horse?" Lyneth walked around the campsite.

"I did." Cabela tramped into the trees where she found a broken lead. "It snapped its line."

Cabela had been gone for three days; the horse could be anywhere. McGuigan walked through the trees skirting the camp to find sign of it, hoping if he did, it'd start a conversation and she'd be grateful to him.

"Its tracks go this way." Deaglan hurried into the forest. "I'll find it for you."

Again, McGuigan cursed under his breath. The boy bragged about tracking and trapping animals; he'd have no problem finding it and bringing it back to impress her.

"McGuigan, go with him," said Lyneth. "Don't go too far. The horse is not worth losing your way."

He grumbled but followed Deaglan across the relatively flat forest floor blanketed with dried orange evergreen needles. The boy hustled, and he had to walk fast to keep up with him. Less than a quarter of a mile away, they came upon a narrow stream meandering through a grassy field that stretched for several hundred feet in each direction.

"And there is the prize." Deaglan trotted towards a dapple-grey mare that wore a leather halter and grazed nearby.

Great! The boy gained popularity with the girl.

"Get on." Deaglan rode bareback and used the mane to help guide him.

He hoisted himself onto the back of the horse and let the boy ride into camp, celebrating his find.

"Shoo-shoo! You found her!" Cabela dropped her rucksack and ran to the horse.

"Shoo-shoo?" Isla squished her nose. "That can't be its name."

McGuigan jumped down beside her.

"You have a better name for your horse?" Cabela hugged the animal and patted its neck.

"Sure do. Two-bit."

"We named it Spindrift," said Liam.

"Two-bit Spindrift," said Isla. "It's better than Shoo-shoo. Sounds like you're trying to scare it away."

"Sounds like your horse is an untrained, broken-down nag."

"She's learning."

"You love this horse?" asked Deaglan standing next to her.

"I do. I've had her since I was a little girl."

He held out his arms. "I'm glad I found her." She made no move towards him, so he slipped his arm around her waist. "I hope it makes you happy."

McGuigan hid his grin. Cabela showed no interest in hugging the boy. They were the same age, but she was more mature than he was.

"Now that we've found the camp," Lyneth stood in the middle of the group, "the offer still stands. You can continue on alone, or you're welcome to travel with us to Allestree."

"Come with us, Cabela." Deaglan patted her horse. "You can leave at any time, but I'd like you to stay. It'll provide a chance to teach you how to steady your arrow."

McGuigan thought Deaglan would fall to his knees and beg her to stay. He'd never stoop to that level. Leaving the conversation for the others to settle, he walked to his horse, pulled out a piece of hard bread and put it into his mouth to suck on until it softened. Seeing Jack resting on a large stone nearby, he sat next to him.

"Looking forward to a warm bed?" McGuigan rolled the hard bread around his mouth and wished he had a mint jelly candy to add sweetness to the flavour.

"I seldom dwell on such luxuries." Jack stretched his right leg in front of him, twisted the toe one way, then the other. He still walked with a limp, but he had assured everyone he'd be fine.

"When we reach Allestree, do you want to share a room?" He'd rather bunk with Jack than Deaglan.

"We'll not be staying, will we?"

"We'll spend one night, enjoy the warmth before we head out again. It gives us a break from each other."

"A break from Deaglan?"

He huffed. "That, too."

"And money is not a problem?"

"For the room?" When he nodded, he continued. "We get paid well for what we do."

"What is it you do?" Jack raised an eyebrow.

"Deliver packages." He frowned in Deaglan's direction. "We were paid to deliver the boy to his aunt, but..."

"You failed to deliver?"

"We delivered, but he trailed us; said he wanted adventure, not study class, and by the time we discovered him, we were a week out of Inglenook."

"Would his aunt not search for him?"

"We're going to send her a letter when we get to Allestree to let her know where he is, so she won't worry."

"And?"

To his knowledge, no one had told Jack about Morwen and Rhys. The man had been relieved to learn he, Kiefer and Lyneth had survived the Tigh na Mare attack but hadn't asked about anyone else.

"Two others survived from..." he leant close and whispered in his ear, "The Mercenaries."

"You don't say," whispered Jack. "Tell me, please."

"Morwen and Rhys."

A smile creased his lips and light ignited in his eyes. "It does the heart good to know the mates live on. How does this tie into Deaglan?"

"Morwen is his aunt."

"Incredible. Did you know?"

"Not until we delivered him."

"You must have been as shocked as I am."

"We were." He grinned. "I prefer these types of pleasant shocks."

"As do I." He placed a hand on McGuigan's shoulder and squeezed it. "I'll share your room. It'll be peaceful with good company."

Isla walked over and when he caught her eye, he saw a hint of frustration. She sat on his knee and rested her arm across his shoulder. "Cabela has decided to accompany us."

"You don't want her to?" asked McGuigan.

"It's not her." She crinkled her nose. "She's a little bossy, but I can sass that back. It's Deaglan. He's pathetic."

"A boy in love." Jack chuckled.

"A boy in foolishness," said McGuigan.

"You were less foolish at his age?"

"I was not like that." He drove his finger in Deaglan's direction.

Liam came to stand near them and rested his arm on Isla's shoulder. "I had to walk away. He's unbelievable. I tried to help gather her things to make packing faster, but Deaglan grabbed them from my hands, insisting he do everything."

"As Deaglan says, I smell opportunity," said McGuigan. "Let's take advantage of this."

"Or maybe you should let it pass." Jack fastened the top button of his jacket. "Young men, I expect you to set a good example."

"Just a wee bit of fun then." McGuigan chuckled until Jack glared at him. "A very small wee bit of fun. Liam?"

He smirked. "A subtle wee bit of fun."

"Great gemstones, I want none of it." Jack stood and stretched his back. "Perhaps a little maturity will help."

"Is that all you have to offer, Jack?" asked Isla. "A *little* maturity?"

He puffed. "You are sassy," he said and walked away.

Liam took Jack's seat next to McGuigan. "What's your plan?"

"I'm thinking. It has to be embarrassing but it can't disturb the group, or Jack will be mad."

Isla moved to Liam's knee and rested her arm on his shoulder. "Is he afraid of squirrels?"

McGuigan made a face. "What do squirrels have to do with this?"

She giggled, and her eyes danced.

Mid-morning three days later, Lyneth stared at the cold blue sky. Below it, the landscape transformed from gigantic trees that obscured the sunshine to an expansive wide-open meadow that stretched for nearly a mile in front of her. She upturned her face to the sun and let its rays seep into her pores, raising the temperature on her skin and blinding her temporarily. Breathing in the fresh warm air cleared her mind and swept away the previous three weeks of cold, snow and shadows. By late tomorrow, they'd arrive at a keep to replenish their supplies, adding much needed variety to their meals.

The two partridges Deaglan had caught the night before had provided them with much-needed meat, and Jack's addition of mushrooms and spices increased the tastiness of the shared ration. Isla added the few potatoes she had stowed away. To break the fast, they ate oatmeal sprinkled with cinnamon.

Halfway across the meadow, Lyneth saw the first dwelling in the distance. It was nestled on the edge of a small wooded area, surrounded on two sides by barren fields that had already been harvested and one side by pasture that supported a flock of sheep. She'd no sooner passed it than from behind her, Cabela asked, "Where's she going?"

Lyneth twisted and found Isla riding the long path towards the dwelling. She halted and twisted farther in the saddle. "Where *is* she going?"

"Does she often go off and not tell anyone what she's doing?" Cabela pouted. "Leave her. She'll catch up."

"That's not what we do." The girl was frank, too frank at times. Lyneth rode back to McGuigan in the rear of the group. "Why is she going to the crofter's dwelling?"

"She said something about eggs."

"We'll be at a keep tomorrow. She can buy them there."

"I don't think she knows that."

Isla dismounted and approached an elf, who came from one of the outbuildings. They talked for a minute, then he led her away, leaving Liam to mind the horse.

"Is she always this open to strangers?" asked Jack.

"Usually," said McGuigan.

"Does she not see the danger in approaching strangers on The Trail? Anyone could live in that dwelling."

"In my experience, people who live in these types of places are not the ones to fear."

"In all your nineteen years of living and two years on The Trail, you've come to that conclusion?"

"Yes."

His answer combined with Jack's expression triggered a grin, and Lyneth turned to hide it.

"We wait and hope for the best?" asked Jack.

"We do." She glanced at Deaglan, who had moved next to Cabela. The pair chatted quietly amongst themselves.

They waited fifteen minutes before Isla came into view, walking beside the elf who had led her away. They shook hands, and she got onto her horse and trotted towards the road. Her hand went to her mouth, and Lyneth peered across the distance, trying to identify what she was eating. As they neared, she rolled her eyes.

"They had biscuits?"

Isla grinned. "With raisins."

McGuigan groaned. "Did they have eggs?"

"They did," she said.

Liam held up a sack. "We have eggs, bacon and bread for everyone."

Isla rode close to McGuigan and pulled a small package from her pocket.

He unwrapped the paper, found two cookies inside and sniffed them. "Mmm, molasses." He bit into one. "Delicious."

"You're welcome," said Isla.

"If my mouth wasn't full, I'd kiss you." He took another bite.

"Let's move on." Lyneth returned to the front of the line.

"She didn't get me anything? Not a cookie, not a biscuit?" Cabela furrowed her brow. "I see how it is. She treats only her men."

"That was mean, Isla," shouted Deaglan over his shoulder.

"She got you bacon, eggs and bread. That's not enough?" Lyneth thought about the past several days; the girl had disturbed the easy-going nature of the group. At Allestree, they'd part ways.

"But no treat. I'm not fond of bacon," said Cabela. "Her foul behaviour is improper. It's disgusting she beds two men."

Lyneth dropped back to ride beside her. "Watch your tongue. She and McGuigan are good friends only. She is Liam's mate." She glared at her. "You're obviously too young to understand men and women can be good friends without having an intimate relationship."

"I don't believe it."

"Do you think I also bed McGuigan? We are good friends. Do you think Isla is also bedding Jack? Are you that daft?"

"She hangs off McGuigan." Cabela considered her. "You were hugging McGuigan after the harpy dropped him. Are you his mate?"

"Seems to me you're jealous." Good grief, was that it? The girl had a crush on McGuigan?

"She's not jealous of McGuigan." Deaglan, who had ridden behind them, came alongside of Cabela. "She doesn't like him."

"I'm making observations." Cabela stuck her chin in the air. "Any fool can see how they interact."

"You may not think of us as such, but we're like family," explained Lyneth. "We're close; we care about each other and what one needs, the other gives willing. We share food, laughs, tears and sometimes, we share beds, but don't ever mistake this for inappropriate behaviour. Any one of us will risk their life for the other. If you had any family at all, you'd know the value of having others who'd be there for you without doubt, without question."

Cabela clamped her mouth shut and as she stared, her eyes grew glossy, and she turned away.

Feeling she'd gotten the message through to the stubborn teen, she moved to the front of the line and led the group into the mixed forest of evergreen and deciduous trees. Gabardine, the large village in their path, was home to wood elves who prided themselves in hardy living, whimsical activities and merriment. Each time she'd passed through, she left happier than when she entered. With Deaglan and Cabela joining them, this one time might be the exception.

৪০ ❖ ୦ଓ

Isla leant against the wall in White Russel Inn listening to Lyneth discuss rooms with the keeper, who stood behind the counter. They'd arrived in Gabardine at dusk to find the first inn they visited full and this one with only two rooms remaining. The lateness of the day coupled with the snow that had started to fall at a steady pace an hour before dusk meant even hardy travellers sought comfort and warmth for the night.

Two rooms meant she'd be squished into one with Lyneth and Cabela, but she'd not be as cramped as the four boys.

Beside her, McGuigan grumbled and whispered out the side of his mouth, "Can I bunk with you?"

"I was going to ask to bunk with you." She poked him in the ribs.

Lyneth turned from the counter. "I took them. Under the circumstances, we might not find an inn with available rooms. That means boys in one and women in the other."

"Boys?" asked Jack. "Have I been demoted, or am I without a room?"

"You can sleep with the men, Jack," said McGuigan. "That's me and Liam."

"While you four sort out your masculinity and bed partners, we'll be in our room." Lyneth gave Jack a key. "This room has two double beds."

"What does our room have?" Cabela squared her jaw.

"Two single beds."

"I call one." The elf picked up her pack and prepared to move.

"Take the other, Lyneth," said Isla. "I care not where I sleep as long as it's warm and dry. The floor is good for me."

"Isla, you are too generous." Lyneth carried the lit lantern and led the way down the hall and to their door.

Isla walked with Liam until the two groups separated. His room was left, two doors down, and theirs was right, four doors down.

"Give me fifteen minutes, and we'll meet for the ration." She walked away but didn't let go, then pulled him to her lips for a kiss. "Maybe I won't let you go."

"That would eventually get awkward." His gaze swept over her face, and he squeezed her hand. "Fifteen."

"Or less." She entered the room and dropped her pack on the floor. The space in the lantern glow was small. Within it was two single beds pressed against opposite walls with a window between them. The floor space was between the beds, leaving little manoeuvring room for those in the beds to walk around her. Great. She'd hoped for a comfortable mattress with lots of space to stretch out, but this would be more cramped than next to a fire. The benefits would be staying warm and dry. Remembering the snow falling outside, perhaps this was better than the campfire but not much.

She propped her bedroll against the wall, unable to set it up until the others were in bed less it be walked on by wet boots. She tossed her jacket onto the rucksack, then sat on the floor next to it and combing her long hair with her fingers to loosen the tangles. She needed a bath, but she didn't know where to find one. Usually, she cleaned herself in her room, stripping naked and washing in a basin of warm water, but she felt too restricted in this space.

"Isla, don't sit on the floor." Lyneth sorted items from her rucksack. "Get on my bed."

She settled on the mattress with her back against the wall. "Thanks. I've slept in worse."

"You and me both."

"At least we don't have to rise at five and get the bread on." She grinned, remembering how she'd mocked 'bread rise at five' when she lived at Blackvale.

"Or sleep six to a room with all that snoring."

"I think that's where I learnt to sleep through anything."

"Six to a room." Cabela groaned. "I'd not do that."

"One day you might have no choice," said Isla. "Better hope those five others are good friends."

"You've got that right," said Lyneth.

"Places we've slept make this room look like a castle chamber."

"It makes me appreciate what I have." Lyneth closed her pack and moved it to the centre of the bed. "Ready to eat a delicious hot meal, one not served with snark?"

"Every day." She hopped off the bed. "Let's get the boys." She cleared her throat on purpose. "And Jack."

"I'm not ready." Cabela stood with a shirt in her hand.

"We'll meet you there," said Isla. "We're eating at the inn tavern."

"Honestly?" Her face bent in disgust.

"It's convenient, warm and prices are fair." She opened the door. "After you, Lyneth."

"Thank you, dear friend." She slipped through the door and pulled it closed behind her.

Halfway down the hall, Isla asked, "Are you planning to let her join us? She's very... How shall I say this politely? Rude."

"I didn't want to throw her on the cold streets at night. We'll do it in the morning."

"Good." She saw Deaglan step from the room followed by Liam and McGuigan. "Where's Jack?"

McGuigan closed the door. "He wants to rest."

She recalled his movements the past few days. His shoulder seemed fine, but he was still limping and favouring his right leg. "Liam, order me something tasty with potatoes and a biscuit. I'll be along in a few minutes."

"He said he was going to sleep." Liam put his arm in front of her. "You should leave him rest. He looks tired."

"I know he does, and that's what concerns me." She dipped beneath his arm and reached the door. "I won't be long. I want to ensure sleep is all he needs."

He nodded. "Porkchop or salmon?"

"Surprise me." She knocked on the door before opening it and then stepped inside. The lantern was set on low and hung near the doorway on an iron hook. This room was larger to accommodate two double beds and had floor space at the end of each bed to lay a bedroll if needed. This was where the boys had dumped their gear. Already, the room was in disarray.

Jack lay on his side on the edge of the bed. He appeared to be sleeping but raised his head when she approached.

"Isla? What is the matter?"

"That's what I'm asking you." She sat next to him. "You appear to be in pain."

"It will settle."

"Travelling has disturbed the healing, hasn't it?"

He nodded. "Efficient healing takes place during long rests."

"Your hip is not healed, is it?"

"It comes along."

"But not while we travel every day."

"I will manage."

"Life is not about managing."

He sighed. "It feels as though it is."

"Please, let me take a peek."

"It will be fine."

"I'm concerned. It was the last I gave my attention, and I was worried for Liam. I may have missed a vital repair."

"Isla, this is unnecessary."

If he was Liam, she'd give him her look and not take no for an answer, but this was Jack. "Elspeth taught me a unique spell," she lied.

"To heal wounds?"

"No, to make you fall asleep against your will. Then I can examine your hip without protest."

He stared at her. "You wouldn't."

"You can willingly show me or take a quick nap, then..." she peered into his face with wide eyes, "I'll do whatever I want, including give you a hair cut and a shave. I might paint your toenails."

"You jest."

"I can make Tam do as I need when I tend to his wounds; you'll be as easy as making a cat dance for a piece of fish."

He paused and gripped the blankets as he tested her threat.

"What will it be Jack Somerled? A yes or a nap?"

"If you weren't an innocent child, I'd confine you to a bubble."

"Good idea. I'll trap you in a bubble from the waist up, then I won't hear you complain."

He furrowed his brow and grumbled. "A quick look. I'm sure it's fine. I need rest." He reluctantly pushed the blankets down past his hip to reveal his singlet and shorts, then he slid the shorts off his hip, exposing a large bruise.

"The colouration is dark," she said.

"The bruise causes the hurt."

"I didn't see this." She gripped the rim of his shorts and pulled them down farther while at the same time pulling up the blankets to cover his front. "Great goodness!" she gasped. "It's infected. Bad." She pulled the blankets up. "Don't move."

She ran to her room, grabbed her rucksack and raced back. "I wish I'd known sooner." She sorted several items on the small table between the beds. "Why didn't you tell me?"

"It should have healed on its own." He lay on the pillow with a blank face. "I'm no healer. I just..." He sighed and closed his eyes.

After organising what she'd need, she drew back the blanket and placed her hand on the wound. It was hot. She closed her eyes and let the energy bounce off her nerves, seeking the damage and finding the best method to heal it.

"What are you doing?" He grunted. "You're generating pain."

"Can I trust you?" She opened her eyes.

"You can." His face flushed from straining against the discomfort.

"Do you trust me?"

"I do."

"Few know what I'm to tell you: Das, Meeme, Liam, Farlan, maybe Tam." She thought of Arthur but dismissed him. "My hands use energy to mend things. The soft stuff, skin, tissue. It's easy for me, but bones are tough."

"You have the power to heal."

"Yes, like the energy inside you. That's what you have, isn't it? Self-healing. Or is it your birth gemstone that does it?" He didn't answer. "You *do* trust me. I'm trying to help."

"It's inside me. The stone channels it."

"Can you heal others?"

"No, can you self-heal?"

"No. I've tried."

"Interesting. This healing drains you."

"No, it doesn't."

"Are you not tired afterwards?"

She hadn't noticed. Her thoughts dwelt on those she'd helped or whatever she was doing.

"The morning afterwards, you were difficult to wake. That night, you were asleep early."

While that was true, she might have been tired for other reasons. "I'm not sure."

"Consider this the next time."

"Are you tired afterwards?"

"No. My healing transpires gradually, and my energy suffers no ill consequences. The injuries I sustained from the fall would naturally mend in two moons. You repair large wounds quickly, and it exhausts your energy."

"What is interesting is when I send forth my energy, your energy mixes with it. I healed you efficiently because they worked together. Let me show you." She closed her eyes and settled her hand upon his skin. His energy found hers quickly, wrapped around it and went to work mending the damage she'd missed the first time.

"Slower." He groaned. "You work too hard, too fast." He clenched his teeth. "It causes great pain."

She slowed her pace and relaxed her nerves, weaving her fingers gently over his skin, tending to the location as if she were touching a baby's face.

"Much better." His voice softened. "Soothes instead of tortures."

Time slipped by, and the peaceful rhythm of their energies weaving together the torn tissues lulled her mind, and she slipped into a trance. When his energy withdrew from hers and settled, the vibration caused her to stir. Jack remained on the edge of slumber.

She picked up the bottle of healing solution from the table. Holding a cloth to catch the run-off, she slowly poured a small amount onto his skin. It seeped into the open wound and sizzled, creating yellow foam.

"Consarn!" He braced his body, and his eyes flew open.

"I'm sorry, but it had to be done." She dabbed the foam, then poured a second helping on the wound. Again, he grunted from the pain. "I'll clean up and put ointment on it. After a few days, you'll be agile as those teenage boys you bunk with."

He released a long sigh. "Not that it matters," he mumbled.

"Excuse me?" She leant close to his face. "It matters to me, and I bet there are others it matters to."

Sadness filled his expression, and he lay still as if he'd never move again. The lines around his eyes grew deep, though she thought him to be a young newlin. Not as young as her, just older than her das. His attitude was positive, but she sensed deep sorrow when he let his guard down. Living on The Trail had drained him, and she wondered if he ever went home. Home. Who would be waiting for him there? A mate? Family? Friends? He'd never said why he travelled The Trail.

"Who are you looking for?" The question startled him. Her das had said Jack had been on The Trail when he began looking for her; to his knowledge, he had no profession. If Jack searched for someone, he'd been searching without success for more than six years.

She applied a generous amount of ointment, then laid a clean cloth over the wound. After adjusting his shorts, she pulled the blankets up to his shoulder.

He didn't answer her question, so she asked again. "If you tell me, I might be able to help? Das found me because he asked everyone, including you."

A tear slipped silently from his eye and left a trail over the ridge of his nose, plopped onto the pillow and seeped into the material. She rested her arm across his shoulder. "Please, tell me," she whispered. "Who do you search for? Another newlin?"

"I've searched everywhere three times. Four times. I've lost count."

"And you're losing hope."

His dark eyes stared at her. "If she had survived, I'd have found her by now."

"Your mate."

His brow bent as if pain raced through his head.

"Is she newlin?" He didn't answer, so she carried on. "The only newlin woman I've met aged enough to be your mate is at Dukedom of Dunakan." She shivered. "I hope it's not her. I don't like her."

He raised his head. "Describe her."

"Dirty blonde. Rotten blue eyes. She almost killed me."

"How?" He sat taller.

"She channelled poyson from the duke's mate to me."

"My mate would never do that. Was she disguised?"

"No. She appeared to be a mixture of dwarf and hauflin but the more I stared, the more curious I became. Then she told me what she was: newlin. She called herself Mystic One, but I don't think that was her real name. She was a foreteller."

"Mystic One?" he mumbled, searching the blankets as if he'd find the answer.

"You haven't encountered her?"

His eyes grew wide. "No."

"Maybe she knows your mate."

"Maybe. A foreteller? I know many, but they are all in..."

"Knavesmire?"

"Did she tell you that?"

"Sir Nyx Humbledon did."

He drew back, and his mouth dropped open. "You know Nyx?"

"I've met him. I don't know him well."

"Great gemstones." He rose to a seated position and reclined against the wall with his legs bent to rest his arms upon. "What is Nyx doing here? And if he's here, where...?" He turned to her. "Was there a woman with him?"

"No, he said he came alone."

"Good. It is best."

"What is your mate's name? Perhaps I've heard of her."

He pressed his lips together and held the name for a moment as if speaking it would drain the final hope of finding her. "Floriana." His voice cracked, and he drew a quick breath.

"I've not heard that name, but I'll keep my ears open." She forced a smile. "We'll learn her fate one way or another. You don't have to search alone anymore."

"Child, when your das praised you, I believed he did it because you were his daughter, but I see it was earned." He blinked away tears and cupped her cheek with his palm. "You make this old heart believe again. It has been many seasons since I've had a friend to confide in, longer since I've hugged another newlin."

"I'm not newlin, but I give hugs." A lump in her throat made her voice sound strange.

He drew her into his arms and squeezed tightly. "You have the power to heal wounds and broken hearts."

The door opened. Liam walked in with a plate of food, stopped and stared. "Is everything okay?"

Isla wiped the corner of her eye with her sleeve and rose off the bed. "Yes. Everything is marvellous. For me? You shouldn't have." She kissed him and took the plate of food. "Jack, do you like potatoes and salmon?"

"I do."

"Good because you need to eat to regain your strength." She set the food on the table. "We've got a long way to go, and I'm dragging you across Ath-o'Lea to see who we can shake from the turrets." She gave him the fork. "Eat or else." She wrapped her arm around Liam's waist. "You gave me back my mate, and I'll do everything in my power to return yours." Her stomach grumbled, and she placed a hand over it. "After I eat. I'll be back for the plate. Make sure it's empty."

She guided Liam out the door. Glancing back, she saw a rejuvenated newlin digging into potatoes. The hope she'd given him worked more magic than her healing hands.

20

Soft Thuds and Muffled Voices

MCGUIGAN CLOSED THE DOOR and followed Liam, Jack and Deaglan down the hall to the inn's tavern. The night had passed quietly since Jack was sleeping by the time they returned to their room, giving Deaglan no chance to talk about Cabela, who had consumed every conversation he'd had since she'd joined the group.

He spotted Lyneth sitting at the far end of the crowded room and pointed her out to the rest. They weaved around tables and patrons to reach the corner and found three chairs available. Deaglan rushed over and grabbed the one next to Cabela.

"Jack." McGuigan pulled out a chair and motioned for the man to sit.

"I'm pampered by these boys." Jack sat down. "Thank you."

"Where's Isla?" Liam stood next to the last seat but didn't claim it.

"Still sleeping," said Lyneth.

"McGuigan, sit." He stepped away from the table. "I'll stay with her until she wakes, then we'll break the fast together."

"My stuff is the room," Cabela said to him. "You can't go in there."

"My mate is in that room, and that allows me to enter at will." He walked away.

"Liam," said Lyneth. He turned, and she tossed him the key, then he continued.

"He better not touch my stuff." Cabela grumbled. "Service is horribly slow here." She stretched her neck to see if the waitress approached.

"They're busy," said Lyneth. "Appreciate their hard work. It's not easy feeding three dozen people at once. Jack." She turned her attention to him. "Isla said it would benefit you greatly if we stayed a second night and leave tomorrow."

"I do not wish to inconvenience you."

"No inconvenience. In fact, it might be to our benefit." She leant close and lowered her voice. "My former group did business in this settlement before; I wish to see if that door is still open."

"I would indeed benefit from a full day of rest, if you are willing. The rest will aid Isla as well. She has over-extended herself on my account."

"Then it's done. We'll stay a second night." She glanced out the window at the snow that still fell. "Seeing the weather, I'll happily sleep under cover for the night."

"I whole-heartedly agree."

"Do you want me to come with you?" asked McGuigan. He saw hot food heading their way, and his eyes drank in the steamy dishes.

"I'd love the company." Lyneth leant back to let the waitress set down the plate of food. "Thank you."

"You're welcome." The young elf smiled as she set Cabela's plate in front of her. "What would the men like to break the fast?"

"Bacon, eggs, potato wedges, toast, ham. Please." McGuigan grinned. He patted his belly, anticipating the warm food.

Jack and Deaglan gave the waitress their order, and she left the table.

McGuigan glanced around the room, searching for familiar faces; he didn't see any, so he followed the pleasant aroma filling the air back to Lyneth's plate. She had strongly-spiced sausages that teased his taste buds. Leaning forward, he ogled the food. She picked up his fork, stabbed a sausage and held it up to him.

"For me?" He accepted the offer. "Did I ever tell you that you were my favourite half-blood?"

"No, but I'll make a note." She bit into her toast.

The sausage was hot and spicy, and when the waitress returned with a glass of water for him, he eagerly drank. His meal soon arrived, and he dug in. The many days with sparse servings had left his appetite unquenched. While the evening ration had taken off the edge, the meal before him would satisfy it. While he was out and about with Lyneth, he'd hunt for a candy store to restock his mint jellies.

Liam watched the gentle rise and fall of Isla's blankets while she slept away the morning. Her soft breathing touched his ear as he gazed lazily upon her face, waiting for her to stir. Three hours had passed since he'd lay beside her and during that time, she hadn't moved. The soft thuds and muffled voices in the hall hadn't disturb her, hadn't caused her to twitch a muscle.

Her need for sleep had confirmed Jack's suspicions. In a private moment before they left their room to break the fast, Jack had suggested Isla's manner of healing others drained her energy, leaving her exhausted. She'd used her ability to heal Jack the night before, and now she lay in dreamland long past her usual wake time.

Seeing he knew of Isla's ability and given he was her mate, Jack had warned him of the permanent damage her generosity of healing others might cause, and that he should be wary to guard against her over-use of it. He also advised him to protect her while she recuperated from the action and to ensure she received proper rest and food to guarantee a full recovery.

Given her sassy and stubborn manner, Jack had said, *the only one capable of talking sense into her and providing the care she'll require is you. As a mate, it is your duty to ensure her safety.*

He gladly accepted that role. He'd safeguard her well-being without hesitation and give her everything she required. It might be his duty, but it was also his honour to keep her safe.

Her nose twitched, and she released a gentle sigh; she'd wake soon. He watched closely, his face inches from hers, as she stirred; the sound of her breathing drowned every other sound in the inn. Her lips moved as if to moisten her mouth, and he fought against kissing them. Instead, he wanted to capture her undisturbed waking, lock it in his memory in case one day he'd not be around to see it. Here, in the silence of the room with her heart beating slowly, he'd savour this moment and forget about the outside world. This was where he wanted to be; she was who he wanted to be with. Nothing else mattered.

Her legs stretched to their full length, and she rolled to her back and shifted her shoulders. Her lips rolled over one another and her eyelids fluttered open, allowing her to scan the ceiling, then the walls to remind her where she lay. When her eyes fell upon him, a smile brightened her face. It ignited his smile and for a long moment, they stared, each drinking in the energy of the other.

She reached out, touched his neck, then drew him to her lips. He savoured her scent, her warm skin and movement of her mouth on his, forgetting all he had done, all that was around him and the danger he put her in. For the moment, it was only them, this kiss, and her gentle hand on the back of his head holding him still.

The poyson sensed Isla and awakened. The chance to claim another victim excited it. Since its last release in Maskil, it had grown anxious and wanted another run at freedom. The itch in his shoulder constantly reminded him that while he was free to travel The Trail, he was still a prisoner of the Mavericks.

Against every desire racing through his blood, he pulled away from her and placed his hand upon her mouth. "Good morning."

She kissed his hand and removed it. "You make it so." She glanced around the room. "Where is everyone?"

"Around."

"Breaking the fast without us?"

"They did three hours ago."

Her brow bent. "What time is it?"

"Must be nine o'clock."

She sat up quickly and rubbed her eyes. "Why didn't you wake me?"

"And disturb your peaceful dream state? Never."

"We should be on The Trail by now." She tossed the blankets aside, rose quickly, then fell back down onto the mounds.

"Take your time. We're in no rush." He slid his arm across her belly. She wore a singlet with thin straps and a pair of shorts. He kissed her bare shoulder and slid closer, tucking his body into hers. The sensations she stirred ignited the fire within and in this moment, if he didn't wear the Maverick scar, he'd remove her meagre clothing.

"You make this claim how?" She brushed her fingers through his hair. "Lyneth has told you this?"

He grinned. "I told me this. Now that you're rested, I'll make sure you eat a hearty meal, and fill this belly." He spread his hand over her abdomen, rubbed it, then slid his finger to her armpit to tickle her. She squealed and tried to escape.

"It's not your birth celebration," she cried through fits of laughter.

"I have five left to make up for." He rolled across her, and she poked him in the ribs.

Gathering her strength, she threw him to the side and came up on top, straddling his waist and glaring down at him. "Enough. I'm fully awake and hungry." She fell upon his lips and kissed them passionately. "Now feed me."

He gazed up at her and again fell in love with her beautiful face and those eyes that sparkled for him. The morning sun pouring in the window danced across her face, highlighting her sensual lips and the gentle curve of her cheek. If he lived a thousand years, he'd not tire of witnessing the happiness that radiated from her being.

"Liam, promise me something." Her voice, soft on the air, suggested a touch of seriousness.

"Anything."

"Promise me you will never let me go."

"I promise." It was the easiest promise he'd made. He'd never let her go. He wanted her more now than he did when he was thirteen, more than he did when they reunited, more than he did yesterday.

She lowered her lips to his and kissed them gently, then stared into his eyes. "I will be heartbroken if you break the promise."

Why would she think he'd consider letting her go? Where had the doubt come from? "Isla, my greatest wish is to hold you for my lifetime. Fear not; I'll never let you go."

"Good." She kissed him on the forehead, then scrambled to her feet. "Now feed me."

"Yes, ma'am." He stood and pulled on his boots.

She slipped into her shirt and buttoned it, then she removed her shorts, threw them on the blankets and pulled on her trousers. She observed him watching her, and her mouth turned up into a mischievous smirk as she fastened her buttons. Without a word, she tugged on her socks and boots, grabbed her vest, then came to stand in front of him.

"See how I dress?" He nodded, and she continued. "Good. When the time comes, you'll know how to undress me." She caressed his chin and went to the door.

He leapt after her, the heat in his neck and groin growing as he followed on her heals. He caught her hand to lead the way to the inn tavern where they'd break the fast together, where he'd spend the morning sitting next to her, enjoying every breath she took.

ഇ ❖ ൯

Lyneth walked next to McGuigan on the shovelled boardwalk. The snow had stopped falling while she broke the morning fast, and now the sun shined brightly upon the land, making her squint and turn her eyes away from the glare upon the snow. The morning business had been favourable, and she'd return to her contact tomorrow and gather a package to be delivered to Bagnio on the foothills of North Hillock. The contact had warned her it was a valuable item, and the reason they entrusted it with her was because of her history with The Mercenaries. They had hesitated when they learnt of the young members of the group, but she convinced them a wiser, more experienced individual also travelled with them, one who matched Elspeth in strength.

They conceded but warned her of the dangers. No one would know about the transaction, but spies had their ears to the ground, waiting for the package to be moved.

McGuigan's strong presence no doubt helped her case. He stood silent, watching and *appearing wise.* That's what she had told him to do: appear wise in his youth. Dwarfs were valued for their strength and determination, and he had pulled it off perfectly. However, a short distance away from the shop, his expression suggested otherwise.

"Are you sure we should accept this assignment?" he asked.

"We've moved more dangerous items. You may not have known about it, but all—most turned out well."

"Not knowing makes it easier."

"You're a senior member now; you don't have the luxury of not knowing," she said. "That spot is reserved for Deaglan."

"And Cabela?"

"She won't be with us."

"I didn't think so."

"You sound disappointed."

He shrugged. "I didn't get to know her. Deaglan is a hog."

"She's rude. You're not missing much."

"I know." He paused and side stepped a pedestrian in a rush. "But maybe there's a reason."

"You're making excuses for her? Do you know what she said about you and Isla?"

"No. What?"

"It's not important. She's bossy and assumes things. She doesn't fit with the group and what we do. She's far from the warrior goal Isla has set for us."

"She's young."

"She belongs at home with her parents, attending study class, not with us on dangerous missions. She'll get in the way and get herself killed."

"Why isn't she home?"

That was the question that had bothered her since she discovered Cabela travelled alone. It was part of the reason she didn't abandon her on the street heartlessly. "Do you think Deaglan knows?"

"I'd ask him, but he's glued to her side."

"There they go now." She pointed to the lane up ahead. "Let's find out because tomorrow, we leave without her." She hurried to catch up to them. "Deaglan," she called out. He stopped and waited. "Where are you going in such a hurry?"

"No where." He shoved his hands into his pockets.

"Good. We need to talk."

"I didn't do it."

Her mouth froze on the words she was about to say, back tracked and asked, "Do what?"

He searched the ground behind her, then glanced at Cabela. "Nothing."

She folded her arms. "What did you steal?"

"I was going to pay for it, but I didn't have the money."

"What was it?" Lyneth studied Cabela; the girl wore a determined expression as if she didn't care about what they talked about.

"A necklace."

"Why did you tell her?" asked Cabela. "She's not your mother."

"I'm his substitute mother until I can return him to his aunt," snapped Lyneth. "Give it to me." She held out her hand, but he shrugged. "Where is it?" His eyes darted between the two women. "Cabela, hand it over."

She grumbled and pulled a gold necklace with a charm box from her pocket. "It's ugly anyways."

"You said you loved it," said Deaglan.

Footsteps approached quickly from behind. "There they are."

Lyneth turned and found a man standing beside a guard. She inwardly growled at the stupidity of the boy. "Are you looking for these two and this?" She held up the necklace.

"They tricked me," said the man, his face red with anger. "Stole it from my shop. I want them arrested."

"Would you instead accept the return of the stolen item and to know I'm going to serve him harsher punishment than he'd receive in lock up?"

"I would not."

"What would please you? Lecturing him yourself, punching him in the mouth? I'm open to suggestions." She handed the necklace to the man.

"You'd let me punch him?"

"I would. He deserves it."

The man considered her and Deaglan. "Hold him for me."

She grabbed Deaglan from behind and held him upright. He struggled to break free, but he was no match for her strength.

The shop owner slapped him across the cheek, leaving a large red blotch. "If you step into my shop again, I'll beat you with a stick and have you thrown into a cell." He huffed, stuck his chin in the air and marched away with the guard beside him.

Lyneth threw Deaglan into the snow. "Boy, you're awfully close to finding yourself behind bars. And for what? A useless necklace that won't keep you warm or fill your belly."

"This isn't your business." He got to his feet and brushed snow from his clothes.

"You travel with me, so it's my business." She turned to Cabela. "If you can't find a place to stay tonight, you can stay at the inn, but when we leave in the morning, you won't be with us." She had struggled to tell the girl this fact, but the current development made it easy. How had Elspeth handled these situations? As leader of The Mercenaries, it had been her responsibility to sort the worthy from the worthless. Elspeth made it look easy, yet Lyneth wondered if she found it difficult at times to turn away those who wanted the safety of the group.

Cabela stood rigid, her mouth and eyes opened slightly, absorbing the words thrown her way.

"You can't do this." Deaglan stood before Lyneth. "She is my friend, and I say she comes."

"You are not a member of this group and as such, you have no say in what we do or who joins us and who we cast aside."

"I *am* a member. Just as much as McGuigan." His stood with his fists clenched, his arms rigid at his side.

"You are no comparison to that man." She stood taller than him, given her human blood, and she glared down, waiting for him to understand his position.

"I told you they were lovers," snapped Cabela, folding her arms. "She'll stick up for him."

"We're what?" McGuigan's jaw dropped.

Lyneth grabbed Cabela by the front of the jacket and pulled her close to her face. "You are so ignorant, you can't see the obvious. Is this why you're not at home, not with family or friends?"

Her eyes grew glossy, and she tried to pull away. "Let go of me."

"Gladly." She shoved her back to add force to her words but not hard enough to send her into the snowbank.

"Get your stuff out of the room and leave now. Your negative attitude is disturbing the balance of the group."

"But...but," she whirled and grasped Deaglan. "I have nowhere to go. Please, don't throw me out."

Deaglan gathered her in his arms. "I won't. You can stay with me in my room."

"Liam's not going to enjoy sharing a bed with the two of you," said McGuigan.

"You want to sleep in a bed with two men, sleep in a room with four men?" Lyneth smirked. "Sounds..." she shivered for effect, "disgusting. What kind of woman are you?"

"Lyneth." Deaglan squared his jaw. "I won't see her outside in this weather. She won't be safe."

"She should have thought about that when she convinced you to steal the necklace for her."

"I decided to take it; she had nothing to do with it."

"Yet, she said she loved it."

Deaglan's mouth closed, opened, then closed again.

Lyneth leered at Cabela. "Get your things and find a place to stay."

"My parents were killed." She blurted the statement so fast, she surprised herself.

"What?"

"My parents." Cabela stared at the ground. "They were killed in a horrible accident." Her hand went to her mouth. "I'm alone. My kinfolk live in Wedgemore. I'm scared." A tortured expression twisted her face. "I have no where to go."

Lyneth fought against letting the story influence her feelings. Leading by the heart instead of the head often ended in disaster. She had no way of verifying the girl's story and had to go by gut instinct except... Isla was excellent at reading facial expressions and body language; she'd detect if the girl was lying. If Cabela was telling the truth, the simple answer was to deliver her to Wedgemore; they were passing through the town on their way to Dougendun. However, that meant enduring weeks of trail life with her snotty attitude and rude accusations.

"Lyneth, listen to your heart," said Deaglan. "We can't abandon her. Let her stay. Her ankle isn't fully healed. Please. I promise I'll stop stealing."

"She was walking fine while you escaped with stolen property."

"Well, she..." He glanced at Cabela. "It must feel better."

"It does. Rest has helped it. And your care." She slipped beneath his arm and rested her head on his shoulder.

Lyneth pressed her lips together as the internal debate raged on. The girl played on his sympathies, making him incapable of seeing through her lies. "Here's what we'll do. The Warriors will hold a meeting in the morning before we leave Gabardine. We'll decide as a group whether you come or not." This would give Isla time to interrogate Cabela to learn more about her past, and time for her to consider the facts without Deaglan's pouty face influencing her decision.

"I'm attending this meeting," said Deaglan. "While I'm with you, I should have a say in what happens. My aunt and uncle would want me to participate."

"You can attend but remember, majority rules." She prepared to leave. "I warn you, if there is any more trouble, there will be no discussion, no meeting; she will remain in Gabardine and we'll carry on without her. Do I make myself clear?"

"Yes, ma'am." Deaglan slipped his hand into Cabela's. "We'll be the most outstanding beings in all the village."

Lyneth huffed. "I didn't ask for a miracle. Just stay out of trouble."

The teens walked away. Cabela glanced back once, a peculiar expression on her face.

"If she is alone and her parents were killed, we could deliver her to Wedgemore." McGuigan tilted his head. "It's not far."

"It's weeks away."

"Not as far as Dougendun."

"Far enough." She walked towards the street, in the opposite direction the teens went.

"We've gone farther."

"You can tolerate me as a lover for that long?"

He cringed. "Why would she think that? That's crazy."

"I know. I'm so hideous; who would want me?"

He glanced at her sideways. "I didn't mean it like that. You're pretty and nice, but we're friends. I don't think of you in that way."

She linked her arm with his. "Friends with benefits, my sweet boy." She giggled.

He pulled his arm free. "Friends. No benefits."

"I'd risk my life for yours."

"I know."

"I'd share my last bite of food with you if we were starving."

He smiled. "I know."

"I look out for your well-being."

"Okay. Friends with those types of benefits. Good friends are important, and I'm lucky to have several."

"She also thinks you and Isla are lovers."

"Why would she think that?"

"You show her too much attention." She exaggerated her happy expression, "And she gave you cookies from the crofter's dwelling."

"Damn. She didn't say anything to Liam, did she?"

"Why does it matter? Liam knows the difference."

"But with that thing in his shoulder, if he gets angry, he might..." His brow bent.

"Are you afraid of him?"

He chuckled uneasily. "I'm told it consumes him. What if he won't listen to reason and attacks because he thinks I want Isla?"

"I'm hoping your friendship will prevent that."

"I still think about it." He put his hands into his pockets.

"What do you think about Cabela?"

"Not what I did before. Too immature. Not interested."

"Do you think she should join us?"

"She needs to go to Wedgemore." He scratched his head. "We could get her there, but we'd have to put up with Deaglan's attitude. I was starting to like the boy, and he had to go all foolish."

"Love will do that."

"It's a crush. I've been there. Wait." He touched her arm. "What about Rod? He's your mate?"

"What about him?" Her nerves pricked at the sound of his name.

"Why would you want to be friends with benefits?"

"I was joking."

He paused. "How do you stay loyal after all these years?"

"It's easy." It was the living without him that was near impossible. "No other man can make me feel as he does. Whether we are together or miles apart, that feeling lives in my heart. You'll know what I mean when you find your mate." Her voice quivered, and she felt moisture building on her eyelids. "I wish for you to know that feeling that fuels a heart like no other, but..." she wiped the corner of her eye, "I hope you never know this missing ache that hums in my chest day and night."

He put his arm around her waist and pulled her close as they walked. "I'm sorry. I didn't mean to make you sad."

She rested her arm across his shoulder. "Sad is not the way I feel. It's more like unbalanced, like walking around with one leg, one arm.

He is the half that makes me whole and without him, I feel an emptiness no other can fill."

"Maybe it's better I don't have a mate. If she were taken away, I'd feel this pain. Without her, I can see any woman and leave without that empty feeling."

She chuckled softly. "The ironic thing about this emptiness is you already feel it."

"No, I don't."

"It's why you look into the face of every woman you meet, searching her eyes to see if she's your mate. If there's a possibility, you explore further, talk with her, kiss her, join with her. When you discover she is not the one you seek, you move onto the next woman." She sighed, remembering those days and the men who'd passed through her life. "Your need to fill that emptiness keeps you searching and when you find your mate and know that feeling of fulfilment, if you are separated, the emptiness is amplified, like a belly that has not had food for many moons and a feast is laid before it. You crave that person who holds the magic to complete you, who makes you feel as if you can take flight and fill the sky with the fireworks in your heart. You'll never regret filling that emptiness even if you become separated."

"Is that only how women feel?"

She squeezed his shoulder. "When we return to Maskil, *young man*, ask your uncle. He's a man of few words, but I bet he'll stumble through a similar explanation."

"Tam would not say such things."

"He might surprise you." Rod had surprised her. His confession of his need for her as they lay in each others' arms was nothing short of amazing. She'd never heard a man speak of love as he had, and it reinforced her belief in the fact both men and women experienced the same emptiness and the same fulfilment. Putting a hand over her belly, she felt the urge though she wore several layers of clothes. Her body craved Rod, and it wouldn't be satisfied until he again lay by her side.

21

A Man Needs Good Friends

ISLA CLOSED THE DOOR behind her and stared at Cabela, who had rolled up her bedroll and was in the process of packing her things into her rucksack and saddle bags. The girl carried too much useless stuff to be efficient on The Trail, and her bags swelled with extra clothes, a small pillow, grooming equipment and two spare pairs of shoes.

Isla would toss half that stuff for one extra blanket to keep warm in this cold weather, but she was a different sort than most girls. In her first five years, she had nothing but the clothes on her back and afterwards, living with her das, she had the bare minimum; he hated clutter in his quarters. At Blackvale, she again was reduced to the clothes she wore and what she scavenged from the castle. Since travelling The Trail, she gathered what served a purpose and discarded everything else.

"Leaving?" Isla sat on the edge of the bed to analyse her expression. She had been sent to interrogate Cabela, to learn the truth from the girl who claimed both her parents were killed.

"Leaving this room." Cabela folded a flimsy, decorative blouse and stuffed it into a pocket on the rucksack. "You can have my bed. You and Liam."

"Liam's fine with the boys for the night."

She turned. "We're switching places."

"Does he know?"

"He will soon."

Lyneth hadn't told her this. "So, you are sleeping with..." She wanted to make a smart remark, but she needed to remain on friendly ground with her until she learnt the truth. "Deaglan is sharing his bed with you? That's kind of him."

"He is and, yes, he's too kind to see me thrown onto the street on a cold night." She tucked a shoe into a saddle bag and the mate to it in another pocket.

"Deaglan is a caring person. He pretends to be tough, but he's a softy." She said the words, but she didn't completely agree with them. Her praise of the boy was limited given their short history that involved him stealing her horse, stealing tarot cards that led Liam to battle an octopus and his newly-found *love* for this girl.

"You see him as I do. He's a sweetie."

"He told me your parents were killed. I'm sorry. You must be devasted." She scrutinised the muscles in her face, waiting for the truth to be revealed. The corner of her mouth twitched; it wasn't the complete truth.

"I am, and he's been thoughtful, helping me through my grief."

Yet, Isla detected little grief. There was sadness in her voice, but no tears pooled in her eyes. A girl her age who'd lost her parents would be overcome with emotion at this point, or at least shed a tear. She'd witnessed the breakdown of many girls older than her when they arrived at Blackvale Castle, girls who'd lost loved ones; Cabela appeared to have had hardships but none that gripped her heart as tightly as the sudden loss of both parents. "Where were you living at the time?"

"Moonsface."

"And you travelled from Moonsface to Yikker Wood by yourself? Why didn't you stick to the main trail? It would have taken you to Wedgemore faster."

"I was scared."

"Of what?"

Cabela tightly gripped the skirt she held. "Bandits." She said it as if it was the first thing that popped into her mind.

"Bandits on the main trail are dangerous. You were wise to take the old trail," she lied and turned away, fearful her expression would give her away. She'd tried to become a better liar, but her das' teachings made her feel guilty.

"Yes, well, I didn't expect to be toted off by a griffin."

"Nor was I." She resumed her scrutiny. "Your kin in Wedgemore must be worried. Have they received news about your parents?"

"Yes–I mean, no. I was going to tell them, but..." she pushed the skirt into her rucksack, "I didn't know how."

"A letter."

"I didn't want to overburden or worry them."

"I hardly think they'd feel overburdened. They'd want to know, want to help."

"I doubt it."

"Not close to them?"

"No. Never met them."

"Yet, you are going to live with them?"

"I didn't say that."

"Why are you bothering to go to Wedgemore? You could have found accommodations at Moonsface with a friend, found work and stayed safe."

"Why are you asking me all these questions?" Her face flushing red. "It's none of your business what I do."

Isla calmed her nerves. She had finally triggered an emotion within the girl; she'd use this to expose the truth. "It might not be my business, but I'm curious. Why wouldn't you stay with a friend of your parents? Didn't they have friends? Weren't they nice people?"

"My parents have friends. They are brilliant people. Better than you and Lyneth."

"If they are so brilliant, why aren't you with them? They left a message at the postal office. They want you to come home."

The colour drained from Cabela's cheeks, and she dropped the bag. "They do?"

"Immediately. They can't understand why you ran away."

She clenched her fists and pursed her lips. "I hate you." She rammed the last of her things into the rucksack, threw it over her arm, grabbed her bedroll and jacket, and stormed from the room, leaving a trail of items behind her.

Isla fell back onto the bed with her head propped up with her folded arms and waited. It didn't take long. After a door slammed down the hall, it opened again, and Cabela soon appeared, gathering the lost items.

"Your parents are not dead, so why are you on The Trail?"

Cabela shook a sweater at her. "You are a liar, a mean person who wants to trick me. You are no better than my sisters."

"You have sisters? How many?"

"Shut up!" She stomped her feet down the hall and slammed the door behind her.

Isla released a sigh. She'd uncovered part of what Lyneth wanted to know: Cabela's parents were not dead. However, she hadn't tricked her into revealing why she was on The Trail. That vital piece of information would determine if the girl would leave Gabardine with them in the morning.

Not wanting to waste time or an opportunity, she jumped from the bed, threw her bedroll onto it and marched out the door; she had business to take care of. Or was it pleasure? It was a little of both.

A few hours later, she slipped between the blankets and wiggled her shoulders into Liam's chest. His arms went around her and tucked her securely against him. He'd already warmed the blankets with his body, so she sank into the heat and relaxed, but she didn't close her eyes.

Lyneth extinguished the lantern and settled into bed four feet away. "I feel like we'll have a quieter night than yesternight. No complaining about the most miniscule thing."

"Maybe." Isla giggled.

"Liam, keep your hands to yourself," said Lyneth.

"I've done nothing." He held up his hands. "She giggles for no reason."

"Oh, I have a reason."

He propped himself up on an elbow and gazed down at her. "That reason is?"

"It'll reveal itself soon. Now hush."

He raised an eyebrow. "Am I part of this? Should I tell a joke?" He spread his hand across her belly. "Or tickle you?"

"No." She slapped her hand down on his. "No tickling. Just resting." She smirked. "Close your eyes and wait."

"I don't like the sound of this," said Lyneth. "What have you done?"

"Shhh. It must be quiet." She closed her eyes, and Liam settled beside her with his cheek pressed against hers.

The minutes ticked by and the anticipation grew until a voice echoed down the hall. A shriek quickly followed, then a high-pitched scream that lasted for several seconds. Isla leapt out of bed and opened the door with Liam and Lyneth on her heels. Others sleeping at the inn came out their door to see what caused the ruckus.

Deaglan stood in his shorts with his back against the wall opposite his open door. He squealed and put him arms up as if something was about to attack him, and Cabela raced out of the room screaming. McGuigan and Jack soon followed, confused more than fearful of what rested inside the room.

"What is it?" screamed Cabela.

"Where is it?" asked McGuigan. He searched from side-to-side to find the thing that had disturbed their rest.

"What has caused this disturbance?" The clerk from the front desk entered the hallway.

"A monster!" cried Cabela, pointing into the room. "It nibbled on my foot."

"It's fierce." Deaglan rubbed his chin with the back of hand. "It attacked while I slept." He pulled back and hid behind McGuigan.

McGuigan glanced over his shoulder and groaned. "That's what you're worried about?"

A grey squirrel the size of loaf of bread shot from the room and down the hall, disappearing into the front room.

"A squirrel?" Deaglan shook himself. "How did that get in there?"

McGuigan stared down the hall at Isla. "I don't know, but you scream like a girl."

"I do not." He huffed and tramped into the room.

"Is it safe?" Cabela still pressed against the wall.

"I believe so," said Jack.

She cautiously entered the room, following McGuigan who walked in without worry.

The rest of the inn occupants returned to their room, the clerk returned to the front desk, and Jack stared at Isla, giving her serious consideration. A smile tickled the corner of her mouth and when it escaped, he frowned. "To bed, young lady. No more mischief tonight."

She giggled and tugged Liam into the room. Lyneth followed and closed the door behind her.

Snuggling into the blankets, she pulled Liam close, rested her head on his chest and closed her eyes. Releasing a gentle sigh, she breathed in his scent and without further thought for the day, fell into blissful sleep.

ೞ ❖ ೮౩

"What dwells on your mind?" Jack stood next to a fallen tree beside the babbling brook they camped near.

Lyneth reached into her pocket for the coins she had separated from those given to her from her contact in Gabardine to deliver the package to Bagnio. "This is yours." She placed the coins in his hand.

"How so?" He furrowed his brow.

"For as long as you travel with us, you're part of the group and will receive a portion of the payment."

He held the coins out to her. "No. I'm not entitled."

She refused to accept it. "You'll earn it."

"It's not my business, and your generosity in paying for my room and food at the keep is more than I expected."

"I've deducted the price of your food. From here on, you pay for your own. I maintain a small fund from our fee to ensure I have money for rooms. It was the way of The Mercenaries. Elspeth had set the rules, and we abided by them because they are fair."

"This is your money, not mine to spend."

"I made the deal to pay six; that included you. I assured them of delivery because two mature individuals led these youngsters. If not for you, they'd have refused the deal."

"What benefit am I?"

"You have already proven your worth in saving Liam's life. I assume you'll help anyone of us if the need arises, and that's what makes you an asset. When the package is delivered, and I collect the second half of the payment, you'll receive a portion of that as well."

"This is how you financially support your travels?"

"Yes. How do you support yours?"

"Not as well as you. Money is scarce and has come from various sources, but I've none to spare or use on acquiring a room."

She considered him, his strengths, wisdom and hidden talents. "I'm glad you're with us. It's not easy adjusting to the leadership position I've been voted into."

"I'm no leader, but I've years of experience."

"Wisdom. I like that."

"And your assessment of Cabela?"

"She has me puzzled. How would you assess her?"

"I believe she needs a friend and guidance. She should not be roaming The Trail with strangers."

"Yet?"

"I feel uncomfortable abandoning her."

"So do I." She sighed and crossed her arms. "It's the only reason I've allowed her to come. I'd like to learn more of her story, but she doesn't trust me or Isla. Can you lend an ear, see if you can coax it out of her if given the opportunity?"

"I'll see what I can harvest. She's not said much in my presence. Given my age, we have little in common."

"You're travelling The Trail together, sleeping at the same fire; there's bound to be common ground eventually."

"No doubt." He slipped the coins into his pocket. "Thank you, and I'll thank the others. I value your friendship more than the money, yet I understand the usefulness of coins."

"I know you do. Thank you for remaining with us. It's not your usual routine."

"While it isn't, my feet grew weary bearing the miles alone." His expression softened. "A man needs good friends to renew what he feels he has lost. I am most fortunate for having found you that stormy night."

She chuckled. "I believe it was us who found you, and we were the most fortunate ones. I was about to give up."

"Yet, you were not as near to giving up as I."

Given he was safe, comfortable and warm beneath his shelter and had plenty of food, she didn't understand why he felt he'd have give up on that cold, snowy night, but she didn't press the matter. He had his reasons, and they were none of her business.

22

Pieces to a Puzzle

THE TOWN OF ALLESTREE rested in a long, flat valley that went on for many miles between a massive mountain range that stretched far beyond the horizon and Skeenie Lake, a body of water so large the other side lay out of sight. Across the vast lake rested Edgewood, the town the Warriors had passed through on their way south towards Moonsface. Allestree was like Edgewood except only elves lived here. Other races were welcome to visit, but the ruling family forbid foreign races from settling. A sign stating this law was posted outside the town gates to inform those who entered, and the four guards at the entrance who recorded names, races and reason for visiting, reiterated the regulation.

After giving the information required, McGuigan waited for the others beside Isla and Liam, who had already answered the questions. "Strict," he whispered out the side of his mouth.

"Unusual," replied Isla. "Been to many places, and I've not encountered this."

"You and me both. It's my first time in Allestree." When the others walked towards them, McGuigan surveyed the town. Besides outbuildings for guards and other official business, the first thousand feet between him and the first town structure were barren. The emptiness on the left, bathed in late afternoon sunshine, appeared to be a harvested field beneath a foot of snow while on the right, several sections of fences indicated livestock pastures. In the distance, several dozen sheep with long, black matted wool trampled snow around a large outbuilding.

McGuigan mounted his horse and quickly travelled the short distance to the start of the wooden sidewalk, shops and dwellings. He scanned the shops, reading the names if they weren't too complicated and searching for a candy store. In his travels, he learnt elves made the best candies in Ath-o'Lea, and he hoped to find his favourite mint jelly candies here so he'd have a sweet treat every day to carry him to Bagnio.

"I think it's him."

McGuigan turned to see who Liam talked about.

"He gave you a strange look," said Isla.

"He's probably still jealous of my position."

He followed their line of sight and saw a mature dwarf, who wore a decorative sword and three daggers, walking on the sidewalk next to a woman of similar age. He recognised the faces, but it took a moment to place them. That was the same man they'd met leaving Legover when they were entering the small village, the same one who made a comment about Liam riding on the back of a horse while Isla steered. Remembering the incident, he chuckled. Liam was quick with his tongue; it was one of the reasons he liked him, though he'd feel better once the poyson was extracted from his blood.

"You needn't worry," she said, glancing over her shoulder at Liam. "He can get as jealous as he wants; I'd never trade you for him. You for anyone."

He chuckled. "I'm not worried. He's no match for me."

McGuigan swallowed hard. According to Isla's report, Liam could easily take down three men the size of that dwarf, which meant Liam wouldn't break a sweat killing him.

"I don't doubt you," said Isla. "He looks rough and gruff; he'd never soft soap his way into my heart. Not like you; you're soft and sweet."

"Hey, I'm tougher than that." Liam laughed.

McGuigan bent his eyebrows; soft and sweet was not how he thought of Liam.

"What do you think, McGuigan?" asked Isla. "Tough or soft?"

He considered the implications of the wrong answer. "Tough?"

"You're unsure?"

"You choose."

"I see how it is. You're thinking sweet or more like sweet shop."

"She knows you too well," said Liam. "If you find a sweet shop, take me with you."

He nodded, then focussed on the street ahead and Lyneth leading the way to the inn, where they'd spend the night. Like many of the villages and towns they'd entered since Moonsface, this town was overly decorated with art. He admired the creativity and marvelled at the construction of elaborate store fronts. He'd tried his hand at wood carving before he left for The Trail two years ago; everything he made resembled a blob of wood.

Lyneth led them to Amoret Lodgings in the far end of town. She said from here, it was a ten-minute travel to the northeast gate, the one they'd leave Allestree through in the morning. After settling into their rooms, McGuigan followed Jack out the front door towards a restaurant they passed on the way in.

"What do I owe this company?" Jack eyed him curiously.

"I'm looking forward to a quiet ration." That was the truth. While eating on The Trail, the number of people around the fire stirred more conversations than he preferred. Deaglan showering Cabela with attention irritated him, but her complaints about the weather, the food, the discomfort and every other inconvenience made it unbearable.

"You wish for me to remain silent?"

"I doubt you'll cause much ruckus."

"I may fool you."

"You can try." They crossed the street, and he caught sight of a shop he'd visit before returning to their lodgings: Bella's Bonbons. Already his mouth watered for the treats he'd buy.

Hasty movement drew his attention to a man who walked briskly towards them. He came so close to Jack, he forced him to step sideways to avoid a collision. McGuigan caught hold of Jack so he'd gather his balance quickly. The haggard, middle-aged dwarf, who wore rugged clothes and had thick mud clinging to his boots, stomped away as if he hadn't seen them.

Jack stopped and watched him disappear into the small crowd. "Did you sense that?"

McGuigan paused. "Sense what?"

Jack sniffed and wiggled his fingers. When he turned, his dark eyes were lost in thought.

"What is it?"

"I sense danger with that man." He pulled him towards the restaurant, leant close and whispered, "Where were Liam and Isla eating this evening?"

"I don't know. Why?"

"I'm uncertain, but I have a strong feeling that man we passed is inflicted with the same illness as Liam."

McGuigan glanced over his shoulder, his mouth open as he searched for the stranger. He didn't see him but feared he might appear at any moment.

"It might be something else, but he disturbs my nerves in the same manner."

"Do you think he's looking for him?"

"I cannot say if he searches for a dead man. He wasn't heavily armed, only a short, slim sword and a dagger, but from what I've heard, it is their strength that is their true weapon."

"That's what I heard, too." The uncontrolled manner in which they killed worried him most. They were deadlier than Tigh na Mare warriors. At least the female warriors maintained control over their actions.

"We'll eat quickly, then search for the mates."

If he had a choice, he'd leave Allestree tonight, hit The Trail without Liam and travel far from Wandsworth. He thought about Isla; he'd not leave her to face this monster alone, and she'd never leave Liam. His path was to stay by their side and hope they avoided the haggard dwarf or defeat him if he attacked.

ಬಿ ❖ ೞ

"I want you up front." Isla held Two-bit Spindrift's bridle and waited for Liam to mount. They'd already given their names to the guards at the gate to put on record they were leaving Allestree.

He leant close to her face and whispered, "Why?"

"I want the best seat. To hold something warm and soft."

"I don't believe you."

"No matter. Get up."

"You're up to something."

She kissed his lips. "I am."

He shook his head, mounted and waited for her.

She climbed into the saddle and settled behind him, pulling close to his back and wrapping her arms around his waist. "Yes, this is nice. I see why you like it back here."

He glanced over his shoulder. "Keep your hands to yourself."

She slipped her hands beneath his jacket and spread them against his chest. "Mmm, warm."

He brought the horse to a trot behind McGuigan and guided it along the dirt road that followed the edge of the lake.

Isla relaxed, tuned her ears to the wind and scanned the forest on the left, the trail ahead and the road behind, searching for the haggard dwarf seen by Jack and McGuigan the night before. His appearance might be coincidence, but she'd take no chances. She'd discussed weapons and spells to use on the man if he possessed the poyson. Their goal was to destroy his body completely. If he carried the full dose of poyson, she feared he had more strength than Liam when it took control. He'd be a force she'd never encountered before.

The foot of snow that had fallen the day before had shrank and melted to half its original height. The trail had been beaten down by traffic that came and went from the town, making travelling easier. From what Lyneth had told her, they would travel the edge of the lake until early afternoon, and then the trail veered into the forest on a well-groomed road. They'd pass the bridge that crossed Blue Myst River, the waterway flowing into Skeenie Lake, by mid-day tomorrow. The bridge led south towards Edgewood. They'd remain on the trail going northeast towards Bagnio. The large village lay in the shadow of North Hillock. They'd reach it in seven days.

By nightfall, they had passed about four dozen travels, some walking, many riding horses and others in waggons. Most were elf, but other races also made their way to Allestree. All appeared friendly. Isla didn't recognise any of them.

Lyneth chose a campsite in a field beside a small stream with fast flowing water where it appeared others had camped the night before, leaving an area around a firepit cleared of snow. Now that everyone knew their routine, they set to work making a fire, gathering wood to last the night and tending to the horses.

Isla's goal was to make the canopy that would be their shelter for the night, the same Jack had made in the mountains to keep the snow off and the warmth in. She'd practised it many times, but she hadn't perfected it. Jack was a patient teacher and when she tired from the lesson, he completed the protective covering to ensure it withstood the weather.

"Your technique is good," he said, "but I think the problem is the number of fingers. The person who taught you to gather energy like this, were they hauflin?"

"No. Alaura showed me first. Then a dwarf."

"So they had five fingers?"

"Yes."

"While Alaura has hauflin blood, her technique doesn't suit you. Dwarf also does not match. Here, raise your hands."

She put her palms out and her fingers up. He placed his hands beneath hers and stretched his five fingers around them.

"Your ability to create the Bubble Spell is amazing. You have efficiency; you need only direct it, shape it to create the canopy. Follow my fingers and feel the energy as I mould it into place."

She closed her eyes and sensed the energy with her fingertips. His magic was similar to Willow's, and it flowed around her fingers, entered their base and flowed freely out the tips to form the Bubble Spell. The shaping confused her, but she allowed his energy to move her fingers and craft the shelter with four open sides and a hole in the roof to allow smoke to exit.

"Good. This finger." He tapped her index finger on her right hand. "Move it, curl it, draw the shape you want."

"Yes. I see it." The energy zipped in the same line she moved her finger and created the opening. Feeling confident, she made the second opening. By the time she opened her eyes, the canopy was completed. "This is incredible."

"Incredible indeed. It's robust and can withstand a boulder strike." He studied the shelter closer. "Your fingers dance in a unique pattern I've not experienced, and you gather particular energy and discard that which fails to hold sufficient charge. Who bestowed on you their wisdom to construct the bubble with such intensity? Mine is vulnerable in comparison, and I learn better from observing you."

"If I told you, do you promise to keep it a secret?"

"You have my word."

She leant close to his ear and in cant, whispered. "A newlin."

His eyes widened. "Do tell a name."

"Willow."

The colour drained from his face. "Follow me." He marched away from the canopy and the fire being built beneath it.

"Is it ready?" asked Deaglan. "Can we put our stuff beneath it?"

"Yes." Jack kept walking.

Isla trailed after him, worried she'd betrayed Willow, but this was Jack; certainly, he'd not hurt her. By the time he stopped a hundred feet into the woods, he'd regained his colour, but his expression was anything but pleased.

"What did I do wrong?" she asked.

"Nothing." He ran his hand down his face and rubbed his thin beard hard. "Where is she?"

"I can't say."

"Why?"

"I'm sorry. I shouldn't have said her name. I promised her I wouldn't tell anyone. I felt safe telling you because, well, it's you."

"Have you told anyone else?"

"No. Except Liam. But I trust him fully. And Nyx. He said they were friends. Are they? He won't hurt her, will he?"

"No. She is safe with him."

"I didn't tell him where she was. He only knows she is here."

"Do you know where she is?"

"I sent her into a portal."

He rubbed his chin with his bent fingers. "Which portal?"

"One at Blackvale. We had returned from Vale of Avoca, and it wasn't safe for her there, so I made her enter another portal as soon as we arrived. I don't know where it took her."

"Great gemstones. She could be anywhere."

"Who is she to you?"

He pressed his lips together and set his eyes on her.

"I trust you," she said. "If you trust me, I can help further."

"She is..." he pressed his mouth to her ear and whispered, "my daughter."

"She'll return to Maskil. She goes often to see someone."

"Why?"

"I shouldn't say; she may want to tell you herself."

"Explain."

"She visits..." she paused, watching the muscles in his face closely, "her mate."

His surprise made him take a step back, and he searched the ground for answers or more questions. "And Nyx is not he?"

"Nyx called himself her sentinel."

Again, he searched his mind, the trees and the ground for his next words. "Do you know this mate?"

"I do. He's a good man."

"Is he newlin?"

"Dwarf."

"Inconceivable." He rubbed his cheeks with his palms and ran his hands through his hair. "I am..." He narrowed his eyes. "Describe this girl? Conceivably a different girl with the same name."

"She's unforgettable. Deep-green eyes, copper-coloured hair that's wild like a wind storm." She brought her hands up to show how thick the hair was on the head.

"It is her. You know her well?"

"No."

"Yet she trusts you to direct you in magic."

"We were in a bind. Stuck in the same dungeon."

"She escaped?"

"We escaped together."

"And she visits Maskil."

"I assume she'd travel there after leaving the portal. I told her to never return to Blackvale."

"When was this?"

"Spring of Leaf."

"She could be in Maskil now."

"She might be, and she might have already been there and gone."

"Why does she not remain by her mate's side? If he was a man of substance, he'd keep her safe at home."

"Your daughter is a determined woman. Sawney couldn't keep her there if he tied her up and chained her to the wall."

"Sawney?"

"Her mate. She was searching for information on the curse, the one inflicting dwarfs and hauflins. What I didn't tell her, but I'm going to tell you is that Lady Alys Kintale at Rhunestone Castle seeks a stone, a brilliant blue one, the same as... You know, and I fear she'll do anything to claim one. Stay clear of her."

"Kintale?"

"Yes. She's Das' aunt, but I don't trust her."

Jack stood straighter, and his face twisted. "Bronwyn is Kintale?"

"His mum is."

"Child, you have many pieces to a puzzle much larger than I imagined. I believed his name coincidence only, but... There are other Bronwyns as there are other Jacks and Islas, but... I am baffled by the path that has led me full circle."

"Now I'm confused. You know another Bronwyn?"

"Yes. Do you know a Bronwyn in the Kintale family?"

"My grandmeeme, Maisie, has brothers, but I don't know their names. I don't even know her dad's name. They've never been to Maskil, or I was too young to remember their visit."

"When our quest is complete, we must return to Maskil. I have questions for your das."

"The one you need to ask is his mum; she didn't-" A hard smack reached her ear, and she looked in the direction of the campsite. Tipping her ear into the breeze, she heard other sounds that didn't belong in the peaceful forest: struggling, grunting.

"What do you hear?" He stared down the narrow path they had travelled.

"Come. We sneak." She crouched low, slipping through the bushes quickly but quietly. When she neared the clearing, she moved slower and crouched lower. By the time she reached the perimeter, she was taking one step at a time. She stopped next to a young evergreen tree and a leafless bush. Jack halted behind her and gazed over her shoulder.

Four men stood amongst the group with swords drawn. Two others had Lyneth and McGuigan pinned and were tying their hands. Cabela clung to Deaglan, and he held her firmly under his arm. Two other men came into sight, making it eight who had attacked the campsite. All were dwarf.

"There are tracks everywhere made by previous campers," said one of the returning men. The dark-haired dwarf wore a cap that covered his ears. "We can't determine which direction they went."

"Watch for them," said the man standing outside the canopy. His sword rested at his side, and he scanned the perimeter of the clearing. "We'll be gone soon and not need to worry about them."

"Got it!" The red-haired man rummaging through Lyneth's rucksack held up a small cloth bag. He opened it and removed a steel box with a built-in lock. He left the canopy and gave it to the man who'd spoken.

Isla felt Jack move behind her, and she put a hand on his chest to stop him. She made eye contact and shook her head. *Let them take it*, she mouthed. Only Lyneth and the person who carried the actual item being transported knew the one Lyneth carried was a replica. When those men discovered the steel box held a worthless stone, they'd return, but the Warriors would be long gone.

Isla scanned the campsite. Everyone appeared well, but... Where was Liam? She searched the edge of the forest, hoping he wouldn't make a move to help the others and reclaim the item.

"Tie them up. Quickly." The man holding the steel box returned it to the bag and placed it in a leather pouch on his belt while four men grabbed Deaglan and Cabela and tied their feet and hands.

"You'll pay for this," cried Cabela. "No one ties me up and gets away with it."

The man chuckled. "Men. Make haste." He mounted his horse, and the others soon followed him down The Trail towards Allestree.

Isla held onto Jack's arm, staring into his face as the horses put distance between the thieves and her. When they had travelled out of sight, she raced into the clearing.

"You were there all this time, and you didn't help us?" Cabela struggled to break free of the ropes.

Isla ignored her and untied Lyneth while Jack helped McGuigan. She scanned the campsite and the surrounding bushes. "Liam," she called. When no reply came, she called louder.

"I haven't seen him since I took the saddle bags from my horse." Lyneth rubbed her wrists, then untied her feet.

Isla moved to Deaglan to untie his hands. "He was tending the horses. I'll check." She flung the ropes free and jogged towards the shelter Jack had constructed for the horses. The animals quietly munched on hay Jack had magically produced from cubes the size of dices. A few still had saddles and bags on their back. "Liam?" Her nerves jumped, and the more seconds that passed, the stronger they bounced against her skin. "Liam?"

A red stain in the snow halted her. The outer edge of the coin-shaped blotch was more pink than red, but the centre was crimson.

"Did you find him?" McGuigan walked towards her.

"No." The word stuck in her throat, and she coughed the rest of it into the air as she studied the footprints in the snow.

"What's that?" He stood over her. "Blood?" He bent and touched it. "That's blood."

She stared into his deep-blue eyes, wide with surprise and wrinkled with lines of concern. His wind-burnt skin pulled tight over his cheekbones and his mouth remained opened as he waited for her answer, but she didn't want to say the words beating around in her brain for fear they may be true.

He stood and examined the area. "They went this way. He must have been carried; I don't see his footprints or sign of him being dragged." He took several quick steps to reach the edge of the bushes. "One set; larger tracks than his. They went that way."

She leapt up and raced towards him, saw the tracks and rushed into the bushes.

"Wait! Let's get the others."

"Go. Get them!" she called over her shoulder. She ran, following the tracks like a troglodyte stalked a fresh kill. If she was fast, she'd overtake the man burdened by her mate, then she'd kill him.

23

Under the Weight of Chains

ALTHOUGH MCGUIGAN WANTED TO stay at Isla's side, he sprinted to the campsite. Informing the others of what had happened was the wise thing to do; they'd easily follow Isla's tracks in the snow.

"Report." Jack stood at the ready on the edge of the site.

"They took him."

"We watched; they took no one."

"Not the dwarfs." He drew a breath to calm his nerves. "One man. It appears Liam was struck, possibly knocked unconscious. There's blood."

"Where's Isla?"

"She wouldn't wait. She ran after them."

"Damn. That's not our method," said Lyneth.

"I doubt Isla cares about decided method or regulations when her mate's life is at risk," said Jack. "Nor do I. The objective is to retrieve Liam as quickly as possible." He turned to the others. "Secure your weapons. We go without wait. McGuigan, show us where to start."

He led them to the horse shelter and where the trail led into the forest. They travelled a few hundred feet before Isla rushed towards them.

"He's on horseback." Her ragged moist breath created steam in the cool late afternoon air. "We have to hurry." She staggered forward and tripped over a snow-covered branch.

McGuigan caught her in his arms. "We will. We'll get him."

"Fortunately, or unfortunately, we know where they plan to deliver him." Jack rested a hand on Isla's shoulder. "Wandsworth."

"Break camp." Lyneth marched towards the campsite.

"Can't this wait until morning?" Cabela whispered to Deaglan.

She may not have wanted the others to hear, but McGuigan had and while his mouth itched to respond, he remained silent. Cabela would never be a member of their group; she was a package to be delivered. She cared about only herself, and she revealed this fact each time they encountered a situation where someone else needed help.

Lyneth guided the band through the forest, following the obvious trail the assailant left when he had abducted Liam. Hiding tracks with a foot of snow on the ground was impossible when travelling over terrain untouched by other travellers. While fortunate for the revealed route, traversing an uncut trail was demanding on horse and rider. Stiff, bare branches whipped both human and animal, and the frigid temperature intensified the sting. Each time she brushed an evergreen tree, snow fell upon her lap or shoulder, making her wetter and colder.

Shortly after they had gotten underway, the sun set, leaving them in shimmering darkness with stars and the half moon in the clear, crisp sky to illuminate the snow-covered land and create soft shadows beneath the trees.

Due to the initial attack by the dwarfs, who had stolen the fake package, they'd have broken camp and travelled through the night to reach a safer location. However, that would have been on the beaten trail, not through the woods.

Brighter conditions loomed ahead, and she leant left and right to identify the reason. It slowly grew and within two hundred feet, she emerged onto an established trail. She examined the hoof prints of the horse she followed; they went left, away from Allestree. This minor trail was less travelled than the main route, but she quickly lost the hoofprints in the dozens of prints that covered the ground.

"I'm certain they went left, but..." Her eyes settled on Isla, who had remained unusually quiet throughout the journey.

Deaglan dismounted and returned to the ditch where the hoofprints they had tracked were distinct, then he followed them to the road and examined the snow-covered surface closely. He paused, then moved forward, then paused again, looking back and forth between different sets of tracks.

"These are them. They went this way." He pointed left.

"Boy, you're earning your keep by your tracking skills alone," said McGuigan. "I don't know anyone who can track like you."

"Thanks." He jumped onto his horse. "My uncle deserves the credit. He taught me all he knew."

"But you retained it," said McGuigan.

"Deaglan, take the lead," said Lyneth. "We'll use your uncle's wisdom and your memory to guide us. Let's keep our eyes open for tracks leaving the trail."

After fifty feet, Deaglan spoke. "He increased his speed. He's moving at a gallop."

"Can you track them if we go faster," asked Lyneth.

"I'll let you know if I can't. Set your speed at a lope."

Lyneth tapped her horse and kept pace with the boy. The philosophy of The Mercenaries, which she kept with this group, was the lives of its members were more important than any mission, and they'd do everything to save the individual regardless of the threat. However, they had never, to her knowledge, faced a force the Maverick poyson generated. It brushed against another philosophy: don't sacrifice the group for one person. Was she leading the Warriors to their death? If the man Jack and McGuigan had bumped into at Allestree possessed a full dose of poyson and he was the one who kidnapped Liam, her small group was doomed. Trading one life for another was not the philosophy of The Mercenaries and wouldn't be for the Warriors either. If that meant sacrificing Liam, then she'd pull back, find another way even if Isla raged onward.

Then again, she possessed what those who had attacked Liam in the past didn't have: Jack. He was a determined man who had left no doubt he'd risk all to rescue the boy. Given his mysterious magical powers, he gave them an advantage to defeat the monster they tracked.

Dawn broke and the bright sun shone into McGuigan's eyes as he stared upon the water of Skeenie Lake. The glare increased the burning sensation he'd felt since midnight, and he pulled his hand from his glove and rubbed his eyes with warm fingers. A cool breeze blew off the large body of water, making his cheeks cold and his nose drip. He enjoyed Harvest at Maskil because he went outside when he wanted, retreated into the warmth of home to thaw and slept in a warm bed each night, protected from the weather. Travelling The Trail in this season was miserable, uncomfortable at best. Under the circumstances, he didn't think he'd enjoy a full day of comfort until Springan, many moons from now.

"My guess is, we're at the lake's most northeast tip." Lyneth stood on a rock overlooking the sparkling water that supported a thin layer of snow-covered ice along its edge. She glanced at the map. "Blue Myst River is less than a mile away. He must be headed to Edgewood. I can't imagine him riding through town with Liam tied to the back of his saddle, so he'll go around it."

"He'll enter." Isla stared down the narrow trail.

"Why?" Jack came to stand beside her.

"There's no sentry. He can enter without question."

"Others will see him, question him."

"Not if he enters after dark."

"So he passes through without stopping."

"He'll stop."

"Where?"

"That, I can't answer, but he'll stop, and they'll let him pass."

"How can you be certain?" Jack's voice remained even, not hinting at his thoughts.

"There's a portal that will take him straight to Wandsworth."

Lyneth climbed off the rock. "Are you sure?"

"I've heard of one, but I don't know where it's located." Isla dragged her glove beneath her nose to wipe away the moisture.

"We need to intercept him before he reaches that portal."

"Will we follow if he does?" Of what McGuigan knew about Wandsworth, he never wanted to visit the city. Not only would he be out of his element, he'd face the entire Maverick gang and more than one monster branded with poyson.

"No." Isla walked to her horse and jumped into the saddle.

He watched the tense muscles in her jaw; she hadn't finished her answer. When their eyes met, he knew it, but he'd never let her go alone. He may not be her mate, but he loved her and would fight by her side.

"We'll decide when the time arrives." Jack mounted.

Deaglan led them on the trail, following the tracks they'd chased all night. Lyneth followed him, then Isla. McGuigan followed her, to ensure she didn't do anything stupid that would get her killed.

Since regaining consciousness shortly after dawn, Liam had bounced on the rump of a horse with his stomach absorbing the hammering and his limbs slapping against the sides of the animal. After an abrupt halt, his captor pushed him off, feet first, and when he struck the ground, pain like that of long needles thrust into his legs brought him to his knees. He cried out in agony and was kicked in the gut for his efforts. The man picked him up by the back of the jacket and forced him to walk. The sharp pain in Liam's legs caused him to fall into the snow where he struggled to rise under the weight of chains and shackles around his wrists and ankles. He lay in the snow, the cold enveloping him while his muscles refused to respond.

He had yet to get a good look at the man, but he knew it to be the haggard middle-aged dwarf Jack had described because of his rugged clothing and boots that still had mud clinging to them despite the snow. The stranger stood nearby, gazing down at the trail they'd left moments ago. The horse was tied a short distance away, shadowed by the dim light of the setting sun.

Darkness creeping upon the land stole the only comfort he clung to and with the light gone, the temperature would drop, leaving him colder than he already felt. He doubted the man would build a fire, giving away his position to anyone who hunted him.

Once again, he rallied his energy to lift himself out of the snow before he became a block of ice and this time, he managed to raise his chest up and settle his butt onto his feet. He gasped for breath and absorbed the ache in his knees. Bending his shoulder forward, he wiped his chin and cheek on his jacket to remove the excess snow.

His nerves settled, but the cold snaked into his bones through his knees that were buried in snow. Bracing his muscles, he gathered strength to propel him upward. The throbbing in his legs defeated his attempt and once again, he fell to his knees. His only chance of avoiding snow was to crawl to the area beneath the evergreen branches, where needles still blanketed the ground. The chains restricted movement of his legs, compelling him to take short, slow strides. By the time he reached the dry needles, exhaustion consumed his body, and he rolled onto the soft bedding and lay on his side.

This position gave him a perfect view of the trail below and of the man who had snatched him from the only friends he had. When the dwarf glanced back at him, the face stirred memories he'd hoped to forget. Hex Sutherland was a man of few words, one who'd served the Mavericks in the shadows for many years. Not all members were introduced to the battle-hardened veteran, but he had been shortly before he was branded. The Mavericks had planned for him to follow in Hex's footsteps, become his apprentice to deal with the trouble that required special attention. He believed this was the reason they wanted him back. Their high hopes had been shattered when he deserted the gang, and according to Faolan Mulock, the leader of the Mavericks, no one deserted them.

His mouth went dry and the growing ache in his heart diverted his attention from his frozen body. If this was a normal man, his friends working together could defeat him, but Hex was far from normal. He was a trained assassin who had been branded with the full dose of poyson. No one had beaten him, and he'd gone up against the toughest thrown at the Mavericks.

A whimper escaped his lips, and Hex peered over his shoulder. The intense stare sent a shiver through his numb body, and he closed his eyes to allow the lids to warm them and to retain the welling tears that threatened to escape and reveal both the pain and the love he endured as he thought about Isla and her friends. They weren't *his* friends; he hadn't earned the right and in truth, he was more danger to them than many they'd meet on The Trail. He had told McGuigan to keep Isla safe, to not give chase if he was captured, but the boy was no match for her determination. It would drive her to do the unthinkable and risk her life for him even when her efforts were futile.

Swallowing slowly, he fought to form a plan. If he released the poyson, it wouldn't break the chains; although it increased his strength, there were limits.

"Hex." His raspy voice caught in the cold air. "What can I give you?"

The man turned back around and watched the trail, while the setting sun drew the last of the light from the land.

"Please. Hex. You must want something." Still, the man ignored him. "Do you want to be a slave to Faolan the rest of your life?"

The man cast him a quick glance.

"You're of a noble race; don't you want your freedom? A mate and to return to your family and friends?"

His top lip twitched, and his eyes darted from one tree to the next.

"Do you have a mate?"

An air of melancholy encased Hex. "There is no escape." He turned back to the road.

"There is. I found the cure."

Hex stomped over, grabbed his jacket and jerked him into the open. The haggard face, inches from his, spewed stale breath upon his cheek. "You still wear the brand."

"I do, but I know where the cure is." His breath came quickly as fire dance in the man's eyes. That fire was fuelled by the poyson. "I'm on my way to get it."

His top lip curled. "Liar."

He shook his head and leant away. "I assure you, it's no lie."

"Faolan said it many times; there's no cure. In all my years of service, no one has escaped."

"Except me."

His top lip twitched, and his eyes roamed over Liam's face as if to find the key to unlock that mystery. "How?"

That one word sent relief to his nerves. "I believed; I had hope."

"Humph. Not enough. What power aided your escape?"

He didn't want to say it and he didn't know if it was true or false, but he had to risk it. "Love."

His face twisted. "For what?"

"A woman."

His grin transformed into a soft chuckle, then laughter. When his entertainment lapsed, he released him and stood back. "The love of a woman is powerless against the brand."

"Have you tried?"

"I love no woman."

"Have you met your mate?"

"You speak nonsense. A mate is no cure."

"No cure, but it's the key to control."

Hex rolled his lips over as he considered him. "Control?"

"After that comes the will to survive and to find the cure."

"I'd need the woman first, and there's no woman who'd desire me the way I'd need a woman."

"But what if there was?" The question hung in the brisk air, giving Liam a chance to form the plan further. "Is there no one from your past you wonder about? Someone who triggered warm feelings. We don't know they are our mates until we explore the relationship further, but our hearts know before we lay with them."

"You found such a woman in Wandsworth, one who'd accept you for the beast you are?"

"I had met her before Wandsworth. I needed only to believe."

"You were a boy, too young for a lover."

"We met when I was seven."

He huffed. "You lie."

"I'd given her my heart the day we met though I was too young to understand. She had given me hers. It's what kept me alive in Wandsworth, made me believe and gave me hope."

"Folk tales for a child." His words, though gruff, did not match the interest in his expression.

"The power of that love and hope gave me the control to leave the Mavericks, leave Wandsworth in search of her."

"Have you found her?"

"Yes."

"She accepts the beast that lives within you?"

"Yes. That's what true mates do."

Seasoned eyes glazed over, and the twitch returned to his upper lip. For many long seconds, the far-off gaze radiated with a deep longing

Liam hadn't seen before. If Hex had a mate, he hadn't been with her for at least five years, probably much longer.

"Impossible. No good woman would accept the likes of us." His voice dipped, revealing an ache in his heart.

"Good women are the ones who will." Liam stood straight, fighting the overwhelming desire to collapse from the strain of holding his body upright. "Is your mate a good woman?"

Hex's eyes flashed, and he struck him across the face, sending him into a snow drift. He stomped through snow, untethered his horse and dragged it forward. With one great arm, he plucked Liam from the snow and tossed him onto the rump of the animal.

Liam's ribs swelled with agony from the rough landing, which expelling air from his lungs and generated bright spots in his vision. The jostling of the horse increased the soreness and extracted the remaining energy from his muscles. He didn't know where he was or how long Hex would travel into the night but a few more hours of this torture, and he'd be beyond the ability to move even if he was still conscious.

24

We're Monsters

DEAGLAN PUT UP HIS hand, and Lyneth slowed. In the dim light of the half moon, she spotted tracks leaving the trail. They weren't the first tracks they'd seen during the day, but the boy paid attention to these ones, getting off his horse to take a closer look.

"It's him." Deaglan jogged up the short hill to the tree line and picked up something from the snow. "The poop is fresh. If the horse relieved himself immediately before they left, they are about fifteen minutes ahead of us."

Lyneth looked in the direction of Edgewood but saw no shadows on the trail. She waited for Deaglan to mount, then reined her horse to follow him. They were half a mile from town, indicating Isla's theory of entering it under the cloak of darkness to avoid suspicious eyes possible. She rubbed her gloved-hand over her chin, then wiped moisture from her nose. Regardless of what happened between here and there, they'd spend the night at Edgewood in a warm inn to recuperate from the two-day non-stop journey. It didn't matter if only one room was available; they'd take it and sleep side-by-side on the floor.

Five minutes later, the faint lights of Edgewood came into view, and between them and the group rode a single horse with one rider. A large bundle rested behind the saddle, but it was too dark and she was too far away to identify the package. It was large enough to be a hauflin, but it might easily be a large bale of blankets to fend off the cold night air near a campfire. The traveller was several hundred feet from the unguarded entrance of the town and appeared in no hurry.

A rush of hooves passed her, spooking her horse and causing it to jump to the side. As she reined it into a straight line, Isla raced forward. The hauflin had better eyesight in these conditions. Did she know it was Liam or was she guessing?

Jack rushed by. "She says its him," he shouted over his shoulder. He sped after Isla, slapping his horse to encourage it to run faster.

He no sooner passed than McGuigan gave chase.

Not wanting to be left behind, she followed, but slowed when she came abreast of Deaglan. "You and Cabela, stay back. Take her to safety if things go bad. Run."

His jaw locked, and he narrowed his eyes. "I'm not a coward."

"No one said you were, but you're too young to die by this monster. Your duty is to ensure that girl gets away alive. Do you understand? This is not your fight."

She kicked her horse, hoping he got the message because she had no time to repeat it. Isla was less than a minute from engaging with the rider, so she'd soon know if this was the man she searched for. Jack was closing the gap, but he was several hundred feet behind her.

Loud hooves beating the ground behind her reached her ears, and she glanced over her shoulder, prepared to curse Deaglan for disobeying. Her eyes locked on dark riders galloping towards them from the forest trail: the dwarfs who had attacked their campsite.

She groaned at the unfortunate turn of events and kicked her horse faster as Deaglan and Cabela sped up. Her mind raced to evaluate the situation but smashed into a roadblock when Isla leapt from her horse and took the kidnapper from the saddle. They wrestled in the dark, rolling through the snow and into the ditch while their horses slowed to a walk. The bundle on the rear of the man's horse remained still. If that was Liam, he was either unconscious or... She pushed the notion from her mind and focussed on the task: reaching Isla.

The solid punch to Isla's face brought stars to her vision, but she ignored them and wiggled her arm free to drive two fingers into the man's throat. He snapped back and pinned her arms in the snow as he leered down at her.

"What business do you have with that boy?" he growled. His face was that of a wild man who'd seen nothing but monsters for years.

"He's my mate!" She spit in his face and bit his wrist.

"Impossible." He gritted his teeth, jerked his hand free and peered closer. "No woman cares for a man like that."

"I do, and I'm taking him back."

Hearing footsteps behind him, the dwarf whirled, taking Isla into his arm and holding a dagger to her neck. "Stop."

Jack and McGuigan froze with their swords at the ready.

"We come for the boy." Jack lowered his sword but held it firmly, ready to defend or attack.

"He's a monster." The man snarled, and his moist, sour breath filled Isla's nostrils. "Why do you want him?"

"He's my son," lied Jack. "I'll not leave without him or her." He pointed to Isla.

"What is she to him?"

"His mate."

"Impossible." He shook his head, rattling the ice that had formed on the tips of his hair. "No woman willingly chooses a man like that."

"You're mistaken. This woman desires him and will sacrifice her life to have him, but I'll not see that happen."

"Die to have him?" He mumbled his words and searched the ground and the faces of those before him. "Why would she die to have a monster in her bed?" he whispered to himself. "Impossible. Can't be true."

"Would I confront you if I didn't love him?" Isla turned her head to look into his eyes. This man appeared to be reasonable. Maybe he wasn't branded with the poyson or at least he had control over it. "I want him by my side, in my bed and in my arms."

He growled, and his face twisted. "Impossible."

"You keep saying that, but mates fight for each other."

"But we're monsters."

"Did your mate abandon you?"

"I didn't give..." He squeezed his eyes shut, and his grip tightened around her. "Calaman," he gasped. His body flinched as if he fought an internal force: the poyson. "I can't face her. She wouldn't..." He shuddered and sharp breaths squeezed between his teeth, spraying spit on the exhale.

"Where is she?" Time was running out. If she didn't break free soon, the poyson would claim him and in the process, her. "Think of her," she said softly. "Let her warm your heart. She can save you."

"Glen Tosh," he said lovingly. "I can never return." He grew hot, sweat formed on his forehead and his eyes flashed open, wild with excitement. "She's gone from me."

"She can save you. Heal the wound. You need only have hope." She swallowed hard and prepared to attempt an escape. "Start with letting me go. Let me take my mate. I need him." Her voice cracked though she struggled to remain calm. "I wish to be with him as you do with your mate. Please." She held the word, filling it with emotion, hoping he'd feel the love she had for Liam.

He tipped his face to the half moon and howled long and hard. By the time he fell silent, tears streaked his cheeks and glistened in the dim light. In one great thrust, he threw her aside, leapt to his feet and onto his horse.

Many other horses arrived in a rush, and she quickly identified the riders as those who had previously attacked the campsite. They skidded their mounts to a halt and drew their swords. The rest of the Warriors stood in a protective circle also with swords drawn. Confused by the whole scene, she tried to ignore it and focus on the bundle behind the haggard dwarf's saddle.

"Hector?" The red-haired dwarf called out to the kidnapper. "Hector Sutherland?"

"Gilmar?" The man's voice was deep and raspy and hung still on the night air.

"We thought you dead."

He scowled, and his eyes darkened. When he spoke, it came out as a low growl. "I am dead." He shoved the bundle from behind his saddle and kicked his horse in the sides, making it lurch forward and speed towards Edgewood.

Isla sprinted to Liam, fell to her knees and lifted his limp body into her arms. Pressing her lips to his, she felt warm breath from his nose on her cheek. While faint, it reassured her; he was alive. His cheeks were cold and stiff, and icicles had formed in his hair. Ice and snow covered the steel shackles on his wrists, and when she pulled back a sleeve, she found the skin blue. He'd lost the glove off his left hand, and she pressed their palms together and wrapped her fingers between his. She sent energy forth, thawing and mending nerves that would die if not warmed soon.

"How do you know him?" The one named Gilmar stared after the man who sped into the darkness.

"I'll tell you if you help us get this man to safety." Isla clenched her jaw. "He's near death, and you'll get nothing from me but trouble if he dies."

"We care not about his fate?" said the dark-haired dwarf who wore a hood and appeared to be the leader.

"But he knows more about Hector Sutherland than any of us." At least she believed he did, given their mutual connection with the Mavericks.

"Why ought we concern ourselves for a man who deserted his family and post?"

"Because he needs to be saved, and we're the ones who can do it." She lowered her voice. "Jack, McGuigan, help me get Liam onto a horse." They stood frozen, unwilling to leave the protective circle. "Now!" she screamed. "Jack, onto your horse. McGuigan, help me get him into the saddle."

Jack kept his eyes on the eight men while he walked to his horse. When he reached it, he sheathed his sword and mounted. He sat to the rear of the saddle and prepared to accept his cargo.

"Easy." Isla held onto Liam's arm to keep it steady while McGuigan heaved him up and into Jack's embrace. "A blanket." She ran to her saddle bag, pulled one out, then returned to Jack. Between the three of them, they spread the blanket over Liam to give him protection from the cold wind generated by riding.

"Go. I'll be right behind you." She pushed on Jack's leg to get him moving towards town, then she turned to the eight men who stood ready to confront her.

"What if they have the package?" Gilmar's horse pranced beneath him, ready to race after the pair if given the signal.

"And what if Hector has already stolen it from us?" She leapt onto her horse. "I value my mate's life more than a stupid package. He can have it," she lied.

"Cameron?" Gilmar stared at the leader, then they both stared in the direction Hector had gone, but the man of mystery had disappeared inside the town, leaving only Jack and Liam on the road.

"Come with us," said Isla, "and I'll tell you where I think he's going." She steered her horse to follow Jack and didn't look back until she was more than fifty feet away. McGuigan, Lyneth, Deaglan and Cabela followed cautiously, watching over their shoulder as the dwarfs discussed their options.

She loped the horse until she came abreast of Jack, then she slowed the pace to see Liam. "Has he stirred?" The question half stuck in her throat as she knew the answer before it escaped, yet she needed to ask it.

"No." He cradled him as if a babe in his arm, guiding the horse with his left hand.

She glanced back and saw the group of dwarfs trailing. "We must buy time, play on their interest with the man named Hector. They seem reasonable, like that of the Rothkin clan."

Jack's brow lowered, obscuring the spark in his eyes in darkness. "Rothkin? What do you know of them?"

"That they are not horrible as some in the Kintale clan will have us believe. The clans seek the same goal, but select members of each seek personal gain. I don't trust the joint efforts, but certain individuals are trustworthy." She released a frustrating breath. "It puzzles me still."

"You can trust many Rothkin."

"And you say this why?"

He considered her a moment before speaking. "Your word?"

"My word."

"I am Rothkin," he whispered.

She raised an eyebrow. "I'm one step closer to solving this mystery." She twisted to see how far the others were behind them. They were getting closer, so she fell silent, thinking of the steps she'd take to ensure Liam recovered fully. Once they were inside the inn, the men who followed would not attack. At least she hoped not.

25

Guide Him into Manhood

THE FIRST NERVE TO awaken told him he lived and that he hadn't succumbed to the conditions on The Trail, yet he feared where he'd find himself when all his senses revived. The second nerve to stir told him his body was far from well and pain was inevitable, and when he braced himself for the onslaught, it opened the floodgate and he twisted from the all-consuming ache that touched every limb and every muscle, including those in his chest that supported breathing. He gasped but froze midway to stall the pain that tortured his ribs and threatened to send him back to unconsciousness.

Warm moist air touched his ear, providing the only relief from the otherwise horrid state he endured. His senses continued to awaken, introducing new aches in his fingers, wrists and ankles. The desire to collapse into the dusk of nothingness grew, and while he fought the pounding in his head, his heart stopped to listen; someone spoke his name softly, warming his ear and tickling the hairs within. Hot fingers on his cheek enticed him to endure the pain and awake fully.

"Liam."

His name once again fell upon his ear. The voice was gentle, low, feminine. The familiar sound stirred warm feelings; Isla? Had she found him? Where was Hex?

"I'm waiting for you."

The whisper brought a smile to his lips, then hot silky skin pressed against them, and he knew without doubt whose skin that was. Her scent filled his air passages, fought its way through the tangled mess in his veins and found his heart. He'd bear pain ten times as much as that pulsating through his body to be with her.

The muscles around his eyes tugged on his eyelids, but they refused to open. He reached up and rubbed one of his eyes, and a warm finger gently rubbed the other. Together, they forced his eyelids open, and he stared into the most magnificent face he'd ever seen. Her dark eyes swept over him, warming his heart and soothing the aches in his muscles momentarily as he held his breath.

"I'd linger 'til the end of my days plus another moon for you." She kissed his mouth and came up smiling and caressing his cheek.

He didn't know how she'd found him or how she came to be with him, but it didn't matter; they were together again. He eased breath from his lungs and gasped for more, clenching his muscles as pain shot through his ribs. The horse. The hours of bouncing on the back of it had done severe damage.

"Breathe easy. Your ribs are badly bruised." She combed his hair with her fingers. "Your chest is black and blue."

He glanced at the blankets covering him and felt them against his skin as if he wore no clothing. Catching sight of his wrist, he rotated his hand in front of him; it was bruised and cut.

"The shackles. They were frozen to your skin." She grasped his hand. "But you'll keep all your fingers." She kissed them, then laid his palm against her cheek.

"Where is...?" The burning in his throat erased his voice, and he winced from the pain of speaking.

"Water?"

He nodded, hoping it would ease the burning. She held a cup to his lips, and he sipped the warm liquid.

"Jack. Tea. Please." She returned her attention to him and held up the cup again as Jack left the room.

He took another sip, swallowed slowly, then relaxed his muscles. "Where is Hex?"

"Hex? Who is that?"

He tensed his muscles and coughed lightly. "The man..." He swallowed. "The man who took me prisoner."

"Hex?" A stout, dark-haired dwarf stood at the foot of the bed. "His name is Hector Sutherland."

"Who are you?" He rested his hand over his throat, hoping to still the hurt.

"Cameron Tumblin of Vale of Avoca, and we seek the item Hector Sutherland stole from you."

"They've searched your belongings and didn't find the package," said Isla, "so we assume it was either lost in the snow or the man who took you had stolen it." She thrust a finger in the stranger's direction. "These men want it." She hid her face from the man at the foot of the bed as well as the red-haired stranger who stood near him. Her eyes endeavoured to send a message and after she winked, she continued. "Do you remember?"

He coughed and gripped his chest for the strain of the action triggered another shot of pain to rip through him. Closing his eyes, he waited for it to subside, but it rumbled through his body to every limb and sparked a whine. He gritted his teeth and slowed his breathing. What item did they speak of? The package they were to deliver to Bagnio? Lyneth carried that, not him.

"Sit down," ordered Isla. "He needs time. He almost froze to death." She slipped her hand beneath the blanket and rested it on his chest. "Take shallow breaths."

Her warm hand pressed against his skin relaxed his nerves, but he felt something else: her healing hand helping him breathe. "No." He removed her hand and held it in his. "Give me time not... Please." He pleaded with his eyes to send a clear message. He didn't want to exhaust her when he'd heal naturally with time.

The men no sooner took seats along the wall, when the door opened, and Jack entered carrying a mug.

"I've added extra cream, so it won't be too hot." He handed the mug to Isla, then went to the other side of the bed and sat next to Liam. "You had us worried, son."

It wasn't the first time Jack had called him that but as the occurrences grew in number, the deeper he felt it. He'd been without a das for six years. Those were the vital years when a boy needed a role model, someone to protect him from the dangers of those who sought to bring him harm and someone to guide him into manhood. Alone, he stumbled, second guessing every move.

Isla tipped the mug to his lips, and he took a good sip, letting the warm, sweet liquid fill his mouth and slide down his parched throat. Resting on the pillow, he grasped Jack's hand and gave him a reassuring smile. "I'm sorry."

Jack clasped his hand between his. "Sorry? Unnecessary. It's the cost of caring, and I've come too far to undo that expenditure."

"In other words," said Isla, "you're not getting away with silly boyish behaviour without him correcting you like a das."

Jack smiled. "That, too. If that's acceptable to you."

Liam squeezed his hand. "I'd like that." Tears warmed his eyes as he thought about his das and how they had sat together many times talking about life. His das would have liked Jack. He blinked away the moisture, but a tear escaped and raced for his ear. Jack wiped it away and patted the side of his head.

"After tea, you'll rest. You've been through a tremendous ordeal."

Cameron stood and came to bedside. "You call the man who captured you Hex. Why?"

"It's what I knew him by," said Liam in a hushed voice to prevent his throat from burning.

"Where was he headed?"

"Wandsworth."

"That's where I believe he's gone, too," said Isla, looking up at the dwarf. "But there is something you should know before you give chase."

"Speak."

"Have you heard of the Mavericks? The street gang in Wandsworth?"

"In passing. Rumours mostly."

"What about their method of branding members?"

"That we have not heard." He looked to the other dwarf. "Gilmar, have you?"

The man stood. "No. What is it?"

Isla explained the branding process, then warned them. "This man Hex or Hector was branded; he'll kill you without mercy."

"Yet, you engaged him," said Cameron.

"He had my mate; I'd have done anything to reclaim him."

"Why did he not transform into this beast you speak of?"

"He didn't?" Liam searched his memory. Hex was branded; that was certain, but what had stopped the poyson from taking control?

"He didn't," said Isla.

"Why?" asked Liam.

"I convinced him his mate had the power to help him."

"His mate?" Cameron glanced at Gilmar. "Calaman?"

"Possibly," said Gilmar. "She's not taken another since his disappearance."

"He said that name," said Isla. "It must be her."

Cameron frowned. "Her family will never accept Hector after his disgraceful behaviour."

"Her family doesn't matter." Isla grasped Liam's free hand. "It's what's in her heart."

Liam knew what she meant. She'd love him regardless of how her das felt. Although Bronwyn had permitted her to travel with him, the man was far from allowing him into the family. If Bronwyn refused to accept those less than ideal, he'd find himself alone with his foolish honour. At the least, he'd estrange his daughter, who would never abandon her mate.

"What's in the steel box?" Isla became serious. "What's so important you'd risk your life for it? And what does it have to do with the dwarf curse?"

The two men stared at each other, neither willing to part with the information.

Isla waited a moment, then turned to Liam and held up the mug of tea. A lone eyebrow rose, and a smile creased her lips. She was up to something.

૭ ❖ os

Lyneth dipped the corner of her toast into the runny egg yolk, then bit off the end as her eyes roamed around her table and to the adjacent table where the dwarfs from Vale of Avoca also broke the fast. Sitting with her, McGuigan, Deaglan and Cabela were Spray and Odart. The four at the other table remained nameless, and she hoped they'd continue as such and they'd be on their way without further fuss, believing Hector Sutherland possessed the package they wanted to steal.

Isla was crafty for making them think Liam had carried the item and it was the reason Sutherland had captured him. The memory of standing in the cold night air surrounded by these dwarfs with swords drawn and facing the branded man put her nerves on high alert. She'd felt as if she had fallen between a dragon ready to breathe fire and troglodytes preparing to feast. Once again, Isla had used her charm to convince the enemy to assist them in their time of need, and they had used their skill and tools to remove the shackles from Liam's wrists and ankles.

With Cameron and Gilmar waiting for Liam to wake to question him about Sutherland, the six others, she presumed, were to keep an eye on the rest of the Warriors. Jack had entered the dining area of the inn moments earlier to fetch a cup of tea. He paused briefly to say Liam had awakened, then retreated quickly to the room.

"Boy, what is your sire's name?" Odart took a drink of tea.

McGuigan chewed on sausage, watching the man who sat across from him.

"We prefer to keep family out of our affairs," said Lyneth.

"I did not address you, but this boy with blue eyes of a family I know well." Odart put his cup down. "Conall Mulryan's family is large and travels afar; I wish to know if he be kin."

"I don't know him." McGuigan took a drink, eyeing him over the rim of the cup.

"Not what I asked. Are you kin?"

"No." He bit into his toast, then filled his fork with egg and slipped it between his lips.

"Conall enjoys news about kin on The Trail." He scratched his beard roughly. "If you were kin, you'd be keen on him knowing you are well."

"I said I was not."

"We don't care what this Conall man enjoys," said Lyneth. "He's no one to us. McGuigan is kin to me, and we have nothing to do with the Mulryan family."

"Kin to you?" He considered both and smirked. "I see the resemblance."

"There's more to kin than the eye beholds." She sipped her tea. "Are you all kin?"

"No. Colleagues on a mission."

"That mission is to gain access to... What is in the package?"

"You were not told?" asked Odart.

"We deliver without unnecessary questions. We ask only the item not cause us personal harm."

"You should be wary of what you deliver."

"Why? Does this item threaten our well-being?" The danger of the package was always a concern, but she was told it wouldn't harm the one carrying it. Whether her contact spoke the truth or not was another matter. Isla remained in possession of the item and so far, nothing had happened.

"It is not my place to say," said Odart.

"Whose place is it? Cameron's?" When he didn't answer, she pressed the matter. "You don't know what's in the box, do you?"

He glanced at Spray, and the two remained silent.

"Hector Sutherland. Was he a member of this fine group you've establish to steal from innocent travellers?"

"You're hardly innocent travellers," said Spray.

"And Sutherland? Was he hardly an innocent thief?"

"He deserted us."

"You're certain." It was a statement, yet one that deserved a response.

"Without doubt."

"Then you'll not hesitate to kill him to obtain the package." Again, they exchanged glances, leaving her wondering about their words. "You don't wish to kill him."

"If it can be avoided, it will be," said Odart. "Our goal is the package; we value life or you'd not have been left alive at your campsite."

Isla had somehow known this and used it to her advantage, as she had on the road from Wirksworth when Tigh na Mare warriors had attacked The Mercenaries. Perhaps Isla's theory about the Rothkin clan not being the enemy to the Kintale clan carried weight.

"Good to know." She dipped a piece of toast into the yolk she'd broken open. "We also value life. Perhaps there's room to work together." She bit off the end of the toast.

"You'd help us track Hector?"

"I didn't say that; we're on our own mission of mercy that will take us in the opposite direction of Wandsworth."

"What are you suggesting?" asked Odart.

"Nothing until I learn what is in the package."

"You'll have to discuss that with Cameron."

"We have plenty of time. The boy will need to recover before we begin for Wedgemore."

"Yet, we are rushed to get underway."

"We'll find middle ground if that is our desire." She once again dipped the toast and brought the soggy bread to her mouth. As Elspeth had done, she'd make allies instead of enemies across Ath-o'Lea, calling on them if in need or avoiding unnecessary conflict due to lack of connection. But unlike Elspeth, she'd work with both Rothkin and Kintale kin to safeguard her and the group as they travelled. No one in the Warriors held alliances with either clan, making it easier for them to remain neutral in the battle for dominance where it concerned the dwarf curse.

26

Provided Little Creature Comforts

THE LARGE VILLAGE OF Bagnio was blanketed in a fresh layer of snow. The traffic earlier in the day had beaten it down on the thoroughfare and churned it brown in the soft ground that was far from frozen. Isla thought of the dirt and slush gathering in the hooves of Two-bit Spindrift and the work it'd take to clean them thoroughly. This was another reason she didn't like travelling in late Harvest, but the foremost one was keeping warm at all times. For now, she was snug in the saddle behind Liam but when they had started the day, she rode in front and the cold seeped between the fibres of her clothes, giving her a chill.

She snuggled into his back and pressed her cheek against his shoulder while she watched the first buildings of Bagnio appear. He glanced over his shoulder and gave a reassuring smile. He'd spent three days in bed at Edgewood before she'd allow him to continue on The Trail. Although Lyneth was eager to get underway after the men from Vale of Avoca left in search of Hector Sutherland, she'd not risk Liam's health to ensure the package arrived safely in this village. His life meant more than a hundred of the packages she carried.

Not Cameron nor Gilmar or the others divulged the contents of the steel box, leaving Isla to wonder about its importance. When she had asked them what it had to do with the dwarf curse, the two had exchanged glances that told her it was vital to its resolution. The contact who had given it to Lyneth was elf, so had no personal connection with the curse; perhaps that was why she handed it to someone else. Isla was required to accompany Lyneth to the drop off location to be her eyes and ears, and to learn more about the item's importance.

She'd been tempted many times over the past seven days to open the box, but it was secure. To open it, she'd have to damage it and that would alert those she delivered it to that it had been tampered with.

Bagnio rested south of North Hillock. It was known to all around as the village of warm baths. Natural springs flowing from the ground provided warm water that filled small pools that accommodated one to twenty people, depending on the pool. She looked forward to soaking in one before sun set. It'd help her weary muscles but more importantly, it'd chase the cold from her bones.

In The Mercenaries' style, the group entered the village in two smaller groups. Lyneth, Liam and she entered first, and ten minutes behind them, Jack led McGuigan, Deaglan and Cabela. The four in the rear would find Wynn's Saddlery in the centre of the settlement and window-browse while she and Lyneth entered the shop across the street. Liam would wait outside, watching the horse, the door and the others.

Lyneth guided her horse to a hitching rail and dismounted.

"Looking forward to a warm bath?" Isla asked Liam as she slipped her foot into the stirrup.

"I've dreamt of nothing else for the past three days." He held her arm to ease her to the ground.

"Nothing? Not even me?"

He grinned. "Who do you think was in the bath with me?"

She hid her smile while she tied the reins to the pole. She'd like nothing better than the two of them in the pool, but public bathes were open to everyone. Looking up, she found Lyneth waiting for her, so she followed her inside Murissa's Delightful Hat Boutique.

Inside the cosy shop hung dozens of colourful hats for all occasions. Many more rested on numerous shelves, some stacked a foot high. Hats for ladies ran down the left-hand side of the shop while hats for men filled the right side.

Isla wasn't a fan of hats unless they kept her head warm on a cold day, but a few on display were cute, and she imagined herself wearing them during hot Sumortide days to keep the sun out of her eyes. She peeked at the price tag of one she liked and quickly released it. She'd have to work a full three days at her aunts' dress shop to pay for it. Given the price of the hats, she wasn't surprised to see the shop empty of customers, leaving Lyneth to discuss business with the keeper without concern for someone eavesdropping.

A stout dwarf in a fine dress and a finer hat tended the embellished counter that held items men and women confined to a village or town would use. Her wide-brimmed hat was made from soft material and flowed in a gentle wave around her head. Delicate lace, colourful feathers and a silk bow decorated the top, giving the woman an air of pretension. Although Isla couldn't see her feet, she imagined she wore fashionable shoes with a heel, making walking awkward and running impossible. Unless this woman knew magic, she was incapable of defending herself. Given the business they conducted, she'd have been wiser to dress appropriately for an attack.

"Good afternoon." The woman's attention left the bowtie she worked on. While she smiled, her eyes revealed her repulsion of two Trail-hardened women in her shop, the mud and slush from their boots leaving tracks from the door to where they stood.

"Good afternoon," said Lyneth. She glanced around the shop before continuing. "We have a package for Murissa Calhoun from Allestree."

The woman's expression changed quickly. "The word is?"

"Sunshine."

"Come with me." She ushered them around the counter and to the door near the rear.

Isla followed Lyneth through the door, then stood off to the side to observe the transaction. Moments before they reached the hat shop, she'd given Lyneth the package for delivery. No doubt Cameron and his men would be sadly disappointed when they discovered they were sent on a worthless hunt. She felt guilty about sending them after Hector, not because she tricked them into believing he had the package, but because Hector might kill them, and she didn't want that to happen. While she warned them of the dangers and told them what to expect, the twinge of guilt lingered.

"The item?" Murissa waited, studying Lyneth with a curious eye.

Isla glanced at the woman's feet. High-heeled shoes. She appeared in no condition to defend against anyone who wanted to steal the package, but it didn't matter. Lyneth would exchange the package for payment, and the safety of the item would fall into the hands of this dwarf.

Lyneth pulled the pouch from her pocket and dumped the steel box into her hand. "We had a group of men from Vale of Avoca attempt to steal it." She handed it to the woman.

"Avoca? Cameron Tumblin?"

"The same."

"They've desired it for years."

"Are they Rothkin?"

"They serve them."

"And you serve Kintale?"

"I serve customers seeking unique hats."

"We hold no alliances."

"You'll never need to choose a side." Murissa looked at Isla. "You will."

"I'm not dwarf," said Isla.

"This curse involves hauflins equally."

"I'll choose those who do right regardless of their sire's name."

"That will be Kintale."

"I've seen good and bad in both. I'll choose the good." Her thoughts went to Arthur. Perhaps she'd judged him too harshly, yet she reacted with the information she had. If he had told her the truth from the beginning, her decision to leave him may have been different, but... Once she'd met Liam, they'd have parted ways.

"Have Cameron and his men followed you here?" asked Murissa.

"No," said Lyneth, "they're heading elsewhere, searching for the package."

The woman raised a curious eyebrow. "They are not fooled easily."

"I didn't say it was easy."

Isla waited silently as Murissa placed the item in a wooden chest and removed from that chest a small sack that jingled with coins. She handed this to Lyneth and thanked her for her service.

On the way out the front door, Isla noted Liam still waited by the horse and the others loitered near the window at the saddlery across the street.

"You can afford to buy one of those pretty hats." Lyneth patted the pocket where she stored the sack of coins.

"I have better places for my takings than in a silly hat."

"I saw you checking them out."

"Checking them out and leaving them behind." She patted her belly. "That's a lot of bacon and eggs."

"And biscuits."

"Yes! We can't forget the biscuits."

Lyneth chuckled. "You can't."

She untied the horse and waited for Liam to mount, then she climbed up behind him. "Ready for that bath?"

"More than ready." He pulled the horse away from the rail and followed Lyneth down the street.

The anticipation of a warm bath, a hot ration and a warm bed warmed her blood. Today would end in a good, warm evening.

⁊ ❖ ⁊

Lyneth removed her boots and wiggled her toes. The mild temperatures along with the warmth trapped beneath the shelter Isla had created made it cosy near the fire though they were well into Forstig. For all the magic Elspeth cast, she'd never crafted such a shelter. Her spells focussed on attacking their enemy. While that was great in battle, it provided little creature comforts on The Trail and in the end, it hadn't saved her from Orenda.

"According to my map," said Jack, "tomorrow we arrive at a footpath entering the mountains."

"Why does that concern us?" asked Lyneth.

"We shall engage it."

"That takes us away from Wedgemore and Dougendun."

"The unique village of Inishmore on the edge of Forest of Caucy has a portal to Dougendun. It's a five-day ride from the trailhead."

"Inishmore?" The name of her hometown rolled lovingly off her tongue. She longed to visit family, but she wanted to keep them secret from outsiders. The only one who knew was Rhys, and that was under special circumstances: to save Isla's life.

"You've heard of it?" he asked.

"I have."

~ 329 ~

"Have you been there?"

"Yes."

"So you know the way."

"I do. Where is the portal?"

"I am not at liberty to say at this time."

She considered the many places within Inishmore a portal might exist, but none stood out more than the other. Did her family own the location? If so, why hadn't she been told of it?

"When will we get to Wedgemore?" McGuigan bit into a slice of bread.

"After Dougendun," said Jack.

"Immediately afterwards," said Lyneth. She was as anxious as McGuigan to leave Cabela at Wedgemore, and the sooner the better. Cabela had proven time and again she was more interested in creating unnecessary drama than learning how to survive on The Trail. In the weeks since departing Bagnio, she'd lost the shine in Deaglan's eyes, leaving him to help only where necessary, but he no longer doted on her and answered her every whim.

"Whoa!" McGuigan's face lit up. "If we travel by portal, we won't camp in the cold and snow."

"Now you understand." Isla slapped his shoulder playfully.

He stared at Liam. "You will be healed sooner."

"It can't come soon enough," said Liam.

"For everyone." McGuigan grinned as he chewed the bread.

Lyneth understood that, too, and she shared his fears of the poyson.

"We agree then," said Jack. "We take the mountain path to Inishmore."

"I didn't agree." Cabela rubbed her ankle.

"You don't have a say." Lyneth pulled off her socks and set them near the fire to dry thoroughly. "We go to Inishmore."

"I'm a part of this group, so my opinion matters."

"You have a say in your destination and if you choose not to go, you are welcome to continue onward alone."

"This is unacceptable." Cabela grasped Deaglan's wrist. "You'll come with me, won't you?"

"He comes with us." Lyneth pulled her food sack near.

"He gets to choose."

"He is under our supervision until we can return him to his aunt and uncle."

"He's sixteen and if he wants, he's welcome to stay with us." McGuigan grabbed a second piece of bread and spread peanut butter on it. "He's to our benefit, and he's teaching us how to use a bow."

"Deaglan?" Cabela pleaded and blinked her sad eyes at him. "You will stay with me, won't you?"

"I like you, but I want to stay with my friends."

"Hmph." She folded her arms and made a pouty face.

Lyneth tried to hide her smile but bathed in the glow of the flames and in tight formation around the fire, it was near impossible. If Deaglan was a little older, she wouldn't mind him staying with the group; he had skills others didn't have. However, he was young, and she felt obligated to Morwen and Rhys to return him. She'd already sent a letter from Gabardine, explaining how he had followed them through the mountain pass and how their mission prevented them from returning him immediately. She assured them he'd be cared for to the best of her ability, but they understood there was no guarantee when travelling The Trail.

27

Versed in Archaic Magic

ISLA SMELT THE SHIRT. If she'd been somewhere warm or at home in Maskil, she'd have tossed it in the wash pile without hesitation, but this close to Wintertide, anything washed had to be hung by the fire to dry and she was unsure if it'd dry by morning. Spending time washing clothes meant less time exploring Inishmore, a village she'd heard little about through individuals who either wanted to protect its secrets or who knew nothing factual about it. She smelt the shirt again. It would do for another day, so she threw it to the foot of the bed.

They had arrived in Inishmore on the edge of Forest of Caucy around noon. If Jack hadn't guided them here, she doubted they'd have found it and instead rode by without thinking twice about the snow-covered mounds. The village existed within a long stretch of mammoth boulders the residents, who were almost exclusively humans and elves interbred, had carved into homes and shops. When they had entered, she thought it small, but as Lyneth led them down the cobblestone streets, she found it never ending. The dwellings not carved into stone were constructed with stone that matched the boulders perfectly. She'd been to many places, but she'd never seen anything like this.

"Is that the wash pile?" Liam held a small bundle of clothes in his hands, ready to drop it on the shirt that had passed inspection.

"No."

He dropped his clothes. "It is now."

A single knock came to the door before it opened, and Jack entered the room. "Lyneth, may I speak with you?" He closed the door behind him.

"Did you arrange for the use of the portal?"

"Yes. We are scheduled in the morning, but there's a second matter I wish to discuss."

"Which is?" Lyneth created her own wash pile on her bed.

Jack glanced around the room. "Cabela's not here?"

"She and Deaglan went for a walk."

"Good." He stepped closer.

Isla pulled another shirt from her rucksack and glanced over her shoulder. Jack sounded strange, and the way he approached Lyneth indicated he was...nervous? Why was he nervous? She continued her sorting with her ears on their conversation and her eyes on the clothes Liam tried to throw into the wash pile.

"I'm torn," said Jack.

"About?" asked Lyneth.

"A woman of unique attributes dwells in Inishmore." He spoke slowly, as if weighing his options with every word. "She may possess the talent to aid my expedition, but I have intense reservations."

"Help you with what?"

"Locate someone."

Isla grabbed her singlet Liam dropped into the wash pile but before she had a chance to rescue it, he snatched if from her hands.

"What is this woman's name?" asked Lyneth.

"Elwyn," said Jack.

"Good grief. Do you honestly want to subject yourself to her mulishness?"

"You know her?"

She released a loud sigh and crossed her arms. "If I tell you, will you tell no one else?"

"I promise."

Isla glanced over her shoulder and found Lyneth staring at her.

"Both of you? Tell no one?" When Isla and Liam nodded, Lyneth continued. "Elwyn is my great great-grandmother."

Jack stood back. "Incredible."

She shook her head. "It's not something I brag about."

"But she is versed in archaic magic and has sight others lack."

"While that's true, more than 150 years of playing with tea leaves and seeing into the lives of others has made her a little edgy."

"Edgy?"

"*Eccentric*, let's say."

"Yet she delivers accuracy?"

"That's a word she misinterprets. She will give you the truth, but you may not understand it."

Jack braced his jaw. "Can you take me to her?"

"You must truly be desperate."

"I am."

"Can we come?" Isla turned. "She sounds interesting."

Jack considered her and was about to speak, when his expression softened. "I believe it will be to my benefit that you come as far as the door, but no farther. My session will be private."

"Understood." She tossed her rucksack onto the bed.

"What about our wash?" Liam grabbed her arm.

"This won't take long," she said. "It'll be here when we come back and if it's not, then we'll thank the person who washes it for us."

"Or you could leave it at the wash woman's shop," said Lyneth.

"They have wash service?" Her eyes widened. "Lead the way." She grabbed the items that had initially passed inspection and threw them into the dirty pile.

Moments later, Isla held Liam's hand and followed Lyneth and Jack down a lane that led towards the centre of the village.

"She knows you're coming," said Lyneth to Jack.

"She does?"

"She will sense your need the nearer you get to her dwelling."

"She is indeed all I expected. Will she know what I seek?"

"No. She'll feel your overwhelming desire for help."

"Incredible. Any advice?"

"If you want to avoid confrontation, drink the tea when she asks."

"Tea?"

"She will offer you a cup, and she'll also drink one."

"Is that all?"

"If her eyes turn red, speak my name."

"And if I don't?"

"You don't want to know."

Lyneth stopped a hundred feet from a mammoth boulder that rested separate from the other buildings. A thick wooden ladder led to an oval door six feet off the ground. A dim light glowed within the dwelling. "You're on your own from here."

"Thank you."

"Don't thank me yet."

Isla scanned the shops along the lane and spotted The Sweet Spot with a sign that suggested chocolate within. She tugged Liam towards it. "While you're getting your question answered, we'll be in here getting my sweet tooth smothered in chocolate."

"Great idea." Lyneth followed her. "I'll get you a few," she said to Jack. "You'll need it." She laughed.

At the door, Isla paused to watch Jack approach the ladder. She believed she knew the question he'd ask, and she hoped with all her might this woman named Elwyn knew the answer. Liam nudged her from behind and she entered the shop, breathing deeply as the aroma of chocolate filled her senses. The only smell sweeter was her mate fresh from a bath.

"Cherry filled," said Liam softly in her ear.

Her mouth watered thinking about biting into her favourite sweet flavour.

"Should we tell McGuigan about this place or keep him in suspense about where we got our treats?" Lyneth chuckled. "There's no green mint jellies."

"But there are chocolate-covered mint jellies." Liam pointed to the display case.

"I've never seen those." Isla took a closer look. "I wonder if he likes them."

"This is McGuigan," he said. "I've never seen him turn down food of any sort."

"Except biscuits with raisins."

"Okay, but that's it."

"I'll get a few. If he won't eat them, I will." She browsed the entire shop before making her decision of which treats she'd buy. In the end, she settled on six cherry-filled chocolates and six chocolate-covered mint jellies.

They exited the shop and stood outside near the window to wait for Jack. He'd been with Elwyn for more than twenty minutes. Unable to stall her taste buds longer, Isla bit into a chocolate, letting the flavour swim over her tongue and around her mouth to touch every tooth before she swallowed it. Liam and Lyneth were also savouring their treats, and she was about to pluck one more from the bag when Elwyn's door flew open.

"Isla!" Jack hung from the opening and searched the area for her.

Lyneth rushed forward and crossed the span in seconds to climb the ladder. "Elwyn. Stop!"

"No. I'm okay. I need Isla." His face was flushed, and his breathing laboured. Sweat dripped from his brow and around his wild eyes. "I need you." It sounded more like a whine than a cry for help.

Isla stared up at the distraught man. Perhaps Lyneth shouldn't have brought him here. She scanned the front of the dwelling and found dandelions and marigolds in full bloom hanging in baskets on either side of the door. How? The frost and snow should have killed them. Then she spotted a wind chime dangling from a bracket ten feet in the air, singing a sweet, gentle tune yet no breeze blew. It reminded her of Beathas' windchime at Moon Meadow.

"Isla, come inside." Jack waved to her to come quickly.

"I'm not sure I want to do this." She took a step back.

"You must." His moist eyes pleaded with her.

A well-seasoned elf stuck her head out of the doorway. Her deep-green eyes reminded Isla of Willow, except these intense eyes felt as though they'd snap her in two if she disobeyed.

"Come inside, child." Her aged voice sailed through the air and pricked Isla's ears. "I've been waiting for you."

"Lyneth?" She looked to her friend for reassurance.

"She provided the cure when you were dying of Geata Syndrome. You can at least thank her."

She took another step back. "Thank you for saving my life."

"The least of my efforts for what you'll bring to me. Come inside."

"I've said my peace."

"Isla, please." Jack's face twisted in anguish.

She clenched her fist; she wanted to help but the chaotic energy the woman radiated sent her nerves racing for cover.

"I'll come with you." Liam walked towards the ladder.

"Evil filth is undesirable in my domicile." Elwyn flung her boney fingers forward, and an invisible force hurled him against a building twenty-five feet away. He slammed against the stone, crashed to the ground and lay in a heap, moaning.

Isla raced to his side and cradled him in her arms. "Liam?"

Shivering, he gripped her as if wind would blow him away. "Don't go in there."

Lyneth knelt beside them, assessing him for injury. "GRAMS, that was unnecessary," she shouted over her shoulder. "He's a friend of mine and means you no harm."

"Hush, child. Bring the girl to me."

"No. I will not force her."

As Isla held Liam, his shaking subsided. "Are you injured?"

"I don't think so."

"Isla?"

Jack waited, hoping she'd reconsider and enter the dwelling. Knowing his question and how long he had searched for his mate tugged at her heart. She had promised to help find her and if this was the course to do so, she had to enter. "Stay with him," she said to Lyneth. She rose and focussed her attention on the haggard woman in the doorway.

"Don't go in looking for a fight," said Lyneth. "You'll get one."

"She started it." She marched towards the ladder and scrambled up the rungs. "Jack, what is it you need?"

"Your presence." He smiled uneasily as he held out a hand to help her over the last step and into the stone dwelling.

"That's it?"

"I am told so."

A gentle aroma of lavender mixed with another herb greeted her senses, enticing her to calm her mind and relax her muscles, but she was far from surrendering to the persuasion of this woman who wielded archaic magic. The warm glow of several candles created a tranquil atmosphere, but Jack was anything but serene, so she'd keep on guard. A neat round table on the opposite side of the room was surrounded by three chairs, each laden with a decorative pillow made of glimmering red materials and golden frills.

"Please, sit." Elwyn directed them to the table as she glided across the matted floor and slipped onto the seat to the right. "Jack." She gestured to the seat across from her. "Isla, the lost child." She tapped the chair next to her.

"I'm not lost." She followed Jack to the table and sat down. The small size of the table meant Elwyn could reach Jack's hands as easily as hers, so she kept hers beneath the surface. Across from her, a round earthen-coloured tea pot, spewing steam from its spout, rested on a cast iron trivet next to a pot of honey and a basket of blooming chamomile. The warm air sent billowing waves of the fragrant flower's aroma into her air passages and for a moment, she enjoyed the delicate scent.

Elwyn set a saucer then a cup in front of her and when all appeared well, she poured hot tea from the pot into it. When she was done, she poured herself a cup of tea, then returned the pot to the trivet. Plucking one chamomile flower from a stem, she dropped it into Isla's cup and settled into her chair to gaze upon her.

"Drink, my dear." She whispered the order, and her eyes grew wide with anticipation.

"Why?" Isla pinched the inside of her thigh, bringing her senses to fully awake.

"It is good for the spirit."

"Whose spirit?"

"Yours."

She picked up the cup, remembered what the woman had done to Liam, and threw it against the wall. It shattered into a hundred pieces and left the liquid to ooze down the stone.

"Isla," whispered Jack, "you were warned to drink the tea."

"I have no question for this woman." She glared at Elwyn. "Only answers."

"Answers I cannot access unless you..." Elwyn's furrowed brow instantly turned upward, and she smiled sweetly at the pair. She walked to a nearby cupboard, extracted an item, then returned to the table.

Isla glanced at the single chocolate the woman placed in the centre of the tea cup saucer. It resembled the ones she'd recently bought. She sniffed the air gently; cherry filled. "Ask me any question. If I have the answer, I'll give it freely."

"You've been asked already." Elwyn tilted her head, and her green eyes sparkled in the candle light.

"What's the question?"

"Where is Jack's mate?"

"I don't know where she is."

"But you do. You've met her."

"I have?" She glanced at Jack, who sat on the edge of his seat, waiting for the truth to be revealed. A jumbled mess of images flashed through her mind as she tried to decipher the faces of those who revealed their true race and those who hid their newlin identity from her. Several women Jack's age came to mind, but she was unsure. "How do you know I've met her?"

"You emanate a fragrance foreign to this land, one that comes from Knavesmire."

"Is that all you have? I've met many newlins who... What do you mean I emanate their fragrance? I've had many baths since I've met them, and the only one I've been with since my last bath is Jack. I carry no newlin scent but his."

"You know much about things you know nothing about." Her smile grew and pressed her cheeks against the bottom of her eyes.

"That clarifies things." She furrowed her brow but when the aroma of chocolate drifted into her nose, she glanced at the treat on the saucer.

"Every being carries an essence, and that essence lingers in the energy of others they've touched." Elwyn sipped her tea. "I can track, follow, identify these essences, and you bear that of Floriana Asuwish."

"Asuwish? Not Somerled?"

"I feared others might find me if I used my real name," said Jack.

"Including your mate." Isla rolled her eyes. "Do you deliberately make it difficult to find each other? Should I assume Floriana also disguised herself and changed her name?"

"You should."

"Can she make herself younger?"

"Yes."

"So she might be the woman at the candy shop across the street, the woman who sold me bacon in Ellswire or any number of people I've met but don't know."

"No." Elwyn took another sip of tea. "I sense more."

"If you sense her, tell me about her." Once again, her eyes went to the chocolate, and her fingers itched to pick it up. The taste of the lone one she'd eaten outside the candy shop lingered on her lips, and it made her crave another.

"It is what I desire." She took another sip of tea and spied on her over the rim of the cup.

Unable to contain her craving, Isla picked up the chocolate and put it to her lips. Before her teeth clamped down upon it, a hand thrust forward and shoved the chocolate into her bottom lip and chin. Her head snapped back and when she came upright, she stared into Elwyn's wild eyes searching for some unknown answer in the chocolate mess on her face.

The intense gaze moved upward over her face and settled on her eyes. Pressure intensified against the barrier of her life force, and she activated her defences, imagining solid wooden doors, thick steal bars and drawbridges slamming shut to keep the woman out.

"Let me in," she cried desperately, her green eyes shining like two full moons in the night sky.

"No!" Her fingers worked beneath the table, gathering energy to build doors to keep Elwyn out of her nwyfre. The almost pure-breed elf would not reach the meadow where her magic dwelt. Each time she blinked, another door went up, securing her inner world, her memories, her desires and fears.

"Who taught you this magic?"

"I did!"

Elwyn slapped her face. "It's Floriana's magic; it is her mark."

"This is unacceptable!" Jack stood and grabbed the woman's arm when she went to strike Isla again. "We're done."

"You have taken me this far; I must know." She ripped her hand from his grip. "Who taught you how to defend your nwyfre?" She peered at the chin, studying the smooshed chocolate. "I sense newlin magic."

"Willow," she growled. She tried to rise from the chair, but her bottom was stuck to the cushion.

"Willow of the Wild fuelled it, but she was not the one who taught you how to construct it."

"Meeme!" She struggled against unseen bonds that held her fast. "Let me go!"

"Your meeme is dead."

A sharp pain struck her. Her meeme was dead, but she had a meeme.

"She means Alaura of Niamh," said Jack. "Now stop this."

"Who taught Alaura?" Elwyn dragged her fingernail through the centre of the smeared chocolate, and her eyes narrowed. "Your aunt searches for you. She needs you."

"Das' sister?" Why? What had happened to her das?

"Your das had no sisters." She grabbed her by the ear and held it firmly.

"My das does." Her mouth hung open realising who she meant. "My real das is Bronwyn Darrow!" She screamed it to ensure she heard without doubt.

"Your meeme's sister searches for you."

"Alaura doesn't have a sister."

"Your real meeme." She boxed her ear, then grabbed it again as she stared into her eyes, weaseling her way past several defensive doorways.

"No!" She screamed loud and long, bringing tears to her eyes. Images of the past fought to escape, ones from long ago of her sleeping in hay beside a woolly animal and ones more recent from Blackvale prison that were shaded in red. No one could see those images as she'd seen them, vividly as if they'd stood beside her when she killed Eveline. Her fingers flew through the air as Willow had taught her, gathering energy from every source, including from Elwyn. Endless doors and gates flew up until the burden strained the energy within her nwyfre, then she wiggled and wedged her feet between her and the table until the chair toppled over and she spilt onto the floor.

"What sorceress guided you?" Elwyn demanded. "She is Floriana. She gave you this power." Orange sparkled in her eyes and surrounded the green like a ring around a Harvest moon.

"I don't know!" Tears streamed down Isla's face and dripped into her mouth, mixing with the cherry-filled chocolate and turning it into a salty mixture she no longer desired.

"Let me in, and I will tell you."

Jack's chair toppled, and he fell to the floor, free of whatever force held him. He jumped to his feet and stood between Isla and Elwyn. "Stop! I demand it." He raised one hand to fend off the crazy woman and wrapped the other around Isla's shoulder. "I do not sanction this method, and neither would Floriana. You must respect my wishes. Stop torturing this poor girl."

Isla wrapped her arms around his waist and buried her face in his chest. Old feelings that had haunted her day and night before she left Blackvale surged through her veins and created an ache in her chest. Kiefer had helped put them in their place but without him here to guide her, she felt lost in the internal storm that raged in her heart.

A glint of steel flashed before her eyes, followed by a waterfall of blood. It stole her breath, and she envisioned Eveline's body quivering at her feet. She jolted forward, and Noemy appeared beside the dying woman, sharing her fate. Their desperate expressions pleaded for the unthinkable. In a blink an eye, Hadena materialized on the floor beside them. Three women who once lived and laughed lay dead because of her sword. She held tighter to Jack, trying to rub the image from her head.

Jack bent to gaze into her face. "Isla." He brushed away her tears.

She gazed into his sad eyes, knowing she caused this pain for not allowing Elwyn into her nwyfre to find his mate. The thought of letting anyone, stranger or friend, see her deeds firsthand terrified her. She cupped his face in her small hands. "I'm sorry."

"You have nothing to be sorry about." He embraced her. "Child, I have benefited more from your friendship in our short time together than all those I've made in Ath-o'Lea. We'll find her. We know you've met her. She's alive, and that gives my heart hope."

"She needs deep healing." Elwyn returned to her chair and fell into a sombre mood. "It will take time to cleanse her mind of the nightmares she locks away, but it can be done."

"Not by your hand," said Jack.

"That is up to you." She yawned. "When she tells you who gave her the tools to create the barrier to her nwyfre, you'll discover your mate." She blew out the candle on the table. "I must rest. Make your leave."

"Gladly." He led Isla towards the door.

"Tell my wonderful granddaughter to visit before she leaves Inishmore. I have news for her."

"I will do that."

"Lost child, you may think me cruel, but life is crueler if you cannot accept yourself."

Isla glanced up at Jack; after all these years, he deserved to find his mate. He had risked his life to save Liam. Yet, letting anyone into her memories felt worse than death. "I'm sorry."

"Hush." He pulled open the door. "Go slowly." He called down to Lyneth at the bottom of the ladder. "Help her."

Isla put one foot on the rung, then swung the other into the air. Through teary eyes, she searched for the next rung and lowered herself towards the ground. Her foot slipped, and she clung to Jack to steady her balance. Hands on her hips made her turn.

"I've got you." Liam held her firmly. "Let's go slowly."

She reached again with her foot, and he guided it to the next rung. Releasing Jack, she took the next step with Liam's help, then the next one. With her feet on solid ground, he pulled her into his arms, and she hid her face against his neck.

"What happened in there?" Lyneth waited for Jack to descend.

He reached the ground and gave her a displeased expression. "I'd rather not say, but a second visit is not in my future."

Isla glanced at him as Liam led her away. She'd never enter Elwyn's dwelling again either.

Lyneth pulled a chocolate from the paper bag she carried and gave it to Jack.

"What's this?" He held it up to the fading afternoon light.

"Mint. You look like a mint boy. Told you you'd need it."

He nibbled the end. "Mmm. I like mint. And you're right; I know not whether to thank or curse you for not talking me out of this."

"Not what you expected?"

"Not the price I intended to pay."

"She doesn't charge."

"In coin."

Isla would rather hand over her entire coin collection than allow Elwyn access to her nwyfre; once there, the unpredictable woman would have seen everything, from her first memories as a baby, to her intimate moments with Arthur to witnessing Liam tear apart the men from Wandsworth. Her only defence was at the entry portal; she knew no other and while her meeme promised to teach her additional methods to safeguard her life force, they had never found the time. When she returned to Maskil, she'd make the time.

"She's resting peacefully, but I don't want to leave her alone." Liam stood next to the bed McGuigan sat on. On the opposite bed sat Lyneth and Jack.

Isla's crying had ceased by the time they'd reached the inn, but an unexplained sadness lingered, one Liam couldn't douse. He had asked Jack for the cause, but he didn't know exactly, only that something that troubled her in the past had been brought to the surface by Elwyn. Jack said she'd fought like a wild beast to keep it locked away.

"Let's compare memories to learn how to best help Isla," said Jack. "Unfortunately, all I offer is my knowledge of her time at Blackvale Castle. She'd been there from the age of twelve to seventeen. No doubt, that's where the horrible memories stem from." He turned to Liam. "Has she confided in you?"

"No. I sensed something had happened; her beliefs are not as they were when we were young; she never explained, and I never asked." He hung his head; he should have asked each time he felt the hurt surface. They had been opportunities missed.

"Guaranteed it happened at Blackvale," said Lyneth. "She's had run-ins and such since she escaped, but she's been with us since; this happened before the Mercenaries. She was reckless at first, as if she didn't value her life. McGuigan, you remember. She acted without thinking, without consideration for her well-being."

"She did. And she had nightmares."

"That's right. After we left Rhunestone. I remember now."

"She's said nothing of this," said Liam. On the nights he lay beside her, she had slept peacefully.

"She constantly twisted and when she had a nightmare, it terrified her." McGuigan glanced reluctantly at him. "She'd jump from our bed and run; all she wanted to do was run."

"Nothing worked to keep her still?" asked Jack.

"Sometimes I'd..." again he glanced at Liam, and released a heavy sigh, "kiss it away, but it didn't always work."

"She never told you what it was about?" Jack rubbed his chin and considered his words.

"Never. She had a far-away look in her eye like she pondered strange things, and Elspeth had Kiefer talk with her. Whatever he said, she slowly came out of it. She started to smile; I mean really smile, smiles that lit up her eyes. He spent a lot of time with her, and they became great friends. On the rare occasion she slipped into that mood, she went to him and they worked it out. Then there was Arthur." He frowned. "As much as I disliked him, he helped Isla come out of her shell. It's like she needed another hauflin. He looks like you." He nodded in Liam's direction. "Same colour hair and eyes. He's a few years older. Maybe that was good, too. She needed the security he offered."

"Sounds like between the three of you, you gave her reason to live," said Jack. "She was lucky to have you."

"I'm grateful." Liam placed a hand on McGuigan's shoulder. "Truly I am. Thank you for keeping her safe and being there when she needed a close friend. Without you, I may not have her by my side today." He hadn't realised this until now. "Kiefer probably knows the source of the problem, but he's too far away to ask. Where's Arthur?" He didn't want to meet the man but would to help Isla.

"Ellswire, probably," said Lyneth. "It's where he's *stationed*."

"Or not," said McGuigan. "He delivered Morwen and Rhys to Inglenook."

"While true, he no doubt returned to his dwelling and profession in Ellswire."

"Let's see how tonight goes," said Jack. "This may be a short-lived episode that will clear by morning with our support. When she returns to Maskil, I'll ensure she gets further help to deal with the trauma."

"I'm hoping she'll confide in me if given time." Liam went to the door. "She needs to eventually."

"I agree. Mates keep nothing between them." He hesitated, then spoke further. "I'm sorry for this. Had I known, I'd never have requested her presence in the dwelling. She..." He shook his head in disbelief. "She presents herself as a cheerful, easy-going girl who loves games. I had no idea she harboured such dark sadness."

"It's not your fault Lyneth's great great-grandmother is a lunatic."

"I warned you," she said.

"That you did," said Jack. "I'll not take your warnings lightly in the future." He turned to Liam. "If you need help through the night, wake me."

"I will." He slipped from the room and went to the kitchen where he had earlier ordered an evening ration for Isla, who had preferred to lay down instead of joining them in the tavern. She had insisted he go with the others because she wanted time alone but now, her time had expired, and he'd spend the rest of the night with her.

With food in hand, he entered the dimly-lit room. "Hey," he said softly, "how are you feeling?"

"Fine." She smiled, but it wasn't a real smile, and it didn't make her eyes sparkle. She curled deeper beneath the blankets and stared at the wall.

He sat on the edge of the bed and placed the food tray on the small table. "Just a few bites? It's your favourite. Pork chop. And a biscuit." When she didn't answer, he slipped off his boots and lay beside her. "Are you warm enough?" He kissed her forehead and combed her hair with his fingers.

"Yes." She closed her eyes and snuggled her nose into his neck. "Stay with me."

"I'm not going anywhere." He slipped his hand beneath the blankets and rested it against her back, pushing her nearer and holding her tighter. Her gentle sobbing moistened his neck and strummed his heart strings. "Isla, please, tell me what hurts you." She shook her head. "I trust you with my darkest secrets. Share yours with me, and we'll bear them together." When she didn't answer, he continued. "Do you trust me?"

She pulled away and rested her head an inch away from his on the pillow. Her gaze swept across his face while her fingers caressed his cheek. "I trust you with my life." She sniffed the moisture in her nose and blinked away tears.

"Do you trust me with your fears, with that which hurts you most?"

Her bottom lip trembled, and her tears refreshed. "Yes," she gasped. "Please. Not now. Not here."

"When? Where?"

She traced his jaw line and rested her finger on his bottom lip. "When we return to Maskil." She kissed his lips. "I will tell you everything."

"Promise?"

"Promise."

"Regardless of your fears, of your hurt, I will love you more tomorrow than I do today." He kissed her. "I will love you more next week than tomorrow. You are mine, and I will always want you. I never want to be without you." He kissed her softer and longer, and his hand slipped beneath her singlet to caress her bare back. She responded in the same, kissing him tenderly and finding bare skin to place her hand.

For several long moments, they shared the intimate position as lovers until the poyson moved towards his lips. While his body ached to continue, he released her mouth and gasped for air, disappointing the poyson and sending it back to his shoulder. He guided her to his chest, where he held her and allowed the ebb and flow of his deepest desires surge through his body unanswered.

Tomorrow, they'd travelled to Dougendun and if luck was on his side, by tomorrow evening, he'd have in his hand the antidote for the brand. Then he'd allow the fires that burnt for this woman to run wild.

This outcome calmed the raging seas and settled him into the harbour of her arms and carried him off to sleep.

28

Dougendun

MORNING IN INISHMORE BROKE crisp and clear with sunlight sparkling on icicles, making them appear like twinkling stars hitched to strands of thick hair emerging from low-lying clouds dyed soft hues of orange and red. They caught McGuigan's attention each time he gazed out the window at the snow that blanketed the land and the glittering flakes that danced in the air as if fairies sprinkled their magic to greet early risers. The scene would have made him shiver if not for the hot meal and drink before him and the knowledge he had to travel only a short distance to reach the shop that held the portal that would deliver them to Dougendun. That portal would save him weeks of sleeping on the cold hard ground and travelling in harsh conditions.

He chewed his sausage and smiled. Today was a good day. He glanced at Isla beside him, breaking the fast as she'd done with him for the past year and a half. Her gloom had departed for the most part, but she was conscious of others knowing she was feeling troubled, so she wasn't her lively self.

She reached for her biscuit, and he grabbed it first.

"Mine." She grasped his wrist.

"But I didn't get one."

"You didn't ask."

"May I have it?"

She pulled his hand closer and licked the biscuit. "You may."

"Never mind." He dropped it onto her plate.

"Your loss." She cut the biscuit in half and spread raspberry jam on it. When she looked up, he caught her eye, and she smirked.

He put his arm across her shoulder, pulled her near and kissed the top of her head. Then he ruffled her hair.

"This is the treatment I get for delivering the sweet chocolate-covered green mints to you?"

"My way of saying thanks."

"Next time, words will do." She poked him in the ribs. "Don't touch my biscuits."

He cut off a piece of sausage, poked it with his fork and popped it into his mouth. The superb flavour made his taste buds excited, and he cut another piece.

Within the hour, he walked through Inishmore with Jack, Isla and Liam. Deaglan and Cabela went with Lyneth to the planned destination. It was better for them to show up in two smaller groups, so they'd attract less attention on the street. He didn't mind. The casual pace was a sharp change to what they had kept since leaving Moonsface several moons earlier, and the layout of Inishmore and the unique way the inhabitants had carved dwellings and shops from stone intrigued him. The cobblestone lanes, which sometimes became narrow pathways, wove their way around the structures. Because of the many twists and turns, he often couldn't see if anyone walked towards him until they were within ten feet. This would be a perfect place to ambush an enemy. Although he didn't anticipate an attack, that possibility kept him alert.

When they arrived at Quadral Bound Book Shop, Lyneth and the others were already inside waiting. The keeper, a seasoned elf who appeared as old as the stone he kept, tapped a bell, and two young, well-armed elves stepped out from a back room. The men ushered them inside and led them to the basement.

The portal consumed most of the ten-foot wall in the small room, and the energy radiating from it made his nerves stand on end. Flashes of bright red and yellow dotted the otherwise swirling blackness that shimmered in the cavity. He'd never seen a portal this large or this active.

How intense was the force that would grab him and throw him into his destination?

"Who will make payment?" The man who stood guard at the portal rested his hand on the hilt of his sword as if to give a show of strength.

"I'll make payment." Lyneth pulled out her change sack.

"I have this." Isla stepped forward and showed her scallop shell.

"You pass without payment," said the man.

"What is that?" Cabela took a closer look.

"A traveller's shell." Isla tucked it into her pocket.

"Where can I get one?"

"You can't."

"We'll see about that." She folded her arms and glared at her.

"Lyneth, please, allow me." Liam placed a hand over hers to stop her from reaching for coins.

"It's unnecessary," she said. "I take these things into consideration for the group."

"I know, but we go because of me."

"While that's true, we often travel because of the needs of one."

"Please."

She nodded and stepped away.

The man told Liam the price, and he paid the necessary coins.

"For your safety," said the man, "ensure all weapons and sharp objects are secure before entering the portal. Once you start your approach, do not hesitate; you're less likely to suffer injuries if you walk quickly forward."

McGuigan double-checked the snaps and fasteners that secured his sword and daggers, then checked his pouches to ensure they'd not flap about.

"We are not responsible for injuries. However, there are trained guards to assist if one occurs." He stepped aside. "Good luck, and enjoy your visit to Dougendun."

"Perhaps I should stay." Cabela took a step back. "I've never done this before, and it sounds dangerous."

Deaglan chuckled. "I've never done it before either, and it sounds fascinating."

"There are no refunds." The guard stood with his hands clasped in front, waiting for them to enter.

"It's easy," said McGuigan. "We've done this many times. I'll go first." He walked towards the portal.

"Will you hold my hand?" She caught his eye.

Lost for words, he was unsure of what to say. He glanced at Deaglan; she usually asked him for assistance. "Sure?" She latched on to his arm with both hands and tightened her grip when he walked forward. The breeze from the portal quickly became a wind, pulling on his clothes and hair. Heading the man's warning, he didn't slow his pace and marched into the centre of the portal.

A quick jerk forward made him stumble, and a rush of air snatched his breath, but he remained on his feet when Cabela screamed and fell to her knees. He pulled her up and searched the room. Three guards stood at the ready. These men were a mixture of dwarf and another race.

"Move forward quickly," ordered one of the men. "Others are coming."

He jumped into action and pulled Cabela out of the way. No sooner had he left the front of the portal than Isla and Liam emerged. They were followed by Deaglan, then Lyneth and Jack.

"This way, please." The man who had barked the initial order ushered them towards a set of stairs.

McGuigan released Cabela and followed the man.

"Thank you."

Her timid voice made him turn. "You're welcome?" Still confused by why she'd chosen him over Deaglan, he turned without additional words and climbed the stairs.

"We prefer you exit through the rear of the store," said the man. "On your return, send one person through the shop door to alert us of your arrival, and we'll enter the rest through the back." He stood at the top of the stairs and pointed down a short hallway.

McGuigan walked past, opened the door to the outside and shivered. Although the sun shone, snow covered the frozen ground and a sharp wind blew into his face, making his eyes water. He stepped onto the cleared cobblestone and waited for the others. A few doors down, two men shovelled snow, clearing a wide path that ran the length of the block.

"I believe the shop we seek is this way." Jack pointed in the direction of the already-cleared alley path. They walked more than twenty feet when he stopped. "Are you coming?"

McGuigan glanced over his shoulder and saw Isla staring at the men shovelling snow. Liam waited for her. "Recognise them?"

"No." She gave Jack an odd expression, then walked forward.

"What is it then?" asked McGuigan.

"I'm unsure. Give me time to think about it."

They travelled to the end of the alley, and Jack steered them right. All lanes appeared busy with citizens coming and going from shops and dwellings in the early morning. He didn't see any humans in the crowd, but he saw the occasional elf. Dwarfs and hauflins were equally scarce, leaving him to wonder why the majority of the population looked dwarf mixed with another race, probably hauflin. In many ways, they were similar to those in Inishmore except there, mixed elf and human blood dominated.

"Incredible."

Isla mumbled the word, but he'd heard it and glanced back at her. "I know what you mean."

"Jack, have you been here before?" she asked.

"Yes. We will talk later, child."

"It's strange," said Cabela.

"In what way?" McGuigan surveyed the people, noting how they stared back as if strangers were foreign to the town.

"They're unhappy."

"Maybe they don't like strangers."

"Everyone?"

He searched individual faces. Sadness or another emotion disturbed their aura. They didn't automatically smile when they met those they knew or strangers. They simply walked and responded in a methodical manner.

"Something's missing," said Isla.

"There is indeed," said Jack.

"What?" she asked.

"Look around. What don't you see?"

McGuigan scanned the area. They appeared to have everything they needed except warm weather, which would arrive in about five moons. "I don't see it."

"It is hidden in plain sight," said Jack.

A long minute passed before Isla spoke in a hushed voice as if she'd break their spirit further if she said it louder. "Children."

"This is the epicentre of the curse."

McGuigan looked in every direction, searching for the youngest person, and all he saw were men and women well above the age of fifty years. In every place he'd visited, children of all ages were seen travelling with their parents, either being carried or running alongside if they were old enough. Kids as young as ten often ran unsupervised in villages and small towns but here, he saw none of that.

A seasoned woman walked by and ogled Isla, giving her full attention to her as she passed. When she went out of ear shot, he half turned and spoke with Isla. "She wanted you to be hers. It's like they haven't seen someone your age in their lifetime."

"More than thirty years," said Jack, "except for visitors."

"Where did the children go?" asked Isla.

"They grew into adults and no more were born."

"This will happen to all dwarfs if the curse isn't erased?"

"Yes. Hauflin, too. It is a shared curse."

"So, elves and humans will rule Ath-o'Lea." Cabela spoke as if that was a good thing, and all eyes turned to her.

"I don't want that." Deaglan furrowed his brow. "What can we do to help?"

"That's a conversation for another occasion." Jack paused at a corner. "Let us solve one curse at a time." He pointed to a shop across the street and about three hundred feet down the wooden sidewalk. Unlike other shops that were painted in light colours, its front was painted in dark-blue, red and yellow. An ornate sign in the shape of a dragon scale hung over the door revealing its name: Mystical Paragons. A blue flag with no other decoration rested in the small mound of snow six feet from the door. It gently flapped in the breeze. "It's time to get into position. Liam and I will wait here."

"I didn't completely agree to this plan." Isla held tightly to Liam's hand with her eyes set on the shop.

"Your agreement sufficed. Now go." When she didn't move, Jack spoke with more authority. "McGuigan, take her."

"It will be okay." Liam kissed her and pulled his hand free. "Jack knows what he's doing."

"But..." His hand went over her mouth.

"If this doesn't work, we'll try your plan."

"Come on." McGuigan wrapped his arm around her shoulder and forced her to walk. "The sooner we get into position, the sooner they get the cure." She opened her mouth to speak, and he spoke quicker. "I'll throw you into a snowbank."

"This isn't a game."

"Exactly. We follow the plan."

She huffed at him but didn't argue further.

They followed twenty feet behind Lyneth, Deaglan and Cabela until they reached their watch spot, almost directly across from Mystical Paragons. Lyneth led the other two a little farther, then window browsed while Liam and Jack crossed the street.

McGuigan leant against a stone wall and waited. The mission sounded simple: Jack and Liam bought the colostrum, they'd rent a room for the night, administer the antidote and wait for it to purge the poyson. By day's end, his fear of being killed by the poyson living within Liam would be gone.

"They're inside." Isla stood at the ready as if expecting the need to race across the street and burst into the shop.

"Relax. You're sending off bad energy."

"You can feel it?"

"No, but anyone within a hundred miles who can, will. That includes the keeper of that shop. Jack can, and you're probably driving him crazy."

She sighed and gave her body a shake. "You're right. I need to think of something else. Did you like the chocolate-covered mint jellies?"

"Not bad. Not as good as plain, but I won't turn them down." He tugged her arm. "Look at that." He pointed down the street past where Lyneth and the others stood. "A candy shop. After we finish here, we'll see what they have." Although he worked to keep her mind busy, his wandered to Mystical Paragons and what might be transpiring inside. He'd think of nothing else until he saw Jack and Liam emerge.

ಔ ❖ ಛ

The overwhelming aroma of herbs simmering over low heat assaulted Liam's nose when he entered Mystical Paragons behind Jack. As instructed by the man who acted more like his das than his friend, he'd follow quietly, observe the surroundings for threats and listen to the keeper who would sell them the dragon's milk to ensure his words were not taken incorrectly. He'd not speak or allow his emotions to reveal their desperation.

Isla had relayed the conversation between her and the strange human named Specks on the streets of Brador. He'd said the keeper, a shifty man of hauflin and dwarf lineage, would possibly charge double or more. They had to be wise, not desperate, or else the man might charge something other than coins. This fact made Jack insist Isla remain outside; he wanted to barter for the lowest possible price in coins.

Given Liam's desperate state, part of him wished McGuigan had entered the shop instead. His desire ran as deep as Isla's, and he feared he'd not keep his facial expression under control.

"It's cold outside," whispered Jack.

He gathered his thoughts and focussed on the task. Any time Jack mentioned the weather, it was code for *remember the plan: be calm, casual and wise.*

The dimness of the shop due to dark-blue lace covering the large front window and the use of four small lanterns to illuminate the interior created a mysterious space where shelves and tables of various sizes and colours, some draped with shiny cloth, packed in tightly left little room for movement. Every surface contained an item, many stacked several high. Thin chains with stones the size of fists, colourful pennants, cones on strings and many more objects hung from the ceiling. Low gurgling, rhythmic hissing and soft thuds resonated from various places in the shop, making him listen for their source. The occasional squishy movement, as if someone stepped in maple syrup spilt on stone, interrupted the chorus.

He leant forward and read a fancy sign beneath a cabinet of small dark bottles: *Aids from the cradle to the grave.* Walking on, staring at the bottles and questioning exactly how the liquid would help him between birth and death, he didn't see the object on the floor and softly kicked it. He cringed and looked to see if he'd broken it. The shiny steel helmet glimmered in the flickering light; it appeared undamaged.

The next table was the height of his chest and held a large glass vessel with bubbling blue liquid that appeared as thick as molasses. Air pockets seeped through it and broke on the surface to send up yellow puffs of air that splashed back down. He peered closer, trying to learn the source of the energy moving the fluid until a face jumped from it and stuck to the inside of the glass. He gasped and sprang back, fearful it would escape and attack. It slowly sunk into the liquid and disappeared.

He stared at the vessel as he walked on, but when a face appeared over the rim of the table from the shadow behind it, he froze. The large brown eyes belonged to a man slightly taller than him, not a pure hauflin but one that appeared more hauflin than dwarf. His short brown hair was kept from his face by a red handkerchief folded and tied above the hairline. He wore a dark-blue shirt and another handkerchief of yellow tied around his neck.

"Do you own this shop?" He pressed his lips together, cursing himself for speaking.

"In a round about way...no." He grinned, revealing large teeth.

"The sun is shining outside." Jack placed a reassuring hand on his shoulder. "Excuse me, sir, are you keeper of this establishment?"

"In a round about way...no."

"Do you work here?"

"Here..." his eyes grew, "and there."

"Can you direct us to the dragon colostrum?"

The man chortled and his large teeth extended over his bottom lip. "I can."

"Wonderful." Jack waited, but the man didn't move, only stared back with the stupid grin. "Can you direct us now?"

The man slowly sunk behind the table and disappeared, leaving Liam searching to see if he scooted away or ducked below, but when he peeked under the table and between two crates, he found him gone.

"Odd little man." Jack walked to the front of the store, and the man appeared and walked before him.

Odd wasn't the word Liam would use. Freaky better described him, but he kept his suggestion to himself. The odd, freaky little man stopped at a dark-red counter that held an array of small wooden boxes, brown sacks, tiny blue bottles and a basket with two dozen fifes sticking in it. The sign before it read: *The Happy Fife for Magical Moments – Cost one arm, one leg.* Who'd be happy with a fife if they had to sacrifice an arm and a leg?

"Oracle Osbern, you have...*customers.*"

The way the little man said the last word made Liam shiver and glance at the door. Was it too late to change his mind? Then again, this was the only place that sold the first milk of green dragons.

A taller man emerged from between thick yellow curtains hanging against the wall behind the counter and stood with his arms awkwardly crossed high on his chest. This allowed the sparkling blue cape he wore to drape in front of him and conceal the shape of his body, his clothing and weapons if he wore any. His straight golden hair rested in a perfect line on his shoulders, each strand combed meticulously. The larger nose and ears, along with his taller statue indicated he was more dwarf than hauflin, yet the smaller race's features were obvious in the smallness of his mouth and chin.

The shorter man waved his hand ceremoniously before him and bowed slightly. "Oracle Ned Osbern, proprietor of Mystical Paragons and foreteller to those who believe."

"A pleasure to make your acquaintance." Jack nodded deeper than he'd normally nod to indicate he acknowledged someone.

Liam stood off to the side, watching the odd pair as Jack conducted their business. He pressed his lips together, and the two dominant fingers on his right hand crossed behind his back as he made a wish to the Welkin nymphs to grant them the colostrum. Isla put her faith in these nymphs though he'd never heard of them until she spoke of them.

Oracle Osbern grunted to get the little man's attention, then pursed his lips as if he'd forgotten something.

The little man jumped into action. "I am Donncath, obedient servant. Please, introduce yourself less you offend Great Oracle Os."

"My apologies," said Jack. "I am Jack Somerled, and this is my son, Liam Fetyplace. Travellers of Ath-o'Lea."

Oracle Osbern moved his head sideways, and his eyes darted between the two. "Son?"

"Adopted."

"A chosen boy." He wet his lips and eyed his servant.

Donncath cleared his throat. "They desire dragon colostrum."

Oracle Osbern raised his eyebrows and leant forward. "It is rare."

"We seek *green* dragon colostrum."

"Rarer still."

"Yet, I am told you peddle it."

"We have."

"Do you have a cup in stock?"

Liam's insides twisted. He hadn't considered it being out of stock. If that was the case, the trip was a waste of time, and all his hope—

"Yes."

"Wonderful." Jack picked up a fife. "I played one of these as a child."

"I doubt you played *one of these*."

"Not exactly but one similar. It did not possess magic." He returned the fife to the basket. "Do you sell un-magical fifes? I might start again."

"No, but for the mere price of an arm and a leg, you may own one of these."

"Maybe next time. Today, my interest is in colostrum."

"As you said. Green dragon. A full cup."

"What is your charge for the item?"

Oracle Osbern lowered his arms and shook them at his side. "It fluctuates. Highly valuable. Rare."

"Of course. Your price today? Or perhaps we shall return next week for your price."

"We'll be out of stock next week."

"You anticipate a rush?"

"It's seasonal."

"So I'll return next Forstig?"

Liam's insides continued to churn as Jack casually chatted about fifes, colostrum and returning a year from now. He couldn't wait that long.

"No guarantee. Dragons are a finicky lot."

"Undoubtably. Your price for this highly fluctuating, rare, seasonal item is three gold coins?"

"One-day sale to a small boy many years ago, but the price is far from that now."

"One gold coin then?"

"Again, once but in my younger seasons when my heart was soft and my skin less wrinkled."

"You haggle honourably." Jack put his hands into his pockets and smiled. "I shall give you the four gold coins you request and, as I'm feeling generous, this precious stone I found high on a mountain trail that glimmered in the sun." He withdrew his right hand and held it open for the oracle to see.

Before they'd left their room this morning, Isla had visited with one more plea for her to accompany them inside the shop and when Jack refused, she offered him the red stone. She'd said it was special in ways she couldn't explain and felt the man they'd meet today would feel a connection to it. Liam had doubts but seeing the expression on Oracle Osbern's face as he gazed upon the unusually stone, erased them; he wanted that stone.

"Storm's coming."

He glanced at the unusual man named Donncath, reflected on the weather reference and focussed on the task. Donncath's eyes revealed his struggled to maintain his composer and his inability to remove his interest from the red stone. Why was it so important to these men?

Sudden movement drew his attention to the counter before them. A black cat with a narrow, dark grey patch of hair extending from its bottom lip to its belly had leapt onto the surface and sat staring at Jack. Its bright red tongue lapped out and licked its upper lip all the while its large dark eyes encircled with yellow never left the man.

"Your pet?" Jack closed his fingers around the stone, made a fist and rubbed the cat under the chin with the side of his forefinger.

"Storm cannot be owned."

"A wonderful name. I see a storm brewing in his eyes." He returned his hand and the red stone to his pocket. "Will I do business today, or shall I return next week?"

"Desperate men should tend to business immediately."

"I am not a desperate man."

"Only desperate men seek dragon colostrum, and only a man more desperate would drink it." The oracle's eyes settled on Liam. "Which of you is more desperate than the other? Which will suffer greatly when he drinks the milk?"

Liam squeezed his fingers together behind his back and concentrated on breathing. Air in, air out, air in, air out... Too fast. He inhaled slowly and allowed his body to hold it a moment before releasing it. He had to clear his thoughts, think of the weather or the cat and not his desperation.

"Interesting," said Oracle Osbern. "You are young, strong; you'll survive, but it will cost you." He no sooner released the words than the cat swatted him in the chin with its front paw, inciting an angry look.

The cat leapt from the counter onto Liam's shoulder. Its claws dug into the material of his jacket, giving it stability. It turned with its tail straight in the air, then sat to knead its claws, plucking the material as if playing a guitar.

The weight of the animal pushed down on his shoulder, making it awkward to stand with his hands behind his back, so he braced them against his hips. A low rumbling noise grew louder in his ear and transformed into aggressive purring.

"Storm has chosen," said Donncath.

"I see." Oracle Osbern frowned. "You have been granted access. You need only make payment."

"Which is?" Jack kept his eyes on the keeper.

"Five gold coins, the stone and...a drop of love."

The last item froze Jack's mouth open and when his lips moved, they fumbled with a few words before they became coherent. "One drop?"

"It's the price of desperation."

"Of whose love?"

"Anyone's."

"Do you desire it in a bottle, on a folded piece of paper or floating in the air for all to see?"

The loud purring made the conversation difficult to hear, but Liam believed they were bartering over love, a drop of it. Where would they get a drop of something intangible, unmeasurable? Why did Jack speak as if he could deliver it?

"In this jar." The oracle produced a small, wide-mouth jar large enough to hold one fenberry. "It must be fresh, pure, young and given willingly."

Jack took the jar and as he brought it closer, he inspected it as if it revealed the secret on how to capture a drop of love. "If I cannot procure a drop today, would you consider another option?"

"No love, no milk."

"You'd have me walk away with my coins and stone?" He presented the red stone again.

"Yes."

"But it's marked by the Inherited One!" blurted Donncath. His fingers scratched the air as if he wanted to grab it for himself.

"Hush!" Oracle Osbern grew red, and he glared at his assistant.

Inherited One? Who was that? The cat leant forward and stretched its neck to peer closer to his face. Would it swat him as it had done the oracle? Its large dark eyes watched him; it sniffed his cheek and licked it once. Its rough tongue left no moisture behind.

A bell dinged, and the background noise of low gurgling, rhythmic hissing and soft thuds ceased. Three seconds passed, and the squishy movement filled the silence, then remained still. All eyes turned towards the door, anticipating a customer to emerge from the dim light. Even the cat stopped purring and waited for the intruder's arrival.

"It appears a drop of love has crossed the threshold."

Liam stared at the man behind the counter; his arrogant stance had returned, and his eyebrow, raised at him, indicated he knew who had entered. The disappointment on Jack's face revealed the same, and as seconds passed and he sniffed the air, he, too, identified the person: Isla.

She emerged around the corner and stared at them bashfully, knowing she was to wait outside and by not doing so had disrupted their plans.

He reached out a hand, and she accepted it to stand near him on the opposite side of the cat that followed her every move with odd head movements.

"If that is the case," said Jack, "then how would you extract it?"

"That's the tricky bit. It must not be coerced or planned but given freely, spontaneously. That's when it's at its most potent."

The cat stretched across Liam's shoulders, settled into a comfortable position and watched Isla. The purring resumed as did all the natural sounds within the shop. He squeezed her hand and attempted to reassure her with his eyes.

"I am a reasonable man," said Oracle Osbern. "The drop you offer is extraordinaire, and I'll give you an opportunity to deliver it."

"Yet, we'd like the milk today."

"Then we have a deal?"

He hesitated. "You will accept the coins and stone and we deliver the drop when we gain access to it, and you give us the milk today?"

"Exactly."

Jack stood straight and stuck out his hand. "Deal."

The oracle shook it. "The coins and stone."

He pulled three coins from his trousers pocket, one from his jacket pocket and one from his chest pocket, then handed them and the stone to the keeper.

Jack had six more gold coins hidden on his body to barter with. They were all the gold coins the group had, collected from everyone with the promise they'd be repaid when possible.

"And the milk." Jack waited.

Oracle Osbern deposited the coins and stone within his pockets, then motioned Donncath forward. "Prepare the transport." The assistant rushed behind the counter and disappeared between the yellow curtains. "Are you the strongest of your band?"

"Yes."

"You've none stronger waiting outside?"

"I do."

"Invite them along. You'll need the support."

"For the purpose of?"

"Gaining access to the milk and holding down your invalid."

"You wish me to wrestle you for it?"

"Not me; the dragon."

Donncath popped out from behind the curtain. "Ready."

"Wait." Jack put up his hand. "I paid for milk you are to deliver."

"Delivery was not in the deal." The oracle leant forward. "Did you believe I milked the dragon myself?"

Liam didn't know how he got the milk but the idea of milking a dragon was both incredible and horrifying.

"I expected a vial of milk in my hand." Jack furrowed his brow and darkened his features.

"Newlin, you are naïve to the way of dragons. You have been granted access to the milk; it is your task to retrieve it from a dragon who has given birth in the past forty-eight hours. Once that milk is in your hand, it must be administered immediately. The longer you wait, the less affective it is, and I sense you need a potent dose to heal this boy." He thrust his finger towards Liam.

"Great gemstones, we are..." He pressed his lips together and cast a defeated glance at Liam. "Green dragons are not my friend."

"Assemble your teammates. You'll require them all." Oracle Osbern crossed his arms over his chest. "I will instruct you to guarantee success." He tapped the counter. "Storm."

The cat leapt from Liam's shoulder and settled on the counter next to the man's hand. It stretched its front paws forward, flexing its long, sharp claws as it yawned.

Liam glanced at the cat as Jack led him and Isla from the shop. They'd done what they'd planned, made a deal for dragon's milk, yet they left empty-handed. While he maintained hope he'd chase the poyson from his body today, the idea of wrestling a green dragon made him feel like he'd die from the cure.

29

We are Far from Home

ISLA CONSIDERED THE ITEMS in her pockets and what she might need while at Dragstone Moorland. Following Oracle Ned Osbern's instructions, she'd removed all her weapons, including a pocketknife, and stashed them in her rucksack, which she'd leave behind at Mystical Paragons. The possessions she'd carry were her map, pouch with special stones and miscellaneous items: flint and steel, two small sacks of healing herbs, grey powder, travelling shell, gloves. Dragstone was a warm location, so she was advised to leave her jacket behind.

"Remove the rope." Oracle Osbern inspected the group.

"But it's rope." McGuigan held up the bundle.

"Considered a weapon. Leave it behind."

He shoved it into his rucksack. "What about my fork?"

"No."

"My scarf?"

"No."

He pulled a short stick from his chest pocket. "And this?"

"You may take your toothpick."

He returned it to his pocket. "I feel naked. Lighter than I've been in moons."

"Good." He held out a stone mug to Jack. "Collect the milk in this. Have him drink it in front of the damsel; she will appreciate the gesture."

"Thank you." Jack tucked the mug into his side pouch.

"Donncath will accompany you to the base but then, you are on your own. If you follow the instructions, you'll have no difficulty."

"I'd like to say that's reassuring, but it's not."

"It reassures me." Isla stepped forward. "I have hope."

"You have more than hope." The oracle motioned towards the small table with the dark-red cloth where the cat sat watching. "You have Storm's approval."

She smiled at the cat; since returning to the shop, it hadn't left her side. When she patted it, it purred loudly and licked the back of her hand.

"I can't say leaving my weapons behind makes me feel comfortable." Lyneth tucked her shirt into her trousers and tightened her belt. "I'm wary about leaving the clothes, too. It's far from Sumortide."

"But isn't it freeing?" Isla stood ready, wearing boots, trousers and long sleeve shirt. "It's like being home. I feel as light as a feather. Springy." She bounced on the ends of her feet, feeling as if she could roll, tumble and flip in the air as easily as she walked.

"While I'm dreading this," said Cabela, "it does feel freeing." She wore a thin pair of boots, a short skirt with leggings to her knees and a blouse. Her hands worked quickly to braid her hair into one long strand.

"When you are ready, stand together, but don't touch one another." Oracle Osbern gripped a staff that measured a foot taller than him.

Isla stood in front of Liam and stared into his eyes. A smile played at the corner of his mouth, grew to his lips and cheeks and spread into his eyes to make them sparkle. "Believe we can, and we will," she whispered. "Remember, a good man is not down until everyone who cares about him has given up hope, and I will never give up on you."

"You are braver than I, knowing we'll face a green dragon."

"Brave or stupid, I'll see the task through."

"I vote for stupid." Cabela stood off to the side with her arms folded over her belly. "Green dragons enjoy killing."

"Hush." Jack stood behind Liam. "Today will be different."

Cabela was right; a green dragon had attacked the search party looking for Isla when she'd been kidnapped by Keiron Ruckle. It had killed two guards and severely injured others, including Farlan. He still wore scars from that attack; the dragon had torn a hole in his side, leaving his skin pinched and twisted around it. Instead of thinking of that incident, she'd think of the green dragon Liam, McGuigan and Deaglan had met in the story book. That was a nice dragon, a reasonable dragon even if it was one from a folk tale. Couldn't dragons be like that in real life?

Oracle Osbern tapped his staff on the floor. "On the third tap, you will be transported to Dragstone Moorland. Be safe, be kind and, above all, be respectful, and you'll see this day through."

Isla stared into Liam's eyes and held her breath. She'd never travelled by transport and had no idea what to expect. The second tap of the staff tensed her muscles. The third tap stole her breath and vision and sent her tumbling through the air at an amazing speed. When she landed, she rolled several times before slamming into a solid force. She no sooner stopped than someone crashed into her.

A loud groan sounded in her ear, and she recognised McGuigan's cursing. She opened her eyes, shook her head and looked around. She lay in a heap with Liam before her, Jack pulling himself from beneath him, and McGuigan on top of her legs. Lyneth, Deaglan and Cabela were tangled up a short distance away.

"Unbelievable." Cabela rose on shaky legs. "No wonder we were not permitted weapons; if we didn't kill each other in the landing, we'd arm ourselves and attack the sender."

"Give me a portal any day compared to this." Lyneth rose and shook herself.

Isla pulled her legs from beneath McGuigan and rolled to her feet. "How many transports can we do a day?" She stretched her back, fearing she'd bruised it.

"As many as you can handle." Jack eased himself upright.

"Excellent."

"Why would you want to travel this way?" McGuigan rubbed his shoulder. "You'd be crippled by the end of the day."

"Once you get the hang of it, it's an enjoyable way to travel."

Isla stared at the little man. Donncath was mostly hauflin, but she recognised the distinct features of dwarf. "We return to Dougendun the same way?"

"You do."

"How do I stay on my feet?"

"Close your eyes." Donncath stepped over a stone and walked towards the base of a steep hill. "Your path takes you up there."

Isla stood beside him and gazed up into the darkness of the mammoth cavern. The size reminded her of caves beneath Blackvale Castle where she'd met Shadow. Brilliant light provided by Donncath illuminated a section of the cavern ceiling, but she was unable to see the top of the hill and where the path led.

"We are to go up that?" Jack put his hands on his hips and grimaced at the climb.

"It is easier than it looks."

Jack raised an eyebrow and considered the man. "When was the last person sent to gather the milk?"

"More than three years ago."

"They were successful?"

"Yes."

His cheeks expanded, and he released the air slowly. "A torch?"

"You'll not need one."

"It's dark up there."

"I will remain until you've reached the top and once there, you'll find your way."

"We return to this spot, and you will be here to transport us home?"

"As planned."

Isla caught Jack's eye. The whole plan seemed incredible, but so did poyson that controlled a man's actions and made him kill mindlessly. Yet, there was something in Jack's expression that hinted at something deeper. He had confessed earlier that green dragons were not his friend; how had they become enemies? "I'll lead the way." She took the first step, but a strong hand held her back.

"I'll lead the way." Liam stepped in front of her. "McGuigan, stay with her. If it goes bad, get her out of here."

"I'm behind you." McGuigan stood beside Isla. "And beside her."

"I'll take up the rear." Lyneth ushered the others forward.

"Walk slowly." Jack trailed McGuigan. "Remember the plan. Stick to it."

"I'm not feeling confident about this." Cabela seized Deaglan's arm. "I don't like heights."

"I'll vouch for that," said Isla.

"You'll be fine," said Deaglan. "Don't look behind you."

She groaned. "Now I must look behind me."

"Watch the dragon at the top," said Isla.

"What?" Her head snapped up.

"It's not there yet, but it might be at any time."

"I don't like you."

"I never noticed."

"Enough chatter." Jack followed Isla closely. "Let's focus on the task, and we'll be home soon."

"Home?" Isla glanced over her shoulder. "It's a nice thought, but we are far from home."

"Yet, with every step, it grows nearer."

She agreed. Even if they were heading away from it, they were getting closer because once this task was done, that's where they'd go from Inishmore: home.

Falling silent, she focussed on placing her feet on solid rocks of the inclined cavern floor. She occasionally kicked a loose stone and sent it rolling behind her. The light Donncath provided lit the entire hill and when she was halfway up, she saw the top and how it bent away from them. Approaching the crest, a soft glow came into view. A hundred feet more, and she looked back to where Donncath had stood; he was gone.

"Is that torch light?" asked Lyneth.

"I don't think so." Liam stretched his neck to see farther.

"It looks like sunshine," said McGuigan.

The source of the light remained a mystery to Isla. Heat spewing from the opening blew upon her, making sweat gather and her hair stick to her neck. She unfastened the top two buttons on her shirt and shook the material to increase air flow. At the top of the crest, she paused to catch her breath and to process the immense size of the cavern she gazed upon. The one they'd left was small in comparison.

"Are they dragons?" McGuigan grabbed her arm as if ready to pull her back.

Her eyes adjusted to the bright, warm lighting and while many ledges and holes took shape, so did the large bodies occupying them.

The dragons, twelve feet or taller, appeared oblivious to their arrival. They lounged in small groups, either sitting quietly or chatting amongst themselves on grassy nooks or beneath trees with lush green leaves.

"Incredible," whispered Lyneth. "Yet terrifying."

"My words exactly," said Jack, his voice wavering. "Let us hope Oracle Osbern spoke the truth."

A loud snort echoed in the cavern, bringing the inhabitants to their feet. Isla searched for the source and found a dragon almost directly across from her sounding the alarm. It pounced into the air, waited for three others to join it and flew directly at them.

"Osbern said nothing of this." Jack took a step back.

"Hold your ground." Isla moved next to Liam. "Do not show fear." She crossed her arms and spread her legs shoulder-length apart.

"I'm with Jack; this was not in the plan." Liam grabbed hold of her arm. "You should go. Let me do this."

"No." She tugged her arm free, lost her balance and tumbled forward.

The lead dragon set its eyes on Isla and glided directly for her.

Fearing the worst, Liam stepped in front. "Get up! Go!" He faced the dragons and put up his hands. "Stop! Please. We mean you no harm!"

The dragon slid to a stop in mid-air, flapping its wings to remain steady. "Where did you get that?" Its deep voice shook Isla's eardrums.

"Get what?" asked Liam.

"The mark."

"What mark?"

The dragon scoffed and landed before him. "The one on your hand."

Liam studied his palms. They were a little dirty, but there was no mark.

"Who marked you?"

"Falkor!" Deaglan pushed his way forward and held up his right hand to expose his palm.

"Falkor?"

Isla swallowed hard. That was the fictional dragon the boys had met in the story book.

"Yes, Falkor. He marked us," said Deaglan. "We are his friend, and he said as long as we're not hostile, no green dragon will attack us."

The dragon's yellow eyes flashed. "Indeed. What favour did you grant him?"

"A stone of fire."

He gasped. "You are the one who returned his fire?"

"We did." He pointed to Liam and McGuigan. "We all wear the mark."

"Do you have other stones?"

"It was our only one."

"Why do you come to our home?"

"We are in search of dragon's first milk." Deaglan stood tall, as if he'd talked to dragons and made deals with them every day.

Isla rose to her feet and stood beside him. "Storm has approved. It is for this boy." She gestured towards Liam.

The dragon leant forward, sniffed Liam and recoiled. "And if we have none to share?"

She glanced at Jack; they hadn't planned for this. Turning back to the dragon, her mind raced with what to do next. "But if you had, would you?"

"We would."

"Do you have a cup of first milk to share?" she asked.

"What will you give to us?"

That wasn't part of the deal either. Again, she looked to Jack, who appeared unable or unwilling to step closer to join the discussion. "What would you like in return of the favour?"

"A fire stone for all of us."

"But we don't have any more."

"Then no deal."

"But, there must be something." She stepped forward. "Something we can give." Her hope of curing Liam would not end because of an impossible request.

"There is nothing. We want fire."

"But...but," she searched the ground for answers. "Where has your fire gone?"

"It was stolen by a man who resembled him." He pointed at McGuigan, who stepped back and held up the palm of his hands.

"A dwarf?" asked Isla.

"Yes."

"If it was stolen, then it can be returned."

"Do you have our medallion, our fire starter?"

"I have nothing. Describe this medallion."

"It has four brilliant blue stones set in gold intertwined with the life course of a dragon."

Isla's mouth dropped open. "Does it have a centre eye of green?"

The dragon peered closer. "Yes."

"Lyneth," she called. "The medallion we delivered to Rhunestone. It sounds the same."

"I've seen similar medallions," said Lyneth. "I can't be certain."

"Druce Rothkin tried to steal it from us."

In unison, the dragons roared, making Isla and the others put their hands over their ears to block the sound, but it was futile. The cries shot into her ears and rattled around inside her head, bringing her to her knees and blurring her vision. When the roar finally ceased, she found herself panting and her eyes watering.

"Druce Rothkin!" The dragon's hot breath spewed over her face. "Our enemy."

"Did he steal your medallion?"

Its eyes grew fierce, and its teeth flashed in the light. "He stole our medallion, our fire, our birth right. Where is it?"

Isla drew a breath and slowly released it to calm her nerves. The mood of the dragon had ignited fear in her heart and if she didn't control her emotions, she'd make the situation worse. "I can tell you where I last saw it. Druce Rothkin has lost it, but he seeks to regain it."

"Where did you see it? Cothromach?"

"I don't know where that is."

"He does." The dragon nudged Jack's stomach with its snout. "You know it well." Its eyes narrowed. "You possess a stone," it hissed. "Will it rebuild our medallion?"

"I think not." The colour drained from Jack's face, and his bottom lip trembled.

"Show me."

"Show you what?"

"Your stone."

"I don't have your medallion."

"But you do possess a stone to rebuild it." When he didn't answer immediately, the dragon's large claw tucked inside the edge of Jack's shirt and ripped it open, exposing the brilliant blue stone imbedded in his belly. Its eyes grew wide as it drank in the glimmering light. In one quick move, the dragon pinned Jack to the ground.

"Wait! Please." Isla fell to her knees and placed her hand over the stone. "Please, don't hurt him. He means you no harm."

"Give us the stone, and we'll grant the milk."

"No." She glanced at Liam. "I can't." Her heart shivered. She couldn't sacrifice Jack; they'd find another way. "It's the medallion you want, not his stone that keeps him alive."

"Bring me the medallion, and I'll let him live."

"The medallion is at Rhunestone Castle, or at least that is where I last saw it."

"It is not in Cothromach?"

"Where is that?"

"Beyond the Myst in Knavesmire."

"I don't know where that is."

"He does." The dragon pointed to Jack. "It's where we seek stones to make another medallion."

"That's why you hunt us?" gasped Jack.

"Hunt you?" Isla stared into his face. She'd never seen the man more terrified, more distraught.

"Green dragons come to my birthplace and take my people. They've taken dozens over the years."

Now she understood the fear. She turned to the dragon. "You seek a blue stone, but not every newlin carries that colour. What you truly seek is the medallion."

"Correct."

"Do you need only the blue stone?"

"We need four blue and one green."

"Have you found either of them yet?"

"No!" Its face twisted in anger. "Not until now." It placed its claw over Isla's hand above the stone.

"Would it not be easier to retrieve the medallion than to make enemies of these good people?" If not for the creature pressing down on her hand, she feared she'd step away and speak from a distance. Droplets of sweat trickled down her back and into her trousers, reminding her of the heat of the cavern.

"We can't find it."

"Maybe we can. If you spare his life."

The dragon glanced at the others, then turned to her. "Why would you help us?"

"We help each other. Isn't it better to make friends than enemies? Better to feel safe in the sky and on the land than live in fear? How many years have you been searching for the stones?"

"Sixteen."

"Sixteen years of hate without success. Perhaps it is time to try a different strategy."

It huffed and a puff of grey smoke billowed from its nose.

"I am Isla of Maura. If you spare his life and grant us a cup of milk, I promise I will search for your fire stone."

"Are you a thief?"

"Yes, for the good."

"I am Benedict Moor, ruler of Dragstone Moorland. Why can I trust you?"

"I have done you no harm, and I'll give you my word."

"Isla, no." Jack seized her arm and pleaded with his eyes. "Never give your word to a dragon."

"Jack, it's all I have." She spoke to Benedict. "If I find your fire stone, I give you my word I'll return it to you."

"Your word is your bond."

"My word is my bond." An odd feeling erupted in her gut and strained to reach her throat. The burning sensation exploded in the back of her mouth, making her gag and sputter. She shook her head to rid herself of it, but it lingered and spread across her tongue. Gathering a wad of saliva, she spit it out. She leant over Jack, shook violently and spit again. Her pendant slipped from her shirt and dangled in the air, swinging over Jack's chest.

"What is this?" Benedict removed his claw from her hand and grasped the pendant. "Who gave you this?"

She glanced at the silver pendent that was slightly smaller than a gold coin. Its blue stones sparkled. "A friend." Now was not the time to be distracted by Elspeth's memory.

"It holds the fire stones... Most of them." His eyes glazed over. "It is much like our lost medallion, but smaller, without the green eye."

"It may work." A smaller dragon leant close. "We must try."

"Work?" asked Isla.

"I am Dancell Moor. Your pendant may create a small fire to allow a few of us to conceive."

"Conceive?" Jack grasped the pendant. "We don't need more green dragons.

"We don't need more newlins." Dancell pushed his face into Jack's.

"We live in peace; dragons have destroyed that."

"If not for newlins, we'd have our fire!" Dancell's lip curled. "And we'd need not raid Cothromach."

"But Druce is dwarf, not newlin," said Isla.

"He stole it to make a deal with the Elders to remove the curse."

"What do the Elders want with it?" Jack pushed closer to Isla when both dragons leant into his face. "Druce is a traitor."

Isla searched his face for the truth. Jack had confided in her that he was Rothkin; Druce was his kin. What deal had been made and broken? "My pendant." She turned to Benedict. "Will it ease your suffering until I find your fire stone?"

"It may."

"I'll leave it and when I find yours, I expect it returned."

"Isla, you can't." Jack pleaded with her.

"I can. We must start mending the wounds somewhere."

Once her hand left Jack's stomach to remove the pendant, the dragons leant close to his stone. Holding up the pendant with one hand, she pulled Jack's shirt closed with the other. "Is it a deal? I loan you my pendant, and you spare this man's life and give us a cup of milk."

"And you will retrieve our fire stone," said Benedict.

"If I find it, I'll return it. Is it a deal?"

He stuck his thick claw into the loop of the chain, lifted it from her hand and gazed at the stones. The stones dimmed, and he furrowed his thick brow. "What happened?"

"They only glow when I touch them."

"Why?"

"I don't know. Do we have a deal?" She tucked Jack deeper beneath her arm.

"What is he to you?" Benedict grasped the pendant fully.

"A dear friend."

"And you'd risk your life for him?"

"Without hesitation."

"Deal."

She relaxed her hold on Jack and while he frowned at her, she didn't share his disappointment. Combing the long strands of his dark hair with her fingers, she considered what might have happened if they hadn't come to a compromise. His stone might have been ripped out, killing him and leaving her with no option but to fight. She kissed the top of his head and rested her cheek against it. This man, so much like her das, was a worthy soul who deserved to live his life fully.

"Will you stop hunting newlins?" The roughness in Jack's voice made her pause.

Benedict considered the idea. "If this works, we'll halt the hunt."

"Stop it now."

"Only if this works." He leered forward. "If it doesn't, we'll take your stone."

"You said you'd spare his life." Isla stood and stepped over Jack. "That was the deal, or is your word unworthy?"

He baulked. "It is worthy."

"Then you will not take his stone."

He fell silent, but his nostrils flared.

"I'm not an expert on dragon reproduction," said Lyneth, who walked up to stand next to Jack, "but if no dragon can conceive without fire, then how are you to give us colostrum from a new mother?"

"Your fortune shines today," said Benedict. "A kit was born yesterday."

"Without the aid fire?" Lyneth crossed her arms and raised an eyebrow.

"Falkor has fire."

"Falkor?" Liam stepped over Jack and grasped Isla's hand. "He's here, not in his lighthouse?"

"He returns to the garden of Dragstone Moorland with his mate to give birth."

"How many little dragons do they have?"

"Six."

"All because I gave him the stone?" asked McGuigan.

"Yes."

"Can we see him?"

"To gain access to the milk, you must." He turned to Dancell. "Go. Tell Falkor we come; tell him what they seek."

Dancell flew off, crossed the span of the cavern and entered an opening midway from the floor.

"I request a mark." Isla stood with her hand out. "If I return with your fire stone, I don't wish to be attacked."

Benedict grasped her hand and held her palm to his snout. Holding it firmly, he released his hot breath, making her cringe in pain. When she pulled away, she shook her hand to try to remove the sting, but it lingered and made her arm shake. The black ring was the size of a coin pressed into her palm.

"I'll take the mark, too." Lyneth raised her hand. "I'll be with her." When he grabbed her hand, her knees buckled, but she stayed upright, pressing her lips together as she absorbed the pain.

"I don't want it." Cabela stood behind Deaglan. "I won't return."

Benedict scowled at Jack. "You will never get the mark."

"I don't want it." He struggled to rise, lost his balance and stumbled into Isla.

"What's wrong?" She found the remaining buttons on his shirt and fastened them.

"The body slam onto stone." He winced and tucked his shirt in to help where the missing buttons kept it open.

She pressed her hand against his chest and tried to convey a message with her eyes more than her words. "We see this through and deal with everything else later. Here, you are not the word of reason, so let me do the talking." She poked him in the ribs. "But don't leave my side."

"Follow me." Benedict led the group along the ridge of the cavern while the remaining dragon waited for them to pass before following.

Isla helped Jack hobble across the stone floor with Liam on the other side for support. They travelled along the rim and down a low incline, passing two levels before reaching the opening Dancell had entered. The large doorway easily accommodated the dragon and towered over her. A warm breeze pushed back her hair and increased her body temperature.

The tunnel went for fifty feet before it opened to an enormous room. Inside was an elaborate nest made from dried grass, moss, twigs and larger sticks. Sitting in the centre of the soft nest was a green dragon coddling a small, winged beast that resembled a hideous creature from folk tales. Another dragon, deep in conversation with Dancell, looked up when they entered. He appeared mirthful and curious. A moment of recognition later, and his face brightened further.

"My allies." He rushed towards them. "Look what you've granted me." He grabbed Liam's hand and shook it with vigour. Then he went to McGuigan and did the same. "The boy who did not die." He grabbed Deaglan and repeated the action. "You have gifted me tremendous joy."

"I see." Deaglan peered closer at the creature in the nest. "We are told this is number six."

"How can that be?" McGuigan scratched his head. "We gave you the stone several moons ago."

Falkor twisted his head. "Impossible. Many moons have waxed and waned. Too many to track."

Coraline, the author of the book, had told Isla she had been lost as a child. Guessing at her age, that was more than fifty years ago. How many *book years* had passed? Six? Ten? Fifty? Did the boys meet Falkor from an age when Coraline wrote the book or when she lived the experience in the book? Or did some other magic play a part?

"It was a magical land," said Deaglan. "We are glad the stone worked for you."

"It has performed better than expected." Falkor beamed. "I hear word someone requires dragon's first milk. Who?"

Liam hesitantly stepped forward. "Me."

"It's my pleasure to return the favour." He put up a finger. "But first, I must introduce you to Magon, my lovely damsel."

Isla kept a firm grasp on Jack while her eyes studied the mother and her offspring. The baby looked familiar, but she couldn't connect where she'd seen a creature like it before. When it poked its head farther over the nest, a memory flickered. It was a smaller version of what she'd found at Vale of Avoca and had given to Merk. She drew breaths calmly and eased the memory from her mind. She'd not think about where that baby came from, nor who in the room might be its parent.

Jack jostled her and gave a curious look.

She squeezed his side where her hand rested and cleared her mind. Milk. Pure, white, creamy milk; that's all they needed.

The introductions out of the way, Falkor opened his paw. "A cup for the milk?"

Jack fumbled with the mug in his pouch and handed it to Liam, who took it but cast a worried glance at Isla. He handed it to Falkor slowly as if he didn't want to give it up.

"The vessel that transports life." Falkor lifted the mug to the light, then handed it to his damsel.

Magon held it to her breast and squeezed the skin around it. A stream of steaming green liquid shot into the mug. Given the size of the dragon compared to the size of the mug, she filled it quickly and handed it to Falkor.

"Anyone else think it's weird he's going to drink breast milk? Green at that." Cabela shivered and scrunched up her nose. "And for what?"

"This is the liquid of life." Falkor sounded offended.

"And is highly valued." Isla pulled McGuigan towards Jack. "Don't let him go," she whispered. She stood beside Liam. "We have travelled far for this opportunity, and we thank you, Magon and Falkor, for sharing this special liquid with us."

Falkor handed the mug to Liam. "Drink, my ally. Without you, we'd not have the milk to give."

Liam held the mug in both hands and gazed at the warm green liquid inside. "I am..." He stared at Isla. "I'm afraid."

"Of...?" She caressed his cheek.

"What if...?"

"It works, and you're completely cured?" She kissed his cheek. "Let us think of that."

He lifted the mug to his mouth and gazed at her over the rim.

"Drink it all. Drink it fast."

He closed his eyes and tipped the cup, exposing his throat and the liquid surging down it. Before he brought down the mug, he began to shake. He lurched forward and gagged, dropped the mug and grasped his throat. His face turned green and beads of sweat formed and dripped down his cheeks.

"Is this supposed to happen?" Isla grabbed him before he fell and eased him to the floor while he thrashed about and gagged on the milk.

"Hold him down." Jack rushed forward with McGuigan's help. "So he won't hurt himself." He grabbed hold of Liam's arm and pinned it to the floor. "McGuigan, his leg. Deaglan, the other."

Isla put her full weight on his other arm, but Liam was strong and pulled it away. Lyneth jumped in to help, and the two of them kept him pinned.

"This doesn't happen." Falkor leant over the group. "This is most unusual."

"It is bad poyson," said Benedict. "The more potent the poyson, the less likely he'll live."

Isla stared at him, not wanting to believe his words. Specks said nothing about this, yet the poyson that infected Liam was potent, the strongest out there.

Liam screamed in agony as if they ripped off his limbs. His body convulsed and threw Jack into the air to crash into McGuigan, who lost his grip and scrambled to get it back. Liam twisted and pulled away, beating the floor with his feet and hands. His contorted face revealed the pain tearing around inside.

Isla closed her eyes and focussed on holding him, fighting against the ache in her heart that whispered the end was near. The struggling reduced and his body slowly slipped away. A single whimper escaped his mouth, and then he lay still. She placed a hand below his nose and waited for breath, but it didn't come. The lump in her throat grew and burnt the back of her mouth. Placing her head on his chest, she listened for a heartbeat. When none came, she pounced on the buttons, unfastening them quickly to place her ear upon his skin. Still...nothing.

She spread her palms over his chest and sent forth energy to find the damage. Through blurry vision she watched his face return to its natural colour and a peaceful expression settle upon his features. Her energy didn't find a heartbeat. She searched further, deeper into his being.

"He's gone."

McGuigan's soft voice floated in the air, kissed Isla's ears and travelled through every nerve in her body. It poked her like stepping on needles upright on the floor and when it reached her heart, it shook it with such force, it knocked the tear sitting on the rim of her eye from its resting place.

A hand passed in front of her. It held a wide-mouth jar small enough to hold one fenberry. It caught the tear, and quick fingers slid a cap onto the jar and twisted it closed.

She blinked and found Oracle Osbern holding the jar. Where had he come from?

A vibration returned to her fingers with the hint of a heartbeat. She closed her eyes and continued to search, pushing her fingertips into his skin. She gasped. The poyson had retreated to his heart, encased it and held it hostage. It made it impossible to beat. Gathering her energy, she focussed it on the heart and punctured an entry point through the poyson to the muscle while surrounding the poyson and fettering it, so it couldn't escape. It feared the milk and as the colostrum spread through the blood, it cowered in a small cavity. She needed only to sustain his life until the milk killed the poyson.

Moments passed and she massaged the heart, increasing the strength of the single beat. The poyson shook and searched for an escape route. She waited until it grew frantic and ushered it towards his gut, then to his throat.

"Get out of the way!" She shoved Liam to his side. "It's coming."

In one violent heave, the dark poyson shot from Liam's mouth and across the floor, creating a steamy flow of gelatine-like material that oozed across the stone like cold molasses on a hot griddle.

Liam gasped and threw himself against her. His body twitched several times, then sprawled across the floor and her lap as he breathed heavily.

"It worked." McGuigan scurried away from the stream of poyson.

"That is the worst smell I've..." Cabela gagged and heaved, then vomited onto the floor.

"That's a smell you never get used to." Lyneth put her sleeve over her mouth and nose.

Falkor drew a deep breath and blew fire over the poyson, igniting it into dark-blue flames.

Isla rocked Liam gently. His weary expression was that of someone who had travelled far, slept little and witnessed horrible sights. Defined lines carved gullies around his eyes and profound sorrow within them gave the impression he'd collapse like a boy who'd been told his das had been killed. She kissed his lips tenderly and stroked his cheek with her fingertips. "You will live a long life by my side," she whispered. "A worthier mate, I will never find." His eyes surged with tears and he buried his face against her chest and wept softly. She squeezed him tighter and the images from long ago in the storage room of the bakery drifted away.

30

It's Home

JOLTING HIMSELF AWAKE, LIAM focussed on the scene before him and the muffled voices. Four guards stood next to a gate, and he forced his body upright to learn why they approached. They wore familiar uniforms, those of... He squinted to find them in his memory. Aruam Castle?

"Name?"

"Isla of Maura, and this is Liam Fetyplace."

"Reason for visiting Maskil?"

"It's home."

"What's wrong with him? Is he contagious?"

"He's not contagious; he's healing from an awful ordeal."

"You may pass."

Liam held tighter to Isla's waist, and they rode through the gates.

"Parnell." Isla nodded at the elf, who stood near the gatehouse.

"Isla." He returned the nod. "Bronwyn is at the castle guard house if you're looking for him."

"Thank you. I hope all is well in town."

"As good as can be expected with the early snow."

"That's one reason I'll enjoy a warm bed tonight."

He chuckled. "I've no doubt you will."

The horse moved, and Liam caught his balance when it slipped. His body craved a warm bed, one that didn't move beneath him. Since extracting the poyson, he'd been exhausted as if the poyson had energized his body and now that it was gone, there was no reserve to draw from. At night, he slept deeply as if death claimed him; Isla found it difficult to wake him in the morning, and he struggled to eat and when he did, he wanted to sleep.

He barely had the strength to walk, and others had to help him in and out of the saddle. Clinging to Isla while she guided the horse on The Trail claimed his meagre amount of strength, and evening found him too tired to eat in spite of Isla's insistence.

His body swayed and his eyes closed, and he found comfort in the warm fluids and gentle rocking that lulled him into a more relaxed state. When the horse stopped, he slipped further into the darkness of slumber.

"We're here."

Someone tapped his leg, and he slowly lifted his eyelids. Jack? McGuigan? What did they want?

"Easy." McGuigan put his arm around his waist and jerked him forward.

The weightlessness lasted a second, and he felt his feet on the ground. He swayed and would have fallen if not for those supporting him. He saw a narrow path shovelled of snow leading to a tidy dwelling. It looked familiar, and he searched his memory. When he recognised where he was, he directed his remaining strength to return to the horse, but McGuigan lifted him up and carried him onward.

The door opened, and Alaura stepped out.

"Goodness, what happened?" She ushered them inside.

"We're not sure," said McGuigan, "but the poyson is gone."

"Gone? Thank the wood nymphs. Can he walk?"

"Not far."

"Put him here." She grabbed a chair and set it near him. "Jack?" Confusion swept across her face. "Jack Somerled, is that you?"

"It is." He pulled the hat from his head. "Alaura, it is delightful to see you well." He hugged her warmly.

"This is fantastic. Please, stay."

"I was hoping you'd share that sentiment since your daughter has already invited me."

"Of course. You're welcome in our home."

Liam struggled to unfasten buttons on his coat. The pleasant conversation between old friends made him wonder if he was equally welcome in the home; certainly, Bronwyn wanted him to stay elsewhere. Larger, thicker fingers pushed his hands aside and unfastened the buttons easily. McGuigan plucked the hat from his head, unwrapped the scarf and pulled off his jacket so efficiently, he was barely aware of the warmth reaching his skin before his boots were also removed. Since the poyson had been expelled, he found McGuigan friendlier, helpful in ways he hadn't considered before. Powerless to do many of the basic activities of daily life, McGuigan had stepped up to do them for him. Given his strength, he did them quicker than Isla.

McGuigan stood and ruffled his hair. "I'll see you tomorrow."

"You're staying at home tonight?" Alaura asked.

"I'd stay no where else while in Maskil. Mum will be happy to see me, and I'll be glad to be with family." He chuckled. "Though I travel with those who are like family." He rested his hand on Liam's shoulder and pulled Isla under his arm. "It's good to have a little brother and a little sister."

Isla rolled her eyes. "He thinks he can boss us around because he's older." She poked his ribs. "We tolerate it because we love him." Slapping his chest playfully, she set her rucksack on the floor. "Help me with the other bags." She walked out the door, and he followed.

Alaura stared at Liam, her hands clasped in front of her. "The poyson is gone for certain?"

"It is," said Jack. "The cure almost claimed him. He has a lengthy recovery but with abundant rest and hearty food, he'll be an energetic lad again by Spring of Leaf."

"Does this mean you'll be staying in Maskil?"

"He'll stay until he's well; me, not so long."

"What?" Liam grasped his arm. "You won't stay?" He hoped Jack to act as a buffer between him and Bronwyn. They were friends; certainly, he could talk sense into the man.

"I'm staying for several days, but I cannot stay indefinitely."

"But..." He stared at the floor and swallowed his words.

"You're in good hands. The best." Jack knelt next to the chair. "You're amongst family and friends."

"But I have no family but you." And he wasn't really family, but he treated him like a son. A lump formed in his throat and though he struggled to control his emotions, his lack of strength made it impossible.

"That is untrue. Son, you have wonderful people here who happily welcome you into their home. Isla is your family, and her family becomes yours." His hand brushed away the tears.

He shook his head. Jack didn't understand.

A gentle hand rested upon his shoulder, and he looked up to see Alaura's kind face. "Liam, you are welcome in our home."

Footsteps followed by bags dropped to the floor brought Isla into view. "What is this sadness?" She wiped away more of his tears. "You will sleep in a warm, soft bed tonight. Does this bring sorrow?"

"Jack's not staying." Liam clenched his fist. The weakness claiming him made him feel foolish.

"Jack, stop lying to the boy." She threw her jacket onto the pile of gear. "You're staying, so get silly notions out of your head. You're part of the Warriors, and you go where we go."

Jack frowned. "I take no orders from a girl."

"Jack Somerled, you have obviously gone without the guidance of a woman for too long. You'll stay and when we set out on our next adventure, you'll be by my side. I made you a promise, and I'll keep it. Do I make myself clear?"

"Isla, do not talk to your elders in that manner." Alaura put her hands on her hips. "Apologise."

Jack put up his hands. "It's unnecessary." He pressed his lips together and shot an unpleasant look at Isla, then he softened his stance. "We will discuss this matter after we've had rest and considered the options."

Liam admired Isla's determination. If she had her way, Jack would stay. Tonight, he'd beg her to make him.

"Let's consider the immediate needs," said Alaura. "Baths, then we'll settle this young man on the chesterfield, where he can rest."

"He'll rest in my bed."

Alaura stared intently at her daughter, waiting for her to yield to the challenge. When she didn't, she tried another strategy. "He will be more comfortable down here if he's too weak to climb stairs."

"I'll help him."

"Your bed is too small to accommodate him."

"It fits us perfectly."

"Your das will not approve of you sleeping in the same room."

"Jack," said Isla, "you will sleep in a warm, soft bed tonight. Mine." She turned to Alaura. "Liam and I will stay at the inn."

"Nonsense." Alaura frowned. "You'll stay here."

"In my bed with my mate, who needs me by his side." She put her hands on her hips to challenge her. "We'll leave the door open if that comforts you. It's not as if the man is up for a game of cards. He's asleep as soon as his butt hits the blankets." She gestured towards him. "He's half asleep now."

He sat straighter to prove he was awake and able to climb stairs, then his body slouched and when they moved him from the chair and he sank into a warm pool of water, he succumbed to the overwhelming serenity. Movement upon his limbs threatened to wake him, but only when the luxury of the warm environment vanished and he felt a chill upon his damp skin, did he stir and help with his clothes. Someone guided him through a dim hallway to a soft mound that beckoned him to sleep deeper.

Warm, soft skin brushed his lips and while he longed to respond, sleep consumed his body. The magnificent scent lingered, giving him a sense of security and tranquility. Rest. It was what he craved, not what he wanted.

Isla put the last bite of bacon into her mouth and listened quietly while her das, meeme and Jack talked of Maskil and friends they knew. The three had shared experiences that had brought them together as life on The Trail had done with many people.

When her das caught her eye, she pondered about his thoughts. His joy of seeing her when he arrived home from the castle the night before was what she'd expected, yet when he stood over Liam, who slept like a helpless babe in her bed, his expression revealed a different emotion. He knew the poyson had been extracted, that Liam would heal and be that same boy he'd known many years ago. What worried him? He made no comment about Liam in her bed as if her meeme had already warned him against it. He simply walked away, telling her to leave the door open.

This morning, his disposition hadn't changed. He was cheerful and chatty around the table as they broke the fast but in moments when he looked at her, she knew he thought of Liam sleeping in his home.

Bronwyn drank the rest of his tea and put the cup near the sink. "I must go. I'm already late though I have an excellent excuse." He jostled Jack by the shoulder. "You're invited to my family's home tonight to share the ration. Tam and Kellyn will be glad to see you."

"As I am them, though I'm not accustom to crowds."

Isla grunted her giggle. When the Darrow family gathered, they were a large crowd.

"Isla?" Jack waited for an explanation.

"You can have my seat. That will be one less."

"I insist you come," said Bronwyn. "Our family wants to see you."

"Liam won't be well to attend; I'll stay with him."

His frown returned. "We'll discuss this later." He leant down and kissed Alaura, then left the kitchen.

Now that he was gone, she wanted to leave, too, and take Jack for a walk to see an old friend. After her discussion the previous evening with her meeme regarding protection spells for her nwyfre, a possibility nagged at her. While preposterous, she needed to rule it out. She wouldn't tell Jack to avoid giving false hope.

"Dishes." Alaura poured warm water into the basin, and the steam rose to the ceiling.

Isla's hand froze with the mug tipped up and the last of her tea sliding past her lips. Did she mean her? Lowering the mug, her eyes rested on her meeme, who stared in her direction; she was talking to her. She put down the cup and licked her lips. "I must go. I'm already late though I have an excellent excuse."

"When you serve the castle as lord, you can escape dishes, but you haven't reached that status yet." Alaura tapped her shoulder. "You wash. I'll dry."

"I should check Liam."

"He's fine. He can't get far while sleeping."

Her shoulders sagged. She didn't mind rinsing her dishes on The Trail, but those that sat before her was a large mound.

"I'll help." Jack stood and picked up his dirty dishes.

Alaura cut him off. "You are a guest. Sit. Enjoy your tea." She took his dishes and set them in the water. "The sooner you start, the sooner you're done." She nudged Isla forward.

She groaned and drove her hands into the water to search for the rag. Being home had its benefits, but it also had its draw backs. Jack chuckled, and she turned to him. He sipped his tea and grinned. "What?"

"The sassy girl meets her match."

"Oracle Os gave me a fife, one he claims is magical." She lowered her brow. "I might try that on you to see what it does."

He laughed. "I fear many things, but you are not one of them."

"A fife?" asked Alaura. "Do you play?"

"Not exactly."

Jack stifled a laugh. "The magic in that fife is the pain it causes the ears when she plays."

She hung her head and began washing the dishes. The sooner she got them out of the water, the sooner she'd escape before her meeme found more chores for her to do.

"After this, we'll start on the wash." Alaura picked up a plate and dried it.

"But..." she thought fast, "it will have to wait. I *need* to take Jack to see someone."

"Who?"

"I can't say." She made a face and confused him further. "I made a promise. I'll wash my clothes when I return. It's important. To Jack."

"When will you return?"

She set the mug on the rack and reached for another dish. "By noon. Will you be home all morning?"

"Yes."

"Good. I don't want to leave Liam alone."

"Will he sleep all day?"

"If I let him. I'll wake him this evening to make him eat."

"While you are gone, I'll discuss his condition with Rhiannon. Between the two of us, we'll get him well."

"I know." That was the reason she was desperate to reach Maskil. Liam would rest in a warm bed and receive excellent healing care. The long days of travelling had exhausted him and hindered his ability to recuperate from the extraction of the poyson.

Twenty minutes later, the dishes washed and her boots on, she rushed out the door with Jack on her heels. When they reached the street, he broke his silence.

"Who are we visiting? Or was that trickery to avoid chores?"

"There's people I want you to meet." She made a bee-line to the bakery. "Perhaps we'll see your daughter."

His eyes lit up. "I've envisioned that, but it is much to ask."

"But first," she hurried towards the shop door, "I'll introduce you to Maisie Kintale." She winked. "And her amazing biscuits." The aroma of the bakery bombarded her senses, and she drew a deep breath. Although she'd broken the fast, she felt hungry all over again. She walked past the three customers in the shop and went to the counter, where Maisie leant over a piece of paper.

"Isla. You've brightened my day." Maisie came around the counter and hugged her. "Does Bronwyn know you're here?"

"I spent the night at home, and I think he noticed." She giggled and gestured towards Jack. "This is a friend I met on The Trail. He also knows Das and Meeme. Jack Somerled. Jack this is Maisie Darrow."

He stuck out his hand to shake hers. "It is pleasant to meet you. I've heard many delightful stories about your raspberry brownies and biscuits. Your reputation as a baker precedes you."

"Thank you. Isla is my biggest fan." She released his hand. "How do you know Bronwyn?"

"We met on The Trail while he searched for this young lady. You might say she brought us together."

"She has a knack for doing that."

"I can't disagree. She's connected me with many wonderful friends, ones I'd miss dearly if I had to live without."

"Today, I'd like to introduce him to your biscuits." She gazed into the glass display case. "Mmm, they look fresh, still warm."

Maisie chuckled. "How many would you like?" She picked up a small paper bag.

"None for me. Thank you." Jack put his hand over his stomach. "Alaura has stuffed me."

"Two." Isla peeked over the counter. "To be on the safe side of fullness."

Maisie plucked two biscuits from the display case, put them in the bag and handed it to her. "Enjoy."

"Thank you." She opened the bag and stuck her nose inside. The aroma tickled her senses. While she was as stuffed as Jack, after their walk she'd be hungry enough to eat one. She'd save the other for Liam. "Jack can try your biscuits at the evening ration. Das invited him."

"He did? I'll ensure there's a place set."

"It was a treat to meet you, Mrs. Darrow."

"Please, it's Maisie. You're not trying to sell me anything."

"Of course. I'll see you this evening."

Isla led him out the door and towards the town gates. "Thoughts?"

"On?"

"Does she look familiar?"

"No. Well, she resembles Bronwyn." He grinned.

"No weird vibes?"

"No."

"But you sensed something."

"Friendliness. She was happy to see you, and she was open to meeting me."

"In a few days, I'll attend a ration and casually say interesting words. You'll understand my curiosity."

"You know key words that disrupt her energy?"

"I do. One is Welkin nymphs."

"That's two."

She poked him. "Newlin."

He raised an eyebrow. "Has she heard of them before?"

"Yes. Das hasn't. Rhiannon has."

"His sister?"

"Yes. There are discussions Das is not invited to." A blinding force swept her off her feet, and she rolled several times in the snow before a body came up on top of her. Prepared to fight, she froze as a happy face beamed down. "Kiefer?" His greenish-blue eyes sparkled, and his dark brown hair whipped around his face as he stared at her. "You are..." The excitement in her heart stole her words.

"Alive?" His open smile revealed most of his teeth.

"Yes!" She grabbed the front of his jacket. "Alive and well!" She tried to sit up, but he straddled her mid-section.

"Thanks to you." He jumped to his feet, grabbed her hand and yanked her into his arms, where he gave her a big bear hug while he swung her around.

"Unbelievable. The potion worked?"

"It did though at first it felt like it would kill me." He brushed the snow from her jacket.

"Incredible." She threw her arms around his waist and hugged him tightly, not wanting to let go. Sniffing back the moisture building in her nose, she thought of the times she believed she'd never see him again. They didn't matter now.

"I admit, when Isla explained what happened, I feared the worst." Jack grabbed his hand and shook it with vigour. "I'm happy to learn I was wrong."

"No one is happier to learn you were wrong than me." He kissed the top of Isla's head. "I live by this girl's philosophy." He ruffled her hair and clipped her nose.

"What's that?" She admired his face; it was young, full of life and made her heart skip a beat.

"A good man is never down until everyone who matters has lost hope."

"That's a noble philosophy," said Jack.

"Come with us." Isla grasped his hand.

"Where are you going?"

"A walk. I want to be with you. Make my brain believe what my eyes see."

"I cannot deny you that." He pulled her under his arm and walked beside her. "I was hoping you'd return soon. My feet are itchy. Delight me with stories of your adventures."

"Since I've seen you last, I've been captured by a griffin and transported to a far-off land." Her eyes widened. "You must try it; you can be transported more than three times a day." Her thoughts tumbled over the past few moons. "I've had my fingers frozen, been lost in snow and endured a blizzard."

"So, the usual stuff."

"Do you know how to play a fife?"

"I do. Why?"

"Good. We'll play later." Approaching the town gates, she saw several guards lingering near it. Two questioned travellers who prepared to enter Maskil. She recognised Farlan, who had his back to her, chatting with several others. Seeing an opportunity she couldn't ignore, she raced forward and planned how to achieve a tackle. Building speed, she judged the slipperiness of the snow. Two yards away, she dropped and pointed her feet between his legs and when she slid between them, she straightened her arms to knock his feet out from under him. Once he was down, she leapt onto his waist and straddled him.

The guards near him jumped into action, and one drew a sword but halted when they saw who it was.

"Isla!" Farlan groaned as he lay in the snow.

"We're even." She poked his cheek.

"Even? Oh, this is not even."

She pulled a biscuit from the bag. "But I brought a treat."

"A biscuit doesn't clean my uniform." He grabbed it from her hand and took a bite. "Is that poppy seeds and lemon?"

"Yes."

"That's new." He took another bite. "Not bad."

Someone cleared their throat roughly above her, and she looked up at Sanderson, the captain of the guard. She hadn't realised he was one of the guards standing in the tight circle. Getting to her feet, she offered Farlan a helping hand.

He brushed the snow from his uniform and took another bite.

She walked towards Kiefer and Jack until Sanderson grumbled. "Biscuits."

"I didn't know you'd be here, Sandy, or I'd have brought you one."

"What's wrong with the one in your hand?"

She was about to bite into it but stopped. Gazing upon the lovely warm biscuit, she sighed and remembered his friendship. She prepared to throw it to him but froze at his rough voice.

"Is that anyway to give a biscuit to a superior officer?"

She hung her head, walked over to him and places it in his hand.

"I'll make a fine soldier of you yet." He bit into the biscuit. "Dismissed."

After she turned away, she rolled her eyes and walked back to Jack and Kiefer.

"You have many allies in interesting positions," said Jack.

She shrugged. "I've known them all my life. Their positions aren't interesting to me."

"And that makes it all the more interesting."

They walked towards Moon Meadow but before they reached it, Isla led them down a narrow path to a small clearing.

"Jack, because of your relationship with Liam, you should know about this place." She pushed her way through bushes.

"What is here?"

"It's where we buried his das. He's been here, and he may come again." The thin blanket of fresh snow made her strain to see the grave. Farlan's simple cross of wood led her to it. The pile of stones beside it confused her until she realised what had happened. She rushed to it and moved away the snow.

"What is it?" Jack stood over her.

"Liam's grave. Someone disturbed it." The pile of stones that marked his spot had been thrown aside and when she moved more snow, she found the jacket he'd worn the night he killed the men from Wandsworth. "Someone came and didn't find him."

He winced. "This isn't good."

"Someone is still looking for him." Kiefer knelt next to the hole. "He'll be vulnerable without the poyson."

She stared at him; he spoke the truth. Liam was only a boy, a hauflin with the normal strength and skill of a nineteen-year-old. He was no longer an equal contender to powerful men.

"We'll rebuild the grave in case others come." Jack took the coat and shoved it into the hole and piled stones over it. "Maybe time will reduce the threat."

She wanted to believe him, but an inner voice insisted the threat wouldn't end until the Mavericks were terminated. Together, they rebuilt the grave, concealing the lie beneath dozens of stones.

Back on the road, Isla turned left.

"Where are we going now?" Jack put his hands inside his pockets.

"A friend who may have something to help Liam heal faster. She's a magic-maiden, and Meeme learnt much of what she knows from her."

"Beathas?" offered Kiefer.

"Yes, have you met her?"

"No, but Catriona talks of her. She dislikes her."

"As far as I know, Catriona has never met her."

"Really?"

"Have they met since you've been here?"

"No, not that I know of."

"Catriona thinks a lot of things. To my knowledge, she's never left Maskil."

"How has she lived within the walls all her life?"

"She's afraid."

He reluctantly nodded. "Her visions keep her fearful."

"They are only dreams." She reconsidered that statement. "Except the one in which Liam was trapped in a tree."

"She saw that vision?" asked Jack.

"She didn't know who was trapped, only that someone was." She saw the narrow path that led to Moon Meadow and left the road. "I have strange dreams; it doesn't mean they come true."

"She's had many lately," said Kiefer. "Ones stained with blood and with horrible smells. Her greatest fear is for me."

Isla glanced back at him. "But you're here with her."

"I remind her of that and tell her they're silly nightmares. It's not as if you'd talk to dragons and live to tell about it."

Isla and Jack stopped and stared back at him.

"She had a dream of Isla talking with a dragon?" asked Jack.

"Yeah. Crazy, isn't it?"

"What colour was the dragon?" asked Isla.

"Green."

She glanced at Jack. "What does this mean?"

"She's a foreteller. I assume she's had no training."

Kiefer fixed his eyes on Isla. "Are you saying you talked to a dragon?"

"Yes. More than one."

His mouth hung open. "Was a cat involved?"

"Black with a grey stripe under the chin?"

His eyes widened. "Bronwyn is in great danger."

Isla stared, trying to read his thoughts. "Tell me."

"It is your das."

"The man named Kieron Ruckle is dead. I saw him killed."

His eye twitched. "Maybe not completely."

"If this woman is untrained, she cannot distinguish between real visions and those that clutter the mind," said Jack. "My aunt is a foreteller, and it took her years to separate the two. I suggest we focus on the task at hand and see if this Beathas woman has something to help Liam. I will not worry about that which may not be our future." He ushered Isla forward.

She focussed on the path ahead, found the bridge that crossed the waterfall and walked the remaining few hundred feet to the cottage. If Catriona foretold the future, she was unsure if she wanted to hear it. Knowing the hardships faced might impede her in unintentional ways.

The familiar sound of the windchime sang in the air as she approached the neat barn where the horses were kept. No one was about, so she kept walking towards the porch of the cottage buried under a white blanket of snow. The door opened and Beathas stepped from the landing. The seasoned hauflin half smiled at her, then looked to the strangers. Her gaze froze on Jack and her mouth opened slightly as if she recognised him but didn't want to see him.

Isla glanced over her shoulder and saw Jack scanning the area before his eyes settled on Beathas. Confusion spread across his face like clouds quickly moving over a valley on a sunny day, casting shadows and constantly changing the lighting. In a daze, he stumbled forward until he stood before Beathas. Then without a word, he grabbed her and sealed his lips to hers.

Isla raised an eyebrow and waited.

"Does he know her?" whispered Kiefer.

"I'm guessing they may have met before." She blinked as the vision before her blurred and shimmered. In a flash, Beathas transformed into a taller woman, one with flowing brown hair twisted in curls. Jack also transformed and the longer she stared, the more she realised they had returned to their newlin form. Jack resembled Nyx, and Beathas appeared like Mystic One.

"Jack, I'm going to make a wild assumption and say this is Floriana, your mate." Jack waved her off, and she grinned. "I guess she's not going to help us with Liam after all."

Floriana pulled Jack towards the cottage.

"We're leaving," she said. "You know where to find me when you're...done. I'll see you in a couple of days." She tugged on Kiefer, then stopped. "He won't remember in his condition. Do you have paper? I'll tuck a note into his pocket."

Kiefer pulled her towards the bridge. "I'm sure they'll be fine."

"More than fine." She snuggled into his side. Late yesternight, her meeme had told her Beathas, not Catriona, had taught her how to protect her nwyfre from intruders. Although unsure Elwyn spoke words of wisdom, she held out hope she did. Leading Jack to his mate completed her promise to him and repaid him for saving Liam. It also made her feel good inside. As good as it felt to be walking beside the man who had miraculously healed from his injuries. She squeezed Kiefer and held him tighter. "So, Kipper, where to now?"

"Maybe we'll head south. Ellswire is nice this time of year."

"I mean today."

He laughed. "Take me to the baker. I've a craving for brownies."

"Brownies it is." When her feet left the bridge, it disappeared.

"Does that always happen?"

"No, only when Beathas makes it so." However, she could find her way if desired but today, she'd give the mates their privacy. After all these years apart, it'd take a major calamity for her to disturb them.

∞ ❖ ∝

The morning sun cascaded through the pane of the small window in Isla's room. Liam stretched his neck and peered outside from his position in bed. Snow had fallen overnight, and the usual morning activity of clearing it away occupied the minds of many citizens in Maskil. He didn't have to worry about the snow or how much fell. After being here for more than three weeks, he was still confined to bed to encourage his strength and energy to return.

Since he'd awakened more than thirty minutes ago, all he wanted to do was move. He'd been up and out of bed several times, but Alaura insisted he remain inactive. She and Rhiannon had given him herbs and different types of food to encourage his health to return, and they insisted on another week of bedrest before he slowly returned to daily activities. Alaura had visited before she left for the dress shop to check on him and to ensure he was following her instructions. Bronwyn had popped in before her, gave that look that told him he wasn't welcome in his home, said he hoped he'd recover soon and left for the castle. It had become a daily routine for the man to remind him he disapproved of his daughter's choice in a mate. Liam had believed that once the poyson was gone, he'd accept him, but now he understood that day would never come.

"Feeling better today?" Lyneth poked her head into the room. Since Jack had found his mate and remained at Moon Meadow, she and Cabela had taken over the spare room at the Darrow home. Deaglan stayed with McGuigan.

"Well enough to head out onto The Trail."

She laughed. "Good. But we'll wait until the weather breaks, so get more rest."

"I think I'd rather ride in this weather than shovel." Cabela stood beside her frowning.

"Think of the money and the muscles you'll make." Lyneth grinned and raised her eyebrows. "Hard work never hurt anyone and today, we've got a lot of snow to shovel. I mean muscle and money to make."

Cabela groaned. "Oh, my poor blisters."

"Come on," she said to her. "Those walkways won't shovel themselves." She waved at Liam and led the girl away.

Liam sank beneath the blankets. He'd rather be snug in bed than hired to shovel boardwalks. He listened to them clamour down the steps, Cabela complaining the whole way, and leave through the front door. Silence filled the dwelling until soft footsteps fell upon the stairs.

Isla walked into the room with a bowl and a steaming cup of fluid. "Maybe tomorrow you can break the fast with us downstairs." She set the food on the small table by the bed.

"I doubt if Alaura will let me leave this room."

"We won't ask." She winked and handed him the bowl. "Porridge. Meeme says it will be less destructive on your belly since you haven't eaten much."

He put a spoonful in his mouth. "Maybe but this doesn't fill me like bacon and eggs." He put another spoonful in.

"I'll fry up a couple of eggs after this." She settled cross-legged on the bed beside him. "Toast, too." She patted his belly. "I can't have you starving under my observation."

He spooned the porridge into his mouth, wishing it was more flavourable than it was. There weren't even raisins, as instructed by Alaura. Simple was best, she'd said. He took a sip of tea, gazing at Isla over the rim. The sun shining in the window caught her eyes, adding sparkle to her being that already radiated beauty. "Is there anyone else home?" The question slipped out without consideration.

"Just you and me. Everyone else is off to work." She straightened the blankets and pulled them higher onto his chest. "Are you warm? I could get another blanket, maybe add a log to the fire."

"No, I'm fine." He put down the teacup and spooned more porridge into his mouth, watching her as he ate. Her lips were slightly parted as if she was about to speak, but they transformed into a gentle smile. His gaze fell to her neck and travelled down the opening of her shirt, two buttons open from the top. Ideas swirled in his head, and feelings erupted in his gut. Intense sensations travelled to his limbs, warming them faster than any blanket.

"If it had been warmer and if it hadn't snowed, I was hoping to get you outside today." She played with a loose strand on a blanket. "But I guess we're stuck inside. We can sit downstairs, give you a change of scenery."

He put the bowl on the table and wiped his mouth.

"Not hungry?" She peeked inside. "You're only half finished." She reached for the bowl, but he caught her hand.

He brought her fingers to his lips and kissed them. Thoughts of what he longed to do overwhelmed him and made him shiver.

"You're cold."

He drew her near and kissed her lips. "Warm me. Feed me."

She raised an eyebrow. "I'm not sure you're well enough."

"I won't know until I try." He pulled her across the bed and into his arms. "Let me try." His lips found hers, and he closed his eyes to better feel her skin upon his and her warm breath on his mouth. Slowly, his fingers unfastened the buttons on her shirt and his hand slipped inside, caressing soft skin. His muscles tensed, and he stretched his full length, anticipating the sensations to come.

"We shouldn't," she breathed. "Not here." She removed her shirt and pressed her bare chest against his.

He unfastened her trousers and slipped them over her hips. "I know." He kissed her hard. "But..." Her scent consumed him, and he buried his hand in her hair and tenderly kissed her breasts. His senses filled with the aromas of their youth while new and exciting smells radiating from her seized his attention.

"The flame for you never died." Her hands roamed over his back and pushed down his shorts. "It smouldered until we rekindled it." Her lips latched onto his and held him firmly as her fingers worked to turn that fire into a raging blaze.

He settled on top of her and pressed her into the mattress. "By the time I was sixteen," he gasped, "I'd heard stories from men and what they did with women they loved." He grinned against her lips. "I started thinking about doing that with you. I've made love to you a thousand times in my mind." His hot breath fell heavy upon her skin. "None of them came close to how you make me feel at this moment."

Her fingers on his skin made him groan as they caressed and squeezed sensitive parts. He bucked and shivered and felt helpless when she rolled him onto his back and straddled him. Her dark hair framed her beautiful face, and her enchanted eyes mesmerised him.

"I've always wanted you to be my first." She kissed him long and hard. "I can't change that, but I can guarantee you'll be my last."

He rolled on top and parted her legs with his knee. She wasn't his first either, but she'd be his last. He'd never be with another woman, never even consider kissing one. He grasped her hand, pressed his palm into hers and squeezed it.

"Isla of Maura, with the fire that rages in my blood for you, I offer a pledge of union. Please, I beg you, accept for if you don't, I will make it every day until you do."

"Liam Jenkins, with all my heart I accept." Her breath came quick and her chest heaved as his hips worked against her. "The fire in my blood burns only for you." She cried out and clung to him.

The sensations she created raced through his blood, sending him over the edge of reason. He fought to maintain control, then surrendered willing to her and the euphorbia of their love.

The bowl of porridge and cup of tea on the bedside table cooled slowly as morning drifted away, and the sun came out and heated the icicles hanging over the window, making them drip and sparkle in the shine.

Epilogue

EUAN FETYPLACE LEANT OVER Willow's shoulder to view the map she'd spread across the large fallen tree. They'd travelled steady since leaving Wyvern three moons beforehand, but they'd only reached Spray Tumblin's Keep due to poor weather, missed trails and two riders on one animal. It had taken eight weeks to get his leave of absence, and another week to prepare for the journey that would take him to Maskil to deliver the pony lent to him to return to the caravan with the baby that had been kidnapped.

Given the time of year and the rugged mountains, Willow had recommended they travel directly south along the Skeoch River. Her estimation of the amount of time it'd take to cover the ground was incorrect and now in early Forstig, they were still weeks away from Maskil. They'd left Wardlow six days ago and while the weather was mild this far south, in about three weeks, they'd be in the middle of Forstig and face freezing temperatures and snow on their journey north.

His experience on The Trail was limited and while he had believed Willow's was better, there were days she proved him wrong.

"Is there a trail that cuts across?" He pointed to a section of the map they'd soon reach. "It'd save us a day."

"No. I've been through there many times."

He sighed loudly. "We'd have been to Maskil weeks ago if we'd taken the route through Pogwa Mountains or cut through Dunakan."

"Dunakan is not safe for me or you, and mountain passes are tricky. I don't like them."

"We didn't go that way because you don't like them." He groaned. "I grew up on the mountains. Passes are nothing to fear."

"They are unpredictable."

"Yes, but only in Forstig. We'd have been through all of them by early Harvest."

"I doubt that." She folded the map. "We'll reach the keep in an hour or so. They have a fantastic inn; we'll stay there."

"Great."

"You don't sound pleased." She tucked the map into her pouch.

"All this travelling with nothing to show."

"You've gained experience on The Trail."

"What good will it do me? I'll return to Petra and guard duty."

"Sounds boring."

"It's not boring; it's an honourable profession." He went to Clover, who grazed on the small patch of grass along the dirt road. The pony proved a worthy beast, one unpredictable and fast. Their time together made him more comfortable with her wild side, and now he felt safe when she took control.

"Don't you want more out of life than guard duty?"

"No." He answered quickly, but he had considered other things. Travelling was one of them but done with a purpose. Putting his foot into the stirrup, he hoisted himself onto the saddle, then waited for her to mount behind him. He gathered the reins and fluttered them in the air. Clover walked and then trotted.

The breeze pushed back his hair and brushed his skin. Passing this close to Ellswire made him think about his brother, but he wouldn't waste more time stopping at the city. He had no idea where he lived or how to contact him. Anyways, his brother may have already returned to North Ridge by now, making the visit useless. No, his goal was clear: return Clover to Alaura and then return to North Ridge where he'd resume his position as a guard at the castle. He'd leave adventuring to those who didn't have responsibilities.

Which path do I take to continue the adventure?

The directions are on the next page.

Which Path Do I Take?

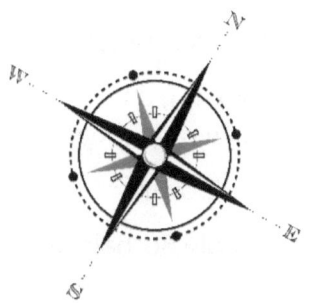

Castle Keepers Series: *Gathered Stones*, Book 5
OR
Mystical Series: Book 3

Cast of Characters

Ailsa, Beathas of: Hauflin, female, sorceress, lives at Moon Meadow

Alvey, Elwyn: Mixed race (7/8 Elf-1/8 human), female, foreseer, magic-maiden, lives at Inishmore, Lyneth's great great-grandmother

Arthur: Hauflin, male, lives at Ellswire

Bess: Elf, female, owner of Ample Bothain at Moonsface with her mate, Harry, Deaglan's grandaunt

Burkenshaw, Farlan: Human, male, sergeant at Aruam Castle, Selina's mate

Cabela: Elf, female, age 16, traveller in Yikker Wood

Calhoun, Murissa: Dwarf, female, owns Murissa's Delightful Hat Boutique at Bagnio

Cronin, Sawney 'Tracker': Dwarf, male, junior corporal at Aruam Castle, Willow Asuwish's mate

Cronin, Willow Althena (nee Asuwish): Newlin, female, Inherited One, magic maiden, Sawney Cronin's mate

Darrow, Bronwyn: Dwarf, male, Lord of Maskil, Aruam Castle guard (private), Alaura of Niamh's mate, son of Maisie and Gaven Darrow

Darrow, Kellyn (nee Mulryan): Dwarf, female, corporal at Aruam Castle, daughter of Lillias and Conall Mulryan, Joris Darrow's mate

Darrow, Maisie (nee Kintale): Dwarf, female, owner of Forest Bakery and Herbs Shop, lives at Maskil, Gaven Darrow's mate

Deaglan: Elf, male, age 15, illusionist, card player, nephew to Valey and Doran Eldon, Oisin and Granger, lives in Moonsface

Donncath: Hauflin more than dwarf, male, assistant to Oracle Ned Oracle at Mystical Paragons in Dougendun

Eldlow, Lady Coraline of Maiden's Way: Elf, female, gardener, author, Weston Eldlow's mate, lives after Brador on the way to Inglenook

Eldlow, Weston: Elf, male, gardener, Lady Coraline of Maiden's Way's mate, lives after Brador on the way to Inglenook

Eldon, Doran Rhys: Elf, male, lives at Inglenook, Valey Morwen Eldon's mate, Deaglan's granduncle

Eldon, Valey Morwen: Elf, female, lives at Inglenook, Doran Rhys Eldon's mate, Deaglan's grandaunt

Gilmar: Dwarf, male, red hair, of Vale of Avoca, second in command

Granger: Elf, male, hunter, Deaglan's uncle

Harry: Elf, male, owner of Ample Bothain at Moonsface with his mate, Bess, Deaglan's granduncle

Isla of Maura: Hauflin, female, age 18, thief, born Maskil, daughter of Maura of Ealasaid and Keiron Ruckle, adopted daughter of Alaura of Niamh and Bronwyn Darrow, former member of The Mercenaries

Jenkins, Liam: Hauflin, male, age 19, thief, born Maskil, lives at Wandsworth, son of Finola of Mallaidh and Warin Jenkins

Kiefer of South Nova: Human, male, healer, former member of The Mercenaries

Lindrum, Merk: Human, male, wizard, owner of Blackvale Castle

Lyneth: Half-breed (elf-human), female, fighter, 31, former prisoner of Blackvale Castle, former member of The Mercenaries, Rod Wheatcroft's mate, born at Inishmore

Moor, Benedict: Dragon, green, male, leader of Dragstone Moorland clan

Moor, Dancell: Dragon, green, male, member of Dragstone Moorland clan

Moor, Falkor: Dragon, green, male, Magon's mate, lives in Blueston Lighthouse, member of Dragstone Moorland clan

Moor, Magon: Dragon, green, female, Falkor's mate, lives in Blueston Lighthouse, member of Dragstone Moorland clan

Mulryan, Conall: Dwarf, male, Lillias' mate, lives at Glen Tosh

Mulryan, McGuigan: Dwarf, male, age 19, sword fighter apprentice, son of Ulette and Laird Mulryan, born at Maskil, former member of The Mercenaries

Mulryan, Rhiannon (nee Darrow): Dwarf, female, seamstress, owner of Sew in Style Clothier with her sister Loran, healer, lives in Maskil, Tam Mulryan's mate

Mulryan, Tamas 'Tam': Dwarf, male, captain at Aruam Castle, son of Lillias and Conall Mulryan, Rhiannon Darrow's mate

Nassen, Orenda: Human, female, lady of Tigh na Mare, leader of the castle's warriors (deceased)

Odart: Dwarf, male, fighter, of Vale of Avoca

Odbern, Oracle Ned: Mixed breed (dwarf-hauflin), male, trader, owns Mystical Paragons in Dougendun

Oisin: Elf, male, owner Ample Bothain in Moonsface

Parnell: Elf, male, junior corporal at Aruam Castle

Ruckle, Keiron: Hauflin, male, thief, Maura of Ealasaid's mate, Isla of Maura's das (deceased)

Sanderson, Zipporah: Human, male, captain of the guard at Aruam Castle

Somerled, Jack: Newlin, male, traveller, magic expert, Floriana's mate

Specks: Human, male, associate of Merk Lindrum, traveller, explorer

Storm: Cat, male, all black except for a narrow patch of dark grey fur running from his bottom lip to its belly, lives at Mystical Paragons in Dougendun

Tumblin, Cameron: Dwarf, male, leader the hunters out of Vale of Avoca

Tumblin, Spray: Dwarf, male, member of the hunters out of Vale of Avoca

Weslia: Elf, female, seasoned, lives at Bannock with her mate, owns Weslia's Wyrd

Wheatcroft, Catriona: Human, female, sorceress, lives at Maskil

Wheatcroft, Rod: Human, male, prisoner of Blackvale Castle, Lyneth's mate

The Castle Keepers Novel Series

Shadows in the Stone

Scattered Stones

Revelation Stones

Healing Stones

Gathered Stones

Origin of the Stones

The Stone Gatherer

Rebellion Stones

Hearthstones

The Lost Journal of Bronwyn Kintale

Mystical Series

Beyond the Myst

Within the Myst

R